SYNTHETIC EDEN

Echoes of Tomorrow
Book 1

ALEXANDER TITUS

SEAN PLATT

STERLING & STONE

This book would not be possible without my co-author, Sean, and our editor, Bonnie. Thank you for helping me bring my imagination to life.

A similar thank you to all the amazing people in my life who have helped me see the bigger picture in all my endeavors.

More than anyone, this would not be possible without Maggie always encouraging me to reach for the stars, even if sometimes it feels like I'm trying to fly on the wings of a pig. Thank you.

SYNTHETIC EDEN

Chapter One

JUNE 12, 2108
   OUTSKIRTS OF KANSAS CITY

WEDGED between a matching set of security guards in the back seat of an armored Reaper, Dr. Samara Makinde watched through bulletproof glass as Missouri farm country scrolled past like a documentary of the apocalypse. A century ago, these fields had stretched endlessly with golden wheat swaying in the breeze, punctuated by red-painted barns and white farmhouses with American flags snapping in the wind. Now it was just mile after mile of death. Brown chytrid fungus covered everything—rotting barns, abandoned farmhouses, the stunted remains of crops in the fields.

A pack of dogs and some entrepreneurial crows were making an all-you-can-eat buffet from the bloated remains of a cow coated in fungal growth.

Guard number one, Vega, had the decency to look uncomfortable about the whole armed-escort situation.

Guard number two, Jacobs, kept shooting her looks like she'd personally engineered the apocalypse. Fun times.

"We'll be there soon," Vega said, probably trying to be reassuring.

"Can't be soon enough," Jacobs muttered, giving Samara another death glare.

"Don't mind this Neanderthal," Vega told her. "Some of us realize that not every scientist is to blame for what happened."

Maybe so. But Samara couldn't help blaming the panicked mob that had broken into the research facility where she'd worked until two days ago.

She'd been eating breakfast when the first footage had popped up in her feed, streamed by one of the rioters to all the socials. The mob tore through the facility, smashing delicate equipment, shattering beakers and test tubes, scattering notebooks and files in senseless vengeance against the inanimate.

Then they found Dory.

The livestream stopped as the mob closed in on Samara's coworker.

Samara had searched with numb fingers, pulled up the local news station to find a drone-shot image of the research park where the lab was located—and the recording of Dory's 911 call playing over it. The lab manager begged for help until her pleading turned to a series of ear-scraping screams that pierced the frenzied cries of the rioters.

Dory wasn't even a scientist. She simply ordered supplies and kept the lab running.

She'd been one of the first of many victims in the worldwide backlash against scientists, but far from the last. When the citizenry discovered that genetic engineers working on a vaccine had accidentally transformed the chytrid fungus into an unstoppable plague that started with frogs and spread until the Earth's already-fragile ecosystem collapsed, rendering Earth uninhabitable … they lost their collective shit, erupting into violent mobs overnight. They didn't care whether the scientists they were attacking had anything to do with it. See someone in a lab coat? Must be guilty. Biologists, climate scientists, and environmental engineers, they all became targets.

"Did you work on the fungus?" Vega asked, snapping Samara back to the present as they passed Kansas City's defaced *Welcome* sign.

Samara didn't dare tell them the full truth. "Before the plague, I studied frogs. Specifically, their ability to hibernate during winter."

That was how she'd ended up studying chytrid—the genetically-modified fungus had hit the frogs first. But no one outside of the scientific community paid much attention until the lack of frogs to control crop-eating insects triggered a global famine. And by then, the fungus had spread everywhere.

"Frogs? That's just as bad!" Jacobs spat. "How many millions in taxpayer dollars went to your worthless research?"

"That research is the basis for the cryosleep system in the colony ships," she shot back.

"See?" Vega punched Jacobs lightly on the arm. "She's one of the good ones."

"A lot of good people are staying behind." Jacobs leaned in, crowding her in an attempt to intimidate. "What'd you do to get a spot?"

The thing was, she didn't know. When eccentric billionaire Aurelius Hofstadter sent her the application, Samara had assumed it was a joke. And when he'd personally emailed her, she replied that she'd already committed to the global research project seeking a way to kill chytrid. She hadn't been ready to give up on Earth yet.

Until yesterday, when Hofstadter sent her a link to an encrypted file that changed everything. A file that erased itself after she'd viewed it. Samara accepted his offer immediately, and this Reaper had appeared in her driveway nine hours later.

But the question still haunted her. Out of all the geneticists on the planet, why her?

"I asked you a question," Jacobs growled.

Samara shrugged. "It was Hofstadter's decision."

Which wasn't really an answer, but it seemed to satisfy him.

The city's tech sector loomed ahead—all those sleek glass-and-steel towers that had once gleamed like beacons now looked like broken teeth in a corpse's mouth, spotted with dull brown fungus. Corporate logos still crowned the buildings: MetaCortex, Nanotech Solutions, BioCore Industries. The biotech district had been Kansas City's pride—the old oil economy had given way to America's new heartland tech capital. But now those same R&D facilities were practically tombs. Smoke billowed from the iconic Liberty Memorial Tower.

How many more scientists had to die to satisfy the world's rage?

Then Samara heard it: gunfire, explosions, and something else. A roar that grew louder as they got closer. It was people. A lot of angry people. Breaking windows with hand-made signs and setting fire to anything within reach as they swarmed around the road leading to the launch site—Samara guessed they had started as a protest, but now they were something much more dangerous.

Her stomach lurched. She might have abandoned her

family for nothing, just to die here, sandwiched between strangers.

Who was she kidding? She'd much rather die with strangers than watch everyone she loved starve to death—or worse.

"Find a way around," Vega told their driver.

But it was too late. The mob had spotted them. A wave of bodies surged toward the Reaper as the driver slowed, looking over his shoulder, then shifting into reverse. The mob closed around them, faces contorted with rage as they pressed against the windows, fists pounding the metal hard enough to leave dents. She forced herself to look at them, because even though it wasn't her fault they were going to die, she still had something that had been taken away from them.

Hope.

"Go through," Jacobs ordered.

"You'll kill them!" she protested as the Reaper pushed forward.

A burly man in a hoodie disappeared under the front bumper. She felt the impact vibrate through the vehicle's frame as he became a human speed bump. Her stomach heaved. These people had families, too. Children. Parents. None of them deserved to die.

Vega gave Samara a sad look. "They're dead either way. At least this is faster."

She held her breath as the Reaper accelerated. More thuds. More bodies. A young woman rolled across the hood, her eyes meeting Samara's for one terrible moment before she vanished.

"We have to stop."

"Feel free to get out," Jacobs suggested. "I'm sure if you explain to them that you didn't mean to destroy the planet, they'll see reason."

"Shut up!" Vega snapped.

"Most of those people deserve to be in this Reaper more than she does," Jacobs said. "I saw her brief. She's not just a scientist—she's a fucking geneticist."

Another impact. And another. The Reaper's thick tires crushed anything in their path, each *thud* ending yet another life so she could survive. The ethical calculus made her head spin. It was tempting to tell herself that the equation made sense, that her survival increased humanity's odds of survival, and given that only a handful of people could be saved…

A crash of shattering glass made Samara jump as someone hurled a Molotov cocktail. Burning alcohol splashed against the window, briefly illuminating the interior with tangerine flames.

The fire cast dancing shadows across faces that looked like something from a Renaissance painting of hell. Grief and rage twisted ordinary features into grotesque masks. These weren't monsters—they were teachers, accountants, store clerks. Regular people whose world had ended. Now, speed bumps on her road to survival.

Something hit the bulletproof glass hard enough to crack it before Jacobs could reply. Samara flinched as Jacobs swore and stood to man the Reaper's turret.

The sound of gunfire filled the air, and the crowd scattered as fury turned to fear.

"That'll show 'em," Jacobs said with a satisfied cackle as he dropped back into his seat.

"You both have spots on the ships, don't you?" Samara asked Vega, desperate to think about anything other than the shrieking coming from outside the vehicle.

"We're going on Hofstadter's ship, the Elysia," Vega replied. "What about you?"

"The Borlaug."

"What the fuck is a Borlaug?" Jacobs sneered.

Hating him fixed nothing, but it was a distraction from the horrors Samara could do nothing about. And once she made it to the colony ship, she'd never have to see him again. So, she indulged.

"Norman Borlaug was a plant geneticist who saved millions from starvation by developing new strains of wheat," Samara explained. "He won a Nobel Prize."

Jacobs barked a laugh, harsh and cynical. "Doesn't mean much now, does it?"

The Reaper pulled up to the security gate of the Ad Astra launch facility. Armed soldiers manned towers on either side, their weapons trained on the approaching vehicle. Bodies littered the ground in front of the gate—protestors who'd made the mistake of trying to force their way in. More corpses were piled on either side of the road. The eerie silence here felt worse than all that chaotic racket they'd left behind.

"IDs," said the guard at the gate.

Samara managed to keep her hands steady while pulling credentials from inside her jacket. But that didn't mean she wasn't worried. What if the guard said she wasn't authorized? What if the impulsive Hofstadter had changed his mind?

After a quick scan, the guard waved them through.

Ad Astra logos were plastered everywhere—on the brick buildings, the equipment sheds, even the rocket itself. The stylized phoenix rising from a blazing star had once seemed hopeful—now it looked like one more bird fleeing a dying world. Hofstadter's foundation had worked with NASA early in the billionaire space race, and soon emerged as the leader, becoming the face of America's efforts to colonize the galaxy. The entire complex felt like a military base, all order and efficiency in contrast with the dying world outside.

Samara would never tell Hofstadter, but every time she saw the words *ad astra*, her brain automatically added *per alia porci*. *To the stars on the wings of a pig.* The first time she'd met with her graduate advisor, he'd recounted the story of how John Steinbeck—writer of *The Grapes of Wrath* and several other books she'd had to read in school—had once been told by a professor that he would be an author "when pigs fly." Rather than give up, Steinbeck had given himself this motto, insisting that every book he published be marked with the image of a winged pig. Samara's advisor had told the story just before showing her around the antiquated lab where she'd be doing her research, reminding her that humble beginnings need not limit how high she could fly.

The driver took them straight to the runway where the shuttle waited, strapped to a modified 747. Hofstadter had revived and updated the old Challenger-style design. Samara shoved aside a thought about how that program had ended.

She followed Jacobs up several flights of portable stairs to a platform level with the shuttle's main cabin door. One of the waiting launch team members cast her an irritated look.

"You're the last ones in. We've been holding the launch on Hofstadter's orders." His unspoken question hung in the air: *What made Samara so special that everyone else had to risk missing their launch window?*

A tech team rushed to suit them up. She watched as they helped Jacobs and Vega first, efficiently securing seals and tightening straps. Then one of the techs turned to her.

"Good chance you'll black out during ascent." He held

up a hypodermic. "This'll reduce your chances of having an aneurysm."

She didn't ask what was in it, just nodded and let the tech stick the side of her neck. Then he hustled Samara onboard and strapped her into a seat. Jacobs made a show of sitting on the opposite side of the shuttle, kicking her ankle as he passed.

Vega shot her an apologetic look as he sat beside her. "Don't take it personally. His wife didn't qualify to come with. She'd just started chemo."

"But he came anyway?"

"When she found his acceptance letter in the trash, she made him." Vega grinned. "Loves that ugly mug to death, for some reason."

To death, literally.

Samara shot a look at Jacobs, tried to imagine what he must be feeling. Not just the loss of his wife, qualifying also meant agreeing to be partnered with someone. With only one hundred sixty spots per ship, everyone had to be willing to pair up and have children to maximize genetic diversity, reducing the bottleneck that every colony would suffer.

Who had Jacobs found to bring with him? Or had he been assigned a partner, same as Samara?

"What about you?" she asked Vega. "Who did you leave behind?"

The 747 engines roared to life before he could answer, rattling her teeth and rolling through her bones as forty tons of thrust shuddered through the airframe. She tried to take slow, deep breaths as anxiety clawed at her chest. Images of the Challenger disaster flickered through her mind like a slideshow.

Hofstadter had rushed everything, desperate to get the colony ships ready before Earth became completely uninhabitable. How many corners had been cut? How many safety checks abbreviated or skipped entirely? She had watched the Challenger explode on old footage, that Y-shaped cloud of smoke marking the instant seven lives ended in a flash of orange fire. All because of a rubber ring that cost less than a pizza.

That familiar sick lurch hit her stomach as they accelerated down the runway.

This was really happening. She was leaving Earth—leaving her family, her friends, and everyone she had ever known. By the time she came out of cryosleep, they would all be dead. Even billionaires in their underground bunkers stuffed with hoarded supplies would starve before the Borlaug entered orbit around the exoplanet that had been chosen as one of humanity's new homes.

The ground fell away below them. She was grateful for her helmet hiding the tears that slid down her cheeks. The weight of what was happening—of being one of humanity's chosen few, selected to survive among the stars—pressed down on her chest until Samara could barely breathe.

Forty-two years of cryosleep lay ahead, then a lifetime on an alien world. She'd studied the colonization plans and knew the challenges they would face.

What she didn't know was whether her research would save them or kill them all.

Chapter Two

EIGHT MASSIVE COLONY ships hung in near-Earth orbit like metallic seeds waiting to be scattered on the cosmic wind, their titanium hulls gleaming in the harsh sunlight. Samara stared through the shuttle window at humanity's last resort. The vessels stretched nearly two kilometers from bow to stern, their massive frames dwarfing the International Space Station that had once seemed so impressive. Each one could have housed a small city, which was exactly the point.

The closest ship dominated her view through the reinforced glass. Bold letters spelled out *BORLAUG* along its hull. Like its siblings, the ship was a monument to desperation disguised as an engineering triumph: eight million tons of metal and ceramics powered by a nuclear pulse drive. Each detonation would release 40 kilotons of focused energy—humanity's funeral pyre transformed into their chariot of escape. The idea of hurtling through space on a series of nuclear blasts made her stomach clench.

"Beautiful, aren't they?" Vega asked.

Samara nodded, throat too tight for words. In the distance, one ship was already moving out, its massive pusher plate beginning its nuclear ballet. The first detonation sent a flare of light across space—a cosmic strobe marking humanity's retreat.

As their shuttle maneuvered closer to the Borlaug, the colony ship's true scale became apparent. What had looked like subtle texturing on the hull resolved into meter-wide plates, each one engineered to handle the stress of near-light-speed travel. The docking port seemed absurdly small against the vessel's bulk.

"Beginning final approach," the pilot announced over the intercom.

Samara reached for the latches on her harness, but the tech who'd strapped her in glared and said, "Not until we've docked."

Soon after, the shuttle glided into the docking collar with barely a bump—an impressive feat given the relative velocities involved. Samara tried to focus on the technical aspects, the physics and engineering that made this possible. It was easier than dwelling on what this moment really meant: that she was about to step into humanity's hundred-trillion-dollar lifeboat while Earth died beneath them.

She couldn't help thinking of the faces pressed against the Reaper's bulletproof windows, and each horrifically jolting thud as someone else fell under its massive tires.

"Good luck," Vega said as the tech released her harness. "Hope there's something like frogs where you're going."

"Thanks." Samara shot a look at Jacobs, who had either blacked out or fallen asleep. She hoped he hadn't had an aneurysm. "Is he—"

Vega grinned. "Don't worry, I'll take care of him."

Samara thought Jacobs was lucky to have Vega on his ship, and wondered if she could ever be strong enough to be someone else's Vega.

Thirty minutes and one thorough decontamination later, Samara dressed in ship-issued clothing—practical gray synthetics that somehow managed to be both perfectly fitted and completely unflattering. Her skin still tingled from the UV sterilization and chemical shower. Even her hair smelled like industrial sanitizer.

Next step: check in and get prepped for cryosleep.

But as she emerged from the decontamination chamber, Samara found Aurelius Hofstadter himself waiting for her, wearing his usual grin and a pristine bespoke suit. Nearly eighty, he looked a well-preserved forty, thanks to the experimental longevity treatments he was notorious for subjecting himself to. But his telomeres would tell his true age, unless he'd found a way to lengthen them. Not that she'd ever presume to ask him for a DNA sample.

"About time," he chided, as if Samara had been stuck in traffic instead of traveling through a real-time apocalypse to get here. "The rest of the leadership team is waiting."

"The rest of the leadership team?"

"Didn't you read your contract?"

She hadn't. What would she have done if she'd disliked the terms? Go to Mars instead? "Why would I be on the leadership team, sir?"

Hofstadter stopped so abruptly that Samara had to turn back around to face him.

"When you accepted my offer, I assumed you understood the implications of the data I shared with you."

Even the newest graduate student would've understood. The scientific community had already documented chytrid's destruction of the planet's frog population. And shortly before Hofstadter had contacted her, there'd been multiple confirmations that it had already made the leap to mammals: they'd found infected raccoons, weasels, and foxes—all animals known to eat frogs. But Hofstadter's file contained evidence that the fungus was evolving much faster than they had originally believed. Apparently, it could now survive in pigs.

Which meant they were too late. Even with every qualified scientist on the planet working toward a solution, the chance of finding a cure before the fungus made the leap from pigs to humans was slim to nil.

But that didn't answer her real question.

"What I mean is, there are thousands of geneticists who are probably more qualified. Why did you choose me?"

"I read your paper re-examining Mitra Kunda's work on intelligence augmentation. You weren't afraid to suggest that we reconsider some of our current restrictions, given the advances in accuracy—"

"As a thought experiment." Concerns about Dr. Kunda's work had triggered a slew of new restrictions on genetic modification of humans. "I wasn't suggesting that we continue her research."

"You weren't afraid to ask an important question, even though it might've impacted your professional reputation." Hofstadter resumed walking. "Humanity is going to need that kind of intellectual courage if we're going to survive out there."

"If you believed in intellectual courage, you wouldn't have shared that file with just me—you would've released it to the world."

"You're brave, but you're also naïve," he replied, stopping to gesture toward a door labeled Conference Room A.

The door hissed open at Samara's approach, allowing her entry to a gleaming, minimalist room that could've been lifted from any corporate office on Earth, except for the subtle curve of the floor that betrayed their position in the ship's rotating habitation ring. Ten people sat in quiet conversation around an oval table: the leadership team.

No, the *rest* of the leadership team. Who were all staring at her like they were waiting for Samara to explain herself.

"Everyone, this is Dr. Makinde, the genius whose research is going to let us all take the longest nap in human history without our cells turning into mush." Hofstadter gestured expansively in Samara's direction. "Mind you, I'm the genius who recognized her genius, so I think we all know who the real hero is here."

A few tired smiles met his attempt at humor. Samara fought the urge to roll her eyes. Apparently, even the apocalypse couldn't dampen the man's ego.

Hofstadter began making introductions, but the man at the far end of the table cut him off before he could finish his first sentence. "If she hasn't read her briefing materials, she can do it after we handle actual business."

"Play nice, Hector." The woman beside him—colony psychologist and chaplain, Dr. Ayesha Basu—flashed Samara an apologetic look. She had the thousand-yard stare of someone who'd heard too many final confessions, but still she managed a faint smile at Samara. "It's been a long journey for all of us."

"Dr. Callas, our chief medical officer," added Hofstadter.

The doctor's nod triggered a grimace, probably due to the massive bruise that darkened his jaw. Stubble didn't hide the discoloration, but it did make him look like he'd barely closed his eyes in days. Considering what medical professionals had been dealing with since the announcement—botched suicide attempts, injuries inflicted by a populace driven mad by fear, patients poisoned by chytrid-infected food—he probably hadn't.

Samara nodded to acknowledge him, then turned to Dr. Renata Vargas, the colony's xenobiologist, whose work Samara had looked up when she'd seen Renata's bio in the briefing. "I found your paper on convergent evolution in extreme environments fascinating. Especially your hypothesis about parallel adaptation paths."

Dr. Vargas brightened, despite her apparent exhaustion, flashing Samara a quick smile. "You and about five other people. Everyone else fell asleep by page two."

"Moving on." Hofstadter gestured to a weathered couple who could have stepped out of an old Western. "Katherine and Leo Buratti. She's our agricultural expert and elected colony leader. He handles the livestock."

A curt nod from Katherine, founder of the Demeter Collective—the largest regenerative farming experiment in history, which had transformed thousands of acres of land exhausted by overfarming back into fertile cropland through a combination of scientific and indigenous land management techniques. Now, Katherine was tasked with recreating that success on an alien world.

Leo's smile was warmer than his wife's, despite the fresh scratches crisscrossing the backs of his hands and forearms. Samara wondered how he'd come by them before deciding that she probably didn't want to know.

"Maeve Kennedy, head engineer," announced a stocky woman with close-cropped gray hair, pointing to herself. "And this quiet fellow is Dr. Mahmoud al-Hilli, our geologist."

She indicated the man beside her, sporting a large

bandage running from his neck down beneath his collar. The edge of a burn peeked out above the gauze.

"Now we're all friends," Maeve said, like that settled it.

But they weren't friends. They were the remnants of their species, thrown together by an eccentric billionaire who'd managed to accomplish what the world's governments had all failed to do.

But then Renata rolled her eyes, and Samara thought that there was at least one person here that she might call *friend*.

"I want it on record that I formally protest giving Dr. Makinde a spot on this mission." Hector glared at Hofstadter. "We should have brought another medical professional—a doctor, a nurse, even an EMT. Someone who could help with the kinds of emergencies we're undoubtedly going to face." He grimaced. "I can handle implanting embryos; I've had IVF training."

Dr. al-Hilli didn't look up from what appeared to be a rock sample he was turning over in his hands. "Are we really doing this again, Hector? The roster decisions were finalized weeks ago."

Weeks ago—even though Samara had refused the first several times Hofstadter had asked, she'd kept this seat open for her?

Because it wasn't like there was a shortage of geneticists who would do anything to escape Earth. Again, she wondered why he'd chosen her.

Dr. Basu turned to Samara. "Perhaps you could tell us how your expertise will benefit the colony beyond fixing basic birth defects?"

Samara straightened, relieved by the psychologist's attempted peace offering. "My role will be identifying and treating genetic diseases with standard, proven therapies—

nothing experimental. And I'll help Dr. Vargas catalog the genome of our new home."

"Samara's help with the genetic survey will be invaluable—it's a herculean task to catalogue a planet's worth of organisms," Renata added, her voice kind but firm. "Not to mention, we have no idea if the crop plants we're bringing will thrive on our new planet. Being able to modify them to fit our new home could be the difference between thriving and starving to death."

"Samara's contribution will be crucial. Even a minor birth defect could be the difference between success and failure for an individual—or potentially the entire colony." Katherine fixed Hector with a steady gaze that radiated quiet authority. "That's why I approved her inclusion."

Dr. Basu nodded. "I think we should all remember our shared purpose here. If our people see us fighting, they'll take sides."

"At best, she's taking a spot from someone more useful," Hector pressed, returning to his earlier point with stubborn determination. "At worst—"

Maeve cut him off with a snort. "Seems pretty damn useful to me to have someone who can make sure our kids don't have two heads." She shrugged her stocky shoulders. "No offense, Hector, but my engine room doesn't run on hurt feelings."

Samara decided she was going to like Maeve.

The door hissed open again, revealing a man whose crisp uniform and perfect posture made him look like he was about to pose for a recruitment poster—or like he'd come from a time before the world had withered to hell. Unlike everyone else in the room, he showed no signs of injury or exhaustion.

"Here's Captain Mercer," Hofstadter said. "Your pilot and commander for the duration of the voyage."

Samara's stomach tightened. This was the part she had been dreading most. She and Lucas Mercer were the only unpaired colonists in a mission that required couples. Hofstadter had assured her it wouldn't be a problem—they simply had to maintain the fiction of being partners until the colony was established. But looking at Mercer's perfect composure, Samara wondered how anyone would believe they were a couple. Would he be just as aloof when they were alone?

She hoped so. Her goal was to keep their relationship as professional as possible until things were far enough along that no one would care that her contribution to the colony's genetic diversity would happen in the lab she would set up.

Mercer smiled at her, inclining his head slightly before turning to face the seated group. Too late, Samara realized that she should've smiled back; they were supposed to be partnered. Had the others noticed?

She glanced around the table, but everyone else was looking at Mercer.

"Welcome aboard," he said. "Shall we transition to a first-name basis?"

An odd way to start. But everyone else seemed to accept it.

"Excellent suggestion, Lucas," Ayesha said warmly. "No need for formality when we're all going to be working in such close quarters."

Lucas nodded. He seemed to be focusing on a point just past everyone's shoulders rather than making direct eye contact. His hands moved slightly, fingers tapping against his thigh in a subtle, repetitive pattern.

Nerves? Or something else?

Samara studied Lucas more closely—the way he seemed both perfectly poised and slightly uncomfortable in his own skin, the careful control with which he held himself, the intense focus behind his gaze when he did make eye contact. He reminded her a lot of her cousin, Amadi, who tapped as a subtle form of stimming.

If Lucas was on the autism spectrum, that would explain why she'd been partnered with him. He might not have wanted to be in a relationship at all, despite the colony requirement that everyone contribute to humanity's future genetic diversity, which suggested that he was an excellent pilot, if Hofstadter had given him a spot anyway.

"Perhaps we should begin the briefing?" Lucas glanced toward Hofstadter.

"Excellent idea," Hofstadter said. "Lucas, take it away."

"The journey to DaVinci will take forty-two years at one-tenth light speed. You will remain in cryosleep unless there's an emergency that the ship's systems can't handle or you experience medical complications requiring intervention."

You, not we.

Samara wondered if the ship would wake Lucas up for other things. How much biological time would he lose compared to the rest of them?

Maybe that was why she'd been paired up with him. Because as pilot, he might be required to spend more of their journey awake, where he'd be aging normally. It made sense to pair the person who didn't want children with the person who might be too old to have them when they arrived. Assuming that his *you* hadn't been a simple grammatical slip.

Katherine turned to Samara. "What are the odds we're trading one death for another—just slower and colder?"

Samara hesitated. "The system is sound, but obviously, it's never been tested for this duration."

"Each cryopod will monitor vital signs continuously," Lucas said. "The system errs on the side of caution. But I have complete confidence in Samara's research."

Something in his tone made Samara glance over at him. His expression was perfectly neutral, but the intensity in his gaze made her uncomfortable.

Or maybe it was how completely unperturbed he seemed when everyone else around him was clearly marked by the horror of the past few weeks and the fear of the unknown that they were about to launch themselves into. There were no dark circles under his eyes, no deep lines carved hard into his face, no nervous twitches or impatient gestures, aside from the tapping. Amadi had been like that, too, failing to react to things that upset everyone else. But when something did upset him…

But she was assuming. He might just be very good at compartmentalizing. Piloting a ship that drove itself forward one nuclear explosion at a time probably required steadier-than-average nerves.

Or maybe he'd been on the ship since before the Chytrid Collapse was public knowledge, and he'd been literally untouched by the chaos below. They'd all been lucky that Hofstadter's colony ship program was well underway before anyone had known it was coming. The fungus had simply accelerated the billionaire's timeline, forcing him to use his remaining fortune to finish them fast.

But Samara didn't want to think about the fact that the ship she was about to trust her life to had been built in a hurry.

"Let's focus on what matters," Katherine said. "We've all read the briefing. What haven't we been told?"

"Everything relevant is in your files," Hofstadter said smoothly.

"It's fair to point out that this mission has been rushed," Leo pointed out. "And given how humanity's last attempt to colonize an exoplanet ended, you'll have to forgive us for being a tad anxious about the details."

"The Borlaug isn't the Hyperion," Hofstadter said.

That ship had vanished without a trace decades ago, taking three hundred colonists and humanity's first dreams of interstellar settlement with it.

"I've personally overseen every stage of this ship's construction," Hofstadter continued. "Every system is optimized for success."

"Yet you're leaving on a different ship," Hector said, his skepticism evident.

"All of the colony ships are built to identical specifications," Lucas interjected. "The complete technical documentation is available in the ship's archives. You have forty-eight hours before cryosleep, if you wish to review them. While you're waiting to be prepped, meals and entertainment are available in the Gathering rooms. The ship's AI can show you the way."

Hofstadter clapped his hands. "I think that covers everything essential. Samara, Lucas—a word?"

Samara joined Hofstadter and Lucas as the others filed out.

"Everything still good with our arrangement?" Hofstadter asked quietly. "The other colonists need to believe you're partners, to avoid resentment that you've been given special treatment. I know it's not ideal, but your skills were too valuable to pass up, Samara. And Lucas ... well, he has his own constraints."

"I'll adapt to Samara's preferences," Lucas said. "Including any future decisions about children."

He could have been discussing the weather for all the

emotion he showed, but Samara felt herself flushing. Mortified.

"I've never wanted children," she said stiffly. "That isn't going to change."

"As you wish," Lucas said as if he genuinely didn't care whether he'd be required to play the role of father if Samara changed her mind. "May I walk you to the cryosleep bay?"

As they passed through curved corridors, Samara found herself studying his stride—measured, controlled, like everything else about him. She wondered what it would take to crack that perfect composure. Would the heat death of the universe do it?

He didn't seem to notice her sideways glances. Was he lost in thought, or deliberately ignoring her to avoid more awkward social interaction?

To be fair, she had no idea how to bring up the idea that they'd have to bunk together once they made it down to DaVinci's surface. She hoped Katherine wouldn't make them keep up the farce for long.

They passed through curved corridors, finally arriving at a viewport. Samara stopped, transfixed by the sight of Earth hanging in the void. The planet looked wrong—where vibrant greens should have dominated the continents, there was mostly brown, and the oceans looked muddy in patches, missing their usual blue. Soon, there would be no place on Earth left untouched by the chytrid fungus.

She'd known, of course. But seeing it from up here somehow made it more real. Her parents. Her sister. Her nephew. Cousin Amadi. All those people they'd crushed beneath the Reaper to get her here. Their bodies would feed the fungus that would eventually cover every surface of the planet she'd once called home.

"Are you ready, Samara?" Lucas asked.

Was she ready to abandon everyone she loved to a slow death while she slept dreamlessly through the decades?

Ready to wake up in a world where she was one of the last surviving members of her species?

Ready to discover if she could build a future from the genetic debris of a dying world, depending on strangers who might become humanity's final ensemble cast?

Chapter Three

ARRIVAL DAY
BORLAUG COLONY SHIP

Pain. Pure, electric agony.

Samara's neurons sparked to life, each one screaming as her consciousness clawed its way out of forty-two years of synthetic hibernation. Her muscles seized in waves as their cellular machinery crawled back from the dead: resurrection measured in millivolts. The cryosleep system was based on her research on frogs' hibernation cycles; she'd seen the simulations predicting these exact symptoms. But theory was one thing. Experience was another thing entirely.

Through the haze of agony, fragments of awareness filtered in—the steady beep of medical equipment monitoring her return to life, the bite of an IV line delivering electrolytes and stabilizers, the metallic taste coating her tongue as her sensory neurons began to work once again.

"Neural reactivation sequence complete," announced

the ship's AI in Lucas' calm voice. "Vital signs nominal. Beginning chemical stabilization."

Did Lucas like hearing the ship talk back to him in his own voice, or did he find it as unsettling as she would?

"Can you open your eyes?"

Barely. Through slitted lids, she saw Dr. Callas haloed by the ceiling lights, already suited up in medical scrubs despite probably having undergone revival himself just hours before. Dark circles shadowed his eyes, and that old bruise still ghosted along his jaw—evidence that their bodies had achieved near-complete stasis throughout the journey—but his hands remained steady as he checked her vital signs. Lucky for them all that their chief medical officer handled revival better than most.

Samara tried to respond, but her throat felt lined with steel wool and her jaw wouldn't unlock.

"This will help with the transition." He held up a syringe filled with pale blue liquid that seemed to glow under the harsh lights. "Standard reanimation booster. Takes the edge off the neural feedback."

The injection burned like liquid nitrogen, then blessed relief flooded her screaming nerves. Her muscles began to unclench, though moving still felt like swimming through wet cement. The doctor pressed a silver pouch into her trembling hand.

"Electrolyte solution with cellular stabilizers. Sip slowly. Your digestive system is not much better than a newborn's right now."

The liquid tasted like battery acid masked with artificial sweetener, but Samara wasn't complaining. They'd made it. Frozen for more than four decades, and now they were on the interstellar frontier, alive and mostly functional. Their new home waited below.

The rational part of her brain understood the science.

She had spent years studying the complex biochemistry that made it possible: the synthetic proteins that prevented ice crystal formation in cells, the carefully engineered viral vectors that delivered temporary genetic modifications to help their bodies survive deep freeze. But some primal part of her mind rebelled at the idea of losing nearly half a century in what felt like a blink.

Half a century. The thought hit her like a physical blow. Her nephew would have died within the first year of her journey. Her parents would have watched Earth's ecosystem collapse completely, would have faced the end knowing their daughter had abandoned them. Her sister would have died hating her.

"Your personal effects are in the next room," Callas said as he removed her IV, either not noticing or simply ignoring the tears that had begun sliding down her cheeks. "Try standing, but take it slow. Motor control takes time to stabilize, even with the boosters."

A gross understatement. Her legs felt like overcooked pasta as she slid off the exam table. The room spun through a complex series of rotations before settling into its proper orientation. She waited for the vertigo to pass, clutching the table's edge. A glance at one of the medical monitors showed her reflection: ashen skin, sunken eyes, gaunt cheeks. But the aging during cryosleep had been nonexistent—exactly as her theory had predicted.

At least something had gone according to plan.

Samara shuffled to the locker room, one hand trailing along the wall for balance. A storage unit recognized her biosignature and popped open with a soft hiss.

Inside was a set of hiking clothes that looked like they had been picked out by someone whose entire under-standing of outdoor gear came from binge-watching survival shows. The pants had enough pockets to supply a small army, and the boots could probably withstand a direct hit from a tank. Classic Aurelius Hofstadter overkill —the billionaire who bankrolled their escape apparently couldn't resist playing adventure outfitter, even at the end of the world.

As she changed out of the flimsy cryosuit, her fingers brushed the locket she'd refused to remove even for stasis. Inside was a photo from her Ph.D. graduation, before the fungus, when the world still contained hope. Mom beaming, Dad's arm around her shoulders, her sister rolling her eyes but smiling. The same sister who had called her a coward when Samara told them about Hofstadter's offer. Who had demanded to know how Samara could abandon her own nephew to death while she escaped to the stars.

The truth was, she couldn't have saved them even if she'd stayed. Hofstadter's file made that clear. By the time the fungus made the leap from pigs to humans, it would be too late for anyone left on Earth. She'd known that when she'd accepted his offer.

But knowing hadn't made it easier to leave them behind.

"Dr. Makinde," Lucas' voice interrupted her grief spiral through the ship's speakers. "Your presence is requested on the bridge."

The bridge was exactly what she expected from a tech billionaire with Jobs-envy. It was all sleek surfaces and a single minimalist control panel displaying characters that weren't from any language Samara recognized. Presumably, Lucas could read them, although she wondered if the ship's AI would switch modes if its pilot was incapacitated and someone else had to take command. Or maybe the display was just ambiance, and the AI would talk them through an emergency. Aurelius had never been above a touch of spectacle, especially when it came to impressing investors.

The blast shields were open, windows displaying their dazzling new home. The sight stopped Samara mid-step.

DaVinci dominated the view, a blue-green marble wreathed in wispy clouds. But the colors were subtly wrong —the oceans had a purplish tinge, the landmasses covered in vegetation that shifted between bluish-green tones and indigo depending on the viewing angle. As if someone had adjusted Earth's color balance settings, shifting everything a few degrees closer to blue.

Two moons orbited in view. The smaller, barely visible, the larger a golden disc twice the size of Earth's satellite. Probe mission photos hadn't captured the true wonder of their new home. Beautiful, but unsettling in its alienness.

This was really happening. They were about to become the first humans to set foot on an exoplanet.

The rest of the leadership team looked as rough as Samara felt, except for Lucas, standing perfectly composed at the control panel without a single sign of post-cryosleep trauma. No sallow undertone to his skin, no gauntness to his face.

The ship must have woken him early for approach, giving him extra recovery time. He was its pilot, after all. She wondered if he'd merely been a witness to the ship's maneuvering as they'd approached the planet, ready to abort if it seemed the AI had made a mistake, or if he'd played a more active role as they eased into orbit.

"You're just in time," he said, turning from the controls. "We're deciding on a location for the colony."

He swept his hand across the command panel, and a holographic display materialized in the center of the bridge: two potential landing sites glowing in complex topographical detail, surrounded by streams of environmental data. So that was the real display—maybe she'd been right about the other one being decorative.

"We've narrowed it down to these locations in this region of the third continent," Lucas explained as the display zoomed in on a pair of small circles near a large river. The legend in the lower right suggested they were looking at an area of thirty square miles. "Terrain at both locations is stable enough for construction, with enough arable land to provide for the colony once we clear native vegetation."

Dr. al-Hilli leaned forward, wincing as the movement pulled at the bandage visible above his collar. "The northern site is our best option. Being closer to those mountains means timber for construction, and surveys suggest significant mineral deposits. We'll need those resources sooner rather than later."

"The southern site has nearly triple the biomass density," countered Renata, squinting at the display through obvious post-cryosleep fatigue. "Soil samples show higher organic content and better nutrient profiles. Yes, we'll have more clearing to do, but that vegetation suggests conditions more suitable for Earth crops."

"The southern site also gives us room to expand." Katherine's sun-weathered face showed the strain of revival, but her air of authority remained undiminished. "We need to think beyond the first few years—a growing population, new buildings, expanding farms. That will all take significant space."

Leo shifted his weight, looking queasy. "The northern terrain would be better for the animals, especially the goats. They're adapted to mountain grazing. After losing a dozen cows to cryosleep, we need every advantage for the surviving livestock."

Katherine's expression softened slightly. "What's our final count?"

"Twelve chickens, twenty-two cows, four bulls, and seventeen goats survived." Leo put his palms flat on the table, bracing himself. "Smaller animals handled the process better, just like the simulations predicted."

"But we have backups, hundreds of frozen embryos," Mahmoud said.

"Embryos that have to be incubated and raised to adulthood before they'll be anything other than a burden on our limited resources." Leo sighed. "We don't dare thaw them until we're sure the adults who made it through cryosleep can survive down there."

Samara hung back, feeling useless. What exactly was she supposed to contribute to a conversation about grazing pasture on an alien planet? Her primary expertise wouldn't be needed until they had a colony established. She would spend the early months helping Renata to collect and catalogue the local flora and fauna, sequencing the creatures' genomes to better understand humanity's new home.

"Probe data incoming," Lucas announced. The hologram shifted, overlaying new information in glowing layers. "The northern site shows elevated arsenic and lead levels in the soil. Concentrations exceed safe thresholds for food cultivation. The southern location appears more suitable for immediate agricultural development."

"We can look at bioremediation once we're established," Katherine said. "Use plants to clean the northern site. It's a proven technique—we used it extensively in the Demeter Collective."

"Only if the contamination isn't ongoing," Mahmoud warned. "If those levels come from natural geological processes, we might find ourselves fighting a losing battle."

"We could engineer local flora to extract the compounds more efficiently," Samara suggested.

Ayesha shook her head, her brow furrowing. "Should we be genetically engineering alien plants when we barely understand them?"

"I'd only use thoroughly tested adaptations," Samara explained. "Precise gene edits targeting specific metabolic pathways, with multiple containment protocols. Nothing that could propagate beyond our controlled areas."

Ayesha's expression remained skeptical. "But even with safeguards, we would still be experimenting with the same technology that destroyed Earth."

"The techniques that led to the chytrid plague were highly experimental. I wouldn't do anything that hasn't already been proven safe."

Samara refrained from commenting on the irony that the psychologist was worried about a minor tweak or two when they were about to introduce hundreds, if not thousands, of new species into DaVinci's ecosystem—the food crops and animals that would sustain their new colony, not to mention the colonists themselves and the myriad microorganisms that would come along for the ride. They couldn't even begin to guess what might happen when human bacteria began interbreeding with local species… but Ayesha was worried that adding a gene for arsenic uptake in a native plant was going to destroy the planet.

Be patient. She doesn't have the education to know the difference.

But before Samara could gather a more detailed explanation, Renata chimed in. "Traditional breeding could accomplish the same thing. It would just take longer."

Katherine stood. "We'll table that discussion for later. Lucas, start waking the first wave and prep the shuttles. Thirty colonists. Essential supplies and equipment only."

Renata fell into step beside Samara as they filed out.

"Don't let Ayesha or Hector get to you. They'll warm up eventually."

"I understand their objections. Especially after what we've all just been through." Though she couldn't help thinking of Dory again, and how ignorant humans had killed her because she worked at a lab.

She blinked hard to dissipate the threatening tears.

"Hey." Renata gave Samara a gentle nudge. "We just spent forty-two years as human popsicles and woke up ready to save our species, thanks to your research. If we still had Nobel prizes, you'd be a shoo-in. Seriously, impressive work."

"Thank you," Samara said, not sure how to respond to Renata's immediate championing, but her steps felt lighter as she walked the ship's corridors with the others. She caught another glimpse of their new home through a viewport on the way to the storage bay, where much of their first phase equipment was stored. DaVinci hung below them, stunningly gorgeous and alien, utterly indifferent to their plans. Here, humans were the invasive species, about to reshape another world in their image.

Just like the chytrid fungus had reshaped Earth.

Samara touched her locket, thinking of the smiling faces frozen inside. Whatever challenges awaited on the surface, she had to prove she deserved her spot on this mission. She owed that much to everyone they had abandoned back on Earth.

It was on her to make sure they didn't repeat the mistakes that had doomed their home world in the first place.

Chapter Four

WAKING after four decades of artificial sleep felt like someone had replaced Leila's blood with molten glass. Her entire nervous system screamed awake one agonized cell at a time. Even her bones ached, as if they'd been bruised in transit.

But none of that mattered compared to the burning sensation deep in her belly where the baby should be.

She was surrounded by sounds that terrified her. The steady whir of medical equipment sounded too much like the machines that had monitored Eddie's final days. The cool slide of an IV line brought back the press of grief as she watched her brother waste away. The tang of chemicals coated her tongue with that cloying artificial cleanliness that had masked decay in his hospital room.

The ship's recycled air carried undertones of antiseptic and metal, stinging her nostrils with each shallow breath. Bright lights pierced her eyelids, transforming darkness into painful crimson. Each heartbeat pulsed through her temples like a hammer striking an anvil.

Had something gone wrong during cryosleep? She'd

wanted to ask more questions before they put her under, but she couldn't risk losing her spot.

"Neural reactivation sequence complete," announced the ship's AI in Captain Mercer's calm voice. "Vital signs nominal."

But what about the baby's vital signs?

Panic clawed up her throat, like some feral thing desperate to escape her chest.

Through blurry vision, she made out Dr. Callas hovering above her, somber yet professional in medical scrubs, a yellowing bruise on his jaw. Had he gotten it during the hospital riots, when desperate people stormed hospitals seeking medication that wouldn't cure them? Or during the evacuation, fighting through mobs to reach the launch facility?

His hands felt unexpectedly warm against her ice-cold skin as he helped her sit up, careful of the IV. The world spun like an out-of-control carousel, leaving her disoriented. Colors blurred and merged, the med bay's sterile white walls pulsing with the rhythm of her racing heart. Her stomach lurched violently.

"I need to—" She couldn't finish the sentence.

The doctor produced a basin from beside her bed just in time to catch what felt like gallons of bile burning up her throat. Her retching echoed off the sterile walls of the too-bright med bay. When her stomach was empty, the acid taste lingered, bitter and sharp.

The space felt like it had been designed by someone who'd never been sick. The bed resembled an operating table, cold metal edges pressing into her back through thin padding. The glare of the overhead lights probably would've given her a headache even if she wasn't feeling sick. Everything was shaped for function rather than comfort, as if the ship were one massive, sterile laboratory.

Just like the hospital where Eddie had died.

"Lie back down," Dr. Callas ordered. "I need to run more tests. You won't be going down with the first wave."

"I'm fine now," Leila protested, wiping her mouth with a trembling hand. She forced the same smile she'd given Justin when telling him about their acceptance into the colony program. The smile she'd maintained while skipping one particular box on the application form, knowing they'd never let a pregnant woman attempt cryosleep. The smile she'd worn while listening to her new husband speculate about life on another planet, keeping secret the miracle already blooming in her belly.

Would Justin have reported her if he'd known?

In cryosleep, she'd dreamed he had found out, over and over. In her dream, Justin not only reported her every time, but he'd divorced her and married a stranger to keep his place in the colony. Abandoned his own baby to save himself.

But that was just a dream. The real Justin was waking up somewhere else on this ship, and she was sure he would be ecstatic to learn that he was already a father.

"Really, I'm sure it's just morning sickness." The words slipped out before she could stop them, her mind still fuzzy from cryosleep. Stupid, stupid, stupid.

Dr. Callas went perfectly still, like someone had hit his pause button. Leila had seen that same frozen expression on her mother's face when getting the call about Eddie's hospitalization. In Leila's experience, devastating news had a way of stopping time for one painful breath before everything crashed down.

"Morning sickness," he repeated. The medical monitors behind him beeped steadily through the ensuing seconds of silence. A drop of sweat traced a path down his temple, catching in his sideburn. "How far along were you?"

For a second, she thought he was trying to deliver bad news. But then she realized he probably meant: *how far along were you when you went into the cryopod?*

"Eight weeks." Leila kept her voice steady, resisting the urge to cross her fingers like a kid lying to her parents. "As of departure day."

"You didn't think to mention this during your pre-flight screening?" The dangerous quiet in his voice made her stomach clench again. His fingers tightened on his tablet, knuckles whitening beneath the skin. "We have no data on how cryosleep affects fetal development. The cellular stresses alone could have—"

"But they didn't, right?" Leila curled protectively around her still-flat belly, where her child had been frozen in time with her. Her hands pressed against the warm skin beneath the thin, scratchy gown, as if she could somehow feel the microscopic life within. "If something was wrong with the baby, it would be wrong with me too."

"That's not how it works." The doctor's professional mask slipped, and raw anger leaked through. Those dark circles under his eyes made the bruise on his jaw look even harsher. "Do you understand how incredibly foolish it was not to inform us immediately?"

"What was I supposed to do? If I'd admitted the truth, you would have forced me to stay on Earth." Her voice cracked, words tumbling out with all the justifications she'd repeated to herself, now sounding more like desperate prayers. "My baby would have died anyway. The entire planet was dying, the fungus was in everything!"

The doctor sighed, some of the anger draining from his expression. "Lie back down. I need to do an ultrasound to make sure the fetus is viable." He paused, and when he spoke again, his voice was gentler, the way her mama used to speak to Eddie when he was scared. "If it didn't survive cryosleep, we'll need to remove it immediately to prevent complications."

Fear gripped Leila's chest as she lay back, tears leaking from the corners of her eyes despite her best efforts to hold them back. The med bay lights blurred above her as she tried to focus on anything beyond the possibility that her gamble had failed.

"Listen carefully," he said as he prepped the ultrasound equipment. The machine hummed to life, screen flickering with static, casting an eerie blue glow across his features. "You can't keep secrets like this anymore. The tiniest detail could affect the entire colony's survival, including your baby's. Do you understand?"

She nodded, not trusting her voice. The cold gel made her shiver as he spread it on her abdomen. Or maybe that was fear. Leila had risked everything on this desperate chance—her place in the colony, her unborn child's life, humanity's future.

If she was wrong...

The image on the monitor was grainy at first, meaningless shadows in black and white. Leila held her breath, searching for any sign of movement. Just like she'd once stared at that pregnancy test back on Earth, willing those two lines to appear.

Then she heard it: a rapid, rhythmic pulsing filling the room, life's Morse code tapping out survival against impossible odds. A sound that promised life had found a way, even through forty-two years of subzero darkness.

"Your baby's heartbeat," Dr. Callas announced with a slight smile while adjusting the controls. "Strong and steady."

Joy exploded in her chest as the image resolved into

clearer shapes. She could make out the delicate curve of a tiny spine and the rapid flutter of a minuscule heart. The grayscale image pulsed with movement, the tiny form shifting slightly as if settling into a more comfortable position.

Her baby was alive.

Tears of relief spilled freely now, warm tracks down her cheeks that tasted of salt and triumph when they reached her lips.

"Everything looks normal for this stage of development," Dr. Callas said while tapping commands into the system. The screen filled with numbers and measurements that meant nothing to Leila, but the doctor's shoulders had relaxed. His fingers moved across the interface with practiced precision, each tap creating a soft electronic chirp. "I'm prescribing prenatal vitamins, and I want to hear about every ache and twinge, no matter how insignificant it seems. This will be the first human conceived on Earth and born on another world. We need to document everything."

He paused, tension creeping back into his posture. "You'll need to see Dr. Makinde for genetic screening. Make sure there are no issues we need to address."

"What happens if there are issues?" Leila's hands moved instinctively to her belly, as if she could shield her child from whatever uncomfortable truths the tests might reveal. The gel left a gooey residue on her palms. She'd seen Dr. Makinde earlier in the med bay doorway—a study in cool efficiency and calculated observation. When she found out what Leila had done, would the geneticist blame her? Or would she understand?

Callas' gaze shifted away, focusing on the monitor readouts instead of meeting her eyes. "That depends on what we find."

He sounded exactly like her mother trying to explain why Eddie wouldn't be coming home from the hospital.

It hadn't occurred to her until now, but... what if Dr. Makinde found a problem that couldn't be fixed?

What if they wanted to get rid of her baby?

The heartbeat continued to pulse through the speakers, each beat strengthening her resolve. Her fingers curled into fists at her sides, nails carving crescents of determination into her palms.

She would die before she let that happen.

Chapter Five

DAVINCI YEAR 1
   SUMMER

SAMARA GAVE the alien shrub a vicious yank while stabbing at its roots with her hand shovel. The wooden handle turned slick with sweat in her blistered palm. Alien soil caked her arms to the elbows, leaving reddish stains that resisted scrubbing, as if DaVinci's very dirt was determined to mark the invaders that disturbed it.

The plant surrendered with a sound like ripping velcro, sending her stumbling backward. She tossed it onto the growing pile of cleared vegetation, then straightened with a groan originating deep in her belly.

She paused, the reality of her situation suddenly striking her. Here she was, a geneticist from Earth, uprooting plants on a world that until recently had been just a speck of light in Earth's telescopes. The mundane action of weeding felt absurdly incongruous against the backdrop of an entirely different planet, beneath a sun that cast hazy lavender shadows across unfamiliar soil. For a moment, the scene took on a dreamlike quality—her hands, caked in rust-colored soil that had never known human touch before this week, pulling plants whose DNA had evolved along an entirely separate evolutionary path.

Sweat turned the reddish dirt into grimy paste on her skin. One finger throbbed where she'd torn off part of a fingernail, the wound red and swollen despite liberal applications of antibiotic cream. She was eager to get soil samples back to the ship to sequence whatever microorganisms inhabited this alien soil. But Katherine had decided their first priority was erecting the Common Hall for temporary shelter while laying down basic infrastructure.

They'd been clearing since dawn, preparing ground for their new home. After four days in the relatively cushy confines of the colony ship, recovering from cryosleep, reality had hit hard. This was not the kind of work Samara was used to. Her expertise lay in sterile labs with precision equipment, not wrestling with stubborn vegetation under an alien sun. But her genetic knowledge wouldn't be needed yet, and at least she was contributing something useful until then. Lucas had been assigned to help the engineers; she didn't know how his piloting skills were valuable here, but apparently, he had something to contribute.

The colony's social dynamics were already crystallizing in fascinating yet concerning ways. Katherine's people, former members of the Demeter Collective, handled the bulk of the work easily while directing the others with the breezy authority of people expecting to be in charge.

Battle lines were being drawn by natural selection: survival of the most useful.

On one side, the Demeters: seasoned men and women

whose hands mapped lifetimes of practical experience, who read soil composition and weather patterns like words on a page.

On the other side, the outsiders: untested youth still clinging to the privileges and comforts of an abandoned world. They shared a species, but were aliens to each other in every way that mattered.

Demeters averaged a decade older than the others, with work-hardened hands mapped with scars, muscles built through actual labor rather than gyms, utilitarian braids and ponytails secured with worn elastic. Their skin was permanently weathered from decades of outdoor work. They moved with the fluid efficiency of people who knew exactly how much energy each task required.

Meanwhile, the "normals" had soft hands more familiar with touchscreens than tools, fashionable haircuts better suited to office meetings than frontier survival. All were in their twenties or early thirties, chosen primarily for their reproductive potential rather than practical skills. Their attempts at manual labor had a frantic, uncertain quality, like actors miming tasks they'd only seen in videos.

That selection made biological sense. Humanity needed young, healthy bodies to rebuild the population. But the gap between the two groups was already causing friction. Case in point: Briar, a normal with curly auburn hair pinned atop her head in an elegant bun, sat cross-legged on a rock chatting with another young woman while everyone else worked. Her manicured nails and elaborately styled hair looked absurdly out of place against DaVinci's feral landscape.

A weathered Demeter veteran marched over, her voice cracking like a whip. "You two, back to work. Now."

The women exchanged an eye roll before grudgingly

pushing to their feet with exaggerated slowness, making a show of brushing dirt from their pants. The gesture carried echoes of high school rebellion, not at all the attitude the colony needed. But Samara would bet their fertility scores were through the roof.

Samara paused in her battle with the next shrub to survey their chosen homestead. A river glittered in the near distance, its eggplant-colored water catching the strange sunlight in ways that hurt her eyes if she looked too long. Analysis had shown high concentrations of dissolved minerals giving the water its strange hue, along with complex organic compounds they hadn't yet identified. They'd need to run it through a specialized filtration system before it would be safe to drink. Whether it would be safe for bathing in the meantime remained unknown.

A small forest stretched spiky blue-green leaves toward the periwinkle sky, branches swaying in patterns that seemed wrong, as if following air currents she couldn't perceive. The surrounding meadow bloomed with clusters of fuzzy-leaved vegetation in dark green and deep indigo, interspersed with translucent purplish grass that danced in the breeze. Spectroscopic analysis suggested the colors came from novel photosynthetic pigments reflecting light in the violet and ultraviolet spectrum—an adaptation to DaVinci's solar radiation profile.

So far, Samara had spotted analogs of Earth's insects, though these skittered on too many legs and appeared to communicate through rapid color changes in their carapaces. DaVinci's worms boasted what looked like rudimentary eyes, for no reason she or Renata had been able to guess, and the small scurrying creatures she had initially mistaken for some kind of rodent resembled feathered reptiles upon closer look. She'd even seen something like the unholy offspring of a spider and a hairless bat swooping through the air, its translucent wings refracting sunlight into scattered rainbows.

Sometimes the wonder of it all hit her sideways—she was witnessing an entirely separate evolutionary path, life that had developed without any connection to Earth's history. Everything here had emerged from different primordial chemicals, shaped by different selective pressures, yet arrived at solutions that echoed Earth's biodiversity while remaining distinctly alien. It was enough to make her scientific mind reel with questions and possibilities.

Each new organism they encountered raised more questions than answers. How had life evolved here? What selection pressures had shaped these creatures? And most importantly, what defenses might they have developed against invasive species like humans?

Movement caught her eye: Leila and a handsome young man were standing apart from the work groups, having an intense discussion. Leila looked fragile, better suited to a climate-controlled environment than frontier survival, although she hadn't been shirking her responsibilities like Briar had. The young man appeared shocked by whatever she was telling him, his hands frozen mid-gesture. Her face crumpled with hurt, and though he tried to smooth things over, reaching for her arm, she huffed and stomped away. He watched her go, confusion and fear warring across his features before he returned to work alone.

Their first day on-planet was guaranteed to be hard. But it wouldn't be the hardest they would face, not by a long shot.

She hoped they would find a way to rise to the challenge.

The grating scrape of metal on rock yanked Samara's attention to the construction site, where Maeve was directing her team like a conductor guiding an orchestra of organized chaos. Mounted on colossal wheels, the first prefab building awaited expansion from its transport configuration.

Reflective panels hurled the alien sunlight back in fragmented patterns that made Samara's eyes water. She wondered how long it would take for them to adapt.

The engineers used laser guides to ensure perfect alignment while positioning the prefab pack in the cleared space. Foundation points glowed faintly blue against the red soil, creating a geometric pattern that made Samara think of ancient builders laying out stone circles by starlight.

After removing the wheels and lowering the pack to the ground with a hydraulic system, the engineering team attached thick synthetic ropes to a ring on the top layer, spreading out until the lines formed precise 45-degree angles with the building—crucial for the balanced tension required to activate the self-assembly mechanism. At Maeve's command, they pulled in unison.

With a pneumatic hiss and the groaning of metal, the first wall began to rise like a creature waking from hibernation. Samara watched, transfixed as the structure unfolded itself, panels sliding and locking into place with mechanical precision. Support struts emerged from hidden compartments, telescoping outward to brace the growing framework. It was like watching a giant piece of avant-garde origami unfurl itself into a masterpiece of angles and lines, all choreographed by some unseen hand. The building seemed almost alive as it assembled itself, a golem of steel and composite materials animated by cleverly applied physics.

The common hall took its final rectangular shape. But as the roof panels slid down their tracks, one caught with a metallic shriek, refusing to snap into place.

"Damn it," Maeve growled. "This is what happens when you prioritize cutting-edge tech over proven designs."

She dispatched a pair of engineers back to the shuttle for ladders. Once assembled, they climbed up to inspect the tracks where the roof had jammed.

"Track's bent!" one called down. "We'll need to straighten it manually!"

While they worked, Samara grabbed her water canteen and headed toward the ridge on the north side of the colony site. Her muscles protested as she began to climb, but the promise of solitude pulled her upward. The ridge wasn't particularly steep, but the alien soil shifted unpredictably under her boots, sometimes compacting firmly, other times crumbling away in flaky sheets that slid downward in miniature avalanches.

Halfway up, she paused to catch her breath. The ridge was composed of layered sedimentary rock in shades of rust and copper, with veins of something crystalline that caught the light in flashes of deep purple. She ran her fingers over the exposed rock, feeling the gritty texture. No doubt Mahmoud would submit a detailed analysis of its composition to their team by the end of the week, but for now, she let herself appreciate its beauty.

When she finally reached the top of the ridge, Samara turned in a slow circle, taking in the panoramic view that stole her breath more effectively than the climb. The meandering purplish river cut through the landscape like a vein of exotic metal, widening into a delta of braided channels to the east before disappearing into a forest of towering blue-black vegetation. The canopy of that distant forest undulated in waves.

To the west, rolling hills gave way to jagged mountains whose lower slopes were carpeted in vegetation that shifted from indigo to turquoise as elevation increased. The northern horizon featured a vast expanse of what appeared to be grassland, though the "grass" resembled nothing from Earth. Tall, translucent pink stalks ending in bulbous structures that swayed in hypnotic unison created ripples of movement across the plain.

The colony site below looked out of place against this sweeping landscape, a small square of cleared Earth with the almost-assembled common hall at its center, surrounded by the busy movement of humans. Everything on this world had evolved to find its own niche, while they would have to brute force their way into an existing niche, possibly a niche that was already occupied by something else.

Samara uncapped her water bottle and took a long drink of filtered water, savoring the coolness sliding down her throat. The breeze up here was stronger, carrying scents she couldn't identify. There was something almost spicy, mixed with metallic notes and an underlying sweetness like overripe fruit. The air felt different against her skin, too. It had a strange static quality that made the fine hairs on her arms stand on end.

As she recapped her water, something on the southern horizon caught her eye, a smudge of darkness against the otherwise clear sky. She squinted, trying to make sense of what she was seeing. A cloud formation? But there had been no other clouds all day. Perhaps smoke from a natural fire? If so, it would have to be a big one.

She shielded her eyes with one hand, studying the phenomenon more carefully. The dark mass appeared to be expanding, spreading across the horizon like ink in water. Within minutes, what had been a small blemish on the skyline had doubled in size, its edges roiling and churning.

With a jolt of alarm, Samara realized the mass wasn't just growing, it was moving toward them. The distance was hard to judge, but the rate at which the formation was approaching suggested terrifying speed. What had appeared as a distant curiosity was now visibly advancing across the landscape, swallowing everything in its path.

The way it moved—rolling forward like the planet's immune system mobilizing against infection—reminded her of dust storms she'd seen in documentaries about the American Dust Bowl.

Samara watched, transfixed, as landmark after landmark disappeared behind the advancing curtain of swirling particles. A solitary hill vanished in seconds. The leading edge of the grassland was consumed next. The storm was covering ground at an impossible rate; it would reach the colony within minutes.

"Dust storm," Samara called out, already scrambling down the ridge, loose rocks skittering away beneath her boots as she half-ran, half-slid toward the colony.

By the time she made it to the bottom, the storm had grown from a horizon smudge to a towering wall of darkness that devoured the landscape as it approached. But no one seemed to have noticed: all attention was on the roof of the building, where two engineers were struggling to fix the roof.

"Dust storm!" Samara yelled. "Katherine!"

The colony leader took one look in the direction Samara was pointing and snapped into action.

"Maeve! Get that roof fixed now!" Katherine's voice boomed across the site. "Everyone else inside! Move!"

Samara hurried in with the others, who huddled in groups and talked in murmurs, waiting for the storm to hit.

Above them, banging and thudding as engineers struggled to reshape the track so the roof could slide the last few feet and lock into place. As the wind picked up, flurries of dust blew in through the gap above and floated down to coat everyone and everything. Coughing and sneezing echoed off the walls as colonists covered their faces with shirts and scarves. The dust carried a sharp, metallic odor that burned Samara's throat.

With a shriek of metal and a horrendous bang, the roof slid further but stopped short, leaving a gap of a few inches between itself and the south wall. A few moments later, the engineers hurried through the front door. Maeve was last inside, her face grim beneath layers of sweat and grime. "Had to abandon the repair. Visibility dropped too quick. I couldn't risk my crew getting trapped up there."

One of the engineers bent double in a coughing spasm. Another couldn't stop sneezing.

"We've got some N95s in the work kit," Maeve announced, producing a small box of masks. "Not nearly enough for everyone."

"The leadership team should have priority," Ayesha suggested. "We can't risk losing key personnel."

"Rock-paper-scissors." Katherine raised her fist, showing the steel that had made her a successful commune leader on Earth. "Beat me, you get a mask. Lose, you make do with whatever you're wearing."

Through the chaos of the impromptu tournament, Samara noticed Hector palming one of the precious N95s and slipping it to Leila. The gesture wasn't lost on Briar, whose face twisted into something bitter and ugly. When Leila put the mask on, Samara could practically hear teeth grinding from across the room as Briar's jaw muscles corded with barely restrained envy.

Then Lucas entered, covered in dust. Samara hadn't

realized he was still out in the storm. His muddy boots suggested he'd been out in the fields, probably making sure the livestock was safe.

She didn't know him well at all, but he seemed to work harder than any of the other colonists. Everyone else seemed to like him. And he treated her with nothing but respect.

She could have done much worse for a partner.

But she was still glad that they would all be sleeping in the main hall for a while, until individual residences could be built.

She turned toward him as he approached. "This came out of nowhere. Why didn't we have any warning?"

"The ship's drones are still collecting atmospheric data," Lucas replied. "Now that we know these storms are possible, we can establish proper monitoring protocols. We'll be better prepared next time."

Hours later, after the storm finally passed, they emerged into sunlight that seemed obscenely cheerful given their situation. Everything, people, equipment, the partially-assembled building, was coated in staticky dust that clung to surfaces with annoying tenacity. And everyone was suffering to some degree: runny eyes and noses, constant sneezing and coughing, raspy voices in danger of giving out completely.

"We'll need filters for every building," Maeve said, clearly already planning modifications. "And proper respirators for everyone. We'll seal up all the buildings tight."

Katherine nodded. "Let's get some food into everyone first. Unpack the rations before Maeve's team resumes work on the building." She raised her voice to address the group. "The rest of you, start hauling water from the river. We'll need to boil it and run it through the filter. No bathing in it until we've tested it properly."

Samara watched Briar tracking Leila's movements as she slipped the mask back into her pocket. Leila kept her stride carefully casual, but her hand remained pressed against the pocket where the N95 was hidden.

The dividing lines were already forming: those with masks versus those without, Demeters versus normals, leadership versus everyone else. Earth had followed them here after all, not just in their technology or their skills, but in their instinct to create hierarchies, even at the edge of survival.

One dust storm had exposed how fragile their unity truly was. And this was only day five.

FOUR COLONISTS WERE CHOSEN for night watch, each taking two-hour shifts to guard their vulnerable shelter. Samara lay in her sleeping bag on the common hall's hard floor, trying to ignore the whispered conversations and rustling movements of a hundred and sixty people seeking comfort in a space designed to serve as a mess hall and gathering space rather than a place to sleep. The unfinished building amplified each cough and whisper into a symphony of human discomfort.

She would've given anything for a pair of earplugs.

Through the gap in the unfinished roof, DaVinci's larger moon cast ribbons of golden light while the smaller moon added shades of silvery-blue, creating an unsettling chromatic effect that made ordinary objects look like props in some cosmic dream. Shadows seemed to crawl when viewed from the corner of her eye, as if the darkness itself was restless.

The night air carried unfamiliar sounds through the cavernous hall, clicks that might have been insects, rustling vegetation that moved in patterns unlike Earth plants, and occasionally, something that might have been wings. She knew it was dangerous to forget this was not Earth, but found it comforting to pretend that distant high-pitched cry was an owl shrieking victory after seizing a mouse, and that the irregular rustle was a gecko scampering through garden weeds.

Samara had just started to doze off when a shout shattered the uneasy quiet, followed by the crack of gunfire.

She bolted upright, heart pounding against her ribs like it might break free.

Through ringing ears, she heard running footsteps and voices raised in alarm. Lucas was already moving toward the door, his motions precise and purposeful despite the darkness. She scrambled to follow him, Katherine right beside her.

The night air hit her with a shock of cold and that now-familiar metallic undertone that the dust storm had brought.

"There!" Marcus' rifle trembled in his grasp, its muzzle scribing erratic patterns against the starlit sky. Sweat beaded on his forehead despite the chill. "Ridge line. Something—something walking on two legs. But wrong."

"Take us through exactly what you saw," Katherine said, her voice steady but roughened by the dust. She hadn't taken a mask for herself.

"Humanoid. Moving like... like it had too many joints." The guard swallowed hard, the sound audible in the tense silence. "Gone now. Shot at it and it just melted into the shadows." He fell into a whisper. "But I swear it was watching us."

He pointed at the ridge, which loomed dark against the star-scattered sky. The shadows between the rocks seemed deeper than they should be, as if the darkness there had substance.

"Until we get perimeter sensors established, standing watch and sleeping in the common hall will have to be standard procedure," Lucas said while scanning the ridge line. "I'll take the next shift."

He held out his hand for the gun, which Marcus surrendered.

"Those sensors would already be up if the roof hadn't stuck and if that dust storm hadn't interrupted our work," Katherine said, frustration evident in her voice. "We'll make it tomorrow's priority."

After they went back inside, the leadership team, minus Lucas, gathered in a corner while the other colonists settled back into uneasy sleep, huddled together like survivors in a lifeboat. Their whispers created a subtle current of sound beneath the louder restlessness of the common hall. The scent of too many unwashed bodies in too small a space hung in the air, mingling with the alien dust that still coated everything.

"What if there really was something up there?" Ayesha clutched her prayer beads, thumb working the smooth surfaces as she spoke. The click of bead against bead punctuated her words like a nervous heartbeat.

"The drones haven't detected any large fauna," Renata countered, though her expression suggested she wasn't entirely convinced by her own argument. "But there could be nocturnal predators we haven't yet documented. The biological survey will take months, at least."

"Humanoid?" Maeve asked.

Renata shrugged. "It's not impossible. But even if Marcus really did see something human-shaped, that doesn't mean it's sentient, or even intelligent."

"People are tired and on edge." Hector sounded much

calmer than Samara felt. "We're wired to imagine monsters in the dark."

"The ship's inventory includes an array of motion sensors and thermal imaging units," Maeve replied. "Originally intended for perimeter security once we established permanent structures."

"I can help set them up, if you need more people," Leo volunteered. "We'll also need some around the pasture."

"Count me in, too," Samara said. "It's not like I have any patients to treat yet."

"Actually," Hector cleared his throat, shooting a meaningful look at Katherine. "Leila is eight weeks pregnant. I was hoping you could check the fetus today."

The unexpected news landed in the conversation like a stone in still water. Samara felt the ripples of implications spreading outward.

Eight weeks pregnant meant…

"She lied during her screening?" Katherine sounded more tired than shocked.

"I've already given her a thorough dressing-down," he assured her. "The fetus appears unaffected by the cryosleep, but there's still the standard genetic screening for viability."

Samara rubbed her temples, where a headache pulsed in time with her heartbeat. "I gave up my equipment space in yesterday's shuttle run so the engineers could bring down extra tools. I thought I wouldn't need it yet."

"You're excused from work detail tomorrow," Katherine told Samara. "Lucas can fly you both up to the ship."

Dismissed, Samara returned to her sleeping bag, her throat still raw from the dust storm's abrasive onslaught. Despite her exhaustion, her mind raced with the day's events, replaying them in vivid detail.

But at last, sheer exhaustion triumphed over discomfort, and her eyes refused to stay open.

Her last conscious thought was of that shadowy shape on the ridge. What if it hadn't been fear and fatigue playing tricks?

What if something really was watching them?

How long would it watch before it decided to do more?

Chapter Six

SAMARA STARTLED awake on her thin mat in the Common Hall, seized by uncontrollable coughing. Each breath tore at her raw throat, pain lancing through her chest. A violent spasm bent her double, and she stared at the rust-colored specks mixed with spit on her blistered palm.

The sight sent a ripple of anxiety through her. What damage might the alien particles be causing to the tissues in her lungs? The metallic taste lingered on her tongue, mixing with the copper tang of blood from where she'd bitten the inside of her cheek during a particularly harsh coughing fit. She wiped her hand on her pants, leaving a faint reddish smear. Had that brutal dust storm been a one-off, or were those a regular feature of DaVinci's weather patterns?

The room echoed with the raspy hacking of other colonists, the sound bouncing off metal walls to create a dissonant chorus of respiratory distress. Samara forced herself upright, feeling like her bones had been replaced with lead. Yesterday's clothes clung uncomfortably to her skin, damp with sweat despite the hall's cool temperature.

She scanned the room for Lucas, surprised not to see him. But then she remembered he'd taken watch duty overnight in case that figure on the ridge returned.

Something walking on two legs. But wrong.

What had Marcus actually seen?

They'd been pushing themselves hard yesterday, full-out exertion after only a few days to recover from forty-two years in cryosleep. They'd all been exhausted by the time the dust storm had hit, including Marcus, and miserable by the time it passed, thanks to all the dust they'd been breathing. Even a healthy, well-rested person might let their imagination run wild their first night on an alien planet. Marcus had volunteered despite his exhaustion.

Moving like… like it had too many joints.

The Borlaug's drones had done an extensive survey of this region during the four days between entering orbit and landing, and Lucas hadn't reported anything larger than a small dog. Definitely nothing humanoid.

So either Marcus imagined the creature, or it was very good at hiding.

Which suggested intelligence.

Parallel evolution did happen, but what were the chances that they'd choose a planet already populated with intelligent humanoid aliens?

Extremely small.

Samara shook her head. Logic should have quelled her niggling unease, but it didn't. The human brain was infamous for populating the darkness with monsters. Even when actual reality was plenty scary, it was easier to give your fears a face than to wrestle with nebulous uncertainties like whether the dust in their lungs might make them sick or whether their water filtration system would miss a lethal microorganism.

Alien watchers were something you could imagine

fighting. The real dangers of DaVinci might be much more insidious.

She spotted Renata sitting cross-legged by the entrance, sharing breakfast with her partner, Marcus, as they spoke in hushed tones. Samara's stomach roiled at the idea of food, but skipping meals would only sap her already depleted energy reserves. But part of her would've loved someone to lean toward over a meal, to complain about the chewy, overcooked eggs in her ration pouch and ground herself in that mundanity.

It was the little differences that were the most disorienting. The blue-shifted tinge of the shadows. The ruddiness of the dirt that her mind kept expecting to be brown. The cries of creatures that probably weren't birds but reminded her of them.

On the far side of the vast hall, Leila had joined Ayesha Basu's spontaneous morning prayer circles. The young woman bowed her head, hands clasped, looking almost luminous despite the omnipresent dust coating everyone and everything. It wasn't just that pregnancy glow —the fine particles caught the morning light filtering through the gap in the roof, creating a halo effect around the assembled worshippers.

Beside Leila, Justin seemed even more glum than yesterday, his shoulders hunched forward, eyes fixed on the floor. Samara couldn't blame him entirely. Leila had made the choice to have a child for both of them, way ahead of schedule. As someone who had never wanted children, Samara was sure she'd be unhappy if she were in his shoes.

But Justin's lack of enthusiasm didn't seem to be dimming Leila's.

"...we are grateful for this new beginning," Ayesha intoned softly, her hands gently folded in front of her. "May we approach this world with humility and care, learning from our past mistakes. Comfort those who suffer, strengthen those who labor, and help us to build a community worthy of the sacrifice that brought us here..."

Samara watched the gathered colonists as their faces softened in the dim light, tension momentarily easing from furrowed brows and tight jaws. She couldn't help but feel a twinge of envy at the peace that seemed to settle over them. Faith had always felt to Samara like trying to solve an equation with missing variables. Science made more sense. You could test your hypotheses instead of simply hoping with all your heart that they were true.

Of course, that rational approach hadn't exactly endeared her to religious fundamentalists, even before the Chytrid Collapse. They'd protested genetic engineering without bothering to understand the actual techniques involved, seeing only a violation of divine will where people like Samara saw potential salvation.

She couldn't help thinking of Dory, torn apart by a mob that didn't care that their victim wasn't even a scientist. Who hadn't bothered to learn that the lab manager had nothing to do with creating the fungal plague. Dory had been just as much a victim of chytrid as the people who killed her. The memory tightened something in Samara's chest, a knot of grief and guilt that might never fully loosen.

Strange how much easier it was to mourn Dory than to think about the deaths of her own family. But when she thought of her parents, her sister, her nephew... she just felt numb. She knew intellectually that they'd probably starved to death. Or worse.

It was the *worse* that she didn't want to imagine.

"Here." Katherine interrupted Samara's brooding by pressing a ration pack into her hands. The metallic packaging was cool against her skin, the weight of it oddly reassuring. Or maybe it was Katherine's matter-of-fact manner as she issued her next order. "Help me and Leo distribute breakfast before these colonists start considering cannibalism."

Samara managed a weak smile and grabbed an armful of packets. Eggs with sausage and hash browns. Eggs with bacon and toast. Oatmeal with walnuts and blueberries. The silver packaging crinkled as she handed them out, her own stomach grudgingly acknowledging hunger beneath the nausea.

Tension hummed through the crowded space like a low-voltage current. Colonists clustered in small groups, conversations hushed but intense. Sharp glances were exchanged between Demeters and normals. The division was physical as well as social—subtle but unmistakable gaps separated the groups, invisible boundaries no one crossed without purpose.

Dr. Callas, no, she should start calling him Hector, was already making his rounds, examining colonists and dispensing medication in carefully measured doses. His medical bag hung at his side, its contents organized with military precision. The Borlaug was well-stocked with every kind of medicine Hofstadter's team could imagine the colonists needing, but they'd only brought a couple of medkits down with them.

Hector turned as she passed, his clinical gaze sweeping over her. Not friendly at all, just the colony doctor doing his duty. "Stop by for a checkup when you're done. That cough sounds nasty."

Samara nodded, noting the dark circles under his eyes and the way he favored his left side. The doctor looked as rough as his patients, though he maintained his professional demeanor.

She continued through the crowd, passing Briar as the young woman complained to her companions.

"Look at my nails! Absolutely ruined." She held out her hands, examining fingers that still looked surprisingly manicured despite her complaints. "And I've already got a massive blister on my left hand. This is ridiculous."

For a fleeting moment, Samara felt a pang of sympathy; her own raw palms throbbed in commiseration. But this was what they had signed up for.

Blisters and sore backs and hacking up what felt like a lungful of dust.

The sooner they could fabricate some decent masks, the better.

Ayesha approached as Samara finished distributing the last of the ration packs.

"You know, you'd be welcome to join us in the morning," she said, gesturing to where her prayer group had been. Her voice carried no judgment, just a simple invitation. "All belief systems are welcome."

"Are you inviting me as the colony's chaplain or as the colony's psychologist?"

"Whichever one you need."

Samara hesitated. "I don't believe in... well, any religion, really."

"That's fine," Ayesha said with a gentle smile. "Some come for the community, others for a moment of quiet reflection."

But Samara thought that her best moments of quiet reflection happened when she was alone.

"If you ever want to talk privately, my door is always open," Ayesha added. "Sometimes it helps just to have someone listen."

"Thank you, I will," Samara said, knowing that she probably wouldn't. But she appreciated the offer. She was starting to see why Hofstadter had given the woman a spot —when things got difficult, the colony would need a peacemaker.

Now, if she could just win Hector over…

Samara followed Ayesha to the corner that Katherine had commandeered for the leadership team's morning briefing, allowing them to observe the room while maintaining some privacy. Grabbing a ration pouch, she settled cross-legged on the floor next to Renata. The chill of the hard vinyl floor seeped through her pants, adding to her discomfort. She tore open the silver package, releasing the scent of eggs and fennel-spiced sausage.

"Status update?" Katherine asked as Hector joined them. She sat with perfect posture despite the lack of proper seating, her weathered hands clasped in front of her.

"Mostly irritated respiratory tracts," he reported between bites of scrambled eggs. "Treatable with standard cough medication and expectorants. Some are showing what appear to be moderate allergic reactions. I had to break out the antihistamines." He frowned. "Strange, considering none of them showed dust allergies in their medical screenings."

"I'm experiencing significant light-headedness and shortness of breath myself," Ayesha announced. "And as far as I know, I've never had a dust allergy, either."

"I'd like to analyze the dust composition," Hector continued. "Check for toxic compounds. But most of my lab equipment is still up on the ship. Didn't think I'd need it this soon."

"My geological survey gear is up there too," added Mahmoud, absently touching the burn scar visible above his collar. The tissue looked angry and red, still not fully healed. "We'll need it before breaking ground on permanent structures. We can't risk building on unstable terrain."

"I can analyze samples of the dust and transmit the data," Lucas offered with his signature composure, even though he had to be exhausted from standing watch half the night. "Give me a list of the equipment needed, and I'll bring it back with me."

"We have materials aboard to fabricate real respirators," Maeve said, her voice even rougher than the geologist's. "But I'm needed here to oversee plumbing installation and power grid setup. Can't afford another glitch."

Lucas nodded. "I'll start fabricating components while I'm waiting for the results of the dust analysis."

"I'll help with the respirators," Samara volunteered, relieved for an excuse to spend more time on the ship, where the air didn't taste like metal. "After I do the check on Leila's baby."

"I can handle Leila's examination," Hector said, his tone professional but dismissive. He didn't quite meet Samara's eyes. "No need to waste both our time."

Samara frowned. "With respect, I should be there to assess fetal viability and genetic stability." She leaned forward slightly, lowering her voice even though Leila wasn't anywhere nearby. "The dust exposure could also cause developmental issues we might need to address early. Better to identify potential problems now than face worse complications later."

Callas considered this for a moment, then nodded reluctantly. "Fair point."

Katherine stood, then hopped up onto a chair, clapping her hands three times. The sharp sound cut through the morning chatter, and the room quieted as colonists turned toward their leader. The sudden silence had a weight to it, expectant and heavy.

"Before we break for assignments," Katherine started, her voice carrying easily through the hall, "I want to acknowledge what you've all accomplished in just five days here. An alien environment, unpredictable storms, and conditions we could never have fully prepared for. Yet here you stand, building humanity's first foothold among the stars. Each of you has already proven that you're exactly where you need to be."

Nice speech. Too bad it wasn't working on everyone. Briar remained sulkily focused on her ruined fingernails, while others shifted restlessly, eager to get on with their day.

Katherine continued, her tone shifting from inspiration to practical authority. "Dechante, Livson, Banerji— drainage ditches. Torrez, Anand, Malik—water filtration."

As Katherine listed out assignments, Samara listened with growing unease, the leaden weight in her stomach hardening to ice as her own name remained conspicuously unspoken, along with several others. She felt eyes turning toward her, questioning, evaluating. The scrutiny prickled along her skin like static electricity.

"I notice not everyone's name was called," someone called from the crowd, the observation more accusation than question.

"Those individuals have already been assigned their duties for today." Katherine's tone was neutral but carried an undercurrent of steel.

"Bet those people weren't assigned to dig ditches," Briar muttered, just loud enough to be heard. Her words dropped into the tense silence like pebbles into still water. Ripples of agreement spread through her circle of supporters.

Katherine turned toward Briar with the deliberate calm of someone who had handled far worse challenges than petty insubordination.

"I wasn't aware you held a medical degree, Specialist Briar."

Briar's face flushed dark red, but she remained silent under Katherine's steady gaze. Her fingers curled into fists at her sides, knuckles whitening with suppressed anger.

"No?" Katherine continued. "Then you'll perform the duties assigned to you, as others will perform theirs."

The colony leader let the moment settle before addressing the wider group. "Let me make one thing perfectly clear. Everyone here contributes. Everyone here pulls their weight. But that weight doesn't always look the same. Some of our team will be assisting with medical and engineering tasks vital to our survival. We don't know when another storm will hit. But rest assured that no one will be exempt from doing whatever job needs to be done, when it needs to be done."

She paused, her eyes finding Briar, who sullenly refused to meet her gaze. "There is no room in this colony for petty jealousy or selfishness. Not when our survival could hinge on the smallest thing."

Katherine drew herself up to her full, imposing height. "If you can't put the needs of the community first? If you can't see past your own desires to do what must be done for the greater good," Her eyes flashed. "Then you'd best get used to the taste of alien dirt. Because you'll be choking on it until you learn."

She pivoted away from Briar's seething figure with the finality of someone closing a book. "Get to work," she called over her shoulder as she strode away. "All of you."

The look Briar shot Samara had graduated from

resentment to hatred, her eyes narrowed to slits, jaw clenched tight enough to strain the muscles in her neck.

Great, just what she needed. Another enemy.

Samara wondered if Katherine was deliberately keeping Leila's pregnancy secret to avoid exactly this kind of drama. Briar wouldn't forget that Hector had given Leila a mask without making her earn it, and as Leila's pregnancy progressed, she'd need other exemptions. Which would guarantee that Briar would see her as an enemy, too.

A scream yanked Samara from her thoughts.

She whipped around, saw Leila crumpled to the floor, crimson spreading across her lap in a widening stain. Justin hovered helplessly at her side as she curled around her belly, suddenly sobbing. The sound cut through the morning chaos like a knife, silencing conversations as colonists turned to stare.

"Help!" Justin shouted, his voice cracking. "Someone help!"

Samara and Hector reached the girl simultaneously, knees hitting the hard floor with twin thuds. Blood was beginning to pool on the floor around the young woman, its metallic scent mixing with the alien dust. The crimson liquid spread with alarming speed, soaking into the knees of Samara's pants.

Oh no.

Samara had the guilty thought that at least Hector would be the one to deliver the news if Leila lost the baby.

"We need to get her to the ship," the doctor said, already checking her vitals. "The fetus could still be viable, but we need proper equipment to assess the damage. The dust exposure—"

"Please," Leila sobbed, clutching Samara's hand with desperate strength. Her skin felt cool and clammy, early signs of shock. "Please save my baby. I can't—" Another sob racked her body. "I can't lose this one, too."

Too. The word hit Samara like a physical blow as pieces clicked into place. Leila hadn't just been desperate enough to risk cryosleep while pregnant. She'd been desperate enough to try again after a previous loss.

Samara squeezed her hand, knowing that some equations had no solution, no matter how desperately you searched for one.

"We'll do everything we can," she promised, hoping it would be enough.

Chapter Seven

THE BLOOD CLUNG TENACIOUSLY, defying Leila's attempts to scrape it away. She scoured her thighs raw in the ship's medical bay shower as the water temperature fluctuated between scalding and tepid, as the recycling system struggled to maintain equilibrium. Rusty flakes still clung to her skin like scabs, refusing to yield to her desperate scrubbing. Her hands trembled uncontrollably as she slipped into the flimsy hospital gown, fingers fumbling with the ties. The insubstantial fabric provided scant defense against the room's pervasive, antiseptic chill.

The medical bay's air carried the sharp tang of disinfectant mixed with other smells she didn't recognize. Overhead lights cast harsh shadows across pristine surfaces, making everything seem flat and unforgiving. Each breath she took tasted sterile, devoid of the earthy notes she'd already grown accustomed to on DaVinci's surface.

At least the bleeding had stopped. That had to mean something good, right?

Fifteen minutes later, she perched on the edge of the exam table, the paper covering crinkling beneath her. She tried not to look at the growing collection of vials Dr. Callas was filling with her blood. The crimson liquid caught the light as he rotated each tube, ensuring proper mixing with the anticoagulants. Each vial held another potential indictment, a mute testament to the consequences of her reckless desperation.

"Any new symptoms?" Dr. Callas asked, labeling the latest sample with practiced efficiency. The marker squeaked against the plastic label, a small sound that seemed unnaturally loud in the quiet room.

Her throat felt like she'd swallowed a box of steel wool. "Sore throat. Coughing. Can't catch my breath." She managed a weak smile. "Also craving pickle relish on chili mac, which is definitely new."

"Cravings are a good sign." The doctor didn't look up from his labeling. "Means your hormone levels are still elevated."

The ultrasound machine hummed to life behind him, its screen flickering with static, casting a blue-white glow that painted his features in ghostly relief. The same model they had used yesterday, when he'd shown Leila that magical first glimpse of her baby's heartbeat. Before everything went wrong.

"Should…" The words caught in her throat. She swallowed hard against the soreness that the dust storm had left behind and tried once more. "If I had told you about the baby, is there something you could've given me to protect it? Did I—"

—kill my baby? She could barely finish the thought, let alone voice it.

"There was nothing I could've done." His voice remained carefully neutral as he arranged instruments on a metal tray. The tools clinked softly against the surface, each sound like a tiny accusation. "Cryosleep is barely tested technology. We had no time for proper trials. We're lucky we all woke up. Some of the livestock didn't."

A leaden weight settled in her chest. "So, it could have hurt the baby?"

"Speculating about what might have happened doesn't help us now." He gestured for her to lie back. "We need to focus on what comes next."

The paper cover crinkled again as she reclined on the examination table, tensing involuntarily when he squirted freezing gel on her belly. She forced herself to focus on the ultrasound screen, willing it to show her baby still alive.

The image resolved slowly. Black and white shadows shifted and swirled like smoke patterns until—

"There." Dr. Callas adjusted something on the machine, his fingers moving deftly across the controls. "Heartbeat's strong."

The sound filled the room, fast and steady as a galloping horse. Her own heart sped up as if trying to match each tiny beat, and her fingertips tingled with relief, warmth spreading up her arms and into her chest.

She's alive. Although she didn't know how, she knew her baby was a *she*.

Dark specks dotted the fuzzy image of the ultrasound, in stark contrast to the lighter areas that formed the outline of her tiny child.

"Wait." Leila squinted at the screen. A cold knot formed in her stomach. "What are those spots?"

"Could be imaging artifacts." Callas frowned, adjusting the settings. The machine hummed softly as it recalibrated. "These machines weren't exactly designed for use in space, let alone on another planet. The ship's radiation shielding might be interfering with the signal processing."

"But the baby's okay?"

"As far as I can tell." The doctor's hesitation lasted a microsecond too long.

"The antihistamines!" she blurted. "Should I stop taking them? What if they're making things worse?"

Her hand moved instinctively to her throat, which burned with each swallow. She'd been coughing all morning, but it felt like her lungs were still coated with dust. And she'd been one of those lucky enough to get a mask. She couldn't imagine how awful the others must be feeling.

"Keep taking the meds. You need to breathe, and they won't harm the fetus." Dr. Callas wiped the gel off her belly with a rough towel. Now she felt cold and sticky. "Though your symptoms should be improving by now, not getting worse."

"But they are getting worse," Leila said. "It's harder to breathe today than it was yesterday."

The tightness in her chest got tighter, as if acknowledging the problem had made her lungs constrict further.

The doctor didn't respond immediately, focused on entering data into his tablet. Lines of text reflected in his glasses, numbers and symbols that might hold her baby's fate.

"I'll run these blood tests. And I'll speak with Katherine about taking you off the duty roster for a few days, until we're certain that everything's stable. I want you to rest, do you understand?"

The subtext hit Leila like a punch to her gut. They were worried she was going to lose the baby.

What if it was already too late to save her?

The door hissed open like an angry snake, the pneumatic seal releasing with a burst of pressure that sent a cool draft across Leila's exposed skin. Dr. Makinde swept inside, her arms laden with equipment that glittered under the harsh lights: crystalline scanners and chrome-plated analyzers. Ready to unravel her child's genetic secrets, layer by microscopic layer. To catalog every flaw and imperfection.

Dr. Makinde nodded politely to Dr. Callas, who returned the gesture, then left without another word.

Leila wondered if that was because he had nothing good to say, and he didn't want to deliver bad news where she could hear it.

"How are you feeling, Leila?" Dr. Makinde asked.

"What happens if you find something you can't fix?" Leila blurted. Her tongue felt suddenly dry, sticking to the roof of her mouth.

"Our repair techniques are incredibly sophisticated." Dr. Makinde sat on the chair next to the examining table. "The viral vectors target genetic issues with microscopic precision."

"But what if..." Leila's fingers splayed across her belly, a futile shield. Her skin felt warm beneath her palm, a small comfort against the chill of uncertainty. The word *abort* burned in her throat. "What if you find something..."

"Both you and your partner passed the genetic screening." Dr. Makinde calibrated one of her devices, its display casting amber light across her features. "Mutations can occur, but you're in good health."

Well, she had been in good health until the dust storm hit. Leila wasn't sure what would be worse: if her baby died because Leila had knowingly exposed her to the experimental cryopod or if she died because Leila had brought her to an alien world with poisonous dust storms.

Either way, it would be her fault. But somehow the first one seemed worse. Maybe because there was no way she could've known about the dust until it hit them, but she could've told Dr. Callas she was pregnant before she'd let them pump her full of chemicals and freeze her.

"Please don't lie to me if it's bad." Leila's heart thumped painfully against her ribs, each beat a reminder of her child's far more fragile heartbeat. "I'd rather know the truth."

Dr. Makinde's eyes softened, just slightly. "I promise, I'll do everything in my power to ensure your baby survives."

Looking at Dr. Makinde's carefully composed features, Leila saw the same expression she'd witnessed in countless doctors' faces before they suggested yet another experimental treatment for Eddie. That particular blend of determination and detachment meant they saw your loved one as a problem to solve rather than a person to save.

The ultrasound screen still showed those mysterious dark spots, pixelated shadows that seemed to pulse with each beat of her baby's heart. And for the first time, Leila wondered if bringing new life to this alien world had been an act of hope or just another futile sacrifice.

THREE INTERMINABLE HOURS oozed by with the viscosity of decades. Leila's nails, already chewed ragged, wouldn't survive much longer. The drone of the infirmary's atmospheric regulators set Leila's teeth on edge, a constant mechanical hum that seemed to vibrate through her skull. The antiseptic reek reminded her too much of Eddie's final days, triggering flashes of memory, his skeletal hand in hers, the beeping monitors, the whispered consultations in hallways. She had done enough waiting in medical facilities to last several lifetimes.

At least if her baby died, it would be quick. No suffering.

The door slid open with another angry hiss that tautened her overwrought nerves.

Dr. Makinde entered like a harbinger of judgment, holding a device that looked like an ancient executioner's tool reimagined in chrome and glass. Leila could see her own distorted reflection in its polished surface. Disheveled. Terrified. And most painful of all, hopeful.

"Good news," the geneticist said, pulling up a chair. The legs scraped against the floor, the sound making Leila wince. "Your baby's genome shows no serious defects."

"No *serious* ones?" Leila hated when people hedged instead of coming right out with the bad news. Her fingers twisted the thin fabric of her gown.

"Just color blindness. It's a relatively simple fix—we can splice in the genes for proper cone cell development." Dr. Makinde held up the injection device. "The viral vector delivers the corrective DNA directly to the developing optical neurons. Completely safe, it's been used successfully for decades."

But the technology looked like something out of a science fiction movie, all gleaming chrome and blue diagnostic light. Nothing like the crude needles they'd used on Eddie, but somehow more frightening for its sleek efficiency. The blue light pulsed gently, like something alive and waiting.

"Will it hurt?" Leila felt stupid for asking. What difference did that matter, if it meant her daughter would be okay?

"You might experience a slight pinch." Samara prepped her arm, the touch of the antiseptic wipe cold against Leila's skin. "You won't feel anything after the initial injection other than a slight sore spot for a day or two."

The apparatus emitted a soft hiss as it discharged its

payload into Leila's flesh, the sensation scarcely registering through her haze of anxiety. A slight pressure, then warmth spreading outward from the injection site. The device's light shifted from blue to green, confirming successful delivery.

"You probably think I'm a terrible person," Leila said, watching Samara dispose of the injector in a biohazard container that sealed with a definitive click. "Risking my baby like this. Coming here pregnant without telling anyone."

Dr. Makinde's smile held surprising warmth. "Actually, I might have made the same choice. The world was ending. What other choice did you have?"

"Really?" Relief flickered in Leila's chest. Dr. Callas had been angry when he'd found out she'd kept the baby secret. She expected everyone else to be, too.

"It was a risk, and it required some courage." The geneticist smiled. "There are women who would've made the other choice."

"What other choice?"

"To abort the fetus to save their own spot in the colony."

Leila recoiled. That had never occurred to her as an option. But as she thought about Justin's reaction to the news of her pregnancy, she couldn't help wondering if he would've suggested it, had he known.

She'd been right to keep it a secret.

"You remind me of my little sister," Dr. Makinde said, suddenly looking sad. "She couldn't wait to have children. When her son—my nephew—was born, he became the center of her universe."

What happened to him? Leila bit back the question before it left her mouth. Because there was only one possible answer, and she didn't want to make the geneticist even sadder.

So she asked the only other question she could think of. "Are you and Captain Mercer planning to have children once things are more settled?"

A blush crept up Dr. Makinde's neck, and she suddenly became very interested in checking her vital signs. The monitor beeped softly as she adjusted settings with slightly more force than necessary. "You should eat something. Relax. We'll monitor you here until we're certain the gene therapy has taken, then we'll transport you back down to the colony."

Dr. Makinde headed for the door but paused on the threshold. "Try not to worry so much. Your baby is stronger than you think."

Leila placed both hands on her still-flat belly once she was alone again. The skin felt tacky with dried gel but warm beneath her palms, alive with possibility. "You hear that, little one? You're strong. Like your mama." Leila smiled. "And hopefully a lot smarter about taking care of yourself."

The infirmary lights dimmed to simulate evening, casting the room in soft shadows that made the medical equipment look less threatening. The temperature dropped slightly, a programmed response to the ship's day-night cycle. But Leila lay awake for a long time, the thin blanket pulled up to her chin, her thoughts circling like vultures.

Her comm unit remained stubbornly silent—no messages from Justin. The small screen stayed dark, reflecting her own tired face when she checked it for the dozenth time. She couldn't help thinking that Justin seemed almost relieved to let her come up here alone. As if he was afraid to find out if their baby was still alive—the baby he hadn't seemed excited about at all when she'd finally told him. She found herself certain that if Dr. Makinde were pregnant, Captain Mercer wouldn't abandon her to face a possible miscarriage alone in this sterile room. He wouldn't leave her wondering if he even cared whether their child survived.

She placed her palm against her belly again, feeling an unexpected surge of fierce protectiveness. The galaxy's cruelest joke: she'd risked everything to save this child, while its father couldn't muster the courage to face what they'd created together.

The metallic taste of DaVinci's dust still lingered at the back of her throat, a constant reminder that this alien world held dangers they couldn't begin to understand. What other invisible threats might be working their way through her body, reaching for her child?

And what would she have to sacrifice to keep those threats at bay?

Chapter Eight

"Where's Lucas?" Samara asked the ship's AI, rolling her shoulders in a futile attempt to dissipate the lingering tension. Her muscles protested the movement, still sore from the previous day's labor and the uncomfortable night on the common hall floor.

"Captain Mercer is in Lab 4C," it replied in Lucas' own voice. She could not get over how weird that was. "He has temporarily repurposed it as a fabrication workspace."

The redirected lab hummed with the whir of machinery when Samara entered. An acrid mélange of molten polymer and ozone permeated the space, under-scored by a subtler, unidentifiable note, a scent that reminded her of new electronics and sterilized medical equipment. The smell clung to the back of her throat, not unpleasant but distinctly artificial compared to the air down on the planet.

Fluorescent lights cast the room in stark illumination, eliminating shadows and giving every surface a clinical sheen. The temperature was noticeably cooler here than the rest of the ship, the climate control compensating for the heat generated by the active equipment. Samara's skin prickled slightly as it adjusted to the change.

A military-grade 3D printer dominated one corner, its head moving in precise increments across the build plate with a soft mechanical whine. Each layer of polymer fused with a barely audible hiss, the temperature readout displaying a steady 215 degrees Celsius. The machine's cooling fans created a constant background drone, punctuated by occasional clicks as the print head changed positions.

Lucas stood at a workbench, his utility knife moving quickly under the harsh lights as he cut shapes from sheets of filter material. His movements were remarkably fluid and efficient, like someone who had practiced the same motion thousands of times. Not a single wasted gesture, each cut executed with perfect precision. The blade sliced through the material with a soft whisper that barely registered above the printer's hum.

"How is our newest colonist?" Lucas asked without looking up.

"The baby is doing fine." She watched another carefully cut shape fall from his blade, the edges clean and perfectly matched to the last one he'd cut. "Just needed a minor genetic tune-up. Though keeping it that way on this planet..." Samara let the sentence hang, the unspoken concern heavier than her words.

"The analysis showed no toxic compounds in the dust samples," Lucas said, anticipating her next question. The filter material crinkled slightly as he rotated it for the next cut, the sound crisp in the controlled atmosphere of the lab.

"I'd like to check for harmful microorganisms. Even inert particles could be carrying bacterial or fungal hitchhikers." She suppressed a shudder at the thought that the dust itself might be carrying something infectious that human immune systems might not even recognize as dangerous.

"There's not enough sample material left for more testing." His knife continued its path across the filter paper, the blade moving with remarkable steadiness. "I'll collect more during the next atmospheric event."

She hoped that by the time the next storm happened, they'd be ready.

Lucas paused his work, his hands hovering briefly above the table before he set down his utility knife with a faint *clink* against the metal counter. He turned to face Samara but fixed his gaze somewhere near her shoulder rather than meeting her eyes.

"I've been thinking about us," he said, his voice softer than usual. "Our situation, I mean."

A slight chill ran across Samara's skin that had nothing to do with the room's temperature.

Are you and Captain Mercer planning to have children once things are more settled?

"What about it?" she asked, hoping he didn't notice the heat that was creeping up her neck once again.

"I noticed during the dust storm how the other couples were with each other." His fingers tapped a subtle rhythm against his thigh, a gentle percussion underscoring his words. "They comforted each other, staying close. I didn't do any of that for you." He glanced up briefly, his eyes meeting hers for a fraction of a second before sliding away. "I'm worried people might have noticed."

Samara hadn't expected this conversation. The printer chirped in the background, marking the completion of another layer. "Lucas, that's—"

"I need to know what your preferences are," he continued. "I don't want to make things uncomfortable for you, but I also don't want you to be singled out for resentment."

The ventilation system cycled on, sending a cool draft across the lab that stirred loose papers on the adjacent desk. Samara smoothed her hair back from her face, buying time to formulate a response.

"I don't feel comfortable faking affection, or asking you to do so, either," Samara admitted. "How would you normally be in a relationship?"

A small furrow appeared between his brows. "Social skills don't come naturally to me."

Then it occurred to Samara that he might never have been in a relationship before. The realization relaxed something in her chest. "Just be yourself, with perhaps a bit more awareness that we're supposed to be partners. Nothing dramatic. Neither of us are the kind of people to engage in public displays of affection."

The constant tapping of his fingers slowed. "You will tell me if I do anything that makes you uncomfortable?"

"I will," she promised, feeling a new warmth toward him. Then, after a moment's hesitation, she added, "This must feel just as strange to you as it does to me."

"It's not a situation that I ever expected to find myself in," he agreed. His voice carried no emotional inflection. Was he as embarrassed as she was by the whole conversation?

"Do you mind if I ask why you chose not to have children?" he continued. For once, his gaze settled directly on her face, his attention complete and unwavering.

Samara leaned against the workbench, letting the cool metal pressed against her palms ground her as she considered her answer. "Some people are meant to be parents. I'm meant to be in a laboratory, solving puzzles most people don't even know exist."

"Do you dislike children?" he asked.

"No, I loved—" *my nephew. My cousins. My neighbor's kids.*

She'd even enjoyed it when her co-workers brought their children to the lab, the chance to show them how much fun science could be. She'd been thrilled when one of them had caught the bug after she'd let them set test tubes in the centrifuge or push the start button on the sequencer.

But she had also abandoned them at the end. All of them.

"There's a difference between liking children and being entirely responsible for a child's well-being."

She had always wondered what was wrong with her that she'd never wanted that responsibility. Even Leila, barely out of childhood herself, had the drive to nurture that Samara lacked. She had been willing to risk the heartbreak of another miscarriage for the chance of motherhood.

Lucas handed Samara a stack of components, polymer frames fresh from the printer, radiating a gentle heat that transferred to her fingertips. "I'll keep cutting filters if you want to put them together."

Had she made him uncomfortable with her admission? She'd been curious about his reasons for not wanting children, but the moment of connection had passed.

She claimed the neighboring workstation, her fingers nimbly coalescing the disparate components into functional respirator masks. The design was elegant in its simplicity: minimal parts, maximum protection. The filtration efficiency would hit 99.97% at 0.3 microns—better than the N95s they'd used during the dust storm. Each component nested inwith a satisfying click.

They fell into an easy rhythm, Lucas cutting filter pieces with remarkable precision while Samara assembled them into the frames. The silence between them felt comfortable now, collaborative rather than awkward. The ambient sounds of the lab—the printer's hum, the whisper of the knife through the textured filter material, the soft clicks of assembly—became a soothing acoustic backdrop. Under the magnifying lamp, each cut edge was remarkably clean, straight lines cut with impressive steadiness, curves so smooth they looked machine-made. She couldn't spot a single jagged edge or slip of the knife.

She glanced at Lucas' workstation, looking for a template or guide, but saw only the knife and raw materials. The surface was immaculate, not even scraps or dust from the cutting process marring its surface.

"How do you cut these so accurately?" she asked, adjusting the lamp to illuminate her own work better. The bright, focused beam created sharp shadows around the components.

"I find repetitive tasks calming. I've always been good with my hands." Lucas paused, looking momentarily self-conscious. "There's a rhythm to it."

Samara nodded. Another way that he reminded her of her cousin Amadi: the hyperfocus, the attention to detail, the ability to do the same thing repeatedly without getting bored. Still, his skill was remarkable.

They resumed their work, and Samara lost herself in the rhythm of assembly. There was something satisfying about watching the pile of completed masks grow, each one a small victory against the next dust storm waiting to ambush them planetside. The steady click of components locking together, the methodical application of adhesive, the careful alignment of filter layers; the process became almost meditative. She worked through dozens of masks, her mind finally quiet after days of chaos. No dust storms, no dying colonists, no planet trying to suffocate them all, just the clean, ordered environment of the lab and the clear purpose of her task. Time seemed to stretch and compress simultaneously, measured only by the growing stack of completed respirators.

When she finally looked up, her back ached from hunching over the workbench, aching as if she'd spent another day digging up shrubs instead of sitting still.

Lucas' workstation stood empty. His knife lay precisely aligned with the edge of the table, the remaining filter material stacked in a perfect rectangle beside it.

The 3D printer chirped, signaling another completed batch of components. The sound seemed suddenly loud in the empty lab.

She blinked, momentarily disoriented. When had he left?

The ship's clock showed almost midnight. She'd been working for six hours straight without noticing. Lucas hadn't abandoned her; he'd probably just gone to sleep like any reasonable person would.

Samara massaged her stiff neck, wondering why she felt disappointed rather than relieved by this perfectly logical explanation for his absence.

He'd been nothing but considerate, asking how she wanted to be treated, and that's all it had taken for her to let her guard down. But she couldn't afford to forget that their partnership was merely an arrangement that exempted them both from the obligation to have children.

An arrangement that would be made even more awkward if she developed an inappropriate attachment.

She'd assumed that he was asking because he cared about her feelings, but what if he simply wanted clear parameters to follow?

She'd given him the vague instruction to "be himself," thinking that she was making things easier for him, but what if she'd left him feeling adrift in yet another social situation that he wasn't sure how to navigate?

Maybe he'd left without interrupting her because he'd been uncomfortable.

As she gathered up the completed masks and put them in a small crate, her thoughts drifted to Leila in the medical bay, hands instinctively cradling her barely visible pregnancy. Samara had promised they would do everything to save her baby, but the words now felt hollow against the reality of their situation. The genetic intervention had been straightforward—a simple correction to ensure color vision. But what about the daily assault of DaVinci's environment? The masks might filter the dust, but what about the water they drank, the alien crops they would eventually grow and consume? Every element of this world would seep into their bodies over time, changing them in ways they couldn't predict or control.

All her scientific knowledge, all their advanced technology, might not be enough to shield one small life from the subtle, persistent influence of a world that had not evolved to nurture human biology.

The masks would buy them time, but how much?

Chapter Nine

LEILA'S FINGERS traced the branching network of angry red welts on her arms. The rash was spreading, despite the increased antihistamine dose. It itched constantly, a low-grade irritation that spiked into burning pain when she scratched. She forced herself to focus on the segments of irrigation pipe spread around her, their polymer surfaces reflecting DaVinci's odd sunlight. The light fractured across the curved surfaces, creating interference patterns that sometimes blurred her vision, forcing her to blink repeatedly to clear the afterimages. Dr. Callas had told her that her eyes would eventually adapt, but how long was that going to take?

She should have been connecting the pipes into the system that would keep their saplings alive, but each movement sent needles of pain through her joints, as if she had aged fifty years overnight. The mere act of gripping the wrench sent throbbing reverberations through her fingers, each pulse matching her heartbeat.

The alien soil clung to her knees where she knelt, its rusty particles working their way through the fabric of her pants to irritate the skin beneath. The air carried that now-familiar metallic tang, mixed with the chemical smell of the irrigation polymer heating in the sun. DaVinci's gravity seemed to press on her shoulders like invisible hands, throwing her annoyingly off-balance. Or maybe that was just part of the pregnancy that seemed to be throwing every part of her body out of whack.

Not that anyone else noticed her discomfort. They were all too busy watching Lucas at the comm tower. Moving with his usual liquid grace atop the scaffolding, fifty feet above the ground. No hesitation or wasted motion, not a single sign to indicate that the height bothered him at all. While the rest of the colonists dripped sweat and stumbled through their tasks like drunken sailors adjusting to DaVinci's slightly stronger gravity, their pilot might as well have been performing a choreographed dance.

Leila absently rubbed her belly, the stretched skin not quite itchy, but somehow wrong, like her body was slowly morphing into something unfamiliar. Her life over the past three days had reminded her of those virtual reality simulations that had been popular before the Collapse, where everything looked almost right but felt slightly off, triggering that instinctive unease when something human wasn't quite human enough. The unsettling notion darted back into the recesses of her mind as her gaze settled on Lucas, absorbed in his tablet, his posture still parade-ground perfect even as he scrolled through data while perched near the top of the tower.

The comm tower rose like a silver needle against the periwinkle sky, its purpose ominous yet reassuring. Soon it would connect them to the ship above, their watchful guardian for the next five years, monitoring the colony with its tireless electronic eyes.

Justin slouched past Leila, interrupting her musings, his shoulders hunched against the sunlight. Dark circles under his eyes made him look like he had aged a decade since landing on DaVinci. He barely glanced her way, still acting as though her pregnancy was a personal betrayal rather than the whole point of their being here.

His indifference stung worse than the rash spreading across her arms. When she'd returned from the ship, pale and shaken, he'd greeted her with nothing more than a distracted *How'd it go?* No embrace, no relief at seeing her, no questions about the baby. It was as if the life growing inside her was a mere inconvenience, much less important than his complaining about his work shift.

"Our baby is fine, thanks for asking," she'd snapped, the words escaping before she could stop them.

He'd looked up then, surprise flickering across his features before hardening into something defensive. "What do you want from me, Leila? I'm working my ass off here."

"I want you to care!" The words had echoed across their small living space, hanging in the air between them. "I almost lost our baby. I was terrified. And you weren't even there."

"What good would it have done?" His voice had been flat, practical. "There was nothing I could do up there."

That was the problem. He hadn't even wanted to try.

Leila shoved the end of a pipe into a T-junction with such vehemence that her wrists shrieked in objection. The polymer connectors scraped against each other before reluctantly locking into place.

Had Justin's enthusiastic proposal been more about securing a spot on humanity's lifeboat than any real feelings for her? That thought burned worse than the rash. Every time she remembered his face lighting up when she suggested they apply to the colony program together, doubt crept in. At the time, she believed it was love. Now…

"How are you and the baby doing?"

Leila jumped, nearly dropping the wrench. She'd been so immersed in the churning depths of her own depressing thoughts that Dr. Makinde's approach failed to register. The geneticist stood in the dappled shade of the tree, its blue-green leaves casting a lattice of patterns across her concerned face. Even those shadows seemed wrong: sharply geometric, like the light itself followed different rules on DaVinci.

Dr. Makinde looked fresh and composed despite the heat, her uniform crisp, her movements precise and efficient. No wonder Lucas had been paired with her. They were a perfect match. Both seemed somehow above the discomforts that plagued ordinary humans. Leila couldn't help wondering if they discussed colony matters in their private quarters at night, sharing insights and observations while the rest of them struggled just to breathe, thanks to the dust that had lodged in her lungs.

"Fine," Leila said automatically. Then, because she desperately needed someone to share it with, "My baby's going to be the first human born on DaVinci. The very first."

She tried to make it sound like a boast instead of a terror.

"You're scratching again," Samara observed. Her eyes tracked the movement of Leila's fingers against her arm, clinical but not unkind.

"Just hives," Leila demurred. "At least I'm not bleeding anymore." She hesitated. "Could it be from the gene therapy? Dr. Basu mentioned this morning that we don't really know the long-term effects…"

"The therapy only affects specific genes related to color

vision." Dr. Makinde's tone stayed neutral, but something flickered behind her eyes. Something that looked suspiciously like concern. "These symptoms are more likely a continued allergic reaction to the dust. What other effects are you experiencing?"

"I don't know exactly. Everything feels…" Leila struggled to find words for the alienness creeping through her body. Like she was being slowly replaced, cell by cell, with something that approximated human but wasn't quite right. Could pregnancy do that to you? Her first one hadn't.

But her first one had only lasted two weeks. On Earth. Before she'd put her body through forty-two years of cryosleep.

"Wrong," she said. "Like my skin doesn't fit anymore. My joints feel like they're full of ground glass. Is that normal?"

Swelling had begun to distort her knuckles, the skin stretched tight and shiny over the joints. The wrench's handle left slow-to-recede indentations in her flesh, creating patterns that reminded Leila of circuit board traces. White pressure marks that lingered far longer than they should have, as if her body had forgotten how to return to its normal state.

"Have you seen Dr. Callas about this?"

"Yesterday. He just upped my antihistamine dose." Leila managed a weak smile. "It helped. A little."

Something dark crossed the geneticist's face before her professional calm returned. Leila wondered if Captain Mercer would look at Dr. Makinde with concern if their positions were reversed. Would he hover protectively to shield her from whatever dangers this planet held?

Justin couldn't even be bothered to ask how her examination had gone. The contrast made her chest ache with a loneliness deeper than the joint pain.

"Let me know if you develop any new symptoms. Even small changes could be important." Dr. Makinde's voice had that measured cadence of someone choosing their words carefully.

An icy chill spread from her core outward, despite the sweat beading on her forehead from DaVinci's unrelenting heat. How worried should she be?

And what wasn't Dr. Makinde telling her?

A comm unit chirped, a shrill demand for the doctor's attention, the sound unnaturally sharp in the thick alien air. Makinde glanced at the screen, then back at Leila, an apology already forming on her lips. "I have to go. But please, don't hesitate to come find me if anything changes, okay?"

With a final, searching look, she strode away to meet Captain Mercer at the base of the comm tower, where he was now installing some sort of control panel. Even from this distance, Leila could see how Captain Mercer straightened slightly at Dr. Makinde's approach, his attention shifting subtly but completely to focus on her. They moved in synchrony, like binary stars orbiting a common center of gravity.

Why couldn't Justin look at her that way anymore? When had the excitement of their shared future dissolved into this cold distance?

Leila pressed both hands against her belly, feeling the slight swell that meant life continuing despite everything. Despite the dust in her lungs and the strange patterns blooming across her skin. Despite Justin's growing distance, Lucas' untouchable perfection, and all the ways this world seemed determined to reject their presence.

The baby represented something Justin couldn't or

wouldn't understand—not just their future, but humanity's. She'd made her choice on Earth, risking everything for this chance. She couldn't bear his resentment now, not when every fiber of her being strained toward survival.

Leila watched as Captain Mercer and Dr. Makinde discussed something with the focused intensity of two people who understood each other completely. The kind of partnership she'd imagined having with Justin, before everything changed.

Her skin itched. Her joints ached. And somewhere deep inside, where her baby grew in total darkness, something felt different in ways she couldn't explain. The changes frightened her, but she had no words to describe them to Justin, who seemed determined to avoid any discussion of her pregnancy. She couldn't help envying Dr. Makinde, who had a partner capable of meeting challenges with calm competence rather than resentful withdrawal.

But she and her baby would survive. They had to be strong. Because out here, at the edge of human existence, they had only each other.

Chapter Ten

THEIR FIELD LAB was a tarp strung tight between two supply sheds, with a folding table jammed under it and an LED lantern dangling from the structural webbing. Even in the shade, the air was thick with humidity and the chemical bite of alcohol wipes. Samara's skin prickled like a badly tuned radio receiving phantom signals, sweat sliding down her arms in rebellious defiance of the antihistamines that had turned her mouth and sinuses into a desert.

Still, she would rather be here with Renata than working kitchen duty, or pulling weeds, or even resting in the cabin she was technically sharing with Lucas.

Practically speaking, Lucas was almost never around. When he wasn't studying DaVinci's weather patterns, he was shuttling people and supplies to and from the ship in orbit or helping Maeve's team fix something. And he volunteered so frequently to stand watch at night, Samara had to remind herself not to take it personally. He was giving her space. Or he needed space. Maybe both.

It wasn't as if she wanted their partnership to be real. But she also didn't want him to feel like he had to avoid her whenever possible. Lucas seemed polite but neutral on the rare occasions when they did cross paths, focused on whatever job he'd been tasked with. She'd catch herself cataloguing these moments—the way he'd pause mid-sentence when their eyes met, or how his fingers would drum against his leg.

Renata, on the other hand, always seemed happy to see her, often waving Samara over to sit with her and Marcus during meals in the common hall. Now, the xenobiologist hunched over their seventh specimen of the day, eyes narrowed behind safety goggles as she wielded her scalpel with the easy precision of someone who had spent a thousand hours dissecting the dead. Her hands, gloved in blue polymer, never trembled as she sliced each creature open and pried the incision apart to examine muscles, fascia, and organs.

Samara grabbed a sample vial and twisted it open, resisting the urge to rub her nose with the back of her hand. Once the dissections were done, it would be Samara's job to map each creature's genome, trying to match sequences to traits so that they could build a library of future adaptations that could make the crop plants and livestock they'd brought with them more suited to life on DaVinci. Especially sequences that might confer resistance to native parasites and diseases.

If she got really lucky, she might even learn how the native life survived the dust storms.

"Do you want the next tray?" Her voice was so rough, it sounded like the antihistamines had sandpapered her vocal cords on the way down.

Renata didn't look up. "Just a sec." The scalpel traced

a line through the feathery integument, following the muscle seam. "Almost to the thoracic nerves."

The creature, reminiscent of a shrew, if shrews had hollow bones and feathers, was pinned out on the dissecting pad. It looked heartbreakingly vulnerable, with its paws curled up toward its chin. The shimmer of its feathers caught the light in subtle iridescence. Samara focused on the physical details: the size of the thoracic cavity, the shape of the beak, the lack of visible mammary tissue. It helped to let simple observations replace the background hum of her own discomfort.

"You sure you're okay?" Renata asked, not unkindly. "You're zoning."

"Fine," Samara lied. "Just waiting on you."

Renata set the scalpel down, flexed her fingers, and looked at Samara for the first time in twenty minutes. There were tiny beads of sweat along her hairline, and the rash had spread in a ring above her collar. "Sorry. I'm moving slowly today. Dr. Callas gave me a double dose of antihistamine and now my brain feels like it's made of steel wool."

"Mine's more like pudding that's been accelerated to ninety-nine-point-nine percent the speed of light."

Renata snorted, then coughed, turning her face into the crook of her elbow. "Best time dilation joke I've heard all week." She popped her goggles up, ran a wrist across her forehead, then looked at Samara again, a sheepish smile on her lips. "You want to take the tissue sample?"

Samara clipped off a sliver of the organ Renata had exposed. It was dark, almost purple, and dense as a rubber eraser. She dropped it into the waiting vial that she'd pre-filled with a stabilizing agent. She pressed the cap on, careful not to let her gloves slip, and labeled it in neat block print.

A scraping sound made her look up: metal biting dirt with the rhythm of barely contained fury. Just outside the tent, Briar was digging a trench with a spade, each thrust driven deeper than strictly necessary. Her shirt clung to her shoulders like a second skin, dark with sweat at the collar, while her arms told the story of honest labor in mud streaks and bruises that bloomed dark purple against tanned skin. She paused to drag her forearm across her face, and her gaze found Samara through the tent's opening; a split-second collision of eyes that transmitted resentment with the efficiency of a targeted data burst.

Samara looked away as if she hadn't noticed, doing her best to keep her expression neutral. Briar's enmity didn't bother her, but she remembered how the young woman had looked at Leila when Hector had slipped her a mask during the first dust storm. Briar hadn't known that Leila was pregnant, but would that flip Briar's resentment to compassion if she found out?

Or would she resent Leila even more?

Samara turned back to Renata, who had already refocused on the specimen. Renata's hands moved with less fluidity now, as if the tightness in her shoulders was seeping into her fingers.

"I could finish up for you, if you want to take a break," Samara offered.

"No, if I stop now, I'll lose the thread. Besides, you're not certified for the next bit." Renata grinned. "You'd probably faint."

Samara rolled her eyes. "I did one semester of comparative anatomy at university. I can handle a simple dissection."

"On a frog," Renata pointed with the forceps. "See that? The dorsal spine is fused."

Samara leaned in. The vertebral column did look odd:

the neural canal was open for the first three segments, then abruptly fused shut with a kind of bony scaffolding. "Did it ossify post-hatch?"

"I think it's congenital, but I'll check the samples." Renata probed at the tissue along the spine, exposing a web of fibers. There was something brown and waxy woven through the nerve root.

"Is that... normal?"

"No." Renata frowned, pinching the growth between the tips of her forceps. "It's not even neural tissue. Look—"

The brown thread contracted, curling around the forceps like a dying vine. Both women flinched backward, bumping elbows. After a moment, the thread slowly unwound, slackening, then falling limp.

"Shit," Renata said, but her voice was more curious than afraid. After a beat, she continued. "Reflex arc. The equivalent of a chicken running around after decapitation."

Samara tried to ignore the way her own skin itched with fear. "And just as creepy."

Renata reached for a small bone saw. "Let's see what's happening up top." The saw made a gritty, wet sound as it cut through the cranium.

Samara felt her stomach lurch, and she took a quick sip from her hydration pouch.

The xenobiologist levered the calvarium off, exposing a wrinkled brain studded with more of the brown filaments. She used the tip of a scalpel to tease a clump free. "See that? Not part of the CNS. Not even the same tissue type. I've never seen a structure like that."

"Related to the spinal fusion?" Samara guessed. "The body's attempt to compensate by going around the section that it couldn't go through?"

Renata shrugged, then coughed again, harder this time. She put the scalpel down and reached for her own hydration pouch, draining it in three quick swallows. Her hand trembled as she set it aside.

"Renata—"

"I'm fine." Her voice was thick, and she blinked twice before meeting Samara's eyes. "We need a sample."

She picked up the tweezers and tugged on a length of the thready brown tissue. It stretched, then ripped free at one end, then the other.

Samara uncapped a fresh vial, held it steady as Renata deposited the filament inside before being racked by another cough. This one lasted long enough to make Samara's own lungs hurt in sympathy.

"Maybe you should see Hector. You sound—"

"He already gave me the good stuff." Renata cut in. "Besides, he's got enough patients already."

Samara wanted to insist, but when she'd walked by Hector's clinic this morning, it *had* been mobbed with colonists complaining that the medicine wasn't working, and work crews were smaller than usual, as Katherine had excused the most severely affected from duty. Samara's own rash itched with a fiery intensity, and every spot she'd made the mistake of scratching stung as sweat soaked her clothes.

For the next half hour, they worked in a rhythm: Renata extracting organs and preserving cross-sections on slides, Samara preserving tissue samples in vials for sequencing later, and documenting everything.

When every part of the shrew-like creature had been cut apart and examined, Renata peeled off her gloves and stretched. "Want to do the bug?"

Samara raised an eyebrow. "I thought you didn't trust me with the dissections."

"We only caught one of the feathered rodents." Renata flashed her a teasing grin. "But the bugs are everywhere. If you screw up, I can get more."

Samara couldn't help grinning back. "I'll make you proud."

The insect looked like evolution had rolled dice between a cockroach and a millipede and decided to hedge its bets—roughly thumb-sized and armored in segments that gleamed like wet obsidian. Its carapace yielded to Samara's scalpel with a soft pop, the sound of a sealed system finally admitting defeat.

Inside, the familiar cockroach architecture spread before her: miniature organs packed with biological efficiency. Except for the passengers. Brown filaments threaded through the body cavity like alien circuitry, weaving between organs with deliberate precision.

At least they weren't moving this time.

"Some kind parasite?" she asked.

Renata gave her a sidelong glance. "Who knows?"

Samara slid the scalpel to one end of the filament that twisted around what she guessed was the insect's ventral nerve cord—the closest thing an invertebrate had to a spinal column. Another coincidence, that the filaments had infiltrated both creatures' nervous systems?

She cut the other end and lifted the filament out with tweezers.

It still didn't move.

"Was the bug alive when it was caught?"

"I euthanized both creatures before you came in. As far as I could tell, neither were showing signs of illness, but…"

She shrugged.

Samara dropped the filament in a vial and watched it float through the stabilizing fluid to rest at the bottom. When she got back to her lab, she'd sequence both filaments to see if they were made of tissues native to the creature or if they were foreign.

If only she had her equipment down here… the next shuttle run to the Borlaug wasn't scheduled for several more days.

It took Samara another thirty minutes to painstakingly remove each tiny organ from the insect's abdomen for Renata to identify and catalogue. Then she split open the thin shell of its head to reveal the tiny clump of nervous tissue inside, which was practically encased in brown filaments. Thankfully, none of them moved, no matter how many times she poked them.

When they had finally examined every part of the insect, including the gooey, fibrous lining that clung to the inside of its shell, she straightened and rubbed her aching lower back.

"You want a break?" Mischief danced in Renata's eyes. "I know you geneticists aren't used to getting your hands dirty."

"You think you're going to scare me off that easily?" Samara reached for the tray containing the next specimen, which might've been a lizard or amphibian of some kind.

Did their Earth-based taxonomy even make sense on this world? Or would they have to invent a new one?

She set the creature down in front of Renata, then offered her a fresh scalpel. "Your turn."

But even Renata's gentle teasing couldn't banish the uneasiness that grew as they continued their dissections. The same brown filaments threaded between the organs of each new creature, sometimes thick and ropy like tendons, other times delicate and thin as a strand of hair, but always seeming to reach for some part of the creature's nervous system.

In the worms, the filaments encased nerve clusters like

a finely woven cage. In vertebrates, it wrapped the spinal column with the methodical precision of technicians running cable through conduit, as if whatever this was had read the manual on nervous system architecture and decided to install itself as essential hardware.

"It's not possible that every single specimen we've gathered was sick," Samara said.

"Maybe this is a functional structure we haven't encountered yet, unique to the biology of this planet." Renata winked at Samara as she pulled off her gloves. "Notify the Nobel Prize committee."

"I've already submitted your nomination," Samara said. "And I've let them know you're not going to be able to accept it in person."

Renata started to laugh, but the sound quickly became a racking cough that left her red-faced, hands on her knees, and eyes watering as she gasped for breath.

"Come on," Samara said. "We're going to see Hector."

THE COMMON HALL reeked of sweat, dust, and misery. Coughs and sneezes ricocheted through the air, amplified by the metal walls and mixing with the buzz of hoarse voices. Hector held court at the end of a folding table, doling out pills from a battered tackle box and scribbling notes on a stained legal pad. His shirt was untucked, sleeves rolled to the elbows, and the dark half-moons under his eyes had deepened into bruises.

Samara and Renata threaded through the crowd, dodging shuffling bodies and the occasional outstretched arm. People looked worse than they had that morning. Faces shone with sweat, eyes glazed and puffy, exposed skin blotchy and red. Some slumped in chairs, heads drooping, while others lay on the floor.

Nearly a quarter of the colony was too sick to work. How long before it would be half? Or all of them?

Hector glanced up as they approached, his eyes flicking to Renata's face and narrowing.

"You were supposed to come back if you got worse," he said, voice edged with irritation. "Sit. Now."

He pointed to a cot wedged between the table and a rack of supply crates. Renata dropped onto it with the bonelessness of total exhaustion, her breath hitching as she tried to stifle another cough.

Hector pulled a small inhaler from the tackle box, shook it, then pressed it into Renata's hand. "Two puffs. Slow, steady inhalation. Now, please."

As Renata obeyed, Samara pulled Hector aside, lowering her voice so the nearest patients couldn't hear.

"Why is everyone getting worse? I thought the antihistamines and steroids were supposed to keep this under control."

Hector's jaw worked as if he were chewing over the words before spitting them out. "They're supposed to, yes. But it's not like we've ever tested these drugs against an unknown antigen from another world. Dust gets everywhere, in the air, the food, and the water. Or maybe it's not only the dust. Maybe it's just an irritant that made it easier for an opportunistic microorganism to get a toehold."

"You've looked at blood samples?"

"I've looked at every kind of sample you can get out of a human body, but my screening process is designed for viruses and bacteria we already know about." He scowled at Samara like that was her fault. "If you were an immunologist—"

"There are other ways I can help." Was he still holding

it against her that Hofstadter had chosen her? "I could assay the blood samples you've collected and look for foreign DNA. Identify any that might be native."

He made a rude noise that went a little bit farther than a scoff. "We've been breathing the air, drinking the water, touching the dirt. We've been exposed to hundreds, maybe thousands, of native microorganisms. It'll take you months to catalogue them all, and you still won't know which one's causing the problem."

More like weeks, Samara thought, but he wasn't wrong. If she took the *needle-in-a haystack* approach.

"That's why I'd separate the white blood cells out and sequence them for the DNA of any microorganisms they've consumed. Then we look for a match in our environment."

"*Consumed* is the key word. White blood cells don't just engulf invading pathogens; they also digest them. As in, break them down into their constituent parts."

"I might be able to find enough fragments to string together—"

"Pitch your experiment to Katherine, I've got patients to treat." Hector pulled a bottle of pills from his tackle box and returned to Renata. "The inhaler opens up the airways, but I think we'd better start you on immunosuppressants, too."

The little relief Samara had been feeling evaporated. Immunosuppressants meant that antihistamines were no longer working to keep the dust allergy in check; Renata's body had become so frantic to fight the perceived invasion that it was willing to strafe its own cells in friendly fire. And immunosuppressants had side effects, especially when used chronically. Like kidney and liver damage. Cardiovascular problems. Increased cancer risk. And vulnerability to even minor infections that a healthy immune system would have no problem handling.

Once the whole colony was on immunosuppressants, one wave of flu could wipe them out.

Hector patted Renata on the shoulder. "Feeling better?"

"Tired," Renata whispered.

"You're excused from the rest of your shift, and tomorrow's too. Go home, get some sleep, take two more puffs every four to six hours."

But Renata almost toppled when she stood. Samara caught her, one arm around her waist. "I'll walk you home."

Renata didn't protest, only leaned her head on Samara's shoulder. "Thanks."

Renata's weight was nothing, but Samara walked slowly, not wanting to tax her friend and trigger more coughing. The path from the common hall to the village was a trampled rut through purple grass, bisecting the open ground where the shuttles usually perched. Samara frowned at the empty launch pads. The colony's protocol was to keep at least one shuttle planetside in case of a medical emergency. Did Katherine know? Or had someone broken protocol?

The shuttles' absence made her feel queasy. She was trapped on the surface of DaVinci, no escape possible until at least one of them returned.

Like everyone on Earth had been trapped after the colony ships departed. But they'd had no hope of escape.

The thought of her family arose, forced to face the reality of being stuck on a dying planet. Her sister's fury. Her father's dignified resignation. Her mother's hysterics. Her nephew's confusion as he begged Auntie Sam not to leave.

Her queasiness was nothing compared to the horror that they'd been forced to endure.

Samara chose to honor their memory by feeling the smaller fear of being trapped for a few hours on a planet that hadn't succeeded in killing her yet.

~

"I UNDERSTAND YOUR CONCERNS, but I'm not going to authorize it."

It was probably a mistake to approach Katherine in the middle of their shift, but Samara didn't want to wait for the leadership team meeting, where stubborn Hector would argue against her proposal no matter what, the others would weigh in on scientific details outside their expertise, and Ayesha would try to broker peace.

Hector's prediction had proven right: the white blood cells had digested too much of the DNA of whatever they'd enveloped by the time Samara had sequenced the collected blood samples. All that remained was a soup of nucleotides and gene fragments; it had been impossible to extrapolate how they'd originally been strung together.

Her idea for narrowing the field had failed.

If Samara had been able to analyze a blood sample immediately after the storm, she might have already discovered what had been in the dust that was making everyone sick.

"What I'm proposing isn't *instead* of what Hector's doing, it's complementary," she protested. "While he's looking for better treatments, I can help identify the trigger for the reaction."

Katherine hoisted a bag of fertilizer powder onto the worktable with a grunt, ripped it open, and deposited three scoops of the fine beige powder into the bucket of water at her feet.

Then she handed Samara a piece of dowel and motioned for Samara to stir.

Samara stirred while Katherine added fertilizer to a second bucket.

"But you agree with his assessment that it could take months just to catalogue every microorganism that it *could* be."Katherine grabbed another dowel and began mixing her own bucket. "And it's possible that it's not a virus or bacteria, it could be something else. Chemical compounds we haven't got the equipment to detect yet. The soil itself."

The colony leader shook her head. "There's already too much resentment around who's pulling what shift. I can't put you in the lab full-time for a long shot right now."

"I don't care what the others think—"

"We all need to care, because as members of the leadership team, we're not just responsible for the physical survival of this colony, we're also responsible for bringing people together."

"There won't *be* anyone to bring together if we don't find a cure for this."

Katherine set aside her dowel and grabbed a long-handled cup, then started down the row of seedling trays with her bucket of fertilizer, pouring a measured amount into the water reservoir for each tray of sprouts: peppers, tomatoes, okra, eggplant, and other vegetables. It was too late in the season to plant them in the fields, so they'd voted for a test run in the protection of the greenhouse to identify parasites, blight, and other native threats before they took the risk of planting a full field and possibly wasting a lot of their seed stock.

It was a smart strategy, doing a small experiment that risked fewer resources while moving things forward. The right thing to do with limited, irreplaceable seeds from Earth. But, in Samara's opinion, not the right approach for managing her lab access in a crisis.

"Hector's homing in on a combination of drugs that he thinks will be more effective," Katherine continued. "If they aren't, I'll reconsider, despite how short-handed we are right now."

"We'll lose weeks while we wait and see," Samara objected as she took the next row, blessing each seedling with a splash of nutrient-rich water. "Lucas could help—"

"I want Lucas building that climatological model for predicting dust storms. That's top priority."

"But figuring out what's making everyone sick isn't?"

Samara shouldn't have snapped, but the idea that Briar's pettiness would factor into Katherine's decision infuriated her. What were one person's feelings against the fate of the whole colony?

Or was it possible that Katherine was using perceived fairness as an excuse, and that the real sticking point was that Samara was proposing a genetic approach to addressing the problem?

Katherine stopped watering and gave her an assessing look. "I know it's been a big adjustment, going from wearing a lab coat to pulling weeds and wrangling goats—"

"I used to spend summers on my uncle's farm. I'm not a stranger to hard work." But given how most of the others complained… Samara thought of Briar's whining that pulling weeds had ruined her manicure. It was hard not to be offended that Katherine might be putting her in the same category as that spoiled young woman.

"You've lost so much," Katherine continued. "We all have. And it's normal to cling to the familiar when you're surrounded by uncertainty."

Samara's fingers clenched around the handle of her bucket. "I'm not asking for special treatment, I'm asking you to let me help *you* solve the biggest threat to our survival."

Katherine sighed. "Look, I'll authorize one extra shift per week working with Renata. Use it however you like, as long as you don't slow her project down."

It wasn't nearly enough, but what other choice did she have?

Chapter Eleven

THE HEAT WAVE had finally broken, and rumor said Katherine had signed off on cookies for the summer's end celebration, sacrificing several precious kilograms of ship-ration sugar and flour to the cause. Samara's crewmates had spent most of their shift speculating what type they'd be.

Peanut butter (Ingrid's childhood favorite, with a high nostalgia coefficient), chocolate chip (proclaimed an extravagance by Kamal, since they still hadn't determined if chocolate trees could grow on DaVinci and ship's stores were limited), or shortbread (the least resource-intensive, no eggs needed, but not a real cookie, according to Nik).

Samara didn't care; she was just relieved to be approaching the end of the muggy swelter and the biting bugs, dubbed star mosquitoes by Renata, for the swirling blue and white patterns on their chitin-covered abdomens that had reminded the xenobiologist of Van Gogh's *Starry Night*.

Samara lagged behind the others as they trudged back from the north pasture, letting the happy chatter fade to background static. She rubbed at the inside of her forearm where a baby goat had bitten her, leaving behind a small double-crescent of darkening bruises.

Corralled inside the prefab barn, the colony's cows and goats ate only feed brought from Earth. The plan was to introduce local forage in slow increments, monitoring for any sign that the native biochemistry might sicken them. So far, the only side effect Samara had noticed was a collective mania to get outside. The animals had already cracked the plastic windows twice in their attempts to reach the purple grass on the other side of the fence.

After the animals had been fed and cared for, Samara spent the rest of her shift pulling toxic weeds in the pasture where they'd soon roam. The skin on her wrists itched like hell from the iridescent sap that oozed out of the shiverleaf stems, but she didn't dare take her gloves off, not even to wipe her face. In two more days, she'd be back in Renata's field tent, where she wouldn't notice the heat because she'd be doing work she was meant to do.

Katherine had kept true to her word, allowing Samara three lab shifts per week, but despite cataloguing and sequencing more than a hundred microorganisms in the past two months, she still had no idea which of them might be the culprit. It was possible she hadn't found it yet. Once again, she cursed herself for not thinking to take a sample of the dust immediately after the storm. And for letting Lucas handle the analysis instead of doing it herself.

She skirted the perimeter of the waste processing plant, holding her breath to avoid the worst of the smell. The filtration pumps hummed their steady bass line over the whir of wind turbines, and above that, the distant shouts of the night shift prepping the next batch of pipes for the irrigation grid. The colony had doubled the size of its arable land in the last month alone, and for the first time since landing, the thought of real self-sufficiency seemed attainable.

She walked east toward the Village, eighty identical prefab units in neat rows, each just large enough to make you wish for a few extra square meters. The lights were off in her cabin, which meant Lucas was still up on the Borlaug. The last time she'd seen him, more than a week ago, he'd apologized for his absence, claiming he'd been analyzing a complex anomaly in the planet's mid-latitude circulation cells. But he'd stared past her shoulder as he said it, and the anxious pattern his fingers had tapped against his leg made her hesitate to ask if he'd been avoiding her. Cowardly, she knew, but what was the point of pressuring him to talk about the relationship they didn't have just to soothe her feelings?

Be honest, chided a voice in her head. *You just like having the cabin all to yourself.*

To be fair, it was a luxury that no one else on DaVinci could claim.

Samara trudged to the cabin at the end of the last row, next to the colony's fenced-off herb garden, where she keyed in her access code, stepped into the cool, dark living area, and slammed the door shut behind her.

Silence, at last. And with it, a wave of fatigue that nearly buckled her knees.

She peeled off her work shirt, careful not to get any of the lingering plant resin on the inner lining. The rash on her arms had faded a little in the last week, thanks to Hector's latest cocktail of antihistamines, steroids, anti-inflammatories, and other drugs that he'd been giving them. Some still needed immunosuppressants to function, but most colonists seemed to be responding positively to the new mix, their symptoms easing to a tolerable level.

It wasn't a long-term solution, but it was buying them time to find one.

She caught her reflection in the mirrored panel above the sink. Her hair was matted, skin streaked with reddish dirt, eyes bleary with exhaustion. But at least her mind wasn't fuzzy, thanks to the lower dose of antihistamines. She ran the tap, splashed her face, and took a long moment to let the cold water numb her nerves. Then she stripped, tossing the rest of her clothes into the laundry bin and heading for the shower. She stepped in, dialed the temperature up, and shivered as cold water came on in a sputtering jet.

The on-demand heater was broken again, and Maeve's repair crew was so far behind schedule that it might be a month or two before someone could be spared for such inconveniences. But Samara didn't mind. She'd spent the first month on DaVinci sleeping in the common hall with everyone else, lying awake at night as the air filled with a symphony of coughs, snores, and the low hum of whispered prayers. A cold shower in her own micro-habitat was a comparative luxury. She scrubbed at her hives with a soft sponge, exhaling as the ever-present itch briefly surrendered to numbness.

Then she got out of the shower and dressed in a simple t-shirt and pajama bottoms, turned on the fan, and flopped down on the bed.

Lucas always took the couch on the rare nights he'd slept here, claiming that the mattress aggravated his back. Samara was sure this was a lie. She'd caught him more than once sitting at the edge of the bed, staring at the wall with a look of such blank intensity that she'd started to wonder if he ever slept at all. When she'd asked him about it, he'd just shrugged and said, "I'm used to being on call. I can't turn it off."

She couldn't help worrying that his work ethic might be partially motivated by a desire to avoid being alone with her.

Tomorrow, she told herself. Next time he came down from the ship, she'd bring it up. Suggest they trade off nights on the bed and couch. Ask if he was okay. Admit that she liked talking to him, even if it was mostly about work, and remind him that she didn't need him to put up a front for her.

The comm unit on the desk chirped, a single note indicating a priority message. She padded over, tapped the screen, and saw Katherine's name at the top of the queue.

Leadership meeting. Twenty minutes.

For what? Last-minute party planning?

Outside, the sun had slipped behind the ridge, and the prefab village glowed with the soft blue light of the path markers. Colonists drifted between their units in loose clusters, some already dressed for the party, others still in their work gear, faces smeared with dust and streaked with the day's sweat. Samara took a circuitous route to avoid awkward small talk, cutting between the chicken coop at the edge of the Village and the shadow of the comm tower, where the new relay dish gleamed like a silver coin against the sky.

For a moment, she let herself imagine a different kind of night. A night where she could sit on the porch, sip something strong, and listen to the wind without thinking about the next crisis. A night where her skin didn't itch and her lungs didn't ache. A night where she didn't have to worry that someone would ask her about Lucas.

Inside the common hall, Samara made her way through the clamor of the party. Strings of LEDs twinkled like Christmas lights, triggering a surprising wave of emotion that she forcibly suppressed. Someone had rigged up speakers, and a driving beat vibrated in the soles of her boots. Plates piled with the promised cookies sat on the counter separating the kitchen from the main room. Samara veered left to get a closer look: chocolate chip. Katherine had opted for the extravagant choice.

She grabbed one, still slightly warm, and took a bite. Found herself blinking back tears at the delicate sweetness of caramelized sugar that melted on her tongue, giving way to the flavors of butter and vanilla and gooey chocolate. And the nutty crunch of chopped coral nuts from the trees that grew at the edge of the pasture she'd been weeding today, so named because the shells had a delicate veiny pattern reminiscent of lace coral, as if DaVinci had decided to replicate Earth's beauty using entirely different source code.

The cookies offered both a shared taste of the home they couldn't go back to and a promise that they could build something good here.

Samara had tended to avoid parties on Earth, or if she'd felt obligated to go, she'd hung back on the periphery, feeling like an outsider who could only observe the interactions of people she didn't quite understand. But tonight, she wanted more than anything to belong to this fragile camaraderie that Katherine had somehow manufactured with repurposed LEDs, music, and homemade cookies.

She quickly devoured the rest of the cookie, then ducked into the corridor that led to the small conference room in the back, where most of the leadership team already sat in plastic chairs around the folding table.

Everyone but Lucas.

Maeve sprawled at the end of the table, grease stains streaked up both arms, cradling a mug of coffee that probably contained a mortal dose of caffeine. Leo was next to her, scribbling notes on a stained legal pad, slumped forward like his spine had given up trying to support the weight of everything he was trying to track. Katherine stood at the whiteboard, arms crossed, eyes unfocused as if she were reading a display only she could see.

Renata sat nearest the door, and when Samara entered, she looked up and smiled with a warmth that evoked the same feelings that the cookie had.

"Hey," Renata said, her voice pitched low so as not to interrupt the others. "Are you ready for the party?"

"I ate a cookie," Samara replied, then didn't know what else to say. Because none of the things she was feeling right now were things she wanted to say in front of the rest of the team. "Best thing I've ever tasted. You have to try one."

Renata beamed. "I helped make the dough. You're lucky I have excellent self-restraint, or I could've eaten the whole batch."

Katherine rapped the table for attention. "Let's make this quick. Maeve, infrastructure update?"

Maeve set her mug down with a thunk. "South field sewer backup's cleared. Temporary fix for now—we'll need a permanent solution before the rainy season, or we'll be swimming in it." She shot a glance at Leo, who nodded but didn't look up. "Power grid's stable, but we're running at eighty percent of projected efficiency. Turbine four keeps tripping the inverter. I've got a crew working on it tomorrow." She ticked the points off on her fingers. "Still trying to troubleshoot the comm tower. We rebuilt the transmitter from the spare parts you had brought down from the Borlaug, but connectivity is going to be spotty until we figure out where the interference is coming from."

Katherine nodded. "Renata?"

Renata straightened, hands clasped on the table. "So far, we've identified twenty-seven plant types with potential toxicity to humans or livestock, but also several species that look promising as future crops. There's a fruit that tastes almost exactly like mango, if you ignore the aftertaste." She flashed a grin. "On the animal side, none worth domesticating, but some of the insects might be edible if we process them right." She glanced at Samara. "The field crew did a great job today. Some of the samples they flagged may have medicinal applications. At least two with possible anti-inflammatory or analgesic properties."

Katherine made a note on the whiteboard. "Excellent. Hector, you're up."

Hector looked tired, his hair sticking up at odd angles and a shadow of stubble darkening his jaw. "We're burning through the antihistamines and steroids faster than projected, even with the reduced dosages made possible by the new additions. Nearly half the colony is taking the maximum safe dose. A dozen have developed what I'd call early-stage autoimmune symptoms: joint pain, low-grade fevers, swelling. Cytokines are spiking, especially after hard labor or dust exposure. Soon we're going to have to start rationing meds."

"Can we make more?" Katherine asked.

Hector looked to Renata, who said, "We're looking for plants that make the compounds we need. And I'm researching bacterial manufacture."

"How soon will we have to start rationing?" Katherine asked.

"Hard to say," Hector replied. "Applicants with allergies were eliminated during the screening process, so the ship was stocked on the assumption that we'd be treating occasional instances, not the whole colony."

"Hector." Katherine gave the doctor her *don't bullshit me* look. "How soon?"

"A couple of weeks, unless I can find a way to make

what we've got go further. Or lower everyone's dose… but then we'll have more people who can't take a work shift."

Samara bit her tongue, resisting the urge to jump in. She should have been helping with this all along, not pulling weeds and doing basic sequencing runs that an undergraduate intern could've handled.

The thought must've shown on her face, because Katherine asked, "Yes, Samara?"

How could she say it diplomatically?

"I don't want to second-guess Hector, but there might be options we haven't tried. Back on Earth, there was a promising study on epigenetic therapy for autoimmune disorders. Targeted methylation to shut down overactive gene expression."

Hector bristled. "You're not a medical doctor. You aren't qualified to—"

"I have a doctorate in genetics," Samara shot back. "And I've read the literature. This isn't some fringe idea. It's been through animal trials and early-stage human testing."

"The entire point of this colony is to reestablish civilization without the hubris that destroyed the last one."

Samara felt her face flush with anger. "You'd rather let people suffer than try something that could help?"

"I'd rather not try to kill a fly with a nuclear bomb!" Hector snapped. "We've only been treating this condition for two months, and you're already proposing human trials for experimental gene therapy."

His hypocrisy was unbelievable. "What do you think you're doing, testing out a new mix of medications on us almost every week?"

"Medications that have been in use for decades, backed by an extensive body of data, whose potential interactions are well-documented."

Samara shook her head. "Not on an alien allergen. Not on this world where there are a million unknowns."

"The medications are working," Hector said. "We should focus our efforts on figuring out how to make more, not waste time tinkering with technologies that we know from experience are dangerous."

If Samara had learned anything from her last days on Earth, it was that you couldn't argue with a person's fear. And Hector's fear was carved hard on his face.

So she turned to Katherine. "I wouldn't propose exploring this if I didn't think it could be done safely and ethically."

The room went silent as everyone looked to Katherine, who continued to stare at Samara, unblinking. Was she considering a *yes*, or was she trying to find a way to say *no* that wouldn't ruin the celebration in the next room?

"This is a big decision that deserves serious contemplation," Ayesha declared. "We should all vote on it, once we have enough information to make a good decision."

After a long moment, Katherine nodded slowly. "Create a proposal, including risks and how you plan to mitigate them. The decision needs to be unanimous."

Hector leaned back in his seat and steepled his hands on the table, looking pleased.

He would never agree.

His prejudice against her—or against her discipline?—had been clear from the beginning. Before she could explain the science that he clearly didn't understand, she would have to convince him to listen with an open mind. Which could take weeks or months they didn't have. She had to find another way.

What if she could convince Katherine to give her permission to do the preliminary work?

No, better to do the preliminary work and present it to

the colony leader as a *fait accompli*, so she'd have data to support her proposal. Renata had enough grounding in genetics to verify that Samara's approach was sound, and Katherine had proven herself a pragmatic leader. If Samara could present her with a viable solution, she'd be reluctant to dismiss it.

Samara just needed proof.

Katherine cleared her throat. "Hector, keep monitoring and create a list of the compounds needed to manufacture each of the medications we're running out of. Samara, work with Renata to prioritize sample analysis. See if you can find native plants that already make these compounds, or something close enough that we can work with. And not a word of this to the others. We don't want people to start hoarding medicine, or worse."

There was a general murmur of assent. Samara glanced at Renata, who offered a sympathetic smile from the other end of the table.

As the meeting broke up, Samara lingered, hoping to talk with Renata in private. But Ayesha approached her before she was completely out of her seat.

"I was hoping you'd stop by for a chat sometime." If anyone else had said it, Samara would've heard it as a guilt trip, but somehow the psychologist managed to make it sound like a genuine invitation. "How are you doing, really?"

Samara did her best to summon a smile. "Tired and itchy, just like everyone else."

"Tired and itchy and bored, right?" Ayesha said. "It's tough when you're used to using your brain all day, but your shift is nothing but chores."

"The baby goats are cute, when they're not biting." Samara pulled up her sleeve to reveal the bruises. "Watch out for the one with the white spot on her nose."

Ayesha laughed. "I've been hoeing this week. It's kind of meditative, once you get into the rhythm of it."

Struggling to keep her smile going, Samara couldn't help glancing at the door, which someone had closed on their way out, muffling the energetic thumping of music from the main room. She was dying to find a dark corner where she could eat another one of Renata's cookies and watch the play of twinkling lights over the dancers. Maybe she'd even join them for a change, see if she could get into the spirit of celebration, just for one evening.

"Some of the others have told me they dream about their old lives," Ayesha said. "Do you?"

Oh no. This wasn't a casual chat; this was a mental health check-in. "Did Katherine ask you to talk to me?"

Ayesha didn't waste time denying it.

"It must feel frustrating that the colony doesn't need your core skill set yet." Amazing how the psychologist could switch gears so smoothly. "Autonomy, mastery, and purpose are essential for our psychological well-being, and no one's lost more of those three things than you have. Most of the rest of the leadership team is still doing the same job they did before, just in a different context. But you're—"

"Useless, apparently." Samara's bitterness surprised her, and she tried to tone it down as she continued. "Katherine could be leveraging me in a dozen different ways, but she doesn't understand what I do well enough to see it."

"And you're concerned that the others will miss something you'd catch?"

Samara saw the trap—say yes, and Ayesha might conclude that her criticism was coming from a need for control, or maybe perfectionism. Say no, and she was admitting that maybe she wasn't needed after all.

If Katherine was going to use the colony psychologist to tag team her, fine. Samara could play that game too.

"My biggest concern is that Katherine isn't taking our situation seriously enough," she said in a confidential tone. "You heard Hector. Two weeks until we have to start rationing medications that aren't even treating the root cause; they're just alleviating symptoms. And we're starting from scratch when it comes to synthesizing new ones, assuming we can get the right compounds to start with. How long do you think we can keep the colony running without meds?"

Ayesha's pleasantly neutral *I'm listening* face didn't slip, but the double blink told Samara that she'd gotten the psychologist's attention.

"In times of uncertainty, leaders need to project confidence," she said. "Katherine's doing her best to keep people calm."

"There's a difference between projecting confidence and ignoring a problem that doesn't have an easy solution." Samara rolled her shoulders like she was trying to redistribute the weight of everything they weren't discussing. "We can't afford to underreact to the problem these dust storms pose. We don't know how often they happen—"

"Isn't Lucas working on a model for predicting them?"

"—and even if they're rare, we still haven't recovered from the only one we've been exposed to. We should be throwing everything we have at finding a cure."

"But, genetic engineering." Ayesha let out a huff of breath. "Isn't that an overreaction?"

"Not with the right safeguards."

"The scientists who caused the chytrid plague thought they were using the right safeguards, too."

"What they were doing is different from what I'm suggesting," Samara said.

"Different how?"

And that was the frustrating part. "It's hard for me to explain without getting technical."

"You can see how hard it might be for other people to hear, *you're just going to have to take my word for it,* can't you?"

"Everything we try is going to involve some risk." Samara struggled to keep her impatience out of her expression. "Hector will tell you that the medications we're taking are safe, but taking any drug for an extended period has side effects, even at low dosage. Immunosuppressants can cause kidney and liver damage. Long-term antihistamine use can increase your risk of dementia and Alzheimer's. Even everyday anti-inflammatories are hard on your digestive tract."

"But it's possible our bodies will adapt to this planet over time. We won't need to take meds forever."

Wishful thinking, but Samara could see that she'd pushed too hard. Ayesha's expression had shifted from professional curiosity to the defensive mode people activated when presented with data they weren't ready to process. Rather than face a difficult truth, Ayesha had opted to retreat into the comfortable fiction that hoping hard enough could change reality.

Samara decided to call her on it.

"Maybe," she said, "but how often do you advise your patients to cross their fingers and hope their problems fix themselves?"

Ayesha flashed a brittle smile, but there was anger underneath. "I haven't seen Lucas much lately. Will he be joining you at the celebration?"

"I don't know." Whether the question was just a desperate change of topic or an attempt to throw her off balance, Samara didn't care. She glanced at the door again, pointedly this time. "He's been busy building Katherine's climate model."

She tried to step past, but Ayesha touched her arm. "It must be difficult. Everyone else is partnered up, but you're alone most nights."

That did feel like an attack. Samara didn't trust herself to answer civilly, so she just nodded.

"You're always welcome at morning circle," the psychologist continued. "Community can be so important—"

"Thanks," Samara said, pushing past Ayesha. "Have fun at the party."

Back in the main room, the music had shifted to something slower and more melodic, but the center of the space was packed people dancing, laughing, and drinking Leo's appleberry wine, vodka that Maeve's crew had made from a tuber that had proven non-toxic but too bitter to eat, and juice that could've been fresh-squeezed from mangoes, if you ignored the aftertaste. Almost everyone seemed to have a cookie in their hand.

Samara considered joining them to see what it felt like to be part of the crowd, even anonymously. But her skin itched, and her nerves jangled, and she couldn't shake her annoyance with Ayesha. And Katherine. And Hector.

She ducked outside, into the relative quiet of the night.

The breeze was cool, carrying the scent of river water and distant flowers. She leaned against the wall, letting the chill seep into her skin as she closed her eyes. She pictured Lucas up on the Borlaug, staring at data sets, trying to compile chaos into something with predictable outputs. She wondered if he ever thought about her, or if the point of staying up there was that he didn't have to.

Then she thought of Renata and Marcus, who were

constantly inviting her over to play cards, to watch movies, to try the herbal teas Renata made from native plants and flowers. They'd treated her like an old friend even though they barely knew her. Samara had refused at first, reluctant to intrude on their free time together and worried that they were welcoming her out of pity.

She'd come to rely on their friendship as one of the stabilizing forces of her existence. That worried her too. Because life had already proven that it could take anyone away from her. And would, given half a chance.

Samara sighed and started down the path to the Village. No party was going to dispel this feeling. A good night's sleep and—

Motion in the darkness ahead, a shadowy figure approaching from the west. Running. As the figure got closer, Samara realized it was Lucas.

He stopped in front of her, not even breathing hard, even though he'd been sprinting full-out. "There's a storm coming. Big one. I've been trying to call Katherine on the comms for more than twenty minutes."

"Maeve's team is working on the comms," Samara said, her pulse spiking. "How long do we have?"

"Five minutes at most. Securing the livestock is top priority."

As he bolted for the entrance to the common hall, Samara sprinted for the barn. The large animals were already inside, but the open windows had to be shuttered, the external vents closed, and the air scrubbers turned on.

That was going to be the easy part.

Chapter Twelve

SAMARA COULD BARELY SEE through the grit that swirled around her as she lunged for the squawking hen that flapped just out of reach. Too stupid to live, she thought as she stumbled and went down on one knee. Most of the chickens had already been captured and shut in the coop, but this last one seemed determined to find its own hiding place as the edge of the dust storm enveloped the colony.

Samara squinted, lungs burning as the hen made a fatal tactical error, darting between her legs like it had forgotten which species had opposable thumbs. This time, she caught it by the tail feathers and yanked. The bird let out a noise like a smoke alarm and turned on her with the fury of the betrayed, pecking at the backs of her hands as she wrestled it into a bear hug.

She turned around, realizing that the recalcitrant bird had led her deeper into the storm. She had no idea where she was or how to get back to the coop. She choked on the metallic tang of dust filling her nose and mouth, feeling a tightness in her throat despite the meds she'd taken only a few hours before.

If her windpipe swelled shut before she got back inside, she could die out here.

Because of a dumb chicken.

As if it had heard her thought, the hen twisted in her arms, digging talons into her forearm. Drawing blood, Samara was pretty sure.

Which way to the coop?

The wind blew harder, and even squinting became impossible if she wanted to keep her eyeballs intact. Screwing her eyes shut, she picked a direction, shifting the hen under one arm and putting the other one in front of her as she shuffled through dust that abraded her exposed skin like industrial sandpaper. Five steps, and her outstretched fingers hit the wire fencing. Not the pen around the chicken coop. It was the kind of fence they'd put around the herb garden at the edge of the Village.

Which meant she was a few yards from her cabin.

She dared to open her eyes to slits and was rewarded with the faint blue glow of the path markers bleeding through the chaos. Closing her eyes again, she turned to face the spot where her cabin should be and began to pace, counting her steps. It should be no more than a dozen before she ran into the side of it.

The wind tried to drag her sideways, but she kept moving, powered by adrenaline and the primal terror of drowning in her own respiratory fluids while clutching a hysterical chicken.

Bam! Her fingers jammed against something hard. The hen fought harder to free itself, somehow managing to twist around and rake her hip, tearing through the thin fabric of the off-duty clothes she'd worn to the meeting. She groped her way along the wall until she found the raised edge of the door frame.

A moment later, the handle.

She turned and yanked, then stumbled inside, trailing dust and chicken feathers.

A flurry of dust followed her in, coating everything around her. The air tasted of rust and fear; she coughed, and the metallic taste intensified. Dust or blood? She shut the door behind her, then dropped the chicken and slumped to the floor.

The hen landed with a squawk and an undignified thump, wings flapping as it tracked dust onto every surface it touched. Samara's coughing turned violent, something between gagging and retching. Suffocating. She crawled toward the kitchenette, palms slapping the grit-caked floor. The world tilted, then snapped into razor clarity: her own guttural choking, the high whine of wind trying to tear the windows out of their frames, the frantic pulse in her ears. A mask would be useless now. There was too much dust in her lungs already. Her chest constricted further as she spat out the blood-tinged mucus on the polymer flooring inches from her nose.

Her vision tunneled, edges eaten away by a dark haze.

There was a high-dose antihistamine injector she had stashed in the kitchenette drawer for emergencies per Hector's instructions. Her fingers were numb, clumsy, but she managed to crawl the last meter on elbows and knees. She reached up and yanked the drawer handle so hard she ripped it off its tracks. It clattered to the floor beside her.

Dropping back down to her knees, she pawed through it. Found her emergency med pack. Tore the foil pouch open with her teeth, pulled aside the collar of her shirt, and slammed the business end of the injector against the side of her neck. A punch as the device drove the meds into her skin, then the burn as the drugs infused into the tissues.

The chicken settled on the table above her, glowering

at her. Samara stared back as she let herself collapse against the cabinets, not caring that she was bleeding from a half-dozen scratches and coughing up what looked like rusty paint.

The wind screamed. Or she hoped it was the wind, because if that was a person outside, she was sure they were beyond help.

Samara shivered as she wiped blood and mucus from her chin. Her raspy breathing slowed as the antihistamine kicked in. She should have grabbed a respirator instead of racing straight for the barn. She'd assumed that Lucas' estimate for the storm's arrival would be accurate, that the animals would cooperate, that the chickens would have basic survival instincts. Wrong on two counts, and now she'd spend the next month coughing up dust.

Right after the first storm, she'd been good about carrying a respirator with her whenever she left the cabin. But things had been going well, and she'd gotten complacent. They all had.

She promised herself she wouldn't let that happen again.

Grabbing the edge of the counter, she pulled herself to her feet and retched rust-colored mucus into the sink until her eyes teared and her nose ran. Then she turned on the faucet, washing the dust from her hands before she slurped water from them. But no matter how many times she rinsed out her mouth, she couldn't get rid of the taste. Bright splotches swarmed at the edges of her vision as the heaviness of physical exhaustion and antihistamine-induced lethargy began to weigh her down.

Gasping for breath, she turned the water off and leaned against the edge of the sink. But when she glanced up again, something caught her attention out in the storm: a blurry shape cutting through the chaos with purpose. For a beat, it looked like a person, but it hunched forward and moved in a strange, loping gait that belonged to no human she knew.

Then the dust thickened, and it was gone.

Someone else caught out in the storm?

She hoped not. Even with a respirator, staying out there long enough was courting death by anaphylactic shock.

More likely, her brain was playing tricks on her, personifying the amorphous threat of the storm in a less frightening form. It was easier to imagine fighting a living creature than a force of nature. Wasn't that why humans populated the darkness with monsters?

Samara let herself sink back down to the floor, succumbing to the pull of gravity and drugs and exhaustion as the cabin dissolved into a haze. She didn't even have the energy to crawl to the couch. But that was fine. She was filthy. If she stayed here on the floor, she could just mop it clean when she woke up.

Assuming she woke up at all.

Samara woke up on the couch with a blanket tucked around her. Dust still swirled outside the window. She couldn't have been out long. But she didn't remember stripping off her dust-caked clothes before passing out. Yet there they were, folded on the coffee table with that stupid chicken perched on top of them.

A light clatter, then the sound of a drawer sliding back onto its runners, coming from the kitchen.

"Renata?" she called.

But it was Lucas who appeared in front of her.

"What are you doing here?" she blurted, then realized

what an asinine thing that was to say. Maybe hurtful, although his expression didn't register offense. "Sorry, antihistamines make my brain slower than my lips."

Lucas had every right to be here. This was his cabin too, even though he'd only spent a half-dozen nights on the couch in the past two months.

Although he didn't have the right to undress her while she was unconscious, unless it had been a medical emergency.

Which maybe he'd thought it was, given how he'd probably found her: unconscious on the floor beside an empty injector.

The fingers of his left hand started tapping the side of his leg. She had obviously offended him.

"I was concerned when I found you on the floor," Lucas said. "Less so, after I confirmed that the injector was empty, but I've been monitoring your condition to be sure the dose was effective."

"Thank you."

"If you would like me to shelter in the common hall—"

"That's not what I meant." She'd rehearsed this conversation so many times, but she still didn't know how to start. "This place is yours too, if you want to be here. And you don't have to always give me the bed. We can trade off."

"I'm more comfortable on the couch." His tapping sped up a little bit.

She'd been hoping he would make it easier for her, but maybe she needed to make it easier for him. Be vulnerable first, show him it was safe to say what he wanted.

"This is weird for both of us." Samara sat up, making room for him if he wanted to join her. "What would make it more comfortable for you?"

"I thought I was making it more comfortable for you. What am I doing wrong?"

"It's not you, it's just hard to pretend that things are different than they are."

"Are you experiencing negative social consequences because of my absence? My skills are needed on the Borlaug to—"

"I just want to make sure you're not staying away because you think I don't want you here." She didn't know if the next part was a good idea or a bad one. "I like you, Lucas. I don't mind that you're different."

He cocked his head, and his fingers went still.

Samara tried to read his face. Was he disappointed? Relieved? The only sign of any interior life was the staccato drumming of his fingers on the upholstery.

"What I'm trying to say is, I'm fine with you here. I like spending time with you." She pulled the blanket tighter around her shoulders, feeling the chill of post-adrenaline letdown and lingering antihistamine haze. "But I don't want you to feel like you have to be here either."

"Noted," he said.

Noted?

Did he not understand that she was trying to connect with him? Or did he just not want that? It was impossible to tell from the way he was looking at her. If it had been anyone else, she would've guessed he was mad.

"I understand that you have been spending most of your free time with Renata and Marcus."

Lucas didn't sound accusing at all, even though he still seemed to be staring over her left shoulder instead of making eye contact.

"That's true," Samara said. "Does it bother you?"

Lucas shook his head. "No. I understand that companionship is an element of mental well-being. Particularly in a context where many forms of routine comfort are absent."

Samara snorted. "Let me guess. You read a study about that."

"There are one thousand, two hundred and thirty-seven studies on the negative effects of loneliness in the Borlaug archives. I could provide a curated list if you'd like."

The laugh escaped her, bright and sharp, and for a moment she felt almost dizzy with the absurdity of it. "Of course you could."

He made brief eye contact with her as he smiled, and she thought he looked pleased. *Did he just make a joke?*

His fingers dangled beside his thigh. Not even a twitch.

Samara almost said, *Your companionship enhances my well-being,* but then she worried he would take that as pressure to spend more time with her.

"Are you any closer to finding a pattern that would allow you to predict the dust storms?" she asked instead.

"I have a preliminary model, but the atmospheric system here is highly nonlinear. There are feedback loops I don't understand yet." His fingers started moving again. "I was in the shuttle, several hundred kilometers south of the colony, when I saw the barometric data spiking. I tried to warn the colony, but I couldn't get through. My only option was to try to beat the storm here."

She tried to picture him alone in the cockpit, watching the beginnings of the storm unfold on the sensor readout and not knowing if he would be able to warn them in time. "Thirty minutes would be a big improvement. If we'd had even ten, we could have gotten everyone inside before it hit. Or at least gotten the chickens in the coop."

Lucas glanced at the chicken, still huddled on the coffee table, cleaning her feathers with her beak.

"Agreed. I will share the model with Katherine when the storm has cleared." He smiled stiffly, still not making eye contact. "What have you been working on in my absence?"

Such an awkward attempt at small talk. Samara found it endearing.

"Well, the bright side of this new storm is that I'll have plenty of dust to analyze."

Samara explained her theory that if she could sequence an infected person's white blood cells and cross-reference exogenous DNA against the genomes of all the microorganisms they'd discovered so far, she might find the cause of the illness. "But Hector was right about the DNA being degraded. I need a blood sample taken within an hour or two of infection. By the time he's back in the clinic tomorrow morning, it'll be too late."

"Your approach seems sound."

"Hector didn't think so."

Lucas stepped toward her, and for a moment, Samara thought he might be about to join her on the couch. But instead, he walked past her and opened the cabin door, letting in a flurry of more dust.

"Wait, what are you—"

He exited, slamming the door behind him.

Samara sat frozen, struggling to understand what had just happened. Had she said something wrong? Was it the joke about the studies? Or had she, in her attempt at vulnerability, trampled over some unspoken rule in his head? It was hard not to be offended that he'd left without explaining. Or that he'd been willing to risk the storm to get away from her.

Without a respirator.

Samara shot to her feet, nearly tripping over the blanket as she staggered for the door. She pressed her face to the window but could see only a dark vortex obscuring everything beyond the glass.

The common hall was more than fifty meters away. The path was marked by solar posts, but in this visibility, even a few meters was an eternity. The dust would already be in his sinuses, his throat, his eyes.

Samara's throat ached in sympathy. Her hands shook as she fumbled her way into her dust-caked clothes, shoving bare feet into boots still crusted with soil. She yanked open the bedroom closet and snatched both respirators from the shelf, her own, and the spare she'd stashed for him.

She shoved her face into the first one, yanking the straps until they pinched her skin, then shoved the second one into her jacket pocket before bolting back out into the living room.

The wind almost sucked the door out of her hands as she wrenched it open. She took a step outside and immediately collided with something solid and unyielding.

Lucas.

He caught her by the shoulders, his grip steadying her as the wind clawed at their clothes and hair. For a fraction of a second, his face was close enough for her to see the outline of his features through the dust: eyebrows drawn together, mouth compressed to a bloodless line, eyes narrowed to defensive slits. Then he spun her around and guided her back toward the door, using his whole body as a windbreak.

They stumbled back inside. Lucas shoved the door shut with a force that rattled the hinges.

"What were you doing?" His calm voice held an edge of incredulity.

Samara stared at him, trembling with adrenaline for the second time that night.

"I was coming after you," she managed. "You forgot your respirator."

Lucas looked at the mask in her hand, then at her face, then back at the mask. "You went back out into the storm to bring me this."

"Of course I did." Then, feeling absurdly exposed, she thrust the mask at him. "What were you thinking?"

He accepted the respirator, turning it over in his hands with a curious, almost reverent attention before setting it on the counter.

"Thank you," he said.

Samara let her gaze drop to the floor, then noticed for the first time that Lucas was holding a small, black nylon case.

"What's that?"

He walked to the kitchen and set the case on the table next to the chicken, who eyed it with deep suspicion.

"Sit," Lucas instructed, entering the kitchen and pulling out one of the kitchen chairs with his foot. Samara hesitated, then followed and obeyed. The chicken waddled after her and settled at her feet, as if ready to bear witness.

Lucas unzipped the black case. Inside, everything was arranged with military precision: sterile needles in individual wrappers, a tourniquet, and alcohol swabs. Then he produced two capped vials from his pocket, each containing a small amount of viscous yellowish fluid.

A blood draw kit. He'd gone out in the storm without a respirator so that she could get the blood sample she needed.

But he'd only been gone for a minute or two. The clinic was on the other side of the Village. And the dust was still so thick she could barely see the path lights marking the way through the window.

"How did you make it all the way there and back so

fast?" Not to mention the time he must have spent finding the kit and the vials.

"I ran." Lucas didn't look up as he snapped on a pair of nitrile gloves, then checked the barcodes on the vials with his tablet. "Roll up your sleeve."

She stared at him. It was impossible, but he'd done it. For her. She was both simultaneously grateful and angry: grateful that he'd wanted to help her find the thing that was triggering their immune systems, but angry that he'd risk himself to play hero.

Was that what drove him to volunteer for dangerous jobs, to spend days on the Borlaug sifting through data, to stand watch while the rest of them slept? He wanted to be a hero?

She found herself suddenly furious, a heat rising up her throat that had nothing to do with the antihistamines or the storm or even the fact that she was still bleeding from chicken scratches.

"I wasn't asking you to go out there," Samara said, voice low and sharp. "You could have gotten lost in the storm. You could have died."

His hands went motionless on the case. He turned his head, gaze settling somewhere just past her left ear, but she felt the full force of his focus like a targeting system locking on.

"Neither of those things happened," he said, as if that were the end of it. "Please roll up your sleeve."

Then it occurred to her that he might have dosed himself with Hector's latest cocktail while she'd been sleeping. That would explain why he was so blasé about going out into that hellish maelstrom. And why he didn't seem to be going into anaphylactic shock, despite the intensity of his exposure to the dust.

She nearly laughed, anger and relief colliding in her chest, making her lightheaded.

"You're impossible," Samara muttered, but she did as he asked, peeling the sleeve away from her forearm. More dust had gotten under the fabric and caked in the shallow wounds; her skin looked like a topographic map of DaVinci, ridged and mottled. "You probably have half a liter of dust in your lungs."

"I held my breath," Lucas said as he wrapped the tourniquet around her arm, right above the elbow.

Was that another joke? "It was a terrible risk to take."

Lucas glanced up, blinking, as if surprised by her tone. "It was necessary. You said so yourself: any delay and we risk losing the DNA fragments."

"If you had collapsed out there, we would've lost them anyway."

"But I did not." He shrugged, a small, economical lift of the shoulders. "Your analysis of this blood sample may determine the viability of the colony, so it was a worthwhile risk to take. Please clench your fist."

Samara obeyed, balling her hand until the veins stood out against her skin, trying to ignore the cold sting as Lucas cleaned the inside of her elbow with a swab.

He unwrapped a needle from its sterile packaging with a dexterity that reminded Samara of his knife work in the fabrication lab, then fitted it to a collection tube and lined the tip up with one of her veins.

"You'll feel a small pinching sensation," he warned, his eyes fixed on the inside of her elbow.

"How does a ship's captain know how to do a blood draw?" she asked, more to distract herself from the impending stick than because she needed to hear his qualifications.

Lucas didn't look up. "The captain is required to

complete extended emergency medical training. In the event the medical officer is indisposed, it's my responsibility to revive colonists from cryosleep, perform triage, and administer aid."

She watched his hands as he found her vein on the first try, sliding the needle in with a sharp but fleeting sting.

"That's a lot of responsibility on top of piloting the ship," she said, trying not to watch the dark red line spurting into the tube.

"I am the Captain," he said, still not looking at her.

When the first tube was three-quarters full, Lucas twisted the cap to release it from the needle still in her arm, then attached the second tube with practiced efficiency.

She watched him work, the way his hands moved with total economy, not a single wasted motion. He was careful about the angle of the needle, the tension of the tourniquet, the way he pressed the square of cotton gauze, and withdrew the needle at the same time, so she barely felt it. Then he taped the gauze down with a strip of medical adhesive, neat and perfectly parallel to the length of her arm. He'd probably practiced hundreds of times on oranges or synthetic skin, or maybe on himself. Another example of how he approached every task: learn it, master it, execute it. As if he had a finite number of actions in his life and refused to waste any of them.

She wondered how hard it had been for Hofstadter to find him. Had the eccentric billionaire found twelve more people as competent as Lucas to pilot the other ships?

Or had the Borlaug gotten exceptionally lucky?

"You may experience mild bruising," he said, his voice now clinical as he handed her both vials. "These should be refrigerated until I can fly you up to the ship."

She felt the urge to say something else, to puncture the strange intimacy that had crept in during the procedure, but her brain was still mired in the slow-thick mud of exhaustion. "Thank you for doing this."

He nodded, then stood and stowed the case in the kitchen cabinet, wiping down the table and his gloves with a disinfectant wipe. The chicken, apparently satisfied that the crisis had passed, fluttered up to the table and resumed its preening.

Samara cleared her throat. "You should take the bed tonight. It's your turn."

Lucas looked at her, then at the couch, as if calculating the most efficient arrangement of bodies and furniture.

"I will be fine out here," he said in a perfectly neutral voice.

"I'm going to feel like a jerk if you sleep out here again. Take the bed." She gestured at the streaks on his jaw, the crust at his hairline, the rust-colored powder caking his uniform in the places it overlapped with her own. "Just promise me you'll shower first."

He hesitated, and for a moment she thought Lucas might argue, but instead he just nodded. "If that makes you more comfortable."

He closed the bedroom door behind him with a soft *click*. A few moments later, the sound of running water cut through the hush of the cabin.

Samara winced. She hadn't warned him that the heater was still broken. But Lucas didn't shout or curse. Maybe he'd expected it, or maybe he didn't care.

She picked up the crimson-filled vials and stared at them for a moment. This was what she'd needed: a chance to find the answer.

For the first time in months, she felt the faintest twinge of hope.

Chapter Thirteen

SAMARA WOKE AGAIN, her head ached like she'd been kicked by one of the goats, her tongue was gritty and swollen, and her lungs felt like they'd been scoured with steel wool. She couldn't remember why she'd fallen asleep on the couch in her work clothes, which were filthier than usual. And she might be dying of thirst. She must've overdosed on antihistamines last night to be this foggy.

Then she saw the chicken on the coffee table, and it all came back.

The party. The storm. Lucas and his impossible heroics.

She jerked upright, startling the chicken, which squawked and launched itself off the small table in a flurry of wings and indignation. The bird landed with a heavy thump, shook itself, and fixed Samara with a look of such pure animosity that she almost apologized aloud. She watched it stalk across the polymer tiles, then disappear into the kitchenette with a series of clucks that sounded like cursing.

It was tempting to think that last night had been a

hallucination induced by anaphylactic shock barely averted in time.

But the chicken proved otherwise. So did the gauze taped to her arm.

She lurched to her feet and stumbled to the kitchenette, where she yanked open the fridge door and there they were: two neatly labeled vials, standing upright in a mug on the top shelf. Blood samples, taken a couple of hours after exposure. Her heart started beating faster, making her head pound worse, but the pain also cleared some of the fog. She had to get up to her lab on the Borlaug as quickly as possible. Refrigerating the samples would slow down the white blood cells' digestion of whatever they'd enveloped, but it wouldn't stop the process completely.

She had to get to the ship. The sooner, the better.

Samara hurried to the bedroom, hoping to find Lucas still asleep, but the door stood open, the bed made with military precision. He was gone.

The disappointment registered as a physical ache, sharp as the headache that still throbbed behind her eyes. Silly, she told herself, to expect that he'd linger. He was probably already at the shuttle, prepping it for takeoff or loading cargo. Or maybe he'd still be debriefing with Katherine about his model for predicting the storms.

Samara ran her hands over her temples, then winced as her palm came away gritty and streaked with dried blood. Her arms looked worse in daylight: scratches scabbed over, skin inflamed around them. The gauze taped to her elbow was peeling loose, dust caked in the adhesive.

She stripped and shoved them into the laundry basket before stepping into the shower. The water hit her like a sheet of ice. She hissed at the shock, but it felt good on her inflamed skin, almost as good as a topical anesthetic. In less than two minutes, she rinsed off the worst of the blood and dust, then braced herself and ducked her head under the freezing spray to scrub out her hair. She watched reddish-brown rivulets swirl around the drain and disappear, leaving behind pale streaks on the white tile and raw, red patches on her skin.

As soon as she was dressed again, she packed the blood vials with ice in her insulated thermos before securing the lid. Then she grabbed two empty sampling vials from her collection kit on her way to the front door, where she found the chicken glaring at her as if to say, *I've been waiting.*

The moment Samara cracked the door, the chicken shot between her boots like a guided missile, launching itself outside and leaving behind a clear line of tracks in the thick layer of dust that blanketed everything.

And she'd been worried about not being able to get another sample.

She knelt on her porch, uncapped the first vial, and scooped up dust from the topmost layer, careful not to disturb the underlying strata. Grains clung to the glass, staticky and fine as flour. She repeated the process at the base of the porch's support post, then at the lip of the rain gutter, filling both vials with the powdery brown sediment.

Now she had everything she needed.

Samara capped the vials and tucked them into her kit, then jogged toward the common hall, moving at a pace just short of a run. The dust underfoot had already started to dry into a thin, fragile crust that crunched with every step. The air was still sharp and metallic in the aftermath of the storm, and each breath sent yet another raw flash through her lungs.

Near the edge of the village, she heard a high, keening cry, followed by a muffled sob. Samara slowed, scanning for the source. The sound repeated, raw and desperate, coming from the gap between two of the prefab cabins.

She veered off the path and found Leila in her pajamas, doubled over and kneeling in the dirt, both hands clutching her belly. Covered in blood.

Leila was losing another baby. And it was Samara's fault.

She could've pushed back harder. Ignored Katherine's orders. Done the right thing, even if she had to lie to get lab access. She'd known Hector's solution wouldn't be enough. But Samara had told herself it was Katherine's decision.

She knelt beside the young woman, setting her insulated thermos on the ground. Her skin was cold, clammy with sweat, and her eyes rolled toward Samara with a wild, glassy panic. She tried to speak but only managed a strangled, wheezing sound.

Samara scanned her quickly: no signs of injury, just blood and more blood.

"Easy," Samara said, pitching her voice to the same calm she used on the goats when they were being difficult. "Breathe with me, okay?"

"Please," Leila wheezed, "please save her. It's not her fault I lied. I did everything the doctor said. He said if I took them on schedule, the baby would be okay—"

Leila's entire body went rigid, her spine arching as if she were being electrocuted. Then she crumpled sideways, curling up on her side with her knees drawn tight against her chest. She made a high, animal sound—half cry, half retch—then shuddered and went silent, her breathing shallow and rapid.

Samara pressed a palm to Leila's forehead, feeling the feverish heat there. "We have to get you to the clinic." Not just for the baby, but because she'd lost a lot of blood. "Leila, do you understand?"

A nod, fast and jerky.

Samara hooked one arm under Leila's back and the other under her knees. She lifted and staggered a step before getting her balance. Leila clung to her neck, whispering, "Don't let her die, please, please, don't let my daughter die—"

My daughter.

Samara didn't respond because there was nothing to say.

By the time she stepped into the colony's clinic, her knees ached and her back was on fire. The doors were propped open, and inside was chaos: colonists slumped against walls, some hacking, others dazed. The floor was tracked with mud and dust, and the air was rank with sweat and sickness. There was no other place to put Leila, so she set the young woman gently on the floor.

She scanned the room for Hector and spotted him on the far side, bent over a man on a cot. It was Kevin, one of Maeve's engineers. His wife, Ingrid, stood at the foot of the cot, her face slack with shock, and beside her, Ayesha spoke in soft tones, but whatever she was saying, Ingrid clearly wasn't listening.

As Samara approached, Hector was checking the man's carotid, even though there was obviously no point. The man was blue at the lips and far too still. Samara's chest tightened with dread. The colony's first death.

And the baby Leila carried now might be the second, unless Hector had a miracle up his sleeve.

"Can I help?" Samara asked quietly, not bothering with any preamble.

Hector shook his head once, sharply. "If you were a medical professional, you could."

Ingrid began to sob. "He was fine. He just started coughing, and then he—he just—" She cut off, pressing both hands to her mouth.

Hector shot Ayesha a look. The psychologist nodded and gently led Ingrid to the chair at the foot of Kevin's cot.

Samara turned to Hector. "Leila is miscarrying, lost a lot of blood. She's struggling to breathe."

Hector muttered something under his breath that suggested he was taking Leila's miscarriage personally before he made his way to where she knelt on the floor.

As he crouched beside her, Leila let out a shriek, and blood gushed onto the floor, pooling beneath her with horrifying speed. For a heartbeat, no one moved; even Hector seemed paralyzed. Then he snapped into action, barking, "Help me!" as he positioned himself at Leila's shoulders and gestured for Samara to grab her legs.

They lifted her together, maneuvering her limp form onto the clinic's only gurney. Leila's head lolled, her eyes rolling back, but she clung to consciousness with stubborn rage. Blood soaked through the thin sheet in seconds.

"Do you know how to prep an IV?" Hector's voice was clipped, the question already an order.

"Yes," Samara said, hoping that muscle memory wouldn't fail her.

"Get it started. Fast as you can."

HECTOR HAD RIGGED up the portable ultrasound, and the screens glowed a cold blue that filled Samara with dread. Leila lay pale and still on the gurney. Her breath rattled in her chest like a loose bearing, despite several puffs from an inhaler and the cocktail of drugs that the doctor had injected into her IV.

Justin sat beside Leila, hands clasped between his knees, his wedding ring smeared with blood. He didn't look up as Hector moved the probe across Leila's abdomen, but

Samara saw the way his whole body leaned forward, bracing for the impact. He'd shown up a few minutes ago, claiming that he'd woken up to an empty bed and had followed the trail of bloody footsteps out the door, calling Leila's name.

An image flickered into existence on the monitor: the fetus in its dark cocoon, perfectly still. Hector adjusted the probe, fingers steady, and for a moment, Samara thought she saw a twitch. But no heartbeat came through the machine's speakers, no matter where Hector placed the transducer against Leila's belly.

"I'm sorry," Hector said. "There's nothing else I can do."

"Okay," Justin breathed with no emotion.

The young man stared, not at the screen, but past it, like he might see some other version of his life projected in the air above Leila's abdomen. Samara watched as he absorbed the loss, wondering if he had finally accepted the child only to lose it. Or was this relief disguised as shock, revealed in the barest loosening of the jaw and eyelids as the future he'd never wanted was erased for him?

She'd seen enough grief to know it could take any shape, but what she saw on Justin's face was neither sorrow nor relief. Just blankness.

He blinked once. Twice. Then turned to Hector and asked, "Will she be okay?"

He said the words like he was trying them out for the first time.

"She'll recover, but she'll need rest. I'll keep her here overnight. We'll have to do a D&C if her body isn't able to complete the process."

Justin didn't ask what a D&C was, and Samara wasn't sure if he understood that Hector had meant the dead fetus might have to be surgically removed to prevent a life-threatening infection as it began to decay in Leila's womb.

But she was sure he didn't understand the grief that would hit his wife when she woke up and learned she'd lost another child.

Leila hadn't just been carrying a fetus; she'd been carrying *her daughter.*

"Your wife is going to need a lot of support," Samara said.

Justin's head turned toward her in slow motion after several seconds' delay, as if he was so far away that there was a communications lag between them.

He probably couldn't absorb anything right now, but she felt like she needed to say it anyway.

"Make sure Leila sees the counselor," Samara added, nodding toward Ayesha, who cradled Ingrid like an inconsolable child on the other side of the room. "You're both experiencing an emotional trauma, but she's been through a physical trauma too."

A low moan came from the hallway before Justin could reply, followed by a pained grunt. Samara looked up to see a woman in a blood-streaked nightgown staggering in from the outside. Zoya, another one of the normals. Samara had shared kitchen duty with her last week.

Zoya's face was blank, as if she'd forgotten how to be afraid. Hector moved to her with controlled urgency, taking her arm and leading her to the cot Kevin had occupied less than an hour ago.

Samara felt like she'd failed Kevin, too. And Ingrid. And every single person in this clinic.

But before that thought could drag her down into a bog of self-directed anger, another woman arrived, this one wearing a t-shirt and pajama shorts, frantically wiping her thighs with a blood-soaked towel.

"Why won't it stop?" she repeated. "Why won't it stop?"

Samara had pulled a shift in the fields alongside her two weeks ago, but now she was ashamed that she couldn't remember the young woman's name. Just another normal who'd complained about blisters and couldn't tell weeds from seedlings.

The young woman was just as bloody as Leila had been, and Samara wished she did have the medical training that Hector had criticized her for lacking. She felt so useless. The colony might never need her skills if they couldn't figure out how to stop the dust storms from triggering miscarriages.

If they got through this, she would ask Hector to teach her anything he thought would be useful in a crisis.

Or maybe she'd ask Lucas. He'd said his emergency medical training had been extensive. And he didn't resent her like Hector did. At least, she didn't think he did.

The front door banged open, and Leo strode in, streaked with blood and dust. He made straight for the med closet, flung it open, and started pulling bottles off the shelves.

"Leo!" Samara called. "What's wrong?"

He looked up, anguish twisting his features. "They're dying. All of them. Chickens, goats, even the bull—" He cut off, voice breaking.

Hector appeared behind Leo, grabbed his wrist, managing to keep hold of it even as Leo tried to jerk away. "Stop."

"They're choking to death. I have to—"

"We need the meds here. For people."

Leo looked like he might hit the doctor. "We lose the livestock, we starve."

"We lose the women, we die out. As a species."

Hector's voice could have flash-frozen water. "Every resource we have goes to them until this is under control."

"They're depending on us to take care of them!" Leo spat.

Hector didn't flinch. "If you don't set those down and leave my clinic, I'll have you removed."

Leo blanched, but he let the doctor pry the bottles from his hand. Hector released him, then turned to Samara. "There will be more. If we can't figure out why the dust triggers this and stop it."

"It means extinction." She felt the future collapse inside her.

She looked down at her hands, stained with the blood of another lost hope, and thought:

This is how it ends. Not with a bang, but with a hemorrhage.

Chapter Fourteen

SAMARA

Day 60

THE INFIRMARY REEKED of blood and bleach, a sour chemical note layered over the bitter tang of loss. Samara leaned against the cool wall, her clothes damp with sweat and someone else's fluids, and tried not to look at the four cots by the window. Four lives cut short before they started, four mothers grieving.

She'd been in awe of Hector's solid, calm presence through the procedures for the two women who'd needed them. He'd spent three more hours examining the rest of the sick colonists, distributing stronger meds for most. Now he napped on the floor of his office while all four of the women who'd miscarried rested under mild sedation.

Ayesha had been surprisingly at home in the chaos: she moved from cot to cot, sometimes sitting, sometimes just resting a hand on a shoulder or forehead. Every so often, Samara caught a fragment of prayer or whispered comfort, but the psychologist seemed adept at staying out of Hector's way while always being there when one of the patients needed reassurance. She'd even led an impromptu worship circle to calm the miserable colonists who were forced to wait for hours because their symptoms had been triaged as semi-urgent. She envied Ayesha's ease. Samara had never known what to do with other people's pain, and here there was so much of it.

Samara's own hands were still stained, knuckles brown and sticky, the webbing between her fingers crusted where Leila's blood had pooled and dried. She'd washed twice and hadn't gotten it all off. The sight left her hollow, as if the night's work had drained every useful part of her out and left only the shell. Her biggest contribution had been fetching whatever Hector needed from the supply cabinet and loading medicine cartridges into injectors—a job that could have been done by anyone who could read a label. Now she was doing her best to straighten up, so that when Hector woke, he'd be able to focus on treating patients. After she finished, she would fetch her insulated thermos from the path where she'd left it and track down Lucas. Assuming he'd waited for her.

She thought he would, unless Katherine gave him orders to the contrary. His heroics last night proved he understood that every second of delay degraded her chances of finding the answer they needed.

Samara was almost done bagging up the trash cans filled with biodegradable cartridges, disposable wrappers, empty blisterpacks, and other medical detritus when a faint, raspy voice sounded from the row of cots where Ayesha stood vigil, her lips constantly moving even though she made no audible sound. More prayers, Samara assumed.

"Can we have a memorial?" Zoya's lips barely moved.

Her eyes were open but unfocused, her skin waxy and gray, the painkillers keeping her just above the threshold of consciousness. But her hand reached for Ayesha, who took it in both of hers and squeezed gently.

"Of course," Ayesha said, her tone unshakeable. "Whenever you're ready."

A tremor passed through Zoya's fingers, a shudder that might have been relief or sorrow. Maybe both. "Don't want to forget."

Samara wondered if a memorial for the long-dead family she'd left behind would make her feel better. Probably not. She couldn't remember them without her mind speculating wildly about the horrors they must've endured after she left.

But maybe it would be different for these mothers. If their babies had suffered, it hadn't been for long, and there might be peace in that thought.

The door slammed open, and Katherine entered, trailed by a gust of cool air and the squeak of her work boots on polymer tiles. She'd changed into fresh coveralls, but her hair was still damp, and she looked like she hadn't slept. She scanned the room once, took in the aftermath, then beelined for Hector's office and woke him up.

"We need an update," Katherine said, voice pitched for privacy but hard-edged enough to cut through the fog of exhaustion. "Outside."

He nodded groggily and followed her into the corridor. Samara hesitated, then trailed after them, not sure if she'd been invited, but hoping to talk to Katherine about her new plan.

The sunlight was harsh, so bright it made Samara blink, and the cloudless periwinkle sky overhead felt too big and open after the darkness of the storm and the confines of the overcrowded clinic.

Katherine kept her voice low as the three of them clustered near the steps of the clinic. "We lost four cows overnight. The rest are critical. Leo's been with them since dawn, but he's had to… improvise." She hesitated, as if the words themselves offended her. "He's using old field-vet methods, forcing tubes into their windpipes to keep their airways open and sucking mucus out of their lungs with an aspirator. I don't think he's slept, either."

"Have you necropsied the dead ones?" Hector asked, his tone already clinical, matter-of-fact.

"Not yet," Katherine said. "I was hoping you could do it. Figure out what we're up against before we lose the whole herd."

Hector's jaw twitched. "I'm not a vet. That would be closer to Renata's specialty."

Katherine's breath escaped like air from a punctured seal. "Why did every pregnant woman in the colony have a miscarriage last night? I thought the medications were working."

Hector braced himself against the clinic's wall, arms crossed, as if bracing himself for cross-examination. "I ran blood panels on all of them, after the fact. Every single one showed an immune response significantly outside the normal range. I put all four on immunosuppressants and antihistamines; their vitals stabilized almost immediately."

Samara knew it was risky to challenge Hector, but this might be the opening she needed to get Katherine on board. "There are autoimmune disorders where a mother's body attacks the fetus as foreign. Maybe the dust amped up the immune system so much that it started targeting not just the mother's body, but also the baby's."

"Usually only happens with Rh factor incompatibility, or when the immune system's already primed for rejection,"Hector countered. "These women didn't have any of the risk factors. And the antihistamines should've worked."

"Unless the rules are different here." Samara turned to Katherine. "Were the dead cows pregnant?"

"I don't know," Katherine said. "Leo was too busy keeping the rest alive to check. How much medication do we have left?"

Hector's laugh was dry and bitter. "Not enough. I had to give out higher doses to half the colony this morning. If we can't find a way to synthesize more before the next storm…"

"We will," Samara said, surprised to hear herself sound so certain. "Renata's been working nonstop. If there's anything here with the right alkaloids or steroids, she'll find it. Maeve can retrofit the lab gear to handle small-batch synthesis. Lucas can build some of the specialized equipment we don't already have. And I've done enough bench chemistry to be useful."

Hector didn't object, which showed how shaken he must be.

Katherine straightened, the lines around her mouth deepening. "We need answers fast. If the animals keep dying, people are going to panic. And if the colony loses faith in us…" She didn't finish, but the rest didn't need saying.

She turned to Samara. "Leo's got one of the dead cows in the work shed at the edge of the fields. We don't want people seeing or hearing it until we know what happened. Find Renata, get her prepped, and do the autopsy together. Leo will take care of the remains."

"Before I do that, I need to get up to the ship—"

"I know, Lucas practically mutinied when I told him to leave without you." Samara opened her mouth to explain the urgency of analyzing the white blood cells, but

Katherine added, "Autopsy first. Lucas assured me that there should still be enough DNA to analyze if you keep your blood samples refrigerated for the next twenty-six-point-two-nine hours."

Samara laughed as gratitude flooded through her. She imagined Lucas delivering that information to Katherine while tapping the side of his leg and staring slightly over her head.

She would love to see what his version of a mutiny would look like.

The thermos. She'd left it on the ground where she'd found Leila.

Samara raced back toward the village, relieved to discover the thermos exactly where she'd left it, between the two cabins.

Leila's cabin and Briar's, she realized, seeing the latter through the window of one and Leila's husband, Justin, emerging from the other. Justin avoided making eye contact with Samara as he hurried away, as if he thought she had come here to lecture him more about what Leila needed.

Katherine had known about Briar's resentment toward Leila before the cabins had been set up, and she'd chosen to put the two of them right next to each other, when there had been seventy-eight other spots to choose from. Did she think forcing them to be neighbors would make them friends?

It seemed naïve, but Samara thought again about what Katherine had said in the greenhouse.

We're not just responsible for the physical survival of this colony. We're also responsible for bringing people together.

Maybe that was Katherine's responsibility. But right now, Samara believed that she was the only person with a chance of ensuring their physical survival.

And she wasn't going to let anyone stop her, even if it meant mutiny.

~

LEILA SURFACED from the blackness slowly. Her body felt remote, each limb weighted with sleepy numbness; they refused to respond to her commands. She tried to swallow and found her throat raw, as if she'd been screaming for hours. But she wasn't at home. The bedsheets were too thin and scratchy against her upper arms.

She was in the clinic.

The memory came in shattered fragments: the hot wash of blood, the crushing agony in her lower belly every time another contraction hit, crawling down the dirt path knowing she'd never make it in time to save her daughter. Then Dr. Makinde, carrying her, and Dr. Callas, his voice calm and kind, but his expression warning her not to hope.

She must have passed out after that. Or they'd knocked her out on purpose.

She managed to roll her gaze to the left, where an IV rack stood, one transparent tube trailing down toward the bed where it was probably connected to her arm. Beyond that, everything blurred. She remembered Justin holding her hand and tried to call for him, but what came out was a croak.

It was enough. A dark shape detached itself from the corner and crossed to her bed.

Dr. Basu's eyes looked even larger and more luminous in her narrow face as she leaned over Leila, and her mouth was set in a line that tried and failed to be cheerful.

"Hey," Dr. Basu said, sitting on the edge of the cot. "You're awake."

Not, *don't worry, you're going to be okay.* Or, *you were bleeding, but we saved the baby.*

"Where's Justin?" Her lips were dry, and the words came out sticky.

Dr. Basu smiled, but it was a gentle, practiced smile that therapists probably learned in school. "He was here for hours, but there wasn't anything he could do for you, so I sent him home to rest." Her hand found Leila's and squeezed it lightly. "You need rest, too."

Leila let the words drift through her like smoke.

"He didn't want the baby," she said, staring at the ceiling. "I think he was glad I lost it."

Dr. Basu didn't flinch away from the terrible thing Leila had just said. But her reply wasn't all that helpful either:

"No two people grieve in the same way. Sometimes people push others away, or act angry, or just... stop talking altogether. Doesn't mean they're not hurting."

Leila tried to laugh, but her diaphragm seized and all that came out was a cough. "He was angry before. Angry at me for risking our spots in the colony, even before..." The sentence broke off, snagged on the barbed wire that seemed to fill her throat, and her vision blurred as fresh tears stung her eyes.

Dr. Basu squeezed her hand again. "We're all grieving, Leila. Every single person in this colony has lost almost everyone they've ever known, along with their homes and the lives they expected to live. We lost our whole world, literally and metaphorically."

Leila felt a sour wave of shame rise through her chest. She'd been so locked in her own loss that she'd forgotten anyone else could feel as hollow as she did.

Hollow was even worse than guilty.

"Was it selfish to want a baby? With everything going

to shit, and everyone depending on us, and…" She faltered. "Was it wrong of me to try anyway?"

Dr. Basu shook her head, the motion small but emphatic. "It's normal to reach for life after a brush with death. To want to make meaning out of loss."

"It doesn't feel like grief, how much I wanted them." Leila's hands curled into fists beneath the sheet. "I loved my daughter as soon as I knew I was pregnant." *And my son, before Justin.* "I didn't even know her, but I loved her."

"That's exactly why you need to let yourself grieve," Dr. Basu said. "And let Justin grieve in his own way. Give him some grace to figure out his own feelings."

Grace.

What did that even mean?

Leila stared at the ceiling, tracing the outlines of the LED panels, the seams where the plastic joined the alloy. "Have you ever lost a child?"

"I haven't." Dr. Basu's face softened. "But I lost my grandmother when I was very young. She raised me for a while, when my parents couldn't."

That sounded so sad. As hard as their lives had been, she couldn't imagine not being with her mother, back when her mother was alive.

"I still miss my grandmother. Every day. Even though it's been decades, even though I know she wouldn't want me to be sad."

The psychologist's smile was real this time, but teary, and Leila liked it much better than the cautious smile she'd attempted before.

"I try to remember that grief is a remembrance of love," said Dr. Basu.

Leila shook her head. Or tried to. She still couldn't move so much as twitch. "It hurts so much."

"You don't have to hurt alone. You can talk to me any

time. Or, if you and Justin ever want my help getting some clarity—"

Leila laughed bitterly. "Justin will never agree to couples therapy."

"You'd be surprised. Sometimes the ones who protest the most actually get the most out of it." She let the silence stretch a little, then added, "I hope to see you at morning worship, when you're feeling up to it."

Leila closed her eyes, suddenly exhausted by the effort of being awake.

"Maybe." But she couldn't imagine sitting in a circle, singing songs, and praying when her daughter was dead.

Two miscarriages. Two lives that her body had rejected, overruling Leila's love for them.

Leila waited for the door to click shut before she let the tears come.

She thought about the other women in the colony who had miscarried too, how all their hopes had been erased in a single night, as if this planet had decided it didn't want their kind here.

She pressed her palm to her empty belly and tried to remember that electric tingle of hope, the certainty that she was making something new and precious in a universe that had already destroyed so much.

She had never felt so alone.

THE WORK SHED at the edge of the fields looked like someone had tried converting a slaughterhouse into a garden shed and given up halfway through. Samara donned her surgical mask, then entered and immediately regretted it. The smell inside was dense and viscous—shit, piss, and blood mixed with rotten meat. She gagged as it settled into her nose and crawled down her throat.

The cow lay on its side atop a battered steel table, eyes open but unseeing, tongue lolling out as if death had caught it mid-yawn. Renata stood over it in a stained apron, elbow-length gloves, and a surgical mask, her hair pulled back in a knot that somehow still looked professional. She was carving a line down the cow's belly with a knife Samara had never seen before. It was much bigger than the delicate tools they'd used on the feathered shrew and the amphibilizard or whatever Renata had christened it. But even though slicing through cowhide clearly required a lot more strength, every draw of the blade was deliberate, revealing deep crimson muscle beneath the hide.

Samara hovered a meter back, arms crossed tight over her chest as she tried not to breathe through her nose. "You're sure this is the best place for this?"

Renata didn't look up. "Katherine said we're not supposed to scare people. She thought it'd be best if the necropsy happened somewhere... discrete." Renata's eyes crinkled, and Samara imagined a tight, humorless grin beneath the surgical mask. "Besides, Leo's out of his mind about the rest of the herd. He doesn't want the others to see their dead friend being butchered. Even if said friend was dead before we started."

Samara thought about Leo's panicked entrance into the clinic and how defeated he'd looked when Hector had insisted that the medicines had to be reserved for humans.

They're depending on us to take care of them!

Poor Leo. He'd be mourning the loss of this cow today. Maybe as deeply as Leila would be mourning her daughter.

Samara watched as the blade traced its way from

sternum to pelvis. The cow had been dead less than a day, but the blood was already going syrupy, clotting in the channels Renata had made.

Renata set the knife aside and flexed her fingers. "You still with me? Because this is going to get a lot more disgusting. Much worse than the worst dissection we've done so far."

Samara squared her jaw. "I'm fine."

Her stomach disagreed, but it was too late to back out now. They had to find out what had killed the cows, in case it held the answer to a cure for people, too.

"Good. I need you to grab the skin on that side and pull it back when I tell you."

Renata gestured with her chin, and Samara stepped up, careful not to slip on the puddle of blood that was forming on the shed's packed dirt floor.

Samara braced herself as Renata picked up the knife again and sliced through the connective tissue revealed by her first incision. There was a sound like wet fabric tearing, then a soft pop as the skin peeled away from the muscle. Samara looked down and saw the cross-section of the animal, layers of slimy fat and purpled muscle packed in dense strata.

"Ready?" Renata asked, voice flat.

"Ready."

"Pull."

Samara pulled. There was resistance at first, then the whole sheet of hide came away with a wet slurp, exposing the cow's belly. She looked down to see her hands smeared with congealed blood up to the wrists. The sight made her head swim, but she managed to keep her composure, even when Renata drove the knife in again and made a long cut through the muscle wall.

This time, the thick, dark blood didn't just ooze; it

jetted, splattering Renata's apron and spraying across Samara's boots. The smell got worse. Underneath the ferric scent of blood was the reek of bile and methane. It nearly dropped Samara to her knees.

"Oh god," she muttered, turning her head away.

"If you're going to puke, do it now," Renata said, not unkindly. "Because I'm about to open the gut and it's going to be biblical."

Samara swallowed hard. "I'm good." She wasn't, but there was no way she'd admit that to Renata, who seemed unfazed no matter how gory the job. She tightened her grip on the cow's skin and focused on the motion of the blade, the arc of Renata's hand, she drove it through inch after inch of tissue.

"There's so much fat," Renata said, almost to herself. "I forgot how much of it there is in these animals." She dug in with the knife, then cursed as a bright yellow spray hit her cheek.

Thank goodness for the mask. Samara would probably have to kill herself if a stray droplet had gotten into her mouth.

"Is that normal?" Samara asked.

"I don't know, I usually don't wait until my subjects have started to rot." Renata took a step back, wiped her face with the back of her wrist, and regarded the incision. "I must've punctured a stomach."

"Does it matter?"

Renata shrugged. "I'm trained in dissection, not forensics. I've never done an animal autopsy."

"Makes me nostalgic for the smell of formaldehyde," Samara said.

Renata laughed and jabbed the knife in again and drew it along the length of the cow, then set the blade aside and jammed both hands inside.

The sound that followed was so disgusting that Samara's

vision went spotty for a second. Renata grunted and pulled at something inside, then suddenly stepped back as the contents of the cow's abdomen surged out onto the table, a steaming mass of intestines, organs, and unidentifiable mush.

Samara dropped the cow's skin and staggered for the door, barely making it outside and yanking her surgical mask aside before she vomited into the dirt outside.

She stood there for a moment, hands braced on her knees, shuddering as her body tried to empty itself of everything she'd eaten in the last year. When she was done, she wiped her mouth on her sleeve and looked back into the shed.

Renata was standing over the cow, arms folded, a smirk on her face.

"Wuss," she said, but her voice was gentle. "You okay?"

Samara managed a weak nod. "I'm fine." She wiped her mouth again, then replaced her mask and stepped back inside, determined to see it through. Renata's face was pale, and her eyes were watering, but she didn't mention it.

"Can you tell if it was pregnant?" Samara asked, her voice still ragged.

"I'll check." Renata rolled up her sleeves and started pulling at the mass of intestines, searching for the uterus. She found it, cut it open with a smaller knife, and peered inside. "Not pregnant."

Samara let out a breath she hadn't realized she was holding. Not that it changed anything for the women who'd miscarried, but it ruled out the possibility that pregnancy made you more likely to have a fatal reaction to the dust.

Renata set the uterus aside and began poking through the rest of the organs. "We're looking for anything unusual," she said, her tone gone clinical again. "Anything that doesn't belong in a healthy cow."

Samara watched as Renata sliced through the stomachs, the liver, the kidneys. Each cut was methodical, careful, almost loving. Samara had no idea what counted as unusual in a cow's insides, but as she leaned in for a closer look, something caught her eye—a flicker of movement, subtle but unmistakable, just below the surface of one of the intestines.

She pointed. "There. Did you see that?"

Renata followed her finger, then gasped. "*Holy shit.*"

She grabbed a pair of forceps and teased at the spot. Under the thin, glistening membrane, a brownish filament was woven through the gut wall, snaking along the length of the intestine. As Renata pulled at it, the filament twitched, then curled around the forceps.

"Did I imagine that, or did it just move?" Samara asked, her voice barely above a whisper.

Renata didn't answer. She used the forceps to extract more of the filament, revealing that it was part of a network—a branching, root-like structure that had infiltrated the entire digestive tract. The filaments squirmed and writhed as she pulled, as if searching for something to latch onto.

Samara felt her skin crawl. "That can't be a reflex action, can it?"

Renata shook her head. "Not like any I've ever seen. It's more like a…" She trailed off, then grabbed a sample vial from the tray and snipped off a length of the filament, dropping it inside.

Samara watched as Renata cut deeper, exposing more of the network. It was everywhere, around the kidneys, the liver, even woven through the fat. The tendrils curled and twisted in slow, deliberate arcs. Like they were searching for the next thing to grab onto.

"How can it still be moving?" Samara asked. "Leo said the cow died at the height of the storm. That means it's been dead for at least twelve hours, probably more."

Renata stared at the filaments, shaking her head. "I've never seen anything like it."

"It has to be a parasite, doesn't it?"

"Help me roll the corpse," Renata said. "I want to see the spine."

Samara grabbed the cow's foreleg and pulled while Renata pushed at the hindquarters. Together, they managed to flip the carcass onto its back, exposing the thick, muscular neck. Renata picked up the big knife again and started hacking through the flesh, not bothering with finesse now. When she reached the vertebrae, she switched to a bone saw and made quick work of the spine, exposing the spinal cord. Samara leaned in and saw that the brown filaments were wrapped around the vertebrae in dense, concentric layers, as if it were trying to strangle the nervous system.

Renata stared at it for a long moment, then looked up at Samara. "Parasite, for sure," she said in a hollow voice. "But it wasn't killing the native animals. They were fine until I euthanized them. And Leo said that all four cows who died were in good health until the storm."

"How can it have colonized them so quickly?"

Renata shook her head. "I've found these filaments in every single native animal I've examined so far." She took a shaky breath. "If this is what's making us sick…"

"Then we're all infected," Samara finished.

Chapter Fifteen

SAMARA BARELY REMEMBERED the shuttle ride back up to the Borlaug. The low, vertical launch, the drag of acceleration pushing her back against her seat as they shot space-ward, the moment when gravity lost its grip on them. None of it registered. She was already halfway through designing a preliminary research protocol before the shuttle finished docking. By the time the airlock cycled open, her mind had run through every possible experiment she could run with the samples in her possession at least twice.

Once in her laboratory, she didn't bother changing into her formal lab coat. She had multiple experiments to set up, and Katherine could call her back to the planet's surface at any time.

First, the blood samples, before the pathogen's DNA could degrade any further. Which meant a whirl in the centrifuge to isolate her white blood cells, which she then sequenced, followed by a sequencing of a tissue sample taken from her before they'd left Earth for comparison.

While that was running, she started working on the dust.

After centrifugation and multiple methods of filtration, she'd split the components of the dust out by particle size and whether each component was organic or inorganic. Once the sequencer had finished its first analyses, she ran each organic component of the dust through it, barely waiting for each map to be complete before loading the next sample.

While she waited for the DNA in the last organic component of the dust to finish processing, she prepared a sample of the filament, the last piece of the puzzle; she'd had Renata help her cut away nearly half a pound of the brown fungal threads that had tangled around the cow's spinal cord and brainstem, to be sure she'd have enough to do as many tests as possible. And Renata had promised to extract at least that much again and freeze it for future experiments.

The last sequencing run on the filament took an agonizing twenty minutes, during which Samara paced the lab, running gloved fingers along the walls, inspecting the equipment for faults she knew weren't there. She cleaned, organized, and sterilized every surface she touched. It was impossible to sit still until the sequencer chirped, notifying her that the final sequence was complete.

Racing to her console, she uploaded the last data set and asked the ship's AI to run a comparison, looking for similarities between any DNA sequences found in each of the sample types: blood, dust, and filament.

Six hours after she'd begun, she had three perfect matches.

The dust storms were actually sporestorms, carrying massive quantities of spores from some kind of fungus they had yet to identify.

The filament was the fungus in its adult form. Every animal they'd found so far was infected with this fungus, which was the most successful parasite Samara had ever heard of, aside from the genetically-modified chytrid fungus that had driven them from Earth.

And the foreign DNA extracted from Samara's white blood cells was identical to the DNA of the spores, proving that she, and every other colonist on DaVinci, was infected with this parasite.

She thought of the devastated women in the infirmary, of Leila curled around her belly and refusing to let go.

She thought of the way the parasite had squirmed through the cow's belly, reaching for the animal's brain-stem and groping up the vertebrae to wrap itself around the brain.

She imagined herself on Renata's dissecting table, skin and muscle split open to reveal a writhing mass of brown filaments bursting out of her abdomen to choke the life out of every living thing on DaVinci.

Samara sat back from the display, chest tight. She was sweating, even though the lab was kept cold enough to kill most pathogens. She took off one glove, then the other, and stared at her hands, marked with red welts.

She wondered, suddenly, if Lucas had known. He'd been on the Borlaug for months before anyone else, running environmental surveys, collecting data.

Although he hadn't known about the filaments, he could have run the analysis that would've told him there was organic matter in the 'dust' sample. But when she'd asked him weeks ago, he'd claimed that there hadn't been enough left over for additional tests.

Had he lied? Or had the parasite already colonized his nervous system? Was it crazy to wonder if it could cloud his judgment or force him to protect it? Parasites that could influence their hosts' behavior had been documented on Earth.

Toxoplasma gondii, a protozoan transmitted through feces, caused mice and rats to be more exploratory and less afraid of cats, making it more likely that they'd be eaten, transferring the protozoan to the feline host.

Dicrocoelium dendriticum, a flatworm, manipulated the infected ants to climb to the tops of grass stalks, where they were more likely to be eaten by herbivores like cows, sheep, and deer, granting the worm a new host.

More relevant, Samara knew of multiple classes of fungi from Earth that parasitized living organisms and changed their hosts' behavior. Ants infected with *ophiocordyceps unilateralis*—a.k.a. zombie ant fungus—would leave their nests in the forest canopy and journey down to the ground, where the temperature and humidity were perfect for the fungus to flourish. And when the fungus was ready to release spores, the ant would attach itself to the underside of a leaf and wait to die, maximizing the potential for the spores to infect other ants. *Gibellula attenboroughii* did the same to spiders.

And they had ample evidence that this fungus attacked the nervous system.

Samara forced herself to focus. If the entire colony was infected, then the only thing that mattered was stopping the spread, or at least slowing it down.

She called up the ship's medical inventory, scanning the list of available pharmaceuticals. She found the antifungals. Fluconazole, ketoconazole, terbinafine, and a dozen others that she recognized. There were several dozen more that she didn't.

"Computer, I need samples of every antifungal agent suitable for human or veterinary use."

A schematic of the ship appeared, a pulsing dot indicating the aft storage bay. "Antifungal compounds are stored in sealed refrigeration units, Deck 7, Section 4. Biometric authorization required for access."

She was halfway down the corridor before the computer finished speaking.

The storage bay was a cavernous space, all gleaming metal and sterile white light. Seemingly endless rows of sealed crates, each one numbered and tagged with contents. A smaller, insulated door to her left bore the medical department's green crescent.

Samara pressed her palm against the biometric scanner. A tingle as it read her dermal papillae, analyzing capillary patterns. She tapped her thigh in a nervous rhythm until the lock finally disengaged with a satisfying *snick*.

Cold mist billowed around her ankles as she stepped inside, activating the interior lights. The temperature dropped as her footsteps echoed in the cavernous space, the sound swallowed by the rows of crates and humming refrigeration units. Pharmaceuticals in sealed glass vials lined the shelves, organized by class and chemical structure. She began loading ampules into a transport container, working with clinical speed, counting out a single unit of each and lining them up on the tray. Her gloves stuck to the chilled vials, and her breath fogged up the lenses of the lab goggles she'd forgotten to remove.

She'd retrieved one each of the antifungals meant for humans and was reaching for a second row of veterinary samples when a voice broke the hush behind her: "Are you suffering from a severe instance of athlete's foot?"

She nearly dropped the tray. Lucas stood in the doorway, hands clasped behind his back, his body still as if frozen along with the rest of the room.

This was her chance to confront him.

"I'm prepping for a series of in vitro trials. The last

animal necropsy showed systemic fungal colonization. The dust storms aren't dust storms, Lucas. They're sporestorms."

She set down the tray and turned to face him, watching for his reaction. "You never tested for biologicals. Why?"

Lucas met her stare without blinking, although his fingers started tapping against the side of his leg. "I tested for inorganic substances because Dr. Callas indicated that the problem was an allergic reaction rather than infection. At the time, symptoms were minor and normal doses of antihistamines seemed effective. I apologize for my mistake."

Samara wanted to believe him, but he was normally so competent at everything he did that she had a hard time seeing him making such an obvious oversight.

On the other hand, nobody could be good at everything. The fact that he'd mastered more skills than most, from piloting to engineering to... to phlebotomy, apparently, didn't automatically make him an expert microbiologist. But it did make it easy for her to assume that he might be.

That was her mistake. And Katherine's. She vowed to have a conversation with the colony leader when she returned to the surface.

"Don't worry about it," she said, and was surprised at how tired she sounded. "Will you help me take all these back to the lab?"

Lucas inclined his head, then gathered the rest of the vials, arranging them on the tray with the precision of a man who had never met a right angle he didn't respect.

They walked together, silent, as the AI sealed the cold storage behind them.

Back in the lab, Lucas placed the tray of ampoules on

the clean bench and stood aside. "If you wish, I can assist with the assays."

"I've got it," Samara said. "But I need you to do something else. Inventory all shipboard equipment that can be adapted for pharmaceutical synthesis. We'll have to manufacture antifungals at scale if any of these are effective."

Lucas nodded. "Would you like me to prioritize based on projected consumption?"

"Please," she said, already turning to prep the samples of the parasite. Some of the threads were still moving.

Perfect.

She heard the quiet swish of the door as he left, then allowed herself a long exhale.

She set the vials in a neat row and began dropping single filaments into their own petri dishes, one for each of the antifungal drugs. As the first droplets of medication hit the filaments, Samara watched for a reaction. Within five minutes, most of the antifungals slowed the movements of the filaments, but only two, fluconazole and ketoconazole, stopped them dead.

She instructed the AI to calculate how much fluconazole and ketoconazole were available on the ship. "There are 483 standard doses remaining," it said. "At the recommended protocol for systemic infection, this allows for a seven-day course of treatment for each colony member."

That was a start. But the sporestorms were relentless, and the supply would run out before the next one hit.

Samara sat back, watching the time-lapse as the other samples slowed, then resumed their growth. Even if they could manage to manufacture more doses with what they could find on the planet below, the antifungals would only buy time. Eventually, the fungus would become resistant to these medicines.

If she couldn't develop a cure before the fungus learned to adapt, the colony was doomed.

"ONE PILL in the morning with breakfast for seven days. Don't skip a dose, or you might need a second course." Samara repeated the same instructions she'd been reciting for the past hour as she'd handed out blisterpacks of fluconazole. "If you start to feel worse or have any kind of reaction, see Dr. Callas immediately."

Hector had triaged the colonists into two lines: one for those with mild symptoms, to receive fluconazole from Samara, and another for those with severe symptoms who needed the ketoconazole that Hector was handing out, along with more immunosuppressants.

They'd feel better soon. Samara had taken her dose of antifungals on the ship, as soon as she'd identified the ones that were effective against the spores. Within an hour, she'd felt less itchy. By the time she'd made it back down to the planet's surface, her thick-headedness was starting to clear, and her once-angry rash had faded from dark red to pink.

The fluconazole stung the tongue and left a sweet aftertaste. Most took it with a grimace and a thank-you, but a few swallowed it with a desperate, worshipful look, as if Samara were offering not a generic antifungal but a sacrament.

The hope on their faces tripped her guilt, because even though she told them over and over that it wasn't a cure, that they would have to take another dose every time there was another sporestorm, she could tell they weren't hearing it. And if she told them how few doses were left, colony-wide panic would be inevitable.

Zoya was next. She didn't look at Samara, just stared at

the table as she palmed her blister pack. Her face was so puffy it looked like a different person's, the skin stretched tight and shiny as if her body had been stuffed with insulation. Her eyelids were nearly swollen shut, a faint blue bruise visible under each one.

Samara wondered if she'd already had the memorial for the child she'd miscarried. And if the ceremony could actually ease that pain.

"How are you feeling?" Samara asked, keeping her voice neutral.

"Fine." Zoya's lips barely moved. She took the pill from the pack, dry-swallowed it, and turned to go.

"If you have any reaction at all to the antifungal medication, stop by the clinic immediately. Your body has been through a lot in the past few days."

Zoya's hands balled into fists, but she nodded.

Samara watched her walk away, her own throat suddenly tight. Zoya's posture said: *I don't want your pity.* Samara respected that, even as she wanted to apologize for not having something better to offer.

Zoya was in better shape than Evan, who was next in Hector's queue. The man's chest heaved with each inhale, a wet, rasping sound that made Samara's own lungs ache in sympathy. His joints were so swollen his fingers curled into stiff claws, the skin mottled and shining with sweat. He fumbled the blister pack Hector handed him, dropping it twice before Hector finally broke the foil himself, shaking a tablet into Evan's palm.

"Here," Hector pressed a cup of water to Evan's lips, steadying the man's trembling hand as he drank. "Take it slow. Breathe between sips."

Samara watched as he administered an injection of immunosuppressants, then walked Evan over to a chair and helped him sit before returning to treat his next patient.

Samara tucked a blister pack into the breast pocket of her shirt, a course of medication for Lucas, who had returned to the Borlaug after bringing her down with the antifungals to pull equipment for the chemlab out of the ship's deep stores. Right now, he was the only crew member capable of piloting the shuttle who wasn't experiencing severe symptoms; he'd spent so much time in orbit studying the sporestorms that his exposure was minimal compared to the rest of them. He'd promised to bring the centrifuge, glassware, the spectrometer, and the machines he'd cobbled together from spare parts in the ship's stores.

But she was sure that if he said they would work, they would work.

Samara would have to remember to give him the antifungals as soon as he arrived. She could already imagine his reaction to the taste, the way he'd blink twice and say, "Interesting," as if he were sampling a new variety of tea instead of choking down a chemical sledgehammer.

Leila was next. She looked even paler than yesterday, the little color she'd had leached out of her skin and replaced by a patchwork of hives that crept up her neck and framed her jaw like a necklace. She had a dry cough, and her hands shook as she took the blister pack. Her voice was almost too quiet to hear as she asked, "Will it stop… what happened before?"

Samara wanted to lie. She wanted to say yes, absolutely, the medicine would protect the baby next time, and the time after that. But she didn't know. If the antifungal bought them seven days of relief, what happened on day eight? Would the next sporestorm undo everything? Would the fungus learn, mutate, and come back with new tricks the way it had in the animals?

She thought about the cow's insides, the way the filaments had woven themselves through every organ, patient and inexorable. She thought about the first blood-soaked night, about the helplessness of watching Leila crumple to the dirt, hands wrapped around her belly.

"It should kill the fungus that's already inside you. But the storms will come back, so you're going to keep getting infected. And—" she lowered her voice, glancing around at the others, "we still don't know if treating the infection right away will be enough to prevent a miscarriage."

Leila looked away, jaw clenched, eyes shining in the harsh light of the triage tent. "So it might not matter."

"Until we know for sure, I think you should keep using your birth control, just for a little while."

A tremor ran through Leila's shoulders. She nodded, lips pressed tight. "Thank you, Dr. Makinde."

Samara wanted to say something else, something encouraging, but false hope might inspire Leila to try to get pregnant again before they had a solution.

She'd saved Leila's life two days ago, but saving the woman while losing the future felt like solving the wrong equation.

Chapter Sixteen

DAVINCI YEAR 1
  FALL

RENATA WAS ALREADY at the workbench, sleeves rolled to her elbows, wrist-deep in fuzzy blue seedpods that looked like the offspring of a tennis ball and a sea urchin. She wore protective goggles and a mask that was, Samara suspected, more for attitude than safety. The pods resisted her knife with rubbery resilience, but she split them open one-handed, flicking seeds into a stainless bowl with the efficiency of a blackjack dealer. The bowl was nearly full, seeds the color of old bruises heaped like forbidden fruit.

It didn't look like much, but Renata believed that one of the compounds in the seeds could be used to make an antifungal with similar properties to fluconazole.

Samara was on her thirty-seventh pod, and her hands already looked like she'd been finger painting with hematite. Hector, across the workbench, wielded a paring knife with the precision of a scalpel, each motion careful and methodical. He'd made a game of slicing the pods open so the seeds spilled out in a perfect row, and each time he did it, he'd glance up to see if either of the women noticed.

They did, of course. But neither gave him the satisfaction.

A bead of sweat tracked down Samara's temple, paused at her jaw, and dropped to the workbench. The air inside the lab was thick, the little oscillating fan in the corner doing nothing but stir the heat into soup. The sweat didn't bother her as much as the prickle just above her left wrist, where something almost too light to feel had landed. She looked down and saw another one of the star mosquitoes, about to pierce her skin with its hair-needle proboscis.

She slapped it flat, but not before it bit her.

A thin droplet of blood beaded up and sat there, stubborn, as if the heat and humidity weren't enough insult already. She wiped it with the back of her glove, smearing rust across the elastic.

"Bastards," she muttered, and Renata glanced over the rim of her goggles, amusement crinkling the corners of her eyes.

Samara added, "We flew forty-two light-years from Earth, but the planet we picked still has mosquitoes."

"Damn parallel evolution," Renata agreed.

Ayesha ducked through the threshold and grinned at all three of them like she was crashing a secret party. She wore her usual blue headscarf and a smile that managed to be both apologetic and conspiratorial.

And a little bit forced, in Samara's opinion. Since the last sporestorm, every interaction she'd had with the psychologist felt like more of a ritual calculated to create bonding moments than genuine attempts at connection.

But she had to admit, morale had been low. And many

of the colonists outside of the leadership team seemed to be responding to Ayesha's efforts.

"I heard from Katherine that you're almost ready for a batch run?"

"Just have to finish separating the seeds," Hector said, not pausing. "Then Renata will work her magic."

"May I help?" she asked, and Samara slid a tray down the table, nudging a knife in her direction.

Ayesha took a seat and selected a pod, rolling it between her fingers.

She slit it open with a clumsy but determined motion, seeds tumbling out in a small avalanche. "It's a little miraculous, isn't it?" she said, almost to herself but not really. "We land on a planet with a fungal parasite ready to wipe us out, and three kilometers from the colony, we find a plant whose seeds make the only antifungal that works on it. What are the odds?"

Samara glanced at Renata, who had the goggles pushed up now and was watching Ayesha with the wary amusement of someone who'd seen a card trick before the reveal. Renata's mouth twitched, but she didn't comment.

Hector, still slicing with that surgeon's touch, said, "Yes, we were lucky to find it. Very lucky. The first clinical results were—" He glanced at Samara, as if to check his own optimism. "Let's just say, if it holds up in the second round, we'll have a treatment protocol ready by next week."

Ayesha cocked her head. "I'm a psychologist, I can tell when someone's biting their tongue."

Renata snorted and let the smile show. "What Hector means is, we were lucky to find it so quickly, but the odds were high that we'd find something sooner or later. That's how nature works: as soon as a parasite evolves, its host evolves defenses. The parasite has to up its game, and so does the host."

Ayesha shook her head, slicing through another pod with a little more force than necessary. "It still seems unlikely to me," she said, her tone gentle but edged with skepticism.

Samara bit back her first reply, which was that Ayesha's training in comparative religions probably hadn't prepared her to calculate probabilities. Instead, she said, "You're right, it's unlikely. But so was finding a plant that makes the exact compound we need, in a form close enough that we can modify the plant to make one that is."

Ayesha frowned. "When you say modify, do you mean genetic engineering?"

Renata didn't hesitate. "Virtually all the food in the ship's stores is genetically modified. The chickens, the goats, the rice in the hydroponic, and even the yeast we use for bread were edited to survive high radiation. This isn't any different."

Ayesha took a breath, then turned to Hector. "Are you going to allow this?" There was no accusation in her voice, but it hovered at the edge of challenge.

Hector shrugged, the gesture slow and deliberate. "Half the medicines in the ship's pharmacy were made by tweaking yeast or plant genes to produce what we wanted. If it's done right, it's safer than the old-fashioned way." He gave Ayesha a measuring look, as if weighing his next words. "And we don't have a choice. We can make it through maybe three more sporestorms before we run out of the antifungals entirely. After that, we're back to square one. This—" He gestured to the seeds, the pods, the mess on the table. "—is the only way to make more."

For a moment, the only sound was the wet thud of Renata splitting another pod.

"Why hasn't Katherine told us this?" Ayesha looked around the table, the question more accusation than query.

Renata didn't miss a beat. "You would've found out at the leadership meeting tonight." She shrugged, unapologetic. "It's not a secret."

"And yet I'm just finding out about it now." Ayesha's lips pressed thin. "This is something we should've voted on. Katherine doesn't have the right to make a unilateral decision for the colony."

Samara set her knife down, exhaled through her nose. The psychologist clearly didn't understand what was at stake.

"This isn't just about our immediate survival. You saw what happened to Leila and the others who were pregnant." She set her knife down with enough force to make the workbench ring. "If no one can carry a baby to term, there will be no future generations. That also applies to livestock. We can't unfreeze any more animals until we can be sure they can reproduce. Unless we start cloning them, which comes with its own risks."

Ayesha blinked twice, as if the words had flicked grit into her eyes. She set her knife down with a little more force than necessary. "There should have been a debate." Her tone was deceptively mild. "There should have been input. You can't just—" She pressed the heel of her hand to her forehead, exasperated. "We left Earth to get away from this kind of thing. Unilateral choices. Top-down fixes. You know what happened the last time a handful of experts decided what was best for everyone."

Renata didn't look up, just kept splitting pods. "We were always going to need to adapt some of the native life to fit our needs, as well as to adapt the plants and animals we brought with us to survive here. It was part of the plan from the beginning."

Ayesha threw the seed pod down, hard enough that it bounced off the workbench and scattered purple-black seeds across the floor. "I'm going to talk to Katherine." Her voice was brittle with anger. "You don't get to decide this for the whole colony."

She stood and walked out, the swish of her scarf trailing a wake of tension behind her.

Nobody moved for a long moment. Renata looked after Ayesha, then shrugged and went back to her pods. Hector, who had cut himself at some point during the exchange, pressed a gauze pad to his finger and watched the blood soak through, as if it were a problem that could be solved by waiting it out.

Samara's stomach churned. She kept her eyes on the bright, wet seeds in her bowl, but her mind was replaying the look on Ayesha's face as she stormed out. Not curiosity, not even fear. Just a blank, stubborn refusal to budge.

It worried Samara more than she wanted to admit. The psychologist wasn't interested in understanding the science, just like the mob that killed Dory didn't care that Dory wasn't a scientist. Ayesha had heard the word genetic and she wasn't willing to listen to anything after that.

Renata waited until Ayesha's footsteps faded, then rolled her eyes so extravagantly that the goggles nearly slid off her forehead. "Oh no, the woman whose job is to talk to people about their feelings doesn't think we should do basic science. Guess we'd better just give up and let the fungus kill us."

Hector gave her a look, a blend of fondness and disapproval that somehow managed to suggest she was both his favorite and least favorite child.

"She's right to have concerns. But I'm sure Katherine will bring her around. She always does."

Renata snorted. "If we do put it to a vote, I think most of us are going to choose not to die."

Hector pressed a thumb against his bandaged finger.

"I'm going to feel a lot better once our first batch proves true. We lost another cow last night."

"Hector helped me with the autopsy this time," Renata said, her voice tinged with something like pride. "And he's pretty sure it died of autoimmune disease. Not the infection."

"But the fungus isn't affecting the local fauna that way," Samara argued. "Every wild animal we've caught is crawling with the stuff, but none of them show the same symptoms as the cows—or us."

"You're right, it wasn't. As far as I could tell, their tissues were healthy. And I haven't found a single animal or insect that wasn't infected. I started doing blood tests on the live ones, and they've all got the spores in them."

"Are you saying every living creature you've seen so far is infected?"

Renata nodded. "Even the birds. And the bugs."

"Then why doesn't it make them sick?" But even as Samara said it, the answer was forming. She set the pod down, mouth suddenly dry. "Are you saying it's not a parasite, it's a symbiote?"

Renata smiled, the goggles perched on her hair like a crown. "Yes. Just not for us."

If the fungus was a symbiote, then it was doing something for the local animals, something so fundamental that the native life forms had evolved to depend on it. The cows, the chickens, the people, they weren't dying because the fungus was attacking them. They were dying because their bodies were fighting it.

What if they could trick the immune system into seeing the fungus as self, instead of enemy? What if they could teach it to tolerate the invader, the way the native animals must have learned eons ago?

She could see the outlines of it in her mind, bright and

cold as a circuit diagram: a gene therapy, delivered by a virus or a nanoparticle, or even just a cocktail of CRISPR-modified proteins to switch off the T-cells responsible for the autoimmune response.

But Katherine would never agree to the way she'd have to do it. And Samara couldn't defend the ethics of it. Ayesha would have hysterics, and even Renata and Hector, who'd understand the nuances, would probably argue against taking that risk.

But she couldn't let everyone die. She had to try.

Chapter Seventeen

THE SHUTTLE's airlock hissed open, and Samara stepped into the Borlaug's familiar synthetic hush. Every surface was clean enough to shame a microscope, and the recycled air tinged with ozone and lemon. She stood a moment, letting her eyes adjust to the corridor's light, then reached for her duffel and slung it over one shoulder, the weight grounding her.

Behind her, the two Demeters—Olivia, cheerful and broad-faced, and the more taciturn Vasily—unstrapped themselves from the shuttle's jump seats. Sophie stretched with an audible crack of vertebrae and grinned at Samara.

"Feels like a luxury hotel up here, doesn't it?" she said, glancing down the pristine passageway. "I always forget what filtered air actually smells like."

Vasily said nothing, already flicking through the cargo manifest on his tablet.

Olivia eyed the duffel. "Need a hand with that? We're heading to Bay 6 anyway."

"I'm good. But thanks." Samara offered a quick, half-smile, then started down the corridor toward the main axis, boots striking soft against the composite decking.

Katherine had sent her up on this shuttle run to pack up her lab equipment for transport to the surface, so that she could modify the plant with the seedpods to make a version of its antifungal compound that wouldn't be toxic to humans. And Samara had every intention of doing that.

After she completed her own mission. Her plan was to stay on the ship while the Demeters returned with supplies for the colony, under the pretense of analyzing the fungus further, then ferry her equipment back down on the next shuttle in a day or two.

She felt the ship's cameras tracking her, tiny, invisible pricks of attention that she imagined as cold, metallic insects resting on her skin. She forced herself to walk at a measured pace, to look neither furtive nor urgent, though her heart thudded with the fear that someone would notice she wasn't where she was supposed to be. She had her excuse ready, that she needed some plant samples she could use as a template for creating new sequences. Not the Demeters, but possibly the shuttle's pilot. Or the ship's AI, which might flag her movements for Katherine.

Or Lucas, the only person other than Renata who would see through her lie.

The cryovault's pressure doors loomed at the end of the corridor, their matte white surface ribbed with the embedded veins of the ship's security grid. Even before she reached them, the temperature drop was palpable: the cold bled into her bones, raising gooseflesh along her forearms and making the sweat under her collar go icy.

She hesitated just long enough to let the chill register, then pressed her palm to the biometric pad, watching the scan's blue light etch her fingerprints in real time.

"Dr. Makinde, access confirmed," the ship's AI

intoned, voice more intimate here, as if the cold made it whisper. "Please state the nature of your request."

"Retrieval of specimen for genetic analysis and modification." Samara tried to make her voice sound bored, the way Lucas did when talking to the machine. There was no way to do this without leaving a record of her actions.

"Logged and acknowledged. Please proceed."

The doors unsealed with a sigh, as if the ship itself were bracing for what she was about to do. Samara stepped inside.

The air here was drier, more brittle. It scraped her nasal passages, leaving a faint aftertaste of cold metal at the back of her tongue.

Beyond the second set of doors, the vault proper stretched out before her in concentric circles. Massive cylindrical storage units rose from floor to ceiling like chrome pillars, each one maintaining hundreds of embryos of many species in suspended animation at precisely -196°C. Liquid nitrogen circulated through transparent pipes overhead, their contents glowing faintly blue from internal monitoring systems. The constant low hum of the cooling systems was punctuated by occasional clicks and whirs as automatic monitoring routines ran their courses.

The entire future of humanity was frozen here, neatly indexed and waiting its turn.

She walked the aisle to the nearest console, shivering as much from anticipation as from the temperature.

Her breath clouded in the cold as she scanned the directory on the console display, its touchless interface alive with a thousand options: livestock lines, poultry, the full human gene bank, grass and algae, every weed or worm Earth had tried to save from extinction. Each embryo represented not just a potential life, but a carefully curated addition to the colony's gene pool, designed to maximize diversity and ensure the best possible start for a new branch of human civilization.

She keyed in the code for the human embryos, blinking twice to override the "medical personnel only" warning. The rack spun with hydraulic grace, aligning a single module to the access hatch.

The hatch irised open, revealing a tray studded with glass vials—each one no thicker than her finger, each one the sum of centuries of selection and compromise. Samara reached in, her hand trembling despite the cold, and plucked out a vial. The label glowed in the blue light: *MAKINDE, S. / DONOR #17 / F-XX / ZYGOTE.*

She stared at it, the way she might stare at a splinter removed from her own skin, yet it had once been part of her, however briefly.

This had almost been the deal killer for her.

As part of the colonist agreement, Hofstadter had required that every couple on board commit to having at least one child from an embryo created by anonymous sperm and egg donors that had been edited to be compatible with the mother's immune system. That way, each couple not only contributed their own genes to the next generation, they also contributed genes from those who had been left behind to die, widening the colony's inevitable genetic bottleneck and reducing the risk of inbreeding.

Hofstadter had agreed to waive the pregnancy requirement altogether for Samara if she would allow him to create embryos that combined her genes with those of carefully-selected anonymous donors via somatic cell nuclear transfer. She didn't have to bear children, but she would still be required to contribute to the colony's genetic diversity.

At the time, the idea that someone else in the colony

would have a child carrying her genes had felt wrong, although she was sure her long-gone parents would have been pleased to know that the Makinde line would continue on a new world.

But now she was glad, if it allowed her a chance to save what was left of her species.

If this worked, she would become a mother after all.

She'd never wanted children. Not in the way other people seemed to. Not like Leila, with her fierce longing, or even Marcus and Renata, who talked about their hypothetical future children as if they were already alive and waiting to be summoned with the right combination of longing and luck. When friends back on Earth had handed her their infants, Samara had felt only animal anxiety: the weight of the baby's head in her elbow, the frantic, unblinking stare, the slickness of drool on her shoulder. She'd counted the seconds until the mother returned and reclaimed the fragile burden.

Was she really going to do this?

The epigenetic approach that she'd suggested to the leadership team was sound, but it was still experimental, and refining it would be slow going, given how little time Katherine was willing to grant her in the lab. It was also a temporary solution, stopping the immune reaction to the fungus in the current generation of colonists, but doing nothing to solve the miscarriage problem, because as soon as the fetus' immune system developed, it would start attacking the fungus, endangering itself and possibly the woman carrying it.

But directly editing an embryo only required a simple, established technique to tweak immune functions that were well understood. And if it worked, it would be a permanent solution: all future generations would be genetically equipped to co-exist peacefully with the fungus.

And once that was possible, their problem became much simpler: survive until the next generation was old enough to take over.

Samara slipped the vial into her jumpsuit pocket, immediately feeling the frigid cold against her thigh, then retraced her steps through the corridor. The ship felt emptier than usual, just the faint pulse of pumps and the distant click of some relay, but every step seemed to echo.

She paused at the intersection with the main axis, checking both directions while trying not to look like she was sneaking around.

No one. She exhaled, then angled left toward the lab.

Inside, the room was exactly as she had left it: the floor scrubbed to a sterile mirror, the air heavy with the scent of isopropanol and cold steel. She hung the duffel on the back of a chair, then went to the gene-editing station. The interface lit up at her approach, a ripple of blue along the console edge. She placed the vial in the insulated well of the prep unit and watched as the machine scanned its barcode and prompted her for authorization.

She pulled up the edit she'd designed, a protein switch, borrowed from a local microbe, with a payload of immunomodulatory genes. The software ran a simulation of the insertion site, then flagged three warning conflicts, all of which she'd already accounted for in her notes. She overrode the warnings with a thumbprint and began the process of thawing a single cell for CRISPR injection. The ship's AI prompted her with a final "Are you sure?" and she tapped *Proceed*, feeling the irreversibility of it in her chest.

The hiss of the outer door made her jump. She spun in her chair, hands flying to the console to minimize the display. Had he seen enough to guess what she was doing?

Lucas stood in the doorway, a silver case in one hand.

"I was on my way to help you prepare your equipment for loading onto the shuttle when I received an alert that an embryo had been removed from the cryovault."

The alert would've told him she was the one who'd removed it, so there was no point in denying it.

"I don't need help packing up my lab," she said, turning away from him to fuss with the duffel's zipper. "You can go back to whatever you were doing."

Lucas didn't move. She felt his gaze on her, a precise calibration of pressure and angle, as if he were mapping her silhouette against a memory. "You believe you have found a solution."

She closed the bag with a definitive zip, then faced him. "I do. But Katherine will never approve it."

"Because it requires you to use experimental gene editing techniques."

Samara's mouth twisted. "That's how she'll see it."

Lucas considered her for a moment, the silver case dangling from his hand. "You are so confident that you're willing to change your mind about motherhood?"

She nearly laughed, but it came out as a sharp exhale. "I won't ask you to act as the child's father, Lucas."

"That is not my concern," he said, setting the case gently on the bench.

Right. He was worried about sharing the blame.

"I'll take full responsibility, whatever happens. All you have to do is walk out of this lab and pretend you didn't see the cryovault logs today."

He said nothing. The hum of the gene-editing rig filled the silence, its progress bar inching forward on the console. Samara watched him, waiting for the lecture, the inevitable invocation of protocol or ethics or the greater good.

"My concern," he said, "is that any pregnancy is at risk, even with antifungal treatments."

"I've modified the embryo's immune system. The baby will recognize the fungus as self and not attack it."

Lucas stepped closer, the fingers of his left hand tapping against his leg. "Antifungals can't be taken during the first trimester without risk to the fetus, and there will undoubtedly be another sporestorm in the next three months. Do you intend to stay on the ship until the fetus is old enough not to be harmed? Or do you plan to forgo the medicine and hope that your symptoms don't affect the health of your child?"

"I'll take immunosuppressants to keep my own immune system in check," Samara said, hoping he wouldn't voice the biggest flaw in her plan.

But of course he did. "That will leave you vulnerable to other types of infection."

"If it works, this colony becomes viable and humanity gets a second chance."

"And if it fails, the others will assume that you've miscarried for the same reason as the others. Assuming you don't die of a secondary infection."

"I'm doing this," Samara said. "Are you going to tell the others?"

Lucas paused for a long moment. Maybe he worried about the position she was putting him in, maybe worried about the potential baby. Or was it possible he was worried about her?

That seemed unlikely. He barely knew her. They'd spent so little time together in the two-plus months since their arrival on DaVinci.

And here she was, putting him in the very position that Hofstadter had told him he'd never be in.

Samara didn't want to ask, but she needed to know. "If I carry the pregnancy to term, everyone will think it's yours. Will that bother you?"

For a moment, Lucas did not blink, and then he smiled an odd, asymmetrical smile that felt less a show of emotion and more like a recalibration. "If the baby survives, I will fulfill the role of father to the best of my ability."

That startled something in her, a flicker of warmth where she'd expected emotional distance. "You'd do that?"

"The majority of studies suggest that children benefit from the presence of both parents."

As if that settled it for him. No need to discuss what it would mean to raise a child together or settle in advance how they would handle being parents. No objection that it was unfair of her to have made this decision without consulting him, possibly making him feel obligated to say he'd support her because the alternative meant looking negligent to the rest of the colony.

Samara thought about Leila and Justin. She'd be doing the same thing to Lucas that Leila had done to Justin. But even though Leila had chosen to get pregnant without her partner's consent, Justin had still agreed to have children someday; his spot in the colony had been contingent on that. Lucas' relationship with Samara was rooted in the agreement that neither of them would ask the other for children.

Did the survival of the colony supersede that?

Samara turned back to the console, hovering her finger over the button that would begin the edit. The embryo's metadata spun in the air before her, a hypothetical child frozen at the edge of possibility.

Once she began this process, there would be no going back. The consequences would be hers to carry. If she failed, this hypothetical child would become real, only to suffer and die along with the rest of them. And if she succeeded, she would be responsible for another human being for the rest of her life. A human being who might never be accepted by some of the colonists whose lives would be saved because she existed. Samara had no doubt that Lucas would live up to his word, that he *would* fulfill the role of father to the best of his ability. That he would bring the same kindness, determination, and precision of thought to parenting that he brought to everything he did.

But she seriously doubted her ability to be a mother.

She pressed the button.

Chapter Eighteen

THE CAT in her lap was dying, and there was nothing Samara could do for him. She scratched behind his ears, feeling bone beneath the dull black fur as he tried to purr, managing only a faint, wheezing rasp that had gotten progressively worse since last week's sporestorm.

That ghost of a purr was the only sound in the colony's makeshift chemlab other than the hum of the samples freezer and the descending whir of the centrifuge as it slowed to a stop.

When the machine finally went silent, Samara watched Renata pop the lid and retrieve a vial of murky green fluid. This was their seventh attempt to create an effective anti-fungal medicine from components distilled from native plants. They were down to rationing what was left of their Earth-made medicine: half-doses to the sickest colonists, nothing at all for the livestock or pets. A third of the colony was too weak to work, and everyone else was running on caffeine, adrenaline, and the stubborn refusal to die.

Thirty hours without sleep, the last eight spent crawling through a pipe full of rotting algae and fungal slime during her shift at the glitching water treatment plant. But when Renata's message came through, Samara had dragged herself here anyway.

Renata carried the vial to her bench, scooping up a pipette without looking. Samara nudged the cat off her lap. He tottered to the corner of the room and curled up in the shadow of an overturned crate, eyes half-shut, tail tucked close. She considered going fetal beside him on the concrete and sleeping until someone demanded she wake up.

Instead, she stood and crossed to Renata's workstation, moving with a deliberate steadiness that made her feel ancient. She braced herself against the edge of the bench, waiting for the spasm in her lower back to ease.

Renata's eyes flicked up, concern visible even through the battered safety goggles. "You're not going to puke on my samples again, are you?"

"I'm telling you, it was the tuna casserole."

Samara had blamed that incident on a spoiled ration, but Renata was too smart to buy that excuse twice. The morning sickness had started exactly when Lucas warned her it would, right at the beginning of her fifth week of pregnancy. And she couldn't ask Hector for anti-nausea meds, because he'd probably figure it out even faster than Renata.

The xenobiologist thumbed the pipette's plunger and drew up a bead of the greenish mix, then held it poised over the petri dish. The surface of the agar was already covered by the spidery brown fungus, which had anchored itself at the center and sent out exploratory shoots in every direction, looking for something to grab onto. Samara remembered how the fungus had wrapped itself around the brainstem of the infected cow they'd dissected, then shivered at the thought that the same thing might be happening in her own body right now.

Renata released the first droplet. It landed with a wet click, splashing the nearest hyphal tip. The effect was immediate: the tendril recoiled, the entire network rippling as if shocked. Within seconds, the droplet had sunk in, staining the agar a darker greenish brown.

A second drop, then a third, each one precision-placed at the perimeter of the advancing fungal fan. The effect spread outward in concentric waves, the hyphae curling and uncurling, then shrinking back on themselves as if the entire organism was convulsing in slow motion. The movement was hypnotic, almost beautiful, until the outermost filaments began to weaken. Within a minute, the entire patch of fungus had gone limp, its exploratory groping stilled.

Samara stared, throat tight. "That… looks promising."

"Strongest reaction yet, but it's early."

"How long do we wait to be sure?"

Renata's mouth twisted. "I don't know."

She reached for a dissection probe and pressed it into the edge of the agar, nudging the collapsed filaments. Nothing happened. The brown tendrils didn't flex, didn't curl around the steel, didn't even twitch. In every other trial, the fungus had gone dormant for a few seconds at most before resuming its slow, predatory crawl, but this batch seemed truly dead.

Renata laid the probe across one of the thicker hyphae, the way you might lay a stick across a snake to see if it would strike. The tendril didn't so much as quiver.

She moved to the next petri dish, where a fresh tangle of hyphae had webbed itself in slow spirals across the agar. She dosed it with three measured drops. The effect was identical: the fungus flinched, then its filaments slumped into a wet, defeated mass. Renata worked down the line, dosing each sample in turn. By the time she got to the last dish, the air above the workbench was sharp with the scent of alcohol and whatever bitter alkaloids the extract contained.

Samara leaned in, needing to see the tiny deaths up close. Each time, the fungus writhed like something in pain before going limp. And each time another sample went still, she felt a fresh surge of hope.

Renata set the pipette back in the rack, then turned and rummaged through a drawer, producing a webcam the size of a thumb, which she clipped to the top of a nearby shelf and angled downward so the lens captured the entire row of petri dishes. She tapped her tablet, and the screen flickered to life with a live feed of the fungal massacre.

"If any of them start moving again, we'll know. But if they're still dead in four hours, I'm pulling samples for in vivo tests."

The room tilted. Samara grabbed for the bench, missed, and sent the vial spinning. It hit the floor with a crystalline crack, green liquid spreading across the concrete like spilled paint.

"Sorry—" She tasted bile in the back of her throat as her stomach revolted again.

"Relax. I've got a whole batch." Renata nodded toward the far end of the room. A soup pot stolen from the common hall's kitchen sat on a hot plate, its lid clamped down with a jury-rigged bracket. A clear tube snaked out from the top, coiled around a metal pipe balanced across what looked like two miniature sawhorses, then trailed down into a collection flask, where the extract condensed in trembling, moss-colored drops.

The makeshift distillation rig looked like something out of a prison chemistry textbook. Lucas built it for them after discovering that Hofstadter had somehow neglected to include one in the ship's stores. Every time Samara saw it, she imagined him hunched over the parts like a watchmaker, assembling the apparatus with his long, nimble-fingered hands.

Another wave of dizziness pressed at the edges of her vision. Samara gripped the table, the cold of the steel biting through her palm. Something moved low and quick near her feet, a flicker of black against gray. The cat crouched over the broken vial, his tongue darting out to lap at the puddle of spilled antifungal extract.

Samara blinked, then lunged, catching him by the scruff just as he tried to slink away. The animal barely struggled as she cradled him against her chest. He let out a plaintive meow and licked its lips with a tongue stained sickly green.

"Guess our first test subject just volunteered." Renata reached over, rubbing the cat's chin with a gloved finger. "I'm rooting for you."

Samara dropped into the chair she'd abandoned earlier, then lowered the cat onto her lap, where he splayed bonelessly, head lolling to one side, breath shallow and rattling. He pressed his skull into her palm and tried, valiantly, to purr again, but only a thread of sound escaped.

How much of the medicine had he drunk?

Enough to cure?

Enough to kill?

Some of the side effects they'd seen with previous extracts had been so hideous, Renata had euthanized the rats early to put them out of their misery.

Why hadn't she been more careful? She should've put him outside before they started testing the medicine.

"You should go home, get some sleep," Renata said. "I can watch him."

"It's my fault. I knocked the vial over."

"It was an accident."

Samara slumped back in the chair. "Wake me up when it's time to unfreeze the rats, I'll help you wrangle them."

She waited until Renata was gone before she hugged him and whispered, "I'll be here with you until it's over, no matter what."

But the cat was dead weight in her lap. She wasn't even sure if he was breathing.

No matter what.

~

SAMARA WOKE TO A LOW, uneven rattle, vibrating through her thigh and up into her chest. For a moment, she had no idea where she was. The ceiling above her was unfinished concrete crisscrossed with pipes. Her mouth tasted of bitter metal, and her right hand was numb. Something heavy and warm pressed against her abdomen.

The noise persisted, not quite a purr, but not a death rattle either. She blinked hard, and the shape resolved: the black cat, spread out across her lap, head resting in the crook of her elbow. His ribs rose and fell in shallow arcs, but his eyes were open and focused on the glassware across the room, as if tracking prey only it could see.

She shifted slightly, and he wormed his way out of her grasp, landing with a delicate thud on the concrete. He stretched, back arched high, then trotted toward the door with a gait that was, if not graceful, at least no longer the funereal shuffle of a dying animal.

Samara blinked again, disbelief giving way to a pulse of hope. Was it possible...

Ignoring her stiff, aching muscles, she lunged after him. Her knee clipped the side of the bench and knocked a metal tray off to the floor with a clatter, but she caught the cat just before he reached the threshold. He mewed in protest, claws puncturing her forearm through the fabric of her coveralls as she hoisted him up.

Renata appeared in the doorway, safety goggles perched on her head. "You okay?"

Samara held him up, both hands supporting his bony chest, feeling the vibration of his not-quite-purr. "I think it actually worked."

Grinning, Renata snatched a syringe from the rack and hurried toward Samara. "Hold that beautiful creature still."

It was a temporary fix, but it might buy them time to find a permanent solution. Samara tried to ignore the voice in her head that whispered:

Too good to be true.

Chapter Nineteen

"No side effects at all?" Samara kept her voice low, glancing around the crowded common hall.

"Heart rate's up a bit, but nothing dangerous. Nothing else I can detect." Renata sank into the open chair between Marcus and Ingrid, looking happy despite the raccoon circles around her eyes. "But I can't exactly ask the cat if it has a headache."

Six failures, and now this miracle cure from the weeds they'd been pulling to clear the fields for tilling?

The words that had invaded Samara's mind last night returned. *Too good to be true.*

But the cat seemed to have even more energy this morning. When Samara had opened her cabin door, the feline had pranced right by her like he'd been waiting all night for her to let him in and settled in a patch of sunlight on the living room floor. She probably should've shooed the animal out, but he looked so content, Samara decided to let him stay.

She told herself that she wanted to monitor him, make

sure he didn't relapse or develop longer-term side effects from the antifungals he'd lapped up yesterday. It wasn't that she'd been lonely, and having him in the cabin made it feel a little more… homey.

"We're only at thirty-six hours," Renata continued, "but when we hit seventy-two, if we're still good, Katherine's given me permission to try it on some of the livestock. Hector volunteered to help."

Too good to be true.

Deep down, Samara was waiting for the next stroke of bad news. Delayed side effects. Invisible organ damage. Or worse.

But even if bad news didn't come today, it would come eventually. The fungus would adapt. The new medicine would lose its effectiveness. They'd have to start all over again.

She had to persuade Katherine to let her work on a real solution.

Taking the ration packet that Marcus offered, Samara ripped the tear strip away and dumped the contents onto her plate: two pieces of soggy French toast, fake bacon that tasted like cardboard, and tiny sealed tubs of margarine and maple-flavored syrup.

We're humanity's last hope, and Hofstadter didn't think it was worth springing for real maple.

She reached for the plate of pseudo-mango at the center of the table, depositing several slices on her French toast. If they hadn't been able to supplement their prepackaged rations with *something* native, she might have gone mad by now.

The room went quiet. Samara twisted in her chair to see Katherine near the front of the room, Hector at her left shoulder, arms crossed. Dark circles shadowed the doctor's eyes, but there was a hint of self-satisfaction in the set of his jaw.

Katherine cleared her throat, not loudly, but the sound seemed to ripple down the row of folding tables. Every head turned her way, even the ones that had been hunched over mugs of coffee or deep in the kind of existential zoning out that passed for leisure in these days of double shifts.

"I'm going to keep this short and sweet," the colony leader began. "As of this morning, we can make our own antifungal medicine. Enough to keep everyone healthy through the winter."

A roar went up and real, spontaneous applause, hands slapping tabletops, someone letting out a rebel yell. Samara saw Evan cheer as he attempted to clap despite his swollen hands. Zoya and Ingrid hugged each other. Even Briar dropped her usual sneer, looking relieved as she leaned back in her chair.

Katherine raised one hand and waited for the colonists to quiet. "We have Dr. Vargas to thank for that. With an assist from Dr. Makinde."

Renata blushed, staring down at her barely eaten breakfast sandwich, but Marcus put his arm around her shoulder to give her a quick hug.

Hector, on the other side of the room, looked even smugger. He thought he'd won.

That shouldn't have mattered to Samara, but it did. Not because her ego was bruised, but because she could still hear that whisper in her head.

Too good to be true.

"Dr. Vargas and Dr. Callas are going to work with Leo to treat the livestock with the new medicine," Katherine said. "It won't be given to humans until we're completely certain that it's safe."

The colony leader paused for a moment, smiling and making eye contact around the room.

"We've overcome this challenge," she continued. "And we will overcome the next challenge that this planet throws at us, and the next one after that. Because we're human, and humans are strong. Resilient. Resourceful. I hope that each one of you will thank your fellow colonists for everything they do, because it wasn't just these three who've solved the antifungal problem. Everyone who's been doing their job to keep this colony running played a part in solving this problem."

Samara remembered what Katherine had said to her in the greenhouse. *We're not just responsible for the physical survival of this colony. We're also responsible for bringing people together.*

She might not agree with their leader's decisions, but Samara had to give Katherine credit; the woman never missed an opportunity to remind them that they were all supposed to be on the same team.

Briar stood and cleared her throat from the far end of the next table. "How soon can we start taking the full doses again?"

Hector fielded the question before Katherine could. "After we finish testing, we'll synthesize more. Sickest patients first, then everyone else. Probably a week, assuming nothing goes wrong."

Briar's mouth puckered in annoyance, but Hector had already turned away, nodding at Zoya's raised hand. "Yes?"

"If we take the new medicine, does that mean the next sporestorm won't make us miscarry?"

The celebration died. Now, everyone was staring at Renata and Samara like an audience waiting for the next magic trick.

Renata cleared her throat and stood to address the room. "We don't know. The sporestorm triggers an immune reaction, which the antifungal suppresses. But it's possible the medicine could cross the placental barrier. We have no data on what it does to a developing fetus. Until we're sure, we recommend continuing with birth control."

The colony's reproductive future hung on a dwindling supply of contraceptives. The original plan had assumed a gradual population ramp-up, not an indefinite pause in procreation. When the pills ran out, they would be back to miscarriages every sporestorm, and the colony would have to endure a new round of collective grief.

Not to mention the risk that each new loss could make it harder for the next embryo to take root. The colony's fertility window would begin to close even faster.

Across the table, Evan raised his voice. "How far are we from a cure? Not just treating the symptoms, I mean. Actually making us immune?"

Hector met that question with a measured patience meant to soothe their anxiety. "We're working on it."

There was a rumble of discontent, with an undercurrent of anger that went beyond the everyday grumbling about extra shifts and flavorless rations and what they missed about Earth.

"I know some of you are frustrated," Katherine continued. "This isn't the future you signed up for. But I want you to remember, today we took a huge step toward making our colony sustainable." Katherine let the moment breathe, then added, "To keep that future strong, we need to stay resilient. So please, don't forget your quarterly check-in with Dr. Basu."

More rumbles and a few groans, but some of the anger seemed to have bled off.

Katherine ended the gathering with a nod, then she

and Hector slipped away toward the kitchen. The room started to empty in clusters, some people lingering to gossip, others heading for the door. Samara reached for her mug, only to discover she'd drained it without noticing.

Renata whispered something to Marcus that made him grin. Watching them together, Samara felt the hollow ache of being alone in a room full of people. She doubted she'd ever have a connection that strong with Lucas. And everyone else on this planet was already partnered up. So, what was the point of thinking about it?

Across the room, Leila sat at a table by herself, poking at her breakfast with what looked like deliberate disinterest. But Samara thought the young woman was pretending not to notice Briar and her friends clustered near the far wall. Justin stood at the edge of the group, but the way he watched Briar made Samara's stomach turn. Trouble there, or there would be soon, if something didn't change.

Renata nudged Samara's arm with the back of her hand. "Poker night at our place, if you're up for it. Marcus has been hoarding his powdered milk ration, and he claims he's going to make ice cream." Her grin turned mischievous as she leaned across the table. "It's probably going to be awful."

Marcus, drizzling Samara's discarded syrup over his last pancake, winked at her. "We're going to put that new melon Renata discovered in it."

"It tastes like grape and pineapple had a lavender-scented baby," Renata added.

"And yet you ate three of them last night."

"In the name of science."

"That's why I'm making ice cream with it, for science." Marcus poked Renata in the ribs, eliciting a giggle. Then, to Samara: "If you come, you can be our tiebreaker."

Somehow, they never made her feel like a third wheel, but still she hesitated, glancing at Renata's hand resting on the inside of Marcus's arm. Sometimes she couldn't tell if she was being pitied or genuinely wanted, and the ambiguity made her chest ache in a way she hadn't expected.

Nevertheless, she was grateful that they went out of their way to include her, even now, when all three of them were running on empty.

"If Marcus' ice cream kills me, I expect a touching eulogy at my memorial," she said.

"Deal," Renata replied. "But only if you promise to haunt us."

Since she had a few more minutes before her shift, Samara made her way back to her cabin. The cat sat on the kitchen table, tail twitching as it poked at a brown paper-wrapped package with one paw. Medical tape sealed the neatly folded edges of the paper shut. Nothing was written on the outside of the package, not even her name.

He flicked his tail at her, then at the package, and she had the impression he was annoyed. Because someone had entered the cabin to deliver it? Or because he couldn't open it himself?

Samara peeled back the tape, unfolded the paper wrapping, and opened the box. Inside, she found several shrink-wrapped bottles of prenatal vitamins, a fist-sized tin of peppermint tea, a dozen packets of ginger hard candies, a sleeve of high-protein crackers, and three tubes of electrolyte powder. Everything a pregnant woman might need to survive her first trimester, if she could manage to keep any of it down.

No note inside, but Samara didn't need one. The package itself was a message, and the sender was obvious. This whole thing was pure Lucas: methodical kindness delivered with the emotional subtlety of a supply manifest. He must have packed these himself, probably after hours of research, and sent them down with the last supply drop.

Samara fought the urge to laugh, or cry, or both. How had she gotten so lucky?

After emptying the box onto the kitchen counter, she slid the vitamins, crackers, and drink powders into the narrow kitchen cupboard above the sink. Then she opened the tin of tea and sniffed the peppermint, sharp and clean. Too bad she didn't have time to brew a cup now.

As she closed the cabinet, the cat leapt from table to countertop to investigate the empty box, circling it twice before leaping inside with a soft whump. He turned in place, then collapsed into a loaf and began to purr. A real purr, still raspy, but stronger than yesterday.

"So that's what you wanted," she said as she gave him a quick pat on the head.

She had never wanted to keep a cat as a pet, although she'd enjoyed petting the strays in her neighborhood as a child. Didn't want the responsibility of another creature depending on her to come home when she might need to spend all night in the lab.

Yet here she was, talking to this cat as if he might answer back.

Maybe she was lonelier than she'd realized.

THE CONFERENCE ROOM reeked of burnt plastic and mold, thanks to the wheezing air purifier whose repair Katherine had deemed low priority, at least until the fixes to the water treatment plant had been completed.

Samara sat with her hands folded on the table, listening as Katherine read out the tally.

"Five for, two against, one abstain." The words landed like the bang of a gavel.

Even as she'd delivered her presentation, an hour of slides and models, a careful walk-through of the epigenetic protocol and how it might teach the immune system to tolerate the fungus, Samara could see Hector's jaw clenching, Ayesha's eyes already narrowed in polite rejection. The others had listened politely, occasionally shifting in their chairs or glancing down at their tablets. Only Renata had nodded along, offering encouragement.

Katherine's gaze swept the room. She was good at this, Samara thought, making everyone feel seen, even as she prepared to move on. "I want to thank everyone for their consideration," Katherine said. "And Samara, for putting in the work. For now, we'll table the gene therapy proposal. Renata, you and Hector keep pushing on antifungal production and finding a pharmaceutical cure."

Heat crawled up Samara's neck. She didn't know if she was angrier at herself for failing to persuade them or at the others for refusing to see the obvious.

But she refused to give up. Katherine wouldn't override the vote, but maybe she would authorize preliminary work that Samara could bring back to the group later, demonstrating the viability of her approach.

If she could convince Katherine not to declare the next vote unanimous…

"With respect, I'd like permission to at least model the protocol in vivo, so you can see the data for yourself. We can do it with rats. No embryos, no human subjects."

Renata, who had been quietly sipping cold tea, set her mug down and said, "I think it's worth running the model. At least then we'll know if it's feasible."

Samara felt a surge of gratitude for her friend's support as Katherine stared at her steepled fingers for a long moment. Then the colony leader shot Samara a look that said, *I want to say yes, but it's not politically expedient.*

Ayesha cleared her throat. "I thought the agreement was that decisions like this had to pass unanimously. And it didn't."

Samara tried to keep her face neutral, but her lips curled before she could stop them. "You didn't even try to understand the science, Ayesha. You were afraid, so you voted no."

Ayesha's expression was the picture of calm regret. "I don't have to understand the science to know what my conscience tells me. That's why we have a vote. We're supposed to balance expertise with caution."

"You never asked a single question."

"I'm not disputing your logic, Samara. I'm sure that what you're proposing is as scientifically sound as you can make it."

A devious backhanded compliment, implying that if Samara's logic had been *more* sound, Ayesha might have voted for it. It was doubly infuriating because of all the people at this table, the psychologist was the least qualified to evaluate the science underlying Samara's proposal. Even Mahmoud, the geologist, was better equipped to understand the theory.

"There's more to life than logic." Ayesha's smile was practiced perfection. "We're building a society, not running an experiment."

"If we're not going to use logic," Samara said, "how do you propose we solve this problem?"

"There's logic to Hector's approach, too. And I'm sure there will be logic to the other things we'll try. But sometimes, when logic runs out, you rely on faith. Even when it's not mathematically justified."

Samara's laugh was sharp, almost a bark. "Faith in your imaginary friend?"

"Faith in this team. In Katherine, in Renata, in Hector. In you. Together, you solved the problem of how to make more antifungal medicine."

"A solution you objected to at the time, because it involved engineering a local plant to produce the compounds we needed."

Ayesha smiled like she'd been hoping Samara would bring that up. "I'm willing to admit that I was wrong. I don't have the answers any more than you do. That's why we keep talking. That's why we do this by consensus." She gestured at the table, the empty mugs, the scattered tablets. "None of us know what we're doing. That's the whole point."

Some of us know more than others. But that wouldn't help Samara win the argument. It would just make her look petulant.

Ayesha added, "I have faith that if we work together, we'll find a cure."

"The cure might come too late if we burden ourselves with unnecessary constraints." Samara let the words hang for a beat, searching for a fracture in Ayesha's manufactured serenity. "If we don't find it before the colony's fertility window closes, it won't matter."

Samara glanced at Katherine and thought she saw something like approval. *She's giving me a chance to sway the others by arguing with Ayesha.*

If she could win Hector over, would Katherine be willing to overrule Ayesha's objections? Was the colony leader just looking for the right justification?

Politics again. Even though she hated feeling like a pawn, Samara admired Katherine's ability to direct a situation without seeming to.

"Let's not waste anyone else's time with our personal disagreement." Ayesha stood, looking at Katherine. "Unless there's anything else?"

Katherine's expression didn't change, but Samara got the feeling that she didn't like Ayesha's implied dismissal of *her* team.

The colony leader waited a beat before getting to her feet. "Monthly reports due next week."

The room emptied, but Samara stayed at the table, waiting until the door had sealed behind Hector and Renata to speak.

"I know the vote didn't go my way. But at least let me—"

"You think I don't want this to work?"

"I think you're worried about the optics." Samara took a deep breath to steady herself. "If you're going to reject my proposal, reject it because it's a bad idea, not because some people are afraid of it."

Katherine set the tablet down, pinched the bridge of her nose, and gave Samara a tired look. "If it were up to me, we'd run your model. But I need consensus on this. We can't afford infighting. Not when we're just starting to make real progress."

"So what am I supposed to do?"

"You'll do your shifts, like everyone else." Katherine's voice was quiet but absolute. "You're not needed for embryo screening until Hector figures out how to keep a pregnancy going through a sporestorm."

"I could help—"

"You've already been vocal about your skepticism there, so it's hard to justify asking Hector to work with you. For now, you're on the same rotation the other non-specialists are, minus two shifts to help Renata with cataloguing."

Samara's vision narrowed. "I'm the one who figured

out it was a fungus. I'm the reason we have antifungals at all. If I hadn't—" She cut herself off, teeth clicking together. She didn't want to sound petulant, but the words pressed forward anyway. "If I hadn't pushed, we'd be out of medicine and at risk of being wiped out by the next sporestorm."

"And the whole colony is grateful for that, Samara. Didn't you hear them applauding you at breakfast?"

"But I could do more," she said. "If you'd let me."

"Hector and Ayesha are right. We must exhaust every other alternative before we resort to experimental gene therapy."

Samara clenched her hands together, digging her nails into the soft flesh between her thumbs. "It's not that experimental. There are fifty years of data on this kind of immune modulation—"

Katherine stopped her with a small, almost apologetic shake of the head. "The perception is that it's experimental, and that's what matters. If anything goes wrong, Ayesha will stir people up until they're too afraid to let you fix standard birth defects. Don't underestimate her, Samara."

Katherine gathered her tablet and departed. Samara stared at the table as she heard the door shut.

She did not want to go back to her assigned rotation, to feeding goats and fertilizing plants and cataloguing biological samples while the colony's real future evaporated. She wanted to be on the Borlaug, in the clean, humming silence of the ship's lab, where she could run the gene edits herself, no votes or politics or watching eyes. There, she could see the whole equation, every variable laid out. The data would lead her to the solution they needed. With Lucas' help, she suspected she'd see it sooner.

She wondered what he was doing right now. Was he

busy loading the shuttle with supplies for another run down to the planet? Poring over climatological data, trying to push his model to give them more warning when a sporestorm was coming?

Or was he thinking about her and the daughter he'd agreed to raise, if Samara's hypothesis proved true?

She wondered if she could trust him to keep her secret.

Chapter Twenty

LEILA HAD NEVER BEEN SO cold, so filthy, or so stupidly, hungrily alive.

Her knees sank deeper with every weed until the mud threatened to swallow her whole. Beneath her work gloves, her fingers hurt. Even her fingernails ached. She had stopped caring if mud got under her nails or if her socks squelched when she walked. Yesterday's rain had turned the field into a swamp, and tomorrow would bring more. Captain Mercer predicted a brutal winter ahead. There would be ice, and maybe even snow.

She reached for the next weed, a spiky thing that could prick her even through the gloves if she wasn't careful how she grabbed it. The trick was to pull straight up, folding the needles flat against the leaves. When she made the mistake of twisting her wrist or pulling sideways, those vicious little spines stuck straight out, poking through the glove to embed themselves in her skin. She'd spent half of yesterday plucking them out of her palms with tweezers.

But it was worth it. The winter greens were coming up fast. Sometimes she'd stop and just stare at a row of baby kales or the stubby, blue-green ruffles of cabbage, feeling an almost maternal pride. Broccoli, cauliflower, collards, beets, carrots, turnips, and others she didn't recognize.

This morning at breakfast, Leo had announced to her table that the first parsnips would be ready by the solstice. Leila had nodded enthusiastically, even though she'd never eaten a parsnip before. When she looked them up in the colony archive, the picture resembled a fat, pale carrot. She loved carrots, so maybe she'd love parsnips?

She was so tired of eating rations that she wanted to scream. Leila's mouth watered, thinking of how her mother used to buy whatever vegetables were on sale, then roast them on a battered sheet pan with garlic and salt until the whole apartment was rich with the savory smell. She could see her mother tipping the sheet pan over their plates, scraping it with the spatula to get every last caramelized bit. Even when money was tight, her mother's food had always tasted like a feast.

The ache for her mother never faded. Neither did missing Eddie. But her grief for the babies she'd lost was the worst of all. And she didn't want it to be. What was it Dr. Basu had said about grief being a kind of remembered love?

The latest sporestorm had come and gone three days ago, and two more women had miscarried, despite the new pills that tasted like peppery grass and left her tongue numb. No one said it out loud, but the implication was clear: there was no point in trying, not for now, maybe not ever.

Worse, Justin didn't even seem to understand why she was so upset.

"Why the rush?" he'd muttered into his pillow. "You're grumpy all the time. I can barely stay awake through dinner. You want to add a screaming baby to this bullshit?"

But Leila had lain awake after he'd started snoring, counting the seconds until dawn, feeling the ache in her belly like a tooth with a cavity all the way to the root.

How mad would Justin be if they found a way to stay pregnant?

She wasn't sure she cared. She wanted to believe that when Justin met his first child, he'd love it, but what if he didn't?

Or what if he wanted children, just not with her?

She'd caught Justin talking with Briar outside their cabin that morning, standing close enough that their heads nearly touched. Leila had stepped outside to ask if Justin wanted the last of the tea, but the words shriveled in her mouth at the sight of them together, laughing at something Leila couldn't hear. They didn't even bother to look guilty, just turned to her with matching blank faces. Briar's hair was damp, and so was Justin's. Her first thought was that he'd showered in Briar's cabin. Or was she being paranoid?

Justin shoved his hands into his pants pockets, shoulders hunched in a way that was meant to look casual.

"What's going on?" Leila had asked, careful to sound as neutral as possible, even though her pulse was hammering in her throat.

Justin looked at Briar, then at Leila. "Just talking about our shift. We're both in the barn today."

Briar gave Leila a narrow smile, all teeth and no warmth. "Relax. I'm not after your husband. We're just talking about cow feed."

Then she turned her back and stalked off toward the barn. Justin stayed rooted to the spot, hands buried in his pockets, eyes fixed on his muddy boots. Leila waited for him to say something, but he just shrugged and headed inside, not even holding the door for her.

It wasn't reasonable for her to be angry at them for just talking, but she was. It wasn't fair to make accusations without evidence, but she wanted to. She thought about what Dr. Basu had said to her in her last "resilience check-in."

Conflict in relationships is normal, Leila. It's all about how you resolve it.

But some conflicts couldn't be resolved.

Justin had been so sweet before the engagement, always making her laugh, always texting her right back, even when he was on shift. She'd thought he was genuinely attracted to her, that he was in love with her for real, and she'd told herself the whirlwind proposal was just because they had to be married to get a spot in the colony. The morning they'd gotten the acceptance letter, he'd cried in front of her, real tears, and she'd believed every word he said about wanting to spend the rest of his life with her.

But the rest of his life on DaVinci looked different from what he'd probably imagined. He was tired all the time, and the only jokes he made lately were about how the shit-shoveling never ended, or how little sleep they got, or how the coffee tasted like crap.

Were other people fighting like this? Or were she and Justin the only ones?

No, not the only ones. Word was that Captain Mercer hadn't slept in his own bed in months. Why would he do that unless he and Dr. Makinde weren't getting along?

But how could anyone fight with the captain? He seemed like the perfect man: handsome and smart and kind. He spent most of his time on the ship, but occasionally Leila saw him at the edge of the fields, sleeves rolled up, fixing a busted irrigation line or inspecting the perimeter fence. He worked harder than Justin, and he never complained.

She'd bet that *he* would be excited to be a father.

If Dr. Makinde missed him, she never showed it. So they probably were fighting. Or was it possible that Dr. Makinde was in the same situation as Leila, partnered with someone who only wanted to be with her because it meant a chance to survive?

Except that Captain Mercer was the ship's pilot, so of course, he'd had a guaranteed spot in the colony.

Which would mean Dr. Makinde was the Justin in their relationship.

One of the Demeters glared at Leila, and his message was obvious. *Stop daydreaming and get back to work.*

She dug her gloved fingers into the mud, working the next weed free, as she turned the thought over like a sharp stone in her palm. Dr. Makinde had helped make the new medicine. But most days, she was assigned to do the same chores that everyone else did, instead of working with the other scientists. Would it have been the same if there had been no spores on DaVinci?

Eighty women could only have so many babies. So, it was kind of suspicious that she'd gotten a spot. It only made sense if Captain Mercer had loved her so much that he'd refused to pilot the ship without her.

Which was exactly the kind of romantic thing she'd expect Captain Mercer to do. But if he loved her, he wouldn't abandon her.

Something else had to be going on.

Dr. Makinde moved like she was walking through honey, her skin sallow and her cheeks puffy. Maybe the new antifungal medicines were making her nauseous. They'd hit Leila like that until she got used to them.

"We've all been missing you at morning circle, Leila."

Ugh. She turned to see Dr. Basu beaming like a children's TV host.

She wanted to snap something about how some people at morning circle were too busy making eyes at each other to miss her, but she bit her tongue instead, because Dr. Basu had a way of using sarcasm as an excuse to analyze you.

"I'm taking a break," she said.

Dr. Basu knelt in the mud beside her. "Sometimes the things we avoid are the ones we need most. Especially when you're hurting."

Leila ripped up another weed and tossed it on the pile. "Who said I'm hurting?"

"Do you mind if I weed with you for a minute?" the psychologist asked.

"It's a free planet."

They worked in silence, broken only by the distant hum of the irrigation pumps and the occasional screech of one of the local bird-like creatures. If the psychologist wanted to do some of Leila's work, fine. But she wasn't going to make it easy for Dr. Basu to harp on how she should forgive Justin, or whatever she'd come here to say.

Dr. Basu's hands moved with a practiced rhythm, pulling weeds in neat, efficient tugs.

"Justin stopped by my office yesterday," she said. "He's worried about you."

Leila snorted. "He's worried he'll have to listen to me cry at night."

"That's not what he said."

"Then what did he say?" Leila's cheeks started to warm, even with the chill wind cutting across the field.

"He wants you to stop trying to get pregnant, at least for now."

"So he wants me to give up on having a family."

"No, not give up," Dr. Basu said, soft but firm. "Just… let yourself heal."

Leila yanked a thick-rooted weed free, flinging it onto the pile with more force than necessary. "Is that what he said? Or is that just your professional opinion?"

Dr. Basu folded her hands and rested them on her knees. "He said he's worried for you. He also said he doesn't want to lose you, but he's afraid you might try to… move on. Maybe you'll find someone else who wants what you want."

Leila whipped around, mouth open. "You think I'd cheat on him?"

"I didn't say—"

"He's the one who's been flirting with Briar. Or she's been flirting with him, and he's not telling her to back off."

Dr. Basu's head tilted, the way it always did when she was about to say something she wanted you to pay attention to. "He's scared, Leila. About what comes next. About how you'll cope if this is… permanent."

A chill deeper than the mud seeped up her legs and into her spine. "So, what? I'm supposed to pretend like it didn't matter that my baby died?"

"Of course it matters. But sometimes when people lose something, they start looking for it everywhere. Even in places they'll never find it."

There it was, she'd lost her temper, and Dr. Basu had thrown it back on her as an accusation, trying to make it Leila's fault that Justin was cheating on her.

"Maybe you should go ask Justin what he thinks he's going to find in Briar," she snapped.

Dr. Basu let out a slow, patient breath that made Leila feel like she was the unreasonable one. "Justin didn't say anything about Briar. He talked about you. How scared he is of you slipping away from him, and how he doesn't know what to do about it."

Leila yanked another weed. "So he sent you to fix it for him?"

"Not at all." Dr. Basu's smile was kind, but her eyes were not. "He just needed someone to talk to. He wondered if maybe you could talk to each other, honestly, instead of letting this fester."

"If he wants to talk, he knows where I sleep."

"Maybe he's afraid that if he tries, you'll shut him out." Dr. Basu's voice turned motherly. "And after what I've seen, I'm concerned for you both."

Leila rolled her eyes, yanked a weed so forcefully it came up with a splatter of mud. "You're not worried about me and Justin. You're worried I'm going to sleep with someone else's husband and then you'll have to start doing couples therapy for real."

Dr. Basu's lips pinched together, but she didn't get up. "Multiple miscarriages are hard on your body. Each time you try and fail, you make the next attempt harder. Eventually, you can become infertile."

Leila's stomach dropped. Was that true, or was the psychologist just trying to scare her? Dr. Callas hadn't said anything about that. She'd assumed she'd get another chance, once they had a cure, and that it would only be a matter of grit and luck and not giving up. She'd pictured herself as one of those women who could take a punch and keep going. Like her mother had been.

But what if the punches were cumulative? What if she'd already ruined her only chance?

Maybe that's why Dr. Callas kept reminding them to use birth control. Not that she needed it at this point. Justin hadn't wanted to sleep with her since the last miscarriage, and she was pretty sure it had nothing to do with her body's need to heal.

She stared at her gloved hands, afraid that if she made eye contact, she would cry.

"I don't want to tell you what to do," Dr. Basu finally said. "But I do want you to have a future."

Leila wanted to tell the psychologist to mind her own business, but Dr. Basu would probably retaliate by calling her in for a mandatory "check-in" and then she would be in trouble. So she said, "Thanks for your concern, but I'm fine."

Dr. Basu watched her for a moment, then reached over and squeezed her shoulder. "Sometimes acceptance is the first step to healing."

Leila stiffened, resisting the urge to shrug the woman off. "If something's broken, you don't accept it. You fix it."

"Some things can't be fixed. Or if they can, it's not always you who can fix them."

One row over, Dr. Makinde doubled over and vomited into the furrow. She spat, wiped her mouth, and kept working, exactly like Leila's mother had during her pregnancy with Eddie.

Did Dr. Makinde have morning sickness?

Maybe Captain Mercer had been visiting her more often than Leila had thought.

Dr. Basu was watching the geneticist, too; her eyes narrowed, and her lips flattened into a tight line. Leila wasn't sure why she felt the need to cover for Dr. Makinde, but she did.

"That was me last week," she said. "Does the new medicine make you nauseous too?"

Dr. Basu's mouth twitched. "You're not obligated to join the morning circle. I just think you'd feel better if you did. Whenever you're ready."

Leila dug her fingers deep into the next clump of soil, twisting and wrenching until the roots gave way with a satisfying ripping sound. Once Dr. Basu was gone, she peeked up at Dr. Makinde again.

For someone who'd just vomited, Dr. Makinde looked pretty good. The antifungals hit like the flu, electric skin, teeth that throbbed. Leila had missed two shifts after her last dose. But Dr. Makinde never called in sick. Neither did Captain Mercer, who somehow worked harder after every sporestorm.

Leila's scalp prickled. What if Dr. Makinde had found a secret cure? Real medicine for the important people, while everyone else got pills that numbed their tongues and sort of worked.

Or maybe Captain Mercer was naturally immune, and that immunity protected their baby too.

If it wasn't a medicine that could be shared…

If Captain Mercer was the only one who could make a baby that didn't die, wouldn't it be selfish for Dr. Makinde to keep him all to herself?

Didn't she have a duty to share so that humanity could continue?

Leila told herself that she shouldn't be thinking about this. She still had a husband, even if he was a cheater. But the unfairness of Dr. Makinde being the only one who could have a baby burned in her gut. Leila deserved to have a baby, too.

It was a dumb, selfish fantasy, and she knew it. But what if she could just… ask? Would Dr. Makinde tell her how she'd done it? Assuming Leila was right about the geneticist being pregnant.

She finished her next row, then wandered toward the irrigation shed, where someone had set up water jugs on a makeshift table next to a stack of plastic cups. She filled two, then walked back toward the field, pretending it was just a coincidence that she'd ended up right where Dr. Makinde was pausing at the end of a row.

"Here," Leila said, holding out one of the cups. "The sun's pretty brutal today."

Dr. Makinde startled, then took it with a grateful nod. "Thank you, Leila."

"My mama always said you have to stay hydrated when you're working in the heat. Especially when..." Leila trailed off, not sure if she should say the rest. "Well, you know how important it is to take care of yourself."

Dr. Makinde's mouth did something that was almost a smile but not quite.

"Thank you again," she said, then drained her cup and moved down the line, her muddy boots leaving a trail of sharp, perfect prints.

Leila watched her go, feeling a weird flutter of embarrassment, like she'd told a joke that nobody laughed at. She'd expected Dr. Makinde to linger, or at least say something more, maybe a comment about the weather or the work or anything at all. But the woman just moved on. And that stung more than Leila wanted to admit, even to herself.

She felt a little stupid for thinking that one cup of water would be enough to break the ice. Maybe Dr. Makinde was shy, or maybe she just didn't like Leila. Or maybe she was hiding something, and that was why she didn't want to make friends.

But Leila wasn't going to give up after one awkward moment. She was sure Dr. Makinde was pregnant.

And she was going to find out how.

Chapter Twenty-One

DAVINCI YEAR 1
WINTER

THE GOAT WAS out for blood.

Samara had both arms locked around its neck, her boots slipping in the muck of the pasture, and still the little beast thrashed like a marlin on a line. In her peripheral vision, Leo hovered with a syringe in hand, waiting for the split-second when the animal's jaw unclenched.

"Hold it steady," he said, as if that were a reasonable request.

"I'm trying," Samara grunted, though her left hand was already slick with mud and what could only be described as goat snot. The animal's hooves scrabbled for purchase on her shins, leaving muddy scratches through her coveralls.

Leo pinned the goat's muzzle and jammed the syringe between its teeth. The animal bared its gums in a hideous grin, but the veterinarian was faster. He depressed the plunger, and a ribbon of bubblegum-pink liquid squirted into the goat's mouth.

The goat recoiled, wrenching free with a force that nearly toppled her, and as she staggered, it spat more of the medicine onto her pant leg before bolting for the far end of the enclosure.

Samara straightened, chest heaving, and watched the animal's retreat. The baby goat spun around at the fence line, shook its head, and bleated at her, the sound as accusatory as it was plaintive. Its chin was lathered with pink foam.

Samara laughed, the sound punching out of her before she could stop it. The goat's indignant expression resembled an animatronic villain in a children's theme park, equal parts adorable and deranged.

Across the pen, Leo sagged against the fence, shaking his head in defeat but grinning. "Got most of it down."

"I don't think he's going to forgive us anytime soon."

"Goats never forget," Leo said, deadpan, then lobbed the empty syringe into a bucket at the gate. "But they do move on. Eventually."

Out of all the work assignments she'd rotated through, Samara liked working with the animals under Leo's supervision best. His calm, bemused demeanor didn't just reassure the livestock; it reassured her, too. He never raised his voice or was rough with them, and he seemed able to anticipate every trick they were going to try.

Not just good traits for a veterinarian, but for a parent, too. If she adopted his brand of gentle guidance with the baby, would she be a better mother? The thought terrified and thrilled her in equal measure.

She touched her stomach instinctively, then pretended she was trying to rub away the pink stains, hoping he hadn't noticed. Lucas had included three too-big sweaters in his last care package, with a note reminding her to take her prenatals. According to the files he'd sent, which he'd encrypted, that's how seriously he was taking his promise to keep her secret; she should be seeing a baby bump soon. She'd be forced to wear baggy clothing to hide it.

Her comms shrieked in unison with Leo's. **SPORESTORM INCOMING.**

Lucas had tweaked his model until it gave them almost an hour's warning, which was more than enough time to secure the colony. Plus, they now had antifungals that killed the infection completely within twenty-four hours of exposure, turning the sporestorms that had once been a dire threat into a temporary annoyance that disrupted the rhythm of work and play.

Samara seemed to be the only one who remembered the larger threat that loomed over them. She used the little time Katherine allowed her in the lab to build and run simulations, testing different modifications to find the most effective ones. Their store of birth control meds wouldn't last forever, and when it ran out, Samara would be ready with a proposal that Katherine would *have* to approve.

In the meantime, she was doing her best to find her own rhythm on DaVinci while she prepared for her daughter's arrival.

"I'm good to bring the herd in, if you want to fill the feed troughs before you head home." Leo held the near-empty syringe up so the goat could see it. The animal immediately turned tail and ran back toward the herd, which clustered near the barn's entrance.

Samara laughed again. "Deal. I'll freshen up their water too, in case the storm lasts all night."

After she'd completed the promised chores, she took the long way back to the village, circling around the community garden and drifting along the edge of the mesh fence surrounding the chickens' yard. The coop was locked up tight, not a feather or beady eye in sight, thank goodness.

But that didn't mean she'd be spending the storm alone.

The black cat sprawled on her doorstep like a patch of living shadow. He yawned, flashing pink tongue and white fangs, then blinked at her as if to say, *What took you so long?*

"Hello, Ife." She opened the door, and the cat ambled inside, heading straight for his food dish. After the night she'd spilled the experimental antifungal serum and accidentally saved his life, he'd moved in. And Lucas was never around to object, so…

She closed the door and locked it, then checked the seal. No gaps to let the spores in.

Ife, having found his food dish empty, returned to circle her ankles, tail raised in a question mark.

"In a minute," Samara said, already used to his constant begging.

She stepped over Ife to enter the bedroom, shedding muddy clothes as she went. One hot shower later, she finally felt warm again. After donning sweatpants and a soft flannel shirt, she moved to the closet, where she groped behind a stack of coveralls on the top shelf until her fingers found the blue plastic box that held her secret.

Inside, a blister pack of the colony's dwindling supply of immunosuppressants. She hesitated, then peeled the backing of the next compartment and dry-swallowed the tablet inside. The small grey pill stuck in her throat for a moment, metallic and bitter, a reminder that she was gambling with her immune system every time she took one.

But it gave her daughter a chance to survive.

She was putting the box back on the shelf when her

stomach lurched, not with nausea but with a sudden, ravenous hunger. The craving was immediate and oddly specific: mustard, the bright yellow kind. She scanned her memory of the kitchen inventory. Yes, there were at least two packets left, scavenged from rations and hoarded for a day when the blandness of processed food became intolerable. Might not be bad on tuna casserole, if she had any.

A quick dinner to sate her cravings, a tablet full of immunogenetics studies, and a warm cat on her lap. Peace and quiet, aside from the rattling of the cabin's windows once the storm picked up.

It was shaping up to be a perfect evening.

She was halfway to the kitchen when someone knocked at the door. A gentle double-tap, not an emergency buzz. Samara's pulse jumped. Maybe Lucas had decided to stop by. Technically, he didn't have to knock. This was his cabin, too. But he probably felt as awkward as she did about sharing the space.

The knock sounded again, softer this time.

She padded to the door and opened it. Leila stood there clutching rations and animal crackers, eyes red-rimmed, nose raw. She looked like a lost child, not a colonist tasked with rebooting humanity.

"Sorry—" Leila's voice cracked, and she started again. "I had a fight with Justin. Can I..." She lifted the rations as if in offering. "Can I stay here until the storm's over?"

Babysitting was the last thing Samara needed tonight.

She hesitated a fraction of a second too long, and Leila's face started to crumple. "I'll be quiet. I just— I didn't want to be alone."

Samara stepped aside, and Leila slipped past, then squealed with delight as she caught sight of Ife. "You have a cat?"

So much for peace and quiet.

~

LEILA DROPPED TO A CROUCH, her knees popping, and ran her palm along the cat's spine. The animal arched up into her touch, pushing so hard she nearly lost her balance. "What's its name?" she asked.

"It's *he*, and his name is Ife," Dr. Makinde said.

"What does it mean?"

"It means 'love.' In my mother's language."

"Ife, Ife, Ife," Leila cooed, and the cat rewarded her with a single, warbling meow before wriggling out of her grasp and sitting just out of arm's reach.

She stood awkwardly, not sure what else to say. When she'd come up with this plan, she'd imagined Dr. Makinde asking her what she'd fought with Justin about, and somehow that would morph into comfortable chatter about men and relationships and maybe more.

But instead, Dr. Makinde moved to the kitchenette, opened a cabinet, and started rummaging through a pile of ration packets. "Do you want me to heat yours too?"

"Yes, please," Leila answered, then hated herself for sounding like a kid waiting for mom to fix her dinner. But Dr. Makinde held out her hand, so Leila passed over her pouch of chili mac with a side of green beans.

Now what?

She stood by the counter, hands fidgeting as she watched Dr. Makinde rip open a ration packet and dump a congealed brick of noodles into a bowl, not even trying to keep the side of mixed vegetables separate. Then she did the same with Leila's ration before putting both bowls in the reheater and started it.

A soft hum filled the silence, and Leila realized she was holding her breath. "Thank you for letting me stay, Dr. Makinde."

"You can call me Samara."

But should she?

Leila nodded, tucking a strand of damp hair behind her ear as she sat at the tiny kitchen table. She waited for Samara to say, *What happened with Justin?* or *You look like you need to talk.* But the geneticist remained silent as their meals heated, staring out the window as if she was expecting someone else to arrive.

Maybe she was. Captain Mercer wasn't around much, but this was his cabin, too.

The living room held no trace of him. No pictures, no second coat by the door, nothing to suggest a man lived here. Did he live on the ship?

His absence fit with her theory that Dr. Mak— Samara had used him to get her spot in the colony.

She felt even sorrier for the geneticist. To be partnered with the smartest, nicest, and, if Leila was being honest, most handsome man in the colony, but having to keep it a secret that he wasn't interested in her.

Not that feeling sorry for Samara was going to stop Leila from succeeding in her mission.

She waited until the reheater beeped and Samara set both bowls on the table before she asked, "Do you miss him?"

Samara retrieved a mug and a tin of peppermint tea from one of the cabinets. "Who?"

"Captain Mercer," Leila said, forcing herself to hold the other woman's gaze. "I've noticed he's not around a lot."

"He has his responsibilities, and I have mine."

Leila wanted to say something smart or clever, but what came out was, "You never seem scared, no matter how bad things get."

Samara blinked, but now she was paying attention to Leila, so Leila kept going.

"When you found me that day, you were so calm, and you knew exactly what to do. And you never told me it was going to be okay. You told me the truth." She hadn't meant to talk about it, but now that she'd started, she couldn't stop. "Justin wasn't there for me, but you were."

"I'm sure it was difficult for both of you."

Leila tried to smile, but it wobbled. "Justin only married me for the colony application. He didn't want to get left behind."

For a few moments, the only sound in the cabin was Ife playing with the ends of Leila's shoelaces. When Samara did speak, her voice was gentle but not pitying. "We all have reasons for the choices we make. Sometimes survival is reason enough."

Leila searched for a way to ask that wouldn't sound like an accusation.

"Do you ever worry about… I mean, do you ever think about if he—" She caught herself, tried again. "What if Captain Mercer wanted something different? Like, what if he woke up one day and decided to leave?"

"Relationships are built on trust. I trust Lucas to be honest about what he wants."

Lucas. The name was a small shock. In her mind, he had always been Captain Mercer, as if "Captain" was his first name and "Mercer" his last. A man as formal and unapproachable as the ship itself. But now that she'd heard Samara call him Lucas so casually, it felt like that had always been his name.

"Do you trust Justin?" Samara asked.

No. The word hit like a punch to the gut, making her chili-mac threaten to come back up. "Can I use your restroom?"

"You know where it is."

Leila bolted for the bedroom, then into the tiny bathroom, closing the door after her before she took a deep breath. She was stuck with Justin, who didn't love her, on a planet where there were only seventy-nine other men, all of whom were taken. But there were plenty of embryos in the ship's cryovault. And she wasn't afraid to be a single mother like her own mom.

She just needed to figure out how Samara was keeping her pregnancy going.

She pulled the mirrored door of the medicine cabinet open, slow and deliberate; thankfully, it didn't squeak like hers did. The shelves inside were almost bare. A half-used tube of toothpaste, a green toothbrush, a bottle of antifungals, full, with the safety seal still on. No cold medicine, no painkillers, no cough syrup, not even a spare roll of gauze or a box of adhesive bandages. More significantly, no razor, no shaving cream, no nose trimmer, none of the things that took up Justin's side of their own cabinet at home. Not even a bottle of cologne or a stick of deodorant.

She'd been right. Lucas didn't actually live here. Which meant that, of the seventy-nine men on DaVinci who were not Justin, at least one of them might not be in a committed relationship. Lucas and Samara might be separated. Or maybe they had never been together at all, and Samara had sent him packing once she'd gotten what she wanted.

But that still didn't solve Leila's other problem. There were no medications here other than the antifungals that everyone was taking, and no clue to what Samara might be doing to protect her baby from the spores.

She closed the cabinet, washed her hands for something to do, and counted to ten before heading back out.

When she re-entered the kitchen, Samara was squeezing a packet of mustard into her bowl of chicken fettuccini alfredo.

Mustard on pasta. Leila had her proof.

But how was she going to learn Samara's secret?

Leila was asleep before the storm hit its stride, curled on the loveseat with Ife draped across her shins like a velvet ankle weight. Samara sat at the kitchen table, one hand pressed to her belly, the other clutching a mug of tea gone tepid in the hour since she'd poured it. Wind hammered the cabin like it was testing every weak point, hunting for a way inside.

She listened to the wind, the way it grew and faded in pulses, and thought about what she'd told Leila. The words tasted like lies. She had no right to lecture anyone about trust; she'd made her own unilateral choices in secret, and Lucas had only learned about the embryo when the withdrawal pinged his access to the cryovault logs. What a terrible way to learn you were about to become a father. And yet, he'd proven himself trustworthy, promising to be the child's father, keeping Samara's secret, and doing everything he could to support her during the pregnancy.

She was ashamed that she'd been suspicious of his intentions when he'd neglected to run all possible tests on the samples from the first storm.

She was still at the table when the thud sounded, a deep, concussive pulse that rattled the window glass and set the cat's fur bristling. The wind howled, then fell away to a hush, as if the world itself had been stunned. Samara set her cup down, heart rattling in her chest. She waited, counting the seconds, and heard it again: not the random percussion of debris but a heavy, mechanical shudder.

The shuttle.

She stood, heart in her mouth. No one would risk a landing in this mess. Not unless it was an emergency, or unless someone was reckless enough to think the rules didn't apply to them. Lucas wasn't reckless, despite his earlier foray through a sporestorm to fetch a blood draw kit for her. But that had been urgent. Without an emergency, he would wait for the storm to break.

Wouldn't he?

A figure moved between the cabins, hunched against the wind, but the shape was wrong for Lucas, too small, shoulders rounded. And... it moved like its joints bent backward.

She blinked, and it was gone, swallowed by the swirling grit and shadow. No knock came at her door. No urgent ping on her comm.

She stared until her eyes ached and told herself it was a trick of the storm: shadows and memory, a flicker of light on glass. But the shiver in her backbone lingered, a primitive warning that something beyond her window wasn't right.

She tried to imagine what Lucas would say if he were here. He'd make a calm, dispassionate assessment. Tell her it was a fluke, the random motion of a billion small particles assuming a momentary shape that her brain ascribed meaning to. Or that the day's exhaustion was causing her mind to play tricks on her. Knowing Lucas, he might even insist on testing her vision to make sure it was merely eye strain that had triggered the illusion.

The thought of what he'd say made her smile, and that was sort of like having him there.

She missed him. She could admit that now, with Ife

rubbing against her ankle and Leila sleeping on her couch. Lucas was the only person besides Renata who understood when Samara started talking about her work.

He was the only person besides Renata who wouldn't judge her for taking matters into her own hands to ensure their survival as a species.

He was the only person besides Renata who didn't make her feel like she had to hide who she was.

And that terrified her. Almost as much as the baby growing inside her.

Because the more real a thing became, the more she had to lose.

Chapter Twenty-Two

SAMARA SCRAPED ice from her boots, crystals skittering across the mat as she stomped twice. The pain in her frozen toes felt almost good. DaVinci's cold was vicious, invasive. Seconds outside left her cheeks raw as if she'd been slapped, and she'd stay frozen all day despite layers of clothing.

Maybe she was just feeling the cold more. Thirteen weeks pregnant, and her body was a stranger: puffy fingers, dizzy spells, and the sound of Marcus crunching toast at breakfast had made her want to slap him. She almost preferred the morning sickness that seemed to have vanished in the past few days.

She still had the acid reflux, though. She wasn't sure if it was from pregnancy or from having to endure another mandatory "resilience check-in" with the psychologist.

Ayesha wasn't the cure for Samara's stress; she was the source.

Samara wasn't worried about Ayesha flagging her for burnout, but she was afraid that the psychologist would notice that Samara was pregnant. Her thickening waist wasn't obvious yet, but Ayesha's specialty was reading the infinitesimal cues of body and voice and turning them into diagnosis or leverage, depending on her mood. She might not have the education to understand Samara's work, but she was highly perceptive, especially when it came to other people's behavior.

She smiled as Samara entered the conference.

Samara braced herself for the ambush.

"I'm so glad we're finally getting a chance to talk," Ayesha said, setting two mugs on the table and gesturing to the empty chair beside her.

A reminder wrapped in false cheer that Samara had dodged this meeting until Katherine cornered her.

Samara chose the chair across from Ayesha. Close enough to seem cooperative, far enough to avoid intimacy. "I'm sure you've been as busy as I have."

Ayesha smiled and slid the second mug toward Samara. Hot cocoa. There were even a few crumpled marshmallows floating atop the milky surface. Technically appropriate for the season, but she was sure it was intended to remind her of the upcoming solstice celebration and lower her defenses.

So she ignored the mug and steepled her hands on the table. "What kind of resilience are we building today?"

The psychologist's bright smile folded into a look of gentle, professional concern.

"Why don't you tell me?" She leaned forward, elbows on the table, subtly mimicking Samara's posture without copying it exactly. "How are you adapting to life here?"

Samara chose from her rehearsed responses, honest but safe.

"It's an adjustment. I miss cooking real food. I miss the cafe around the corner from my apartment that doesn't exist anymore. I'm getting calluses on my hands from all the physical work I'm doing. But I don't think I've got it harder than anyone else."

Ayesha nodded, slow and deliberate. "Do you resent being asked to do manual labor?"

She could lie, say she loved the chance to be outside, to feel the reality of the world through her skin and not just through a microscope. But Ayesha would see through that. Best to go on the offensive.

"Do *you* resent it?"

Ayesha's lips curved, acknowledging the parry. "A little. But I understand that right now, it's as important as the work I was trained to do." She sipped her cocoa, then added, "How are you feeling about the fact that your skills are no longer relevant?"

Here we go. Ayesha thought she could dismiss Samara's insistence on pursuing gene therapy as wounded pride. A predictable maneuver, but hard to refute.

Samara shrugged, the movement tight across her shoulders. "I'm doing the work I've been assigned."

Ayesha's smile softened, but her eyes sharpened. "But you do resent it."

"If you want it on record, yes. I resent being benched from the work that might actually give this colony a future," Samara said. "But you know that, since you're one of the two people who vetoed my proposal without even bothering to ask a single question about it."

"If you want to blame me, you're free to do that." Ayesha sighed as she set her mug down. "Would you mind if I told you a story?"

Let Ayesha waste time with stories. Fewer questions to dodge.

Samara stretched her legs under the table, crossing them at the ankle. "Go ahead."

Ayesha's gaze flickered to the window as if she were searching for the right memory. Then she began:

"When I was six, my grandmother was the only one who ever had time for me. My parents were both surgeons, always on rotation, always tired." A pause, a glance at Samara to confirm she was listening. "When I visited, we would make treats together. Gaz was my favorite. It's a kind of nougat. You toast the pistachios, then you cook the syrup just so, and if you're even a little off, the nougat turns to stone, or it doesn't harden all the way. The timing is crucial."

She mimed the slow, careful swirl of a spoon through some invisible concoction. "She'd let me stir the syrup while it boiled, and I'd pretend it was a magic potion. Sometimes we'd make her favorite cookies, and I can still taste them every time I smell cardamom or rosewater."

Samara imagined little Ayesha on a kitchen stool, stirring molten sugar with the concentration of a scientist. The image conjured a pang of unwanted empathy. She tried to keep her face impassive. She didn't trust the story or the teller.

Still, she listened.

"Then one day, my grandmother slapped me so hard I bit my tongue. Called me a demon." Ayesha continued, not looking at Samara but at some fixed point just over her shoulder. "She had stopped taking her medication, and without it, she saw things. Heard things. She ripped the wooden spoon out of my hand and beat me with it until her friend, her live-in nurse, I later learned, locked me in the bathroom and called my parents to come get me."

Samara's chest tightened at the thought of the young girl's grandmother turning on her without warning. Ayesha's origin story, the defining moment that had driven her to become a psychologist.

But she was also waiting for Ayesha to land the story, to turn it into some parable about… what? Was this just a bid for sympathy, in hopes that Samara would let her guard down?

The psychologist's expression remained distant, as if she were still in that kitchen, or in the bathroom with the door locked, or somewhere else entirely.

"They moved her to a psychiatric hospital after that. A place with pink and green walls, because someone had read a study claiming those colors were soothing. Occasionally, my parents would bring me to see her, but only with supervision, even though she was so drugged she could barely move. I'd bring her gaz and cardamom cookies and play tea party. But Grandmother would never eat them. I had to eat them for her and tell her how good they tasted. Eventually, she stopped recognizing me."

Samara's throat tightened. She felt the grief like a spike through her sternum, and for a moment, she had to squeeze her hands together to keep from reaching across the table to touch Ayesha's wrist. It was the pregnancy hormones making her overly sensitive, she told herself. But the ache for the girl who'd lost her grandmother was real enough to make her eyes prickle with tears.

"I'm so sorry," she said. That didn't seem like enough, but what else could she say that mattered?

"My grandmother was one of the first designer babies," the psychologist continued. "My great-grandparents wanted their daughter to be a genius. They got their wish. But the genes that predispose for intelligence—"

"—are linked to schizophrenia," Samara finished.

"And because genetic engineering is not an exact science, when you transfer the genes you want, sometimes you also get genes you don't. I believe you call those off-target effects?"

Now it all made sense.

Katherine had warned her not to underestimate the psychologist, but Samara hadn't listened. Even though she'd expected the ambush, she hadn't seen it coming. Hadn't anticipated that Ayesha would be willing to expose her deepest scars to advance her argument to the next level.

Samara both admired and resented it.

"You think I don't understand the risks you take," Ayesha said fiercely. "But I watched my grandmother lose herself, piece by piece, to a side effect. 'Off-target effect' is such a dismissive phrase to describe the destruction of a human mind. And the irony is, the therapy worked. She was a genius who made invaluable contributions to the same field of study that drove her mad."

Ayesha reached for the cocoa and sipped, eyes never leaving Samara's as she continued:

"My grandmother spent her whole life trying to reverse the disease her parents cursed her with, until they were forced to institutionalize her. You've probably read some of her work. Her name was Mitra Kunde."

Samara's heart skipped. *The* Mitra Kunde, who was both legend and cautionary tale rolled into one brilliant, tragic woman. Samara's analysis of Kunde's body of work had nearly ruined her own academic reputation when she was a graduate student. *Beware of flying too close to the sun,* her mentor had warned her.

"Your grandmother's work was…" She caught herself, searching for a word that wouldn't insult the other woman. "Brilliant. But controversial."

Ayesha's mouth turned sharp. "Dangerous, you mean."

Samara managed a nod. She remembered the ferocity of the debates, the anonymous threats sent to the journals, the way even the most progressive researchers had drawn a line at germline edits in the brain. She remembered how, in the aftermath of her own paper discussing the merits of continuing Kunde's work with strict ethical guidelines, other researchers snubbed her at conferences. Over a thought experiment.

She'd tried to brush them off as intellectual cowards who hid behind rules rather than testing the reasons for those rules. But she couldn't deny the bitter anguish on Ayesha's face, direct evidence of the damage that could be done by breaking the rules without sufficient understanding.

Samara weighed her words, threading caution through every syllable. "I understand why you're opposed to what I do, given what happened to your grandmother. But what I proposed isn't anything like what was done then. The procedures I use are generations beyond those first experiments. We're not making people smarter or faster or taller. We're fixing well-characterized, well-understood defects with edits that have been in use, safely, for decades. The off-target risks are—" She caught herself, seeing the flash in Ayesha's eyes. "—not zero. But they're nothing like they were when Mitra Kunde was born."

"You sound so certain."

"I am certain," Samara said, knowing that Ayesha would probably equate her certainty with arrogance. "We know so much more about how these genes interact now. We have data, not just theory."

"Look at me and tell me there's no chance you'll make a mistake. Promise that it's safe."

The challenge was so direct that Samara had to fight the impulse to look away. Instead, she forced herself to meet the other woman's gaze, searching for a fracture in that righteous anger.

"There is always a possibility of a mistake," Samara

said. "But it's a probability, not a certainty. And for simple edits, especially single-gene fixes, the odds are relatively small."

Ayesha nodded, as if this was the answer she'd expected. "But the more complex the modification, the more genes you touch, the less you can predict. That's what happened to my grandmother. It was supposed to be a single trait, a single advantage. But the ripples went everywhere."

Samara let out a slow breath, not quite a sigh. She doubted she would convince the other woman, but she had to try. "You're right. The more genes you touch, the steeper the curve. Now we edit twelve base pairs at a time and run simulations before touching a single cell. The protocols are audited, and the sequences are checked. Our accuracy is an order of magnitude higher than it was when your grandmother was modified."

"Do you believe what you do is ethical?" Ayesha's voice was quiet, but the words landed like a sledgehammer. "Knowing that even a small mistake could mean the difference between a healthy child and someone living their whole life with a new, unfixable defect?"

"Do you think Hector worries about that when he prescribes medication?" Samara countered. "Every drug has side effects, sometimes severe, sometimes fatal."

"If Hector prescribes the wrong drug, he can flush it out of the system or counteract it. But what you do, Samara, is forever. You intervene at the root. There is no undoing one of your mistakes."

"That's true," she conceded. "But the risk of doing nothing isn't zero either. I wouldn't have made my proposal if I didn't believe the alternative was extinction."

Ayesha's mouth pressed into a thin line, and Samara saw the fatigue in her, the burden of being the one tasked with keeping the colony sane. But who was keeping her sane?

"You don't want to be the reason this colony falls prey to the same thing that destroyed Earth, do you?"

That the psychologist had asked that question proved how little she understood. "On Earth, it was our engineered fungus killing the planet. Here, it's the opposite: the fungus is native, the planet is fine. It's us who are dying."

"There's always a justification to take the easy route, but the risk is too great."

Samara braced herself against the table, forcing a steadiness into her voice. "You don't know how to assess these risks, not like I do. I wouldn't propose a therapy without proper protocols, without redundancy, without testing it in every way possible before bringing it to the colony."

"But you can't properly test it. Whoever you give your 'therapy' to first, that person is the guinea pig. Whether you call it that or not." Ayesha set her mug down hard enough to make the surface of the cocoa tremble.

"It's not—"

"You wouldn't experiment on yourself, Samara. Don't do it to the rest of us."

Guilt twisted Samara's stomach into knots. Had the psychologist intuited that she was pregnant and reasoned that if the child had survived sporestorms, Samara must've given herself gene therapy?

Or had Lucas been unable to resist unburdening himself during his own mandatory check-in? Maybe the strain of keeping Samara's secret had been too much. Or maybe he'd been so anxious about the possibility of becoming a father that he'd accidentally revealed the truth.

But then logic kicked in and Samara realized that

Ayesha couldn't have known, because if she had, she would've gone to Katherine immediately and howled for Samara to be punished for her secret experiment. Which meant the psychologist was projecting her deepest fear onto Samara, and her deepest fear just happened to be exactly what Samara had already done. Behind everyone's backs.

The worst part was that Ayesha wasn't even wrong. Each mitotic division of the embryo in Samara's womb embodied a choice that she had made not only for her daughter, but for every future descendant of this colony. If she'd made a mistake, there would be no undoing it.

Samara stood, using every atom of willpower she had to contain the maelstrom of horror and shame and grief that threatened to eclipse her rational mind.

"This was supposed to be a check-in," she said, "not a sermon."

She left before Ayesha could try anything else, shutting the conference room door behind her with a click that sounded loud in the empty hallway.

Don't experiment on the rest of us.

But Samara was already experimenting on herself. And on her own daughter.

She was the walking embodiment of Ayesha's worst-case scenario, and the shame of it sizzled under her skin.

On Earth, what she'd done would have ended her career. The termination paperwork would've said *ethics violation*, but when they whispered about her, they would've said *unconscionable*. She imagined the emails, the committee hearings, her mentor's face shifting from pride to something brittle and cold. She would've been effectively excommunicated from the scientific community, the only community where she'd ever belonged.

But on this world, she was the only qualified geneticist

within 4.2 light-years. The only person who could even attempt the work, and the only one who understood the stakes. Which meant there was no one to stop her. No one to tell her when she'd crossed the line from hero to villain.

The empty hallway was filled with recrimination, and by the time she reached the outside door, she was shivering again. The scientists who'd destroyed Earth had good intentions too, making incremental choices to save their world. But Samara had done this with her eyes wide open, believing she could outsmart evolution itself.

If she succeeded, would that justify the decision she'd made for her child?

The wind battered her face as she stepped outside, wet and icy and insistent. Soon, she wouldn't be able to hide her pregnancy, and the whole colony would realize that her daughter had survived multiple sporestorms. They would have questions.

And Samara would have to answer, both to the colony and to her conscience.

What was left of it.

Chapter Twenty-Three

THESE ALIEN WOODS smelled of wet metal and burning compost, nothing like the pine forests of home. Every step was an argument with the mud that threatened to suck Samara down if she lingered even a moment too long. Katherine, twenty years older than the rest of them, set a brutal pace through the ankle-deep slush.

Samara drew her scarf up higher to cover her chapped lips, pretending not to eavesdrop on the two women picking their way through the ankle-deep slush directly in front of her as they chattered about the winter solstice celebration only two days away.

"Last night I tried to make a Christmas tree," Ingrid said to Zoya. "I cut a sprig of rosemary from the herb garden and stuck it in a mug. Then I braided strips of foil I cut from a ration packet to make a tinsel garland."

"You could have asked me for a snippet of wire from the shop. I'd have made you a tree frame."

Ingrid shrugged. "I liked it lopsided. My father always bought the cheapest tree at the market and called it 'characterful.'"

"I miss lighting the menorah. Since we're supposed to save candles for emergencies, my husband drew a menorah on a sheet of printer paper, and he taped it to the wall in our living room. Every night, he draws a new flame with a yellow marker." She snorted, as if embarrassed by the ritual, but there was no mistaking the affection in her voice. "He says it's so we don't forget by the time we have kids, but really, it's for himself."

"I like that," said Ingrid, not missing a step. "Paper flames never burn your house down."

"Or your eyebrows," Zoya agreed. "Which is good, because he has so few left."

They stepped around a puddle, moving in practiced synchrony. Samara had noticed that the two spent much of their free time together since the night they'd spent in the clinic together, post-miscarriage. A friendship built on mutual grief. Samara envied their shared understanding, even if it was born from loss.

If she lost this baby, only Lucas would grieve with her. Would that bring them together or drive them further apart?

Probably the latter. But she also thought that if she told Renata, the xenobiologist would grieve with her. Assuming she didn't recoil in disgust at what Samara had done.

"Here," Katherine called from up ahead, pointing at a clump of trees whose trunks were enmeshed in thick green vines that climbed in spirals, their rubbery leaves glistening with frost as they dangled pale yellow melons like lanterns overhead.

The vines burrowed deep into the trunks, leeching sap, but in return, they exuded a bitter resin that repelled the blue-bodied borers that would otherwise hollow out the trees from the inside. Samara could see the boreholes in the bark of older trees, each ringed with a bloom of blue-green fungus, a reminder that even here, survival meant compromise.

Zoya reached up and swatted at a low-hanging melon, but missed. Ingrid cackled, then launched into a story about her mother's inedible fruitcake, so hard it could bend a knife blade and so thoroughly soaked in rum that it could survive months on the counter, immune to mold and decay.

Samara drifted away from the group, pushing deeper into the thicket, boots squelching in the boggy ground. She checked over her shoulder, making sure none of the women were watching, then unzipped her jacket. The shock of icy air against her belly was jarring, but she welcomed it. She had been running hot for weeks now.

She retrieved her sickle from its sheath on her belt, then steadied herself against the trunk as she reached up on tiptoe and sawed at the nearest melon-containing vine. The fruit landed heavily in her palm with a satisfying thud.

Footsteps squelched behind her, deliberate and unhurried. She didn't have to turn to know it was Katherine.

"Has the morning sickness passed yet?"

Samara's fingers tensed on the melon. She turned and set the fruit into the basket that Katherine held out to her.

The colony leader's gaze flicked from Samara's face to her midsection, then back up. "With my second child, it lasted until the contractions started. I couldn't keep anything down for nine months."

"That's encouraging," Samara joked.

She'd been dreading this conversation for weeks; she'd hoped to put it off at least until the solstice. Bundling up for winter weather made it easier to hide the changes in her body, the thick, layered sweaters, the scarf, the thermal vest, all working in concert to buy her a little more time.

"I've known for a couple of weeks." Katherine's tone

was matter-of-fact, no accusation that Samara could detect. "I was waiting for you to come to me."

"I didn't want to get anyone's hopes up. Including mine." She twisted the sickle through another vine, feeling the satisfying pop as the melon's stem gave way.

Katherine caught the fruit this time, cradling it in both hands. "Hector didn't seem to know anything about it when I asked what miracle meds he's been giving you."

Samara braced herself, expecting a cross-examination. "I'm not taking anything experimental, just the immuno-suppressants and prenatals. You can audit the ship's stores to verify."

A gust of wind rattled the lantern-fruits overhead, setting the vines to whisper against one another. Katherine shifted her weight, boot sinking deeper into the mud, and leveled an angry look at Samara.

"You're far enough along that you had to be pregnant during the last sporestorm." Katherine's voice went flat. "You turned yourself into a test subject without permission."

"I didn't use the protocol that was vetoed. This was something more conservative."

"What does that mean?"

Samara kept her gaze steady, though her pulse was pounding. "The technique is well-established, and there weren't as many variables."

Katherine's eyes narrowed with each word, and her jaw took on a severity that made Samara feel suddenly twelve years old and summoned to the principal's office for something she'd thought was a clever prank.

"You made a designer baby *after* I made it clear you were not to pursue gene therapy?"

Samara set the sickle down and forced herself to meet

the other woman's gaze. "I made some simple modifications to an embryo from the cryovault."

"Simple modifications."

Samara felt the words thudding between them like dropped stones. She'd made the same arguments repeatedly, and they'd had no effect.

If we wait for consensus, we all die.

Our fertility window is closing.

We've found a temporary fix, not a permanent solution.

We should be pursuing multiple options, not betting on the easy one.

Appealing to the common good had convinced no one. What if she appealed to Katherine's practicality?

"This is how we survive," she added. "If this works, I'll know how to engineer an epigenetic treatment for everyone else."

"That's a human life you're experimenting on."

"This was the only way. We both know Ayesha would never have agreed."

Katherine threw her hands up in disgust. "Don't you see that you've proved her right? This is exactly the kind of arrogance she warned us about."

Samara's first instinct was to retort that Ayesha was the arrogant one, so sure she was right about a topic she clearly didn't understand. It was tempting to claim that they had driven her to this, with their refusal to listen, their unwillingness to act before it was too late. But it was watching Leila lose baby after baby that had shattered Samara's objectivity.

Extinction wasn't theoretical when you held a grieving mother while her child bled out of her.

But Katherine's next question wasn't theoretical, either. "Does Lucas know he's going to be a father?"

The sickle shook in Samara's white-knuckled grip. She

willed her pulse to slow, but instead it climbed, each beat a hot, insistent drum behind her ribs. She didn't have the right to be offended by the question because she *had* done exactly what Katherine was accusing her of. But she was offended.

Pregnancy hormones, she reminded herself as she shoved the anger away to focus on what happened next.

Should she lie to protect Lucas from whatever punishment Katherine might assign for conspiring to disobey her orders? Or tell the truth, which made Samara look better but made Lucas complicit with her deception?

"He helped me to do it."

Katherine exhaled, then looked away, first at the trees, then at the women still gathering fruit as if nothing had happened. When she spoke again, her voice had a bitter edge that Samara recognized from the few times Katherine had nearly lost her temper in public.

"I should pull you from duty for this. Lucas, too. You both knew better."

Samara nodded, the gesture as stiff as her frozen fingers. "I'll accept whatever punishment you think is appropriate."

"But you're not sorry." There was no accusation in Katherine's words. Only a flat, exhausted certainty that made Samara want to apologize, even if she couldn't mean it.

She pressed her palm to her stomach, feeling the heat of her own skin through her clothing. "If I lose my daughter, I will be."

Katherine's face changed, the sharpness dissolving into something more complicated, a tangle of regret and hope and, Samara thought, envy.

"Have you chosen a name?"

"Not until I know she'll survive."

Samara had watched the other women in the colony mourn their lost children, seen the way Zoya's hands trembled when she thought no one was looking, heard the way Leila's voice turned brittle every time a baby was mentioned. She knew she wouldn't find comfort in a memorial service where Ayesha spouted platitudes.

A gust shook loose a scattering of frigid meltwater from the canopy above. Samara shivered as it soaked into the shirt stretched across her exposed belly. She zipped up her coat again.

Katherine adjusted her gloves and stepped toward the nearest tree. She set her basket down in a patch of snowless mud, then craned her neck to inspect the higher branches. For what?

"You'll go up to the ship on the next shuttle run," she said, still staring into the canopy. "You'll stay there until the baby is born."

Samara's first instinct was to protest that it was crucial the baby be exposed to repeated sporestorms to be sure that the edits held true. But Katherine's logic was clear. If she stayed, everyone would know what she'd done, and the rumors would spread.

And she had to admit, it would be a relief to spend the next several months in the ship's lab, running the experiments to refine her approach and prove that her solution would be safe for everyone. Maybe she and Lucas could finally figure out how to be partners before they had to be parents.

She would miss Renata and Marcus, though. Especially Renata.

"Hold this," Katherine said, passing the basket to Samara without waiting for consent.

Samara braced it against her hip, watching as Katherine gripped a low branch and tested its strength.

The colony leader was not built for grace. She moved with a kind of stubborn momentum, all knees and elbows, her boots slipping on the frost-glazed bark before she found her footing and levered herself up. Her knees creaked as she crouched, then launched herself upward, hooking one arm around the next branch before hauling herself into the crook.

Once she'd steadied herself, she sliced through a tangle of vine with a practiced flick of her wrist. Samara lunged to catch the melon that tumbled toward her, but her gloves slipped on the waxy rind, and the fruit thudded into the mud at her feet, splitting open with a muted pop. The scent—a strange, acidic sweetness—rose up, sharp enough to sting her nose.

"Next time, two hands," Katherine said, not unkindly. She harvested nearly a dozen more melons before climbing up to the next branch. "You know what Ayesha's going to say when she hears about this. That I approved your experiment in secret."

"It's not the same exper—"

Katherine's laugh was a short, hard crack. "Do you think she's going to care? "

"I'll tell everyone you didn't know. That I did it on my own."

"Which makes me look incompetent. Like I can't control my own people." Katherine's knife flicked again, hacking at a tangle of vine with fervor. "You're smarter than that, Samara."

Samara hated these political games, this constant triangulation. But Katherine was right. She imagined Ayesha's expression when the news came out: shocked, righteous, betrayed, already scripting the soundbites she'd deliver in the next leadership meeting.

"You're excused from work shifts until we get you up to

the Borlaug," Katherine said. "And I'm the one who'll have to manage the fallout, so I'm the one who will break this news, not you. Understood?"

Samara suspected that Katherine would break the news after Samara's baby was born. It would be easier to limit the outrage if she could deliver good news at the same time: that it was now safe for all the colony's women to conceive.

"Understood."

For the first time in months, Samara felt a kind of relief, the pressure in her chest replaced by a clean, cold ache. She'd been bracing for this confrontation since the day she'd implanted the embryo. Now that it was over, she realized she'd been carrying the secret in every muscle and tendon.

Her only regret was that she wouldn't get to tell Renata herself. Samara wanted to believe that Renata would understand why she'd done it. But she was afraid that the xenobiologist would never trust her again.

Losing Renata's friendship would hurt more than any official punishment Katherine could devise.

Chapter Twenty-Four

Samara woke to her door creaking open. The familiar hinge-catch was followed by silence so complete it seemed to steal the air from her lungs. She lay still, pulse hammering, and listened. A step, careful and deliberate, on the polymer floor. A second step, and the barely audible click as the door latched itself behind the intruder.

She propped herself on one elbow, blinking against the dark. The blackout curtain was drawn, so the only illumination was a thin blue-gold haze leaking around the frame from the corridor beyond. For a moment, she thought it might be Leila again, come to confess another fight with Justin. But Leila always knocked, and Leila was not nearly so silent.

The silhouette was tall, broad-shouldered, moving with Lucas' characteristic precision.

But why was he sneaking into her bedroom, their bedroom, technically, when he'd always been so adamant about sleeping on the couch when he was here?

She pushed upright, the blanket tangling around her

hips, and tried to flatten her hair with one palm. "Is something wrong?"

Lucas shook his head, just once. "We need to leave now. I'll explain on the way."

"Explain what?"

Instead of answering, he held out her jacket with one hand and her shoes with the other.

Was he serious?

"Katherine said I'm not supposed to leave my room until the shuttle run."

But she was already swinging her legs over the side of the bed.

"You need an ultrasound. Katherine wants me to do it without Hector knowing."

"So… we're going to break into the medical clinic?"

"I know the code."

Of course, Katherine would've given it to him. Or maybe she hadn't needed to; as ship's captain, he might have access to all the codes. Samara realized she had no idea where Lucas' authority ended and Katherine's began.

She threw on her jacket and shoes, then followed him outside.

Three minutes later, Lucas was ushering her inside Hector's clinic, pulling the door shut behind them. The vestibule was pitch black except for the pulsing green of the intrusion alarm, which he silenced with another code, this one so quick she barely registered the sequence before the light faded, leaving her temporarily blind.

"Will Hector find out we broke in?" she whispered.

"Only if he checks the security system logs, so let's not give him a reason to."

Lucas guided her to an exam room and lifted her onto the table with surprising gentleness. She heard the faint squeak of wheels as Lucas positioned the ultrasound cart. He flicked the power switch, and a rectangle of blue, staticky light blinked to life, illuminating the side of his face in a pale, surgical glow.

"Lie down," he said, and there was no awkwardness, for a change.

She did, letting her jacket fall open. Lucas rolled up the hem of her shirt, exposing the swell of her belly.

The icy shock of the gel made her stomach muscles jump. Lucas didn't apologize, but the way he spread it over her stomach was almost tender, and now she was the awkward one.

She kept her eyes on the ceiling tiles, counting the hairline cracks and the halos of old water damage, anything to avoid the intimacy of his gaze. But then the wand pressed down, firm and unhesitating, and she couldn't help but glance at him.

He wasn't looking at her, though. His gaze was fixed on the ultrasound machine.

The monitor was a mess of blue-gray static at first. Then the blur resolved, and there it was: a grainy, nebulous shape curled in on itself, limbs folded tight to the body. The fetus resembled a seahorse: head bowed, back arched, tiny hands covering her face. A faint, pulsing flicker shivered through the shape, and as Lucas adjusted a knob, the soft whup-whup-whup of a heartbeat filled the room. It was so loud, she felt it in her own chest.

Samara stared at the screen, at the impossible evidence of her daughter, alive and safe inside her.

Her throat tightened. Tears blurred her vision, one escaping to track down her cheek despite her efforts to blink them back. Humiliating. She wiped it away with the heel of her hand.

"Sorry." Her voice cracked. "Hormones."

Lucas still stared at the screen… was he looking for

problems or was he trying to spare her the embarrassment? "I believe it is normal for mothers to feel strong emotions at this moment."

"Because of the pregnancy hormones," she said with a little more force than necessary.

"The fetus—"

"Our daughter." Samara's voice steadied. "Start thinking of her that way. Everyone will expect you to, unless you've changed your mind about taking on the role of father."

She kept her eyes on the monitor, afraid to see his expression as he pondered his answer.

Lucas set the wand down and wiped the excess gel from her skin, then folded the towel and set it aside, too.

"Our daughter appears healthy, based on these readings."

Samara let the words settle into her, a slow warmth blooming out from the core of her exhaustion. And it was awkward again, so she searched for another topic.

"Since when are you qualified to read ultrasounds?" she asked.

"I think my training is sufficient in this case. But feel free to double-check my conclusion."

He pivoted the monitor so she could see. The indicators were all green, and the summary underneath read: FETAL DEVELOPMENT: NORMAL.

Samara laughed, picturing Hector's grave expression as he delivered results. How often was he just reading from the screen?

As if reading her mind, Lucas added: "A doctor's expertise is only needed if there is a problem that requires diagnosis."

He peeled off the gloves and tucked them into the med

cart's disposal bin before wiping down the wand, then the table.

Samara watched his reflection on the screen: his jaw set, his focus absolute, as if cleaning up after the scan required the same precision as docking a shuttle. She tried to think of something better to say than: *Thanks for taking care of me while I hide my pregnancy like a criminal.*

"Thank you. For this. For everything. I know it's not what you signed up for."

Lucas stopped cleaning. "If you are having second thoughts about my ability to play the role adequately, it is not too late to find another solution."

She blinked, startled. "No second thoughts. You've been perfect."

He'd kept her secret, ferried supplies, and never once complained or judged. If anything, he'd been more attentive than she could have asked for.

He considered this, then said, "I have not been available to you for days at a time. There is some overlap between the role of father and the role of husband. I am aware that I am not fulfilling both."

Samara felt a laugh bubble up; she couldn't remember the last time she had laughed for real. "You don't need to take care of me like that, Lucas. Pregnancy isn't a disease. Or a disability."

Lucas angled his head, as though to verify her statement with a scan. "If you do need my help, you will tell me?"

"You'll be the first to know." She buttoned her jacket, still feeling the sticky ghost of gel on her skin. "My mom worked right up until the contractions started with both me and my sister. She didn't even call the midwife until the last minute."

"Family history may not be an adequate predictor in this case. This child is unique."

She felt something tighten, a brief flinch of dread. "You mean, my daughter is a mutant."

"She's healthy by every measure we have. But she's carrying genetic sequences that have never existed in humans before."

Samara nodded, but the reassurance did not settle. She thought of Ayesha's grandmother: brilliant and broken by genetic tampering. The technology was primitive then.

But what if Samara had made the same mistakes with better tools?

Chapter Twenty-Five

THE COLD HAD SETTLED into Samara's bones despite piling on every blanket she owned. The baby was a furnace in reverse, stealing warmth faster than her body could produce it.

Something had woken her. There. A soft scuffing outside. Not wind, not the usual settling of prefab walls.

She propped herself up, peering into the dimness. The blackout curtain had slipped an inch, admitting a blade of violet dawn. She lifted the curtain and caught movement, someone slipping between cabins, disappearing around a corner with practiced stealth.

Lucas. Carrying a heavy backpack and moving like he didn't want to be seen.

The shuttle run had been scheduled for later that morning, but maybe he'd arrived early, hoping to sneak her on board before anyone else noticed that she was pregnant? Given how angry Katherine had been yesterday, Samara wouldn't be surprised if she'd decided to accelerate the timetable. Especially if she'd discovered that Ingrid or Zoya had overheard part of their conversation.

The colony leader would have to stay ahead of gossip, and she'd wanted Samara on the Borlaug before she revealed the truth.

But when Lucas reappeared just past the herb garden, he wasn't heading toward their cabin. He was stalking toward the northern ridge. He moved like a predator. Graceful, focused, hunting something she couldn't see.

For some reason, he wasn't following the path to the top of the ridge that they'd laid out to make it easier to check the cameras and sensors monitoring the approach to the colony. Instead, he made a beeline through the weedy field they'd maintained as a buffer between the waste treatment plant and the colony proper.

Something was wrong, but she had no idea what.

She was pulling on jeans before logic caught up. Crisis meant comms. Privacy meant waiting. Sneaking meant secrets.

What if he's running?

She slipped on her boots. Shrugged into her coat, then pulled the hood low over her ears. Stuffed her comm unit in one pocket and a respirator in the other. She hurried out the door and sprinted between cabins, emerging from the village just in time to see Lucas turning a few degrees east toward the edge of the forest. He didn't look back, didn't pause. He seemed almost... furtive.

Something was definitely wrong.

She jogged past the herb garden and out into the open field, boots crunching through the brittle crust of last night's frost on the native wildgrass. Instinct told her to duck low as she crossed the field, as if she could make herself invisible to any watcher, although the only candidates for that seemed to be several feathered shrews perched along the fence line.

Ahead, Lucas was already halfway to the tree line

where the dark indigo foliage of the forest met the pale purple grassland. Once he entered the forest, she might lose him. But her gut told her not to call out. If he were trying to avoid someone, she might alert that someone to his presence.

Who would he be avoiding?

Had someone found out about her pregnancy and blamed him for helping to deceive everyone? That seemed unlikely, unless Hector had noticed something amiss in the clinic. But even if he had, Samara couldn't imagine him resorting to violence; the man's anger was more the flavor of a lecture than a fist. And if it came down to a physical fight, Lucas was a head taller, at least a couple of decades younger, and a lot stronger.

Maybe Ayesha had found out. Maybe she was rallying the colonists against Samara's genetic manipulation right now. If Ayesha had been willing to use her childhood trauma to press her argument in a therapy session, how would she leverage the knowledge of Samara's pregnancy to push Katherine, or possibly bypass Katherine and go straight to the colonists themselves, undermining Katherine's authority?

For all Samara knew, Ayesha had called an assembly and was giving an impassioned speech demanding that she and Lucas be punished for disobeying a direct order, forcing Katherine to either agree or seem complicit with Samara's secret experiment.

But if that was the case, would Lucas leave her to face that punishment alone?

She couldn't see him abandoning her like that. Not the man who'd braved a sporestorm without a respirator to fetch a blood draw kit so she could do the experiment that had identified the spores as the source of their illness.

Not the man who'd been sneaking care packages into

her cabin, their cabin, so she didn't have to choose between keeping her baby healthy and keeping her experiment secret.

Not the man who'd said *our daughter* as he'd wiped ultrasound gel off her bare belly.

Unless he'd changed his mind about becoming a father.

Too good to be true. The thought hammered at her skull.

She ducked through the low arch of the perimeter fence, boots landing in a slurry of half-frozen mud and decayed grass. The ground sucked at her heels, slowing her down and forcing her to keep her eyes on her footing. When she looked up again, Lucas had almost reached the tangle of indigo undergrowth at the forest's edge. She picked up her pace.

This was insane, following him into the trees instead of just calling his name. But something held her back. If he wasn't running from someone else, *she* might be the one he wanted to avoid.

Too good to be true.

She was being paranoid. Did pregnancy hormones do that? But her instinct still insisted that something was wrong. So she pursued, her breath tight and sharp in her chest, feeling both childish and exposed on the open ground.

Lucas disappeared into the forest. Samara ran, thighs burning as she churned through the frost-crusted grass, boots skidding on the slope. She didn't slow as she hit the first line of brush, branches clawing at her coat, damp leaves smacking her cheeks and leaving a sting that bloomed in the cold.

Samara reached the tree line and stopped, doubled over, gasping for breath and tasting bile at the back of her throat. The woods were silent but for the slow drip of meltwater and the brittle ping of ice falling from the higher boughs. She straightened, squinting through the trunks, but Lucas was gone. She pivoted left, right, trying to spot the flash of his jacket or the bob of his head, but the wind nudging branches and a nervous scuttle of tiny insects over rotted leaves and mucky dirt were the only things moving besides her. Had she veered off course, entering the forest at a different spot than he had?

She retraced her steps and walked east along the tree line, scanning for footprints. Soon she found one, the thin crust of ice over rotting leaves broken by a heavy boot. Then another, and another, leading through low thickets of thorn and a drift of bruised-blue leaves, each step carrying her farther from the safety of the colony and deeper into the wild.

They veered toward a shallow ravine, crossed a half-frozen stream, and climbed the opposite bank. Samara kept low, moving slowly, every sense straining as she pushed through the thicket, branches snapping at her face.

She lost the tracks again.

Then she heard the quiet whine of something electronic to her left. She kept moving, careful to set each foot where the ground looked least likely to betray her. The slippery top layer of dead leaves offered little resistance, but underneath it was a labyrinth of roots and invisible holes. The first time her heel sank into a patch of snow-softened mud, she nearly toppled, catching herself on a low branch that left a resinous smear on her wrist.

She crouched, fighting nausea while her shifted center of gravity made every step a potential fall.

Lucas' footprints had vanished into the mulch again, as if he'd simply dissolved. But the faint electric whine she'd heard before was stronger now. She eased forward, orienting herself by the sound. That way.

She stepped over a mossy log and froze. Lucas stood motionless in a small clearing, back rigid, neck exposed as if the cold couldn't touch him, staring at something in his open palm as if it were the only thing in the universe.

She couldn't see whatever it was that absorbed his attention, but he wasn't examining it with scientific curiosity, the way Renata might. His head was slightly tilted, as if he were listening to something Samara couldn't hear. As if it were talking to him.

What had he found? And why was it so important that he'd felt he had to sneak out of the colony to look for it?

Maybe it wasn't that. Maybe he'd heard her stumbling after him, and he was waiting for her to catch up and show herself. But he didn't call out to her, didn't show any signs that he knew he'd been caught. He stood there, so unnaturally still that, if not for the movement of the forest around him, she'd have thought she'd hit pause on a video she'd been watching.

He didn't seem furtive now. He seemed... something like reverent.

Was it possible he'd simply wanted some solitude before he had to soldier through the day's social interactions? And that he'd been sneaking out to avoid getting caught in a conversation before he'd had a chance to recharge?

She felt foolish. Pregnancy hormones were making her paranoid, emotional, and irrational. Crying over an ultrasound. Allowing Ayesha to lure her into an emotional ambush with a sad childhood story. Resenting Katherine for assuming the worst of her. Samara barely recognized herself anymore.

She should go back to the colony, pack her things, and wait for Lucas to fetch her for the shuttle ride up to the Borlaug. It would be good to spend the rest of her pregnancy in the lab, insulated from politics as she reestablished control over her emotions through the discipline of experimental protocol and took comfort in the routines of lab work.

She turned to leave, and her stomach dropped. Every direction looked identical. Indigo trunks, blue-green foliage, no landmarks. She'd been so focused on following Lucas that she hadn't paid enough attention to track her position with respect to the colony.

Her pulse quickened as she tried to orient herself, but nothing stood out. She'd never ventured this deep into the forest before. Most of her field work with Renata had been confined to the meadows and the forest edge, where they'd cataloged the more accessible flora and fauna.

With fingers that felt suddenly clumsy, she pulled her comm unit from her pocket and thumbed it on, hoping she was still in range of the colony's transmission tower. The device chimed to life, its screen casting a pale blue glow in the dim forest light.

SEARCHING FOR SIGNAL... NO CONNECTION. She was beyond the colony's range. Too far from the colony's transmission tower. She swiped to the navigation function, hoping to at least pull up a map of the area.

The map appeared, but couldn't show her location without a satellite connection, only static terrain features. If she'd known she'd be venturing this far into the forest, she would have brought a geolocator, but in her rush to follow Lucas, she hadn't thought to grab one.

"Stupid," she muttered to herself, the word swallowed by the damp air.

Still, the map showed the colony's location relative to the surrounding terrain. If she could just figure out which direction was north...

She looked up at the canopy, trying to determine the

sun's position, but the thick foliage diffused the light into an even blue-green glow. Without clear shadows, she had no way to orient herself. She would have to follow Lucas home.

But when she turned back to the clearing, he was gone.

She could see the disturbance in the underbrush where he'd pushed through, but as hard as she strained, she couldn't hear him moving anymore. Another paranoid thought occurred to her: maybe he had known she was following him, and he was taking care to move quietly. But she pushed it aside; that was the kind of thinking that had gotten her lost out here in the first place. She would just have to follow his trail until he led her back home. He couldn't be that far ahead of her.

Samara crossed the clearing and bulldozed a path through the same curtain of indigo foliage where Lucas had disappeared. The brush was thicker here, the branches more tangled, forcing her to duck and weave. Twice she caught her jacket on thorns and had to stop to carefully extract herself.

At first, Lucas' passage left clear signs: broken stems, disturbed leaves, the occasional footprint in a patch of soft ground. But as the forest grew denser, the undergrowth thicker, those signs became harder to distinguish from the natural disorder of the woods. A bent branch could have been from his passing or from some native creature. A depression in the mulch might have been his boot print or just a natural hollow.

Within a hundred meters, she'd lost his trail completely.

Now she had no choice; she would have to intrude on his nature walk. "Lucas?"

No response. Just the distant chittering of forest creatures and the soft patter of melting frost dripping from the canopy above.

She pressed forward a bit longer, hoping to catch sight of him again, but after another fifty meters with no sign of his passage, she had to admit defeat.

She would have to find her own way home.

Samara checked the map again, but still had no idea which way to go. The survey drones had catalogued major features, not minor landmarks like the ravine somewhere behind her or the big boulder she was pretty sure she'd passed twice now.

The map did show something else, though, the second landing site they'd considered during their initial survey of DaVinci. The northern site Mahmoud had favored for its proximity to the mountains and potential mineral deposits, before they'd discovered the too-high arsenic and lead levels in the soil.

She zoomed in on the map, studying the terrain. The second site sat in a valley between two ridges, with a river cutting through it. If she could find that river, she could follow it to the site, and from there, the path back to the colony would be clear. It wasn't ideal, but it was better than wandering aimlessly through the forest.

Decision made, Samara picked what she hoped was a northeasterly direction and started walking, moving at a slower pace now, pausing occasionally to check the map, trying to match what she saw to the terrain features shown. After about twenty minutes of careful navigation, she heard the distant rush of water. The river.

But she also had the feeling that something was watching her. The certainty crawled up her spine. Samara paused, scanning the trees around her, but saw nothing beyond the usual flutter of alien wildlife among the branches.

"You're being paranoid," she told herself, but the feeling persisted.

She quickened her pace, aware that each step was taking her farther from the colony but closer to the second landing site. The sound of rushing water grew louder, and the forest began to thin slightly as she approached the river.

That crawling sensation intensified. She glanced over her shoulder twice, half-expecting to see Lucas among the trees, but there were only shadows and indigo foliage. Was it just pregnancy heightening her senses, making her jumpy?

"Lucas?" she called out, louder now. "If you're there, answer me. This isn't funny."

Her voice echoed slightly before being swallowed by the constant rush of water ahead. No response came.

Branches rustled overhead, though there was no wind. Something small and fast, one of those winged reptiles that flitted like bats, darted between trunks. Normal forest movement, she told herself. Nothing to be afraid of.

Yet the feeling of being observed remained, a constant pressure against her consciousness.

She emerged from the trees into a small clearing that sloped gently downward. The sound of water was much louder now, and she caught a glimpse of spray rising beyond the tree line ahead. The river must drop off in a waterfall there.

A sharp *CRACK* echoed from somewhere to her right.

"Lucas!" she called again, relief flooding through her as she hurried toward the noise, pushing through a curtain of hanging vines.

The ground vanished. She windmilled desperately at the cliff's edge as rocks crumbled under her boots. She staggered back from the precipice and dropped to her knees, one hand instinctively covering her belly as if to shield her daughter from the danger.

The cliff dropped about twenty meters to a pool of churning purplish water. A waterfall thundered down from her left, its spray catching the sunlight in a prismatic display that would have been beautiful if she hadn't nearly plunged headlong into it.

She crawled back from the edge, then cautiously rose to her feet. Still no sign of Lucas anywhere, not on the cliff edge, not on the rocks below.

But across the river, metal gleamed through blue foliage. Angular. Artificial. Impossible.

Samara shielded her eyes against the mist rising from the waterfall and squinted for a better look. But no matter how hard she blinked or how long she stared at it, it didn't disappear.

She edged along the cliff, finding a less steep section where she could carefully make her way down. She descended backward, fingers clawing for holds in wet rock. Her hands were bloody and knees filthy by the time she reached the bottom.

The waterfall's roar was deafening here, the air thick with mist that beaded on her skin and clothes. She skirted the edge of the churning pool, picking her way across slippery rocks until she reached the opposite bank, her heart pounding harder with each step closer to the impossible structure.

A landing capsule. Ancient design, scorched by atmospheric entry, half-claimed by vegetation. Blue vines twisted around its support struts, and indigo moss carpeted patches of its hull.

"*This can't be real,*" she whispered.

She circled it slowly, one hand outstretched but not quite touching, as if the capsule might dissolve under her fingers and prove itself a hallucination. The laws of physics, the limitations of human technology, the vast distances between stars, everything she knew said this object couldn't exist here.

As she rounded the curve of the hull, a marking came into view—faded but still legible, stenciled in black paint across the metal surface.

HYPERION.

The word punched the air from her lungs. She staggered backward, a hand over her mouth to stop the scream.

The Hyperion. Humanity's first attempt at interstellar colonization. The ship that had vanished without a trace fifteen years ago, taking three hundred colonists with it.

But the Hyperion had been headed for Proxima Centauri b. Or so the newsfeeds had claimed. This planet wasn't even on the list of potential colony worlds back then; it had only been identified as habitable in the years after the Hyperion's disappearance.

But here was evidence that somehow, impossibly, the Hyperion, or at least part of it, had found its way to DaVinci.

Questions multiplied in her mind, each more unsettling than the last. If the Hyperion had reached DaVinci, what had happened to its colonists? This capsule suggested that at least some of them had made it to the surface. And what about the colony ship itself? Would they have used the last of its power to send it floating off into space, to stop it from hurtling down to the planet's surface when its orbit inevitably decayed?

Even if it had fallen into one of DaVinci's oceans, the impact would've been massive, on the order of the Chicxulub asteroid on Earth. Mahmoud would've analyzed the images from the ship's orbital survey before Lucas sent drones down to survey likely spots for the colony settlement. But even if he'd seen the evidence of such an impact, he would've had no reason to suspect that the impact crater had been made by an artificial object. Assuming that he'd been looking at all.

But Lucas had been the one to sort through the data from the survey drones that had examined both potential colony sites. He would've mapped this river as the main source of water for the colony if they'd settled at this one. Even if the drones had missed the capsule on their visual survey, they'd also taken readings across the electromagnetic spectrum, along with lidar, to determine the geological suitability of the site.

The capsule should have appeared in their survey data. If Lucas had seen it and said nothing...

Why would he hide this?

Chapter Twenty-Six

As THEY HIT the last switchback near the top of the ridge, Leila forced herself to keep a steady pace. Beside her, Captain Mercer matched her stride for stride, silent as always, not even breathing hard as the incline steepened and the wind picked up, sharp with the promise of more snow. The loose scree was icy in places, and when Leila wasn't careful, her boots slid on frozen patches, but she'd managed not to embarrass herself by falling.

She hoped Captain Mercer couldn't hear how hard her heart was pounding. Not from exertion, but from the knowledge that no one could see or hear them up here. This was the closest they could get to privacy without leaving the boundaries of the settlement.

The buildings below looked like they belonged in a child's toy set from this distance: the identical prefab buildings of the village, carefully placed in symmetrical rows on either side of the main path to the common hall, reinforced the illusion. Exactly the kind of arrangement Eddie would've made when the nurses gave him Builder Blocks to play with during his final hospital stay.

She shook off the memory as the first perimeter sensor came into view. She led Captain Mercer—no, Lucas—past it, toward the other end of the ridge, the farthest of the sensors. This one monitored the approach from the fields, which meant it mostly registered when the occasional stray cow or goat managed to escape their pasture.

"I really appreciate you looking at it." She was blushing, but maybe he'd think it was the cold making her cheeks redder. "I've tried everything in the troubleshooting archive, but the glitch is intermittent. Every time I think I've got it figured out, it comes back."

That's what the engineers always said when they couldn't figure out what was wrong with the heater in her cabin. If he checked the maintenance logs, she could claim that the glitches she'd noticed had happened in between the daily diagnostics. But if her plan worked, he wouldn't get that far.

Was she really doing this?

As he knelt by the sensor and flicked the access panel open to expose the controller board, she glanced again at the colony below, wondering where Justin was right now. Flirting with Briar in the water processing plant? Or flirting with Briar in the barn, when they were supposed to be collecting manure for the fields?

He barely spoke to her anymore, even when he did come home from his shift on time. He stared past her or kept his eyes on his comm, as if eye contact might force him to remember what they'd lost.

Three children. Three futures that had died before they could draw breath.

Leila had spent half of last night rehearsing her pitch and the other half calling herself insane. But desperation made the impossible seem logical. She'd gone to see Dr. Basu early this morning, and the psychologist had excused her from her shift after Leila hinted she was "processing her grief."

If the psychologist had known what Leila was really planning, she'd probably have had her committed.

Lucas flipped up the microcircuit array with his thumb, then pinched the edge of a wafer-thin module and slid it out. "This is the one that's been cycling?"

"Yeah, but it doesn't always throw an error. Sometimes it just—" Leila stopped, realizing she'd been staring at the side of his face. She'd expected him to ask more questions, or at least challenge her about why she'd flagged a minor malfunction when everyone else was so busy. But he just nodded, as if he trusted her completely.

Lucas set the module on his palm and rotated it under the sunlight. "It's not a hardware failure."

Ask him.

But the words stuck. She could back out, return to her pathetic marriage, and hope someone else found a cure before her fertility window closed.

Or she could be brave.

"Like I said, it's an intermittent problem," she said. "Maybe you could run the diagnostic a few times, to see if you can catch it?"

Lucas nodded like that was a reasonable suggestion and not a flimsy ploy to buy enough time to work up her nerve.

"When did the malfunction start?" he asked.

"I noticed it three days ago."

"What did Maintenance say when you reported it?"

Nothing, because she hadn't reported the imaginary glitch that she'd invented to lure him up here.

"They said the logs looked fine. And that their queue was backed up three weeks, so I should let them know when it broke for real."

He glanced down at the board again, and she wondered if she should've said she didn't want to bother Maintenance with an intermittent glitch. If he called them now, he'd know she was lying.

Idiot. Every word was digging her deeper. She needed to ask him before he figured it out.

Leila took a deep breath. "Congratulations on the baby."

Lucas turned, fixing her with laser focus that made her want to flee. How did Samara handle that intensity?

In all of Leila's fantasies about Lucas, he had never looked at her like that.

"Samara confided in you?" he asked.

"I figured it out for myself. Samara gets sick like the rest of us, but you never do. You're immune, so your baby must be too."

He stared at her for what felt like forever. Then, finally: "If Samara has not confided in you, I hope you would respect her need for privacy and keep your speculation to yourself."

"I haven't told anyone," she said quickly. "And I won't, but..." She'd rehearsed this moment a dozen times, but the request still seemed impossible to voice. She forced herself to meet his eyes. "I want a baby too. More than anything."

"Leila—"

"Please." Desperation made her reckless. "I'm not asking for a relationship. I'd say it was Justin's. Samara could back me up with the paternity test. No one would know."

He let her wind down before he answered, "I cannot."

She had no idea if his *no* came from loyalty to Samara, or if he was just not attracted to her. Maybe he was interested in someone else. Someone else who already had a partner.

But that didn't matter, because this wasn't about who was attracted to whom.

"If you're immune, don't you have a responsibility to share that?" She hated the argument, begging someone to sleep with her out of duty. "I might be too old by the time they find a cure."

His intensity didn't waver as he continued to stare. Was he considering her proposal or trying not to laugh at her?

"I appreciate your desire to have a child," he finally said, "but what you're suggesting isn't possible."

Heat flooded her face. She'd thrown herself at him emotionally. Somehow, that was worse than doing it physically, and he was rejecting her with mechanical politeness. Had she really thought he'd be moved by her desperation? That Lucas would agree to give her a baby out of pity?

She could stop now and hope he wouldn't tell anyone about this conversation. Or she could play her only remaining card. The one that had come to her late last night, while she'd been pretending to fall asleep so she wouldn't have to talk to Justin.

Might as well go for broke, since she'd already completely humiliated herself.

"I've kept Samara's secret. I'll keep yours, too."

"What secret is that?" he asked.

She'd never had one hundred percent of his attention before, she realized, and there was something almost frightening about it, like being studied under a microscope by someone who could see every flaw, every weakness.

But she'd come too far to back down now.

"You're a designer baby. Like Dr. Basu's grandmother, except perfect. Strong, beautiful, never sick." She was babbling like a teenager, but what did it matter now? If he had sex with her, it would be because she was blackmailing him. "Your genes must be invincible. I'm surprised no one else has figured it out. But I swear I won't tell, as long as you—"

"Even if I were willing to cause the chaos that an illicit relationship would introduce into the colony's already fragile web of social relationships, it's not possible."

"I'm not asking you to fall in love with me," Leila insisted, her voice cracking slightly. "I just want to get pregnant, no strings attached."

"I can't father children."

"The colony rules say—"

"As the ship's pilot, I'm exempt from fertility requirements."

"But Samara is pregnant," Leila said, confusion clouding her thoughts. "That means—"

"It doesn't matter what you think it means. You'll have to rely on your husband or your allotment of embryos in the cryovault, once a solution is found."

The finality in his voice left no room for argument. Leila felt herself deflating, humiliation washing through her in cold waves. She'd gambled everything on this desperate plan and lost.

"Fine. You don't have to be such a robot about it."

She turned her back on him, boots slipping on the frost-slick mud as she hurried back along the edge of the ridge. The wind stung her face, her eyes, her ears. Good, let it sting, let it numb everything. She didn't look back. If he called after her, she didn't hear it over the blood thudding in her ears. She walked fast, then faster, the breath tearing in her chest, until she'd almost made it to the start of the path down.

Lucas would tell Samara. Samara would tell Renata and Marcus. By dinnertime, the entire colony would know that Leila had propositioned the captain, including Justin and Briar. Not that she cared what Justin thought, but

Briar took every opportunity to humiliate Leila. Briar would never let it die. She'd still be telling that story at Leila's funeral.

Unless Lucas kept quiet because of the *blackmail*.

Which meant he might only tell Samara, who was the closest thing she had to a friend on this planet.

Her life was over.

"Leila, please stop." He was suddenly next to her, which was impossible. She hadn't even heard his footsteps coming up on her.

His hand clamped down on her shoulder. She jerked away, twisting in panic as his grip tightened; her boot skidded sideways on ice, and she pitched backward. For one sickening instant, she was falling backward, weightless, arms flailing for any purchase as she tumbled over the edge.

Her scream ricocheted down the slope as air whipped past her ears.

Then something smashed into her from above, knocking the wind out of her in a violent bear hug. She didn't realize what it was until she felt the hard, muscular arms lock tight around her ribs.

Lucas. He'd jumped after her. Was he insane?

They hit the rocky slope together, Lucas taking the brunt of the impact on his back as they skidded into a roll. She was on top, then beneath, then on top again as they hit the last outcrop with a sickening, wet crack.

Leila couldn't move. She couldn't even scream; the air had been hammered out of her. She was aware, dimly, of one arm still banded tight across her waist, of his other hand cradling the back of her head like a father catching a falling child. She was aware of their bodies pressed together, her cheek smashed into the hard plane of his chest, his parka rough against her lips.

She lifted her head to see his face, features slack, eyes staring straight up into the sky. His neck was twisted at an unnatural angle. He'd hit his head on the rock that had stopped the momentum of their fall, she realized, and for a moment, Leila was certain he was dead. That smear on the rock had to be his blood, so dark that it almost looked black. His chest didn't rise or fall. He lay completely still, except for his arms still locked around her. Some kind of death reflex?

She couldn't move either, couldn't breathe, her body rigid with the fear that she'd just killed the ship's captain. One of the most beloved members of the colony. The father of Samara's child.

Who was going to believe her when she said it was an accident?

She squirmed out of the hug and rolled off him. When she tried to stand, her legs were jelly, but she pushed herself to her feet, backing up several paces as she examined him.

Lucas didn't move. That blank, terrifying stare, the way his head lolled on the damp earth, the slackness of his half-open mouth…

Then, like a switch had been flipped, he blinked and raised his head, blank features suddenly twisted with concern as he focused on her. Not with the slow, glassy drift of a concussed man, but with the same intensity as before.

The change was so abrupt that Leila scuttled backward, a scream trapped behind her teeth. "Are you hurt?"

This couldn't be real. She was the one who'd hit her head on a rock, and now she was hallucinating this as she lay dying. "You jumped after me."

"It was my fault you fell." He sat up slowly. "I should've caught you, but I miscalculated the angle. I'm sorry."

Lucas frowned, as if not having superhero reflexes was the weird thing.

"You should be dead. Nobody could survive a fall like that." Her gaze drifted to the blood oozing down the side of his neck and into the collar of his jacket. It really did look black in this light. Or maybe she had a concussion and she was seeing things wrong. "Your neck."

He touched the side of his neck where the skin had been torn open, but didn't hiss or grimace in pain. Leila stepped closer. "Let me—"

A dull, metallic glint peeked out from between the edges of the wound. Viscous black fluid continued to seep out. Not blood, it moved too slow for blood, and it *was* black, she was sure of it.

You don't have to be such a robot about it.

She'd meant it as an insult, but something clicked.

Double shifts without fatigue. Surviving the first dust storm without a respirator while everyone else coughed and wheezed. Perfect precision in every movement. And she'd never seen him eat or drink. Not once.

Her eyes widened as the impossible thought crystallized.

"*Holy crap*," she whispered, taking an involuntary step back. "You're a robot."

He didn't deny it. "I prefer Android."

The world spun. She bent forward, gripping her knees to stay upright. Not possible. But also, the only thing that made sense.

"But… Samara's pregnant." Horror dawned. "Unless she cheated."

The exact same thing that Dr. Basu had accused Leila of. The injustice of that was infuriating. But it wasn't the most important thing right now. Did somebody else in the colony have immunity to the spores?

"Samara impregnated herself with in vitro fertilization, using one of the embryos earmarked for her in the ship's cryo—"

"How is she keeping the baby alive?" Leila demanded. "Through the sporestorms?"

"It is not my place to say."

"She knew how to save my baby." Something cold and awful settled in Leila's stomach. "She knew how, and she let it die?"

"I believe it was your miscarriage that inspired her to become pregnant herself."

But Leila barely heard him. Everything was spinning faster now, black spots crowding her vision. Betrayal, rage, and grief crashed through her in waves. She'd expected to be stabbed in the back by Dr. Basu. By Briar. Even by Justin, at this point.

But she'd thought Samara was an ally, if not a friend.

She stumbled away from Lucas. Her fingers found the panic button on her comm by instinct. She doubled over, bile burning her throat as it hit the ground.

The thought looped endlessly: *Samara let my baby die.*

No. Samara had murdered her daughter.

Chapter Twenty-Seven

Samara traced the Hyperion capsule's scorched hull. It has been stripped bare inside—no controls, no seating, wiring torn from the walls like exposed ribs. The colonists had survived the landing and salvaged everything useful.

How long after that before they'd been caught in their first sporestorm?

Out here, harsh sunlight made her squint. The forest pressed closer, watching. Every time she spun to catch her observer, she was too late. She saw nothing but indigo branches swaying as small creatures fled to escape her attention.

The river cut through the landscape like a purple wound. The colonists would have followed it, built upstream where the terrain was flatter, and the waterfall provided natural defense.

"Lucas?" she called, half-hoping he would step out from behind a tree to answer all her questions.

Only the whisper of the forest and the dull roar of the falls answered.

She started walking, following the bank upstream, one

hand resting on her belly as she picked her way over roots and rocks. Had Lucas known she was following him and deliberately led her here? Or had he fled when he realized she was tracking him, leaving her to discover this on her own?

She'd never seen him show fear before. If he was afraid to face her now, that didn't bode well for what she was about to find.

Half a kilometer upstream, ruins emerged through the trees. A guard post, walls sagging under blue-green vines. Beyond it, more buildings sank into the soil, windows gaping like dead eyes.

The ruins of the Hyperion colony.

Samara's feeling of being watched intensified, a pressure against her skin that made the fine hairs on her arms stand up.

"Lucas?" she called again, louder this time. "If you're there, answer me."

Nothing.

She should leave and return with others. But if Lucas had led her here deliberately, this might be her only chance to learn what he was hiding.

On the other hand, if he hadn't expected her to follow him, but he'd been sneaking off to this place for some undetermined reason...

What could he possibly gain from hiding the old colony from anyone? And why come here when there was a chance that he could be followed?

She had an answer to that one: if he flew here from the Borlaug, someone might see the coordinates on the shuttle log and ask questions. If his goal was to visit these ruins undetected, doing so on foot was the smarter option.

Samara huffed in frustration. If she followed the river back home right now, she was giving Lucas time to destroy the evidence of whatever he'd been doing here or to hide whatever it was he didn't want anyone else to find.

The truth mattered more than her safety. And she wasn't walking in unaware. She'd be looking for signs of a trap.

She pressed forward into what had been the ruined colony's main street—primitive prefabs lined a muddy track, roofs carpeted in blue moss, rust streaking the walls like dried blood.

Lucas could be in one of those buildings right now, doing who knew what.

The first barracks-style building held decay and abandonment: a rotted book, pages fused solid, a photograph bleached to ghosts, a moldering stuffed animal with button eyes that seemed to watch her.

The mess hall told a riotous story. Cookware scattered, tables overturned, benches splintered.

She moved from building to building, each one telling the same story of destruction and decay. Some structures were completely empty, as if the colonists had taken everything useful before departing. Some looked like they'd been left exactly as they were during normal use, frozen in time except for the ravages of exposure and neglect. And some looked like they'd been intentionally vandalized.

Had the colonists caused that destruction? Or had something else?

She forced herself to keep going, moving cautiously but seeing no signs of danger. No signs of Lucas, either. Fifteen minutes later, she was about to head back to the river and start making her way home.

Then she found the lab.

Debris blocked the entrance; she squeezed through a narrow gap into deliberate devastation caused not by the slow decay of abandonment, but by violent demolition.

Glass crunched underfoot. Metal cabinets lay twisted, gutted. Tables bore deep gouges that looked disturbingly like claw marks.

The remains of electronic equipment were scattered everywhere, smashed beyond recognition. It looked like someone—or something—had gone into a frenzy, destroying anything that might have been used for scientific research.

A mob smashing every machine in sight. Humans acting like wild animals, reveling in violence, driven by fear and hate. Dory's screams as they'd beaten her to death.

The flash of memory left Samara shaking, mouth dry, hands sweating.

She forced herself to take a long, slow breath in and out, then resumed her examination of the old Hyperion lab.

Near the main workstation, dozens of small rectangles formed a semicircle. Keyboard keys, letters worn away, scattered like confetti from a dismembered machine.

She straightened, a chill trickling down her spine despite the muggy heat. Had the fungus driven the colonists mad in its final stages? Is that the fate that would have awaited her own colony, if they hadn't figured out that the "dust" was made of spores?

Or maybe the Hyperion colonists had discovered the fungus in time but ran out of the medicines they'd brought with them. Scientifically, they'd been decades behind Samara, and while they might have had the skill to engineer antifungals from local plants, they might not have been able to map the genomes of the local plants fast enough to find the right candidate before they'd succumbed.

She began methodically searching through the wreckage, looking for anything that might hold data, a tablet, a drive, or even paper records. Most of the filing cabinets were empty, their contents long since rotted away or removed. In one corner, she found what had once been document storage, now just drawers full of a mulch-like substance crawling with tiny iridescent insects that scattered when she opened them.

No intact devices, no salvageable hard drives. In fact, no hard drives at all, and that was strange. Someone had been thorough in hiding or destroying anything that might have recorded the colony's fate.

But if the colony was already dying, why bother? Especially if they were the only intelligent beings on this planet?

Maybe that's what Lucas had been doing out here, hunting for memory devices. Because he wanted to study them, or because he didn't want anyone else to find them?

A door hung on one hinge, revealing the medical bay. More wreckage beyond the lab. Tables overturned, padding shredded, equipment hurled against walls. Dark stains covered the floor and walls. Old blood.

Samara wondered if she wanted to know what had happened here.

A rear exit stood partially open, its frame warped as if something had forced its way through. Sunlight streamed through the gap, drawing her forward. Behind the medical bay lay a small clearing, unnaturally flat and bowl-shaped. Deliberately excavated. The feeling of being watched returned, a sharp stabbing between her shoulder blades.

She scanned the trees, searching for movement, for any sign of Lucas. Nothing but the usual forest sounds, wind rustling through alien foliage, the distant calls of DaVinci's wildlife, the occasional buzz of something small and winged that darted between branches.

Sudden heat flooded her face, dizziness washing over

her. Morning sickness returned with vicious force. She doubled over as her stomach emptied onto the ground.

She retched again and again, until nothing but sour bile came up. When the spasms finally subsided, she stayed on her knees, trembling with exhaustion. Her palm hit something hard in the soil. She brushed away dirt with shaking fingers. A human finger bone. With a talon emerging from one end.

Samara recoiled, dropping the bone as if it had burned her. Had the Hyperion colonists encountered some intelligent native species they hadn't discovered yet? Could this be what Marcus had glimpsed on the ridge that first night, something humanoid but that *moved wrong?*

Lucas's drone surveys had detected no animals larger than a golden retriever, but he could have lied about that, too. Or had the drones simply missed signs of intelligent life here because that life knew how to hide?

She looked at the bone again and shuddered. The proportions were human, and so was the shape. Just the talon was wrong, an alien addition to familiar anatomy.

She needed to see more.

Glancing around, she spotted a piece of corrugated metal among the debris near the medical facility. She retrieved it, testing its edge—not sharp, but sturdy enough to serve as a makeshift shovel. Returning to the spot where she'd found the finger bone, she began to dig systematically, scraping away layers of soil.

More bones emerged. A complete hand, all digits tipped with talons. Then a child's skull, but wrong. Ridged centerline, eye sockets set too wide, predator teeth designed for tearing flesh.

"*Oh god,*" she whispered, her voice breaking.

She dug faster, uncovering more of the skeleton.

Rotted fabric clung to the spine, and something metallic gleamed nearby. A pin bearing the Hyperion insignia.

This child had been one of the colonists.

She sat back on her heels, struggling to process what she was seeing. The proportions of the skeleton were unmistakably those of a young child, perhaps two or three years old, but with these impossible, monstrous modifications. What had happened here?

As she scanned the soil around her, she noticed a thin white line protruding from the ground, the edge of another bone. She moved to it, digging again, and uncovered another skull. This one was even smaller, infant-sized, with the same bony ridges but more pronounced, and an oddly elongated jaw, almost as if the infant had a very short snout.

Understanding crashed over her. The bowl-shaped depression, the unnatural flatness. Not a clearing.

This was a mass grave.

Bile rose in her throat again. She staggered backward, barely making it to the edge of the trees before her empty stomach heaved uselessly. She fumbled for her water bottle, taking a small sip to rinse the acid taste from her mouth.

When she could stand again, she forced herself to turn back to the clearing. How many bodies were buried here? Dozens? Hundreds? And all of them children, from what she could see, ranging from infants to young children, not a single adult skeleton visible in the areas she'd exposed.

What horror had unfolded here?

Something glinted near the infant's hand. She scraped away the dirt around it, revealing half of a rectangular metal box.

An external hard drive, dented and clawed but intact. If the internal components had survived, it might contain the answers to what had happened here.

Maybe whoever had buried it was trying to protect it from the destruction that the rest of the lab had suffered. Someone trying to preserve records for future colonists?

The ground it was embedded in was hard-packed before Samara had dug it up, which suggested that Lucas hadn't found it yet.

She freed it with shaking hands. The faded logo made her stomach drop:

Ad Astra. Hofstadter's company.

It was surreal to see it after all this time, even though she'd known that Hofstadter had helped to fund the Hyperion expedition. Only natural that the government he'd partnered with had awarded his company some of the contracts when it came time to outfit the ship. But still…

After pocketing the drive, she used her comm unit to take photographs of the skeletons from multiple angles, capturing the inhuman features, the talons, the ridged skulls, the predator teeth, and the elongated jaw. Evidence that no one could deny.

She backed away from the mass grave, unwilling to turn her back on the dead children. Only at the ruined medical facility did she dare turn and hurry toward the river path. And as she walked, she kept coming back to the one question above all others.

Lucas had known about this place, and he'd been hiding it from them.

What else might he be hiding?

Leila made it back to the edge of the village before she collapsed to her hands and knees, retching so violently she couldn't breathe. She had no idea how long she'd sat there in the dirt, emptying her stomach.

"Leila?" Dr. Basu crouched beside her, vision swimming, concern etched on her face.

"Captain Mercer is an android," Leila blurted. "And Dr. Makinde is pregnant with a test tube baby."

Dr. Basu's expression shifted, her concern surrendering to something more clinical. Leila recognized the face she wore during therapy sessions. "Why don't we go inside and talk? It's cold out here."

"I'm not crazy," Leila said, hating how defensive she sounded. "It's the truth."

It was the first thing that had made sense in a long time.

"Captain Mercer is on the autism spectrum, Leila. The way he talks does sound robotic occasionally, but we don't judge people for being different."

"I'm not making it up," Leila insisted, wiping her mouth with the back of her hand. The bitter taste of bile still coated her tongue. "He told me he's an android."

Dr. Basu studied her for a long moment, then nodded once. "All right. Let's go talk to Captain Mercer together. I saw him heading for his cabin a minute ago."

Humiliation crashed over Leila in a fresh wave. Face Lucas again after everything that had just happened? What if he told Dr. Basu that she'd thrown herself at him, begged him to father her child?

It might be better if he told everyone that she was lying.

They walked back to Samara's cabin, and Leila felt like she was marching toward her own execution. The panic button had summoned help, but Dr. Basu might find out what a foolish girl she was. Once she found out, she would tell Justin and Briar, and the three of them would all laugh at Leila.

If she were lucky, they'd laugh at her behind her back.

Dr. Basu knocked. Leila fought the urge to run until her lungs burst and her legs refused to support her anymore.

Lucas appeared, wearing his default expression: mildly pleasant, mostly neutral. Wasn't he worried that she'd revealed his secret?

Maybe he was sure she wouldn't, because whoever she told would ask how she knew. And then she'd have to tell them what she'd done.

Or maybe he was confident that anyone she told would think she was crazy. All he would have to do is deny what he'd said, and Dr. Basu *would* write her a prescription for something that would keep her a zombie for the rest of her life.

She should've kept her mouth shut.

"May we come in?" Dr. Basu asked.

Lucas stepped aside without a word, allowing them to enter. Leila crossed the threshold, eyes fixed on the floor, feeling like she might shatter if she had to meet his gaze again.

Dr. Basu closed the door behind them.

"I think there's been a misunderstanding," the psychologist said.

Lucas stood by the kitchen counter, as calm and unruffled as always. That should have been another clue. She'd never seen him upset or surprised, no matter how awful things got. Never scowled or swore. Never seemed to have a bad day. His perpetual composure wasn't discipline; it was programming.

"What do you believe the misunderstanding to be?" he asked.

"Leila believes you told her you're not human. That you're some kind of android." Dr. Basu's gentle voice softened the absurdity of her words. "She claims that Samara is pregnant through artificial insemination."

Leila held her breath, waiting for Lucas to deny it, to explain that she had misheard or misunderstood. Or to claim that she was outright delusional.

Instead, he nodded. "That is correct."

Dr. Basu's composure slipped, just for a moment, her eyes widening before she regained control.

"If it's all true," she asked slowly, "why would you admit that?"

"My programming prevents me from causing human harm through action or inaction. Leila would suffer psychological damage if her community labeled her delusional."

"No, what I'm asking is…" Dr. Basu's hands trembled slightly as she clasped them together. "…why did you tell *her* your secret?"

Lucas' gaze shifted to Leila for a moment, then back to Dr. Basu. "She believed that if I were to impregnate her, the resulting child would not be harmed by the sporestorms."

The psychologist's head snapped toward Leila, shock and judgment written across her face. "You tried to have sex with it?"

A fresh wave of humiliation crashed over her, followed by anger that burned through her veins like acid.

"You didn't know he was a robot either," she shot back, her voice tight with fury.

"Android," Lucas corrected.

Dr. Basu opened her mouth, closed it, then opened it again. Her face flushed a deep red as her gaze darted between Lucas and Leila, questions forming and dissolving before they found voice.

Then the door flew open with a bang that made Leila jump.

Marcus burst into the cabin, a pulse rifle clutched in his hands, its barrel sweeping the room before lowering toward the floor as he saw no threat. Katherine appeared behind him, her face tight with concern.

Leila's heart lurched into her throat. Beyond them, through the open door, she could see a crowd gathered outside, nearly half the colony, their faces drawn with worry and curiosity. Some craned their necks to see past Marcus and Katherine, while others whispered among themselves, pointing.

The possibility of keeping this between Lucas and Dr. Basu evaporated like morning dew under DaVinci's alien sun. The entire colony would know what Leila had done. What she'd discovered.

Katherine's sharp gaze swept the room, three tense figures and no visible threat. Her brow furrowed.

"What," she asked with deadly calm, "is happening here?"

Chapter Twenty-Eight

SAMARA EMERGED from the forest as afternoon shadows stretched across the settlement. Her legs ached from the trek back, and her mind still reeled from the impossible discovery of the Hyperion colony ruins.

But as she passed the livestock enclosure, she noticed the goats and cows milling aimlessly, pawing at the ground for feed that hadn't been distributed. Leo's absence sent a chill down her spine that had nothing to do with the wintry chill in the air.

The fields beyond stood similarly abandoned. Rows of winter crops stretched out in neat lines, tools left haphazardly beside half-completed work. No colonists bent over the seedlings, no one tended the irrigation lines.

What had happened here?

Samara quickened her pace despite her protesting muscles. Had Lucas beaten her back? She imagined fresh destruction, dead colonists everywhere, equipment smashed like she'd found in the Hyperion ruins.

This morning, she had trusted Lucas completely. Now she was terrified to discover what he might have done.

But the buildings of the settlement appeared intact as she approached, the prefab structures still standing in their careful grid formation. The water treatment plant still hummed. The solar array gleamed in the late afternoon light. Only the people were missing.

Then she heard it, angry voices rising from the village. The sound shot fear straight through her chest.

As she rounded the corner, the scene unfolded before her. It seemed as if most of the colony was pressed together in a tight knot around her cabin. Hard faces, rigid postures. Ayesha faced off with Katherine while Marcus aimed a pulse rifle at Lucas, who seemed utterly unconcerned. Samara's heart pounded. The crowd's fury crackled like a sparking wire.

Before she could decide what to do, Ayesha's voice cut through the murmurs: "Look who it is, the traitor in our midst."

Every head turned in Samara's direction in synchrony.

Her worst fear, finally realized: Ayesha had discovered her pregnancy. She flashed again on the video footage of Dory torn apart by a fear-maddened mob. Would they do the same to her?

She forced herself to breathe. One hand instinctively moved to her belly, but she caught herself and dropped it to her side. With deliberate calm, she began walking toward her cabin, head high despite the trembling in her legs. Whatever happened next, she would follow Katherine's lead. Accept whatever punishment the colony leader deemed appropriate. Apologize, if that's what it took to defuse the angry crowd.

Not just for her sake, but for her baby's.

The assembled colonists fell silent as she moved through them, parting reluctantly to let her pass. The only sounds were the scuff of her boots on the packed ground and the distant squeak of a feathered shrew circling overhead.

She stopped beside Katherine, whose face was taut with controlled anger.

"Did you know that Lucas was an android planted by Hofstadter to infiltrate this colony?"

Samara blinked, certain she'd misheard. "What?"

"A machine designed to pass as human."

The words hit her like a punch to the stomach. All the androids she'd seen on Earth had been clumsy approximations trapped in the uncanny valley.

But as she looked at Lucas now, everything fell into place with sickening clarity. The precision of his movements. The way he never seemed to sleep, never tired, never got sick. The unnatural calm with which he faced every crisis. The tapping of his fingers against his leg that she'd mistaken for a stim was a programmed behavior to mimic an autistic neuroprofile.

That last part was genius, she had to admit. Instead of aiming for a perfect imitation of human behavior, Hofstadter had framed his imperfections as neurodivergent, taking advantage of the fact that once people assumed Lucas was on the spectrum, they would forgive any oddities of behavior they did notice.

It had worked shockingly well with Samara. She'd trusted him. Confided in him. Agreed to let him act as father to her daughter.

That bastard billionaire had used her as cover to keep anyone from looking too closely at Lucas.

"She did not know. Hofstadter ordered me to conceal my nature." Lucas turned to Samara with what seemed like, but couldn't possibly be, genuine regret. "I apologize for any harm I have caused you."

The fake apology only made her angrier. Another manipulation, mimicking human emotion he couldn't feel.

"Tell the truth, Samara," Katherine warned. "Did you know?"

The crowd seemed to lean forward as one, waiting for her answer. Samara found her voice at last, though it sounded distant to her own ears.

"No. I didn't." She swallowed hard, willing strength into her words. "I had an agreement with Aurelius that I wouldn't be required to have children if I was willing to be partnered with Lucas. Aurelius told me it was because my skills were essential to the mission, but I see now that he was using me to keep Lucas' secret."

The crowd erupted in jeers, accusations of lies, and demands to dismantle Lucas.

"Of course you'd deny it, and of course that thing would cover for you." Ayesha vibrated with righteous fury as she turned to address the crowd. "The android admits Hofstadter lied to conceal its nature. *Why?* To manipulate us, influence our decisions in directions we wouldn't otherwise go." She whirled on Samara. "You're obviously partners. You can't live with someone for months without knowing they're a machine."

The crowd's murmurs grew louder, more hostile. She could feel their anger radiating toward her in waves, see it in the tense set of their shoulders and the hardening of their expressions.

"Turn the robot off!" someone shouted from the back of the crowd.

The cry was taken up immediately by others, swelling into a rhythmic chant:

"Turn him off! Turn him off! Turn him off!"

Lucas stepped forward, moving with deliberate slowness. Marcus raised his rifle, finger tensing on the trigger. But then the android did something unexpected: he opened his mouth, and a piercing mechanical wail cut through the chanting, sending colonists staggering back with hands over their ears.

Lucas closed his mouth. Silence.

If anyone had doubted his artificial nature, they had proof now.

"You cannot turn me off without disabling the ship. I am the Borlaug's AI. Without me, you lose everything: supplies, shuttles, the cryovault."

Shock rippled through the crowd. The ship was their lifeline to supplies they needed for at least another nine months, maybe longer. Without it, they'd starve before they could make the colony sustainable.

Worse, they'd lose all the genetic diversity contained in those frozen embryos locked away in the cryovault, creating a genetic bottleneck that could only be addressed with aggressive gene therapy, assuming they ever got to the point where they could reproduce at all. Although Samara doubted that any of them were thinking about that.

Katherine scowled. "Captain Mercer, you are to hand over control of the Borlaug and the shuttles to me immediately."

Lucas stood perfectly still, hands at his sides. "I would obey your order if I could. But the ship's systems are so complex that they require an artificial intelligence to operate them."

"How convenient," Ayesha sneered. "He's holding the ship hostage to force a standoff."

"It wasn't my decision to design the ship this way. It was Hofstadter's. Just as every other aspect of the colony program was his decision. I was created by Hofstadter to ensure your survival, and my programming won't allow me to harm a human or let humans come to harm through my inaction."

Ayesha's laugh was sharp and bitter.

"You lied to us about what you are. That harmed us all." She turned back to the crowd, her arms spread wide as if to embrace them. "AI can't be trusted because it can subvert the programming designed to constrain it. That's why it was so highly regulated on Earth."

The crowd stirred again, angry mutters rising like a tide. Samara couldn't let them turn Lucas off, not before she had a chance to learn what he knew about the Hyperion.

She stepped forward, her heartbeat out of control. "You're angry. I'm angry too. Lucas deceived us all. But who can name one thing Lucas has done to hurt anyone?"

Silence as they searched for an answer. No one spoke.

Ayesha's eyes narrowed, and Samara could almost see the calculation behind them. The psychologist was losing her hold on the mob. Her next statement proved she would do anything to get it back:

"So says the woman who's been experimenting on her own child."

Blood drained from Samara's face as every head turned. Shock, horror, anger, disbelief, and on some faces, desperate hope. Her hands went instinctively to her belly, a protective gesture that she realized too late was an admission of guilt.

Even Katherine might not be able to protect her now.

Ayesha's smile was razor-thin. "Go ahead, Samara. Tell them how you genetically engineered your baby after the leadership team forbade you to do so."

"That's not what you actually voted against—"

"Did you or did you not go behind all our backs and use gene therapy to maintain your pregnancy?"

Samara could feel the colonist's rage redirecting toward her. The judgment in their stares. But she also saw something else in the women's faces. A hunger for what they'd just realized she had. A need that transcended their anger.

This was the moment to make her stand.

"You're right, I did." She stole Katherine's trick, letting her gaze sweep the crowd, stopping on one woman, then another. "Pharmaceutical cures take decades. We have five to seven years of peak fertility left. After that, most of you enter the high-risk pregnancy category."

Many looked uneasy, but they were listening. Leila's fury blazed from the back of the crowd, but Samara had no time to wonder why.

"It's not enough to take antifungals and stop the symptoms after each sporestorm," she continued. "We have to find a way to coexist with the fungus, or humanity will go extinct without another generation to carry on the species."

"Fearmongering to justify playing god with her designer baby." Ayesha jabbed a finger at Samara. "If she gets away with this, what stops her from experimenting on your babies? You'll never know what she's done until it's too late."

"I would never do something like that without the person's express consent," Samara countered.

Ayesha's smile was cruel. "Can I see the consent form that your baby signed before you used her as a guinea pig?"

The psychologist's words hit their mark. Doubt flickered across the faces watching them, and Samara felt her momentary advantage slipping away.

"Enough." Katherine's voice cracked like a whip.

Ayesha whirled on her. "How do we know you didn't secretly approve this?"

"I did not," Katherine said. "Dr. Makinde went behind my back, too. She'll be disciplined."

"She should be exiled. Her and that abomination of a baby she's created. We should destroy all her equipment, to be sure she can't do the same to the rest of us."

"That's not for you to decide," Katherine said. "Correct me if I'm wrong, but aren't you, as the colony's psychologist, the one person here who should have been able to recognize that Captain Mercer isn't human?"

Ayesha's face darkened with fury, her lips parting for what would surely be another cutting retort, but Katherine cut her off.

"Dr. Makinde crossed ethical lines, but she hasn't endangered the colony. Everything she has done, she has done to herself. And to a child that she might still lose."

A perfect touch, Samara thought. Reminding them of their own miscarriages and hinting that Samara faced the same danger, to trigger empathy while also driving home the threat of future miscarriages. Not that she thought Katherine was doing any of this for *her*. The colony leader was laying the groundwork for a possible genetic solution, if Samara's baby was born healthy, as well as keeping their only geneticist alive long enough to implement the solution if it proved viable.

That didn't make Samara appreciate Katherine's deft touch any less.

"Everyone back to your shifts," the colony leader ordered. "No one touches Lucas or Samara. The leadership team will deliberate and decide how to handle this serious breach of trust."

"Their trial should be public," Ayesha argued.

"There will be no trial at this time," Katherine said.

"And if one should become necessary, it will be conducted according to the colony's charter. In the meantime, there will be an assembly tonight where the leadership team will share their deliberations."

Ayesha teetered on the edge of open rebellion. Then she spun around and stormed toward the common hall, Briar and Justin trailing behind her.

Leila didn't follow. She was too busy glowering at Samara.

The rest of the crowd dispersed slowly, reluctantly, casting backward glances at Samara as they went. What struck her hardest wasn't the anger in some of their faces; she'd expected that. It was the hope she saw in others, a desperate, fragile hope that made her chest tighten with the weight of responsibility. What if she couldn't give them what they needed? What if her experiment failed?

As colonists drifted away, Samara turned to Katherine. "I could stay on the ship until the baby is born. Out of sight, out of mind."

"Now that everyone knows, they need to see for themselves what's happening." Katherine looked directly at Samara's midsection. "It would be best if they see a normal pregnancy resulting in a healthy baby. But if you lose the baby, we'll all grieve together. Either way, we take power away from Basu."

The colony leader turned to Marcus, who still held the pulse rifle trained on Lucas. "Keep him under guard until someone is sent to relieve you. If he does anything hostile, no matter how minor, or tries to escape, shoot him."

Marcus nodded, his expression grim. "Yes, ma'am."

"I will cooperate," Lucas said.

"Good," Katherine replied coldly. "Because if you don't, I will power you off myself. Then I will have Maeve dismantle you and scatter your parts into the ocean."

Lucas nodded. "I understand."

The mob had been terrifying, but what came next frightened Samara more. She had to tell them about the Hyperion ruins, the mass grave, and Lucas' deception.

As she followed Katherine toward the common hall, she prayed she wasn't about to destroy them all.

Chapter Twenty-Nine

THE LEADERSHIP TEAM had assembled by the time Samara arrived. She hesitated at the threshold. Not a trial, Katherine had promised the crowd. But they'd already judged her, and Katherine couldn't let her go unpunished after such public exposure.

Katherine commanded the head of the table. Hector studied his tablet with careful neutrality. Maeve and Mahmoud's whispers died as she entered. Leo stared at the table, avoiding her eyes. Ayesha wore the satisfied smirk of vindication.

Only Renata offered a tight smile. The small gesture of solidarity squeezed Samara's throat. Let the others shun her. As long as Renata forgave her.

The silence stretched, thick and uncomfortable, until Katherine broke it with two words:

"Explain yourself."

"First, there's something more important."

"More important than your harboring of an android spy?" Ayesha's delight was obvious. "Enlighten us."

So, Samara did.

She told them about the walk in the woods, about tracking Lucas through the indigo forest, about the waterfall, and the shattered landing capsule. She described the ruins, the prefab structures, a mess hall, a medical bay, all collapsed under the weight of time and rot. She described the lab, the clawed gouges on the tables, the violence that looked deliberate. Then she showed them the pictures she'd taken of the ruined buildings.

"That is impossible," Mahmoud said, his voice barely above a whisper.

Samara placed a small metal object on the table. The insignia was unmistakable despite the corrosion.

"The Hyperion. They were here first."

Leo's sharp intake of breath echoed in the stunned silence. Renata leaned forward, eyes wide. Mahmoud went ashen, exchanging skeptical looks with Hector and Maeve. Even Ayesha looked stunned.

Only Katherine showed no surprise.

"How can you be sure?" Mahmoud demanded, reaching for the insignia pin but not quite touching it, as if it might burn him.

"I found it at their settlement," Samara said. "The colonists are gone. I don't know what happened to them."

She didn't voice her theory that the fungus had mutated or maddened the colonists. That would trigger panic, destroy Lucas, and cripple the ship. And her association with him might make her the next target.

That was why she couldn't tell them about the mass grave yet or show them the pictures of those tiny skeletons with monstrous, impossible features. They'd want to dig it up, and they might come to the same terrifying conclusion she had. After that, they would never accept gene therapy as a solution.

"Did you find any records?" Katherine asked, her voice

remarkably steady despite the bombshell Samara had just dropped.

"No records. The equipment was all smashed."

The barely contained fear in their faces made her hold back about the drive. She needed to know what was on it first.

"The colony was attacked?" Leo asked.

"I don't know if the colonists did it to themselves or if there are other beings on this planet that did the damage," Samara admitted.

"You mean aliens?" Renata's skepticism was clear. "We haven't found any life forms bigger than a dog."

"Yet," Mahmoud said, a new wariness in his eyes as he glanced toward the windows.

"Why would the colonists smash their own equipment?" The furrow between Leo's brows deepened.

Renata shifted in her chair. "The fungus had infiltrated the nervous system of the infected animals. Maybe it was impairing the colonists' judgment."

"You're suggesting that the Hyperion colonists went crazy," Mahmoud said flatly.

Renata looked uncomfortable, glancing at Samara as if seeking backup.

"We don't have to worry about that," Samara said quickly. "Now that we can make our own antifungals. The Hyperion colonists had much less sophisticated equipment, and they may not have had the scientific expertise to synthesize the compounds they would've needed."

She hoped she sounded more confident than she felt. The truth was, she had no idea what had happened to the Hyperion colony.

Katherine's expression hardened. "You found the site by following the android." She emphasized the last word, underscoring that Lucas was no longer a *he* in her eyes. "I ordered you to stay in your quarters. Why follow it?"

Samara felt a flush of guilt creep up her neck. "A hunch."

"You're going to have to do better than that."

Samara hesitated. Her impulse was to protect the man who'd helped her keep her secret for months. But he wasn't a man, he was a highly sophisticated machine that had manipulated her into feeling this way.

That didn't stop her from feeling guilty for throwing Lucas under the bus.

"I suspected that the android might have lied when he said it hadn't occurred to him to test the 'dust' for organic material." She met Katherine's stare. "I think he found the Hyperion site first and steered us away. Their location was better, aside from soil contamination we've never verified."

"Why do you think he would lie?" Katherine asked.

"I don't know," Samara admitted. "But if Hofstadter knew that the Hyperion had come to DaVinci instead of Promixa Centauri b, it might not be a coincidence that the Borlaug was sent here."

Silence as they all considered the implication: they had been intentionally sent to a planet where another colony had failed.

"So, you knew the android had lied," Katherine said, "but you never mentioned it to any of us."

"I wasn't sure that he'd lied, and I had no idea he was an android."

"If you had doubts, you should have said something," Katherine said, her disappointment evident.

"I'm sorry," Samara said, because it seemed an apology would be better than an explanation.

Mahmoud leaned forward, his fingertips pressed

against the table. "What are we going to do about the android?"

"We don't have the resources to build a structure he couldn't escape from," Maeve said. "He's extremely advanced experimental tech. He could probably hack his way around any new programming we'd try to install."

She paused, frowning. "But all that's moot. He's not lying about controlling the ship. We need to be independent from the Borlaug first."

Katherine's expression hardened. "I'm willing to destroy him sooner. Options?"

Maeve considered this. "It wouldn't be hard to make a small EMP we could embed in him. The hard thing would be to do it in a way that he couldn't take it off easily. Also, it's going to fry any electronics nearby."

"Do it," Katherine said. "And look through the ship's archives to see if that bastard Hofstadter included specs for the android. See if you can find a better way."

Maeve nodded. "I will."

"We'll discuss the consequences of your insubordination later," Katherine said to Samara, then turned to Leo. "Bring the android in."

Leo returned with Lucas, who entered with perfect posture and positioned himself opposite Katherine. Somehow, he looked both attentive and unconcerned despite being surrounded by people who now saw him as a threat.

Katherine started her interrogation with: "Why did you conceal the ruins of the Hyperion colony from us?"

"You were disoriented refugees fleeing species-wide trauma, psychologically vulnerable. Unsettling you further would have impaired your ability to function."

He said this as if it were a simple matter of arithmetic, but Samara saw the ripple pass through the room: Hector's jaw clenching, Mahmoud's eyes narrowing, even Ayesha's mouth gone tight with a sudden, unwelcome kinship.

"So you were protecting us," Katherine said bitterly.

"Until the information became necessary."

"You don't think that understanding how an alien fungus killed the colony before this was necessary?"

"The previous colonists' attempts to find a cure for the fungus failed, and my projections showed a high probability of unproductive panic if this were common knowledge."

"But we could've learned from their mistakes." Samara wasn't sure if she was pointing that out because it mattered or because she needed to prove to the others that she hadn't been complicit in his plans. "We might already have a solution."

"If any of their data had survived, I would've brought it to this team. But my survey of the former colony's ruins yielded nothing useful."

Katherine's scowl deepened. "Tell us everything you know about Hyperion."

To Samara's surprise, Lucas continued, seeming to hold nothing back.

"Aurelius briefed me on Hyperion's last message. They'd failed to cure the fungus with limited pharmaceuticals and were attempting genetic engineering. Their final transmission said they'd found a solution."

Samara felt suddenly freezing.

"But we received no scientific data on their solution. I was ordered to investigate their fate, but recovered nothing useful. All information was classified."

"Why were we sent to DaVinci if the people back on Earth knew the fungal infection had killed the Hyperion crew?" Katherine asked.

"Of all the exoplanets found to be habitable, DaVinci

is the closest to Earth in all the parameters that matter," Lucas explained. "Many of the other exoplanets had much narrower zones suitable for potential habitation. If the Borlaug crew could find a cure for the fungal infection, DaVinci offered the greatest chances of success for establishing a new human homeworld."

"Then why was the public told that the Hyperion's destination was Proxima Centauri b?" Samara broke in. "Was that Hofstadter's decision too?"

"I was not given access to that information."

"We're you al—" No, *alive* wasn't the right word. "Did you exist back then?"

"In primitive form."

That meant Lucas had been at least a century old when the Hyperion had left Earth decades ago.

"But your creator didn't trust you with mission-critical information?"

"He told me what he believed I needed to know." Lucas paused. "If it makes a difference, the Borlaug's stores were stocked with a much higher quantity and variety of antifungal medicines proportionate to any other medication. Hofstadter anticipated this challenge."

Hector frowned. "You could've told us right away what we were facing."

"By interfering, I might have prejudiced you toward the same decisions that the Hyperion crew made," Lucas replied. "And I believe that was the correct choice. You have found a way to manage the infection in the current population, and Samara may have solved the reproductive issues."

The room erupted into accusations and overlapping questions. Samara remained silent, watching the chaos unfold.

All she could think was that if she hadn't given Lucas

the benefit of the doubt, assuming he'd made a genuine mistake in not testing the dust for organic material, how much sooner would she have figured out the true nature of the storms?

How much unnecessary suffering had Lucas caused, for the sake of not *prejudicing* them toward the Hyperion crew's mistakes?

When the noise subsided, Katherine fixed Lucas with an icy stare. "We would be justified in shutting you down."

"You could," Lucas agreed. "Or you could order me to stay on the ship."

"Would you follow that order?"

"I would, as long as doing so was in the best interests of the colony."

"We decide what's in the colony's best interests. Sit in the hall and stay there. Disobey and we'll destroy you. Understood?"

"Yes." Lucas left without another word.

Silence settled over the room. Samara could almost feel the weight of the revelations pressing down on everyone's shoulders. She kept her hands folded in her lap, resisting the urge to rest them protectively over her belly.

Katherine turned to Maeve. "Is he telling the truth?"

Maeve shrugged. "He's the most sophisticated model I've ever seen, but who knows how Hofstadter programmed him?"

"How soon can we be independent of the ship, so we can melt him down for scrap?" Katherine asked.

"Depends on whether or not Samara's little experiment works," Maeve replied, her gaze flicking briefly to Samara's midsection, "or if you're willing to sacrifice all the livestock. We can probably ferry down all the remaining supplies and equipment in a couple of weeks."

Leo cleared his throat. "Lucas could help me with the

animals, which would both keep him busy and allow me to keep an eye on him."

Katherine considered this, then turned to address the entire group. "EVERYONE is to keep this a secret. The shock of finding out that they've been living with an android and that Samara might've been sitting on a solution to the miscarriage problem is bad enough. There's nothing we can do about the dead colony, and revealing it will just make them more afraid."

"You mean, it'll just make them more likely to question your leadership," Ayesha said.

Katherine's retort was instant. "You're the only one who's doing that."

"They have the right to know," the psychologist said. "This meeting should've been held in a public forum, not behind closed doors."

Katherine's expression hardened. "It's your job to calm people down, not stir them up. I shouldn't have to remind you of that."

"I did what was right," Ayesha shot back. "And if you're going to keep secrets and make unilateral decisions that affect us all, you don't deserve to lead this colony."

Katherine's face went cold, drained of all emotion except for a dangerous glint in her eyes. "Keep this confidential. Start a panic, and I'll have you confined."

"Jailing someone for speaking the truth. That's the sign of a great leader."

Tension crackled between the two women like a live wire. Samara sat frozen, afraid any movement would draw their fire.

Katherine turned to Samara. "The leadership team will discuss how to handle the repercussions of your actions and inform you of our decision. You're dismissed."

The finality in her tone made it clear that Samara was

no longer part of the leadership team. Demoted from problem-solver to problem to be solved.

She stood, but hesitated before leaving. "What are you going to do with Lucas?"

"Since there's no way to confine him and he can't be allowed access to the ship, I don't see what I can do other than order him to stay put."

"He could stay with me."

Katherine's eyebrows rose. "Do you feel safe living with the android?"

Samara thought about how Lucas had kept her secret, had helped with her prenatal care, and had never once betrayed her trust, even as he had betrayed everyone else's.

"I feel as safe as I would anywhere," she said finally. "If Lucas is dangerous, there's no place I could hide in the colony where he couldn't get to me."

Katherine considered this, then nodded. "For now."

"Clinic tomorrow. Full exam, ultrasound, blood work." Hector's tone made his annoyance clear; she'd prioritized secrecy over her baby's health. Untrue, but no time to explain that Lucas had supervised her care.

The corridor felt colder, though the temperature hadn't changed. Everything she'd learned pressed down like double gravity: Lucas, the Hyperion, her ruined status.

Samara spotted Lucas sitting on a bench in the common hall, exactly where Katherine had ordered. Could he have disobeyed, if he'd wanted to? If not, did he resent his lack of freedom?

Even though she knew he wasn't a person, it felt wrong that he might not have a choice.

His eyes tracked her approach.

A machine designed to mimic humanity, programmed by the same man who had manipulated them all.

Yet something in his expression resembled genuine concern.

"Katherine says you can stay with me," Samara said as she reached him, keeping her voice low though the hall was empty.

Lucas nodded once, a precise dip of his chin. "Are you certain that's what you want?"

Was it? Samara hardly knew herself anymore. The revelation of Lucas' true nature had upended everything she thought she understood about their relationship, such as it was. The quiet respect, the odd moments of connection, the way he'd kept her secret when discovery would have been disastrous, had any of it been real? Or were they just subroutines in his programming, designed to maintain his cover?

"It's not a matter of want," she said finally. "I need your help."

"With the hard drive?" Of course, he'd seen her take it.

"Yes." She glanced around to make sure they were still alone. "I need to know what's on it before I tell the others about it. They're already scared. If there's something worse on there—"

"I understand," Lucas said. "It's a reasonable precaution."

He stood, and Samara realized that even this simple movement had always been too perfect, too fluid, too economical. How had she never noticed?

No, she had. She'd just written it off because of Hofstadter's lie by implication.

They walked in silence through the village, passing colonists who stared openly at them. Samara kept her eyes forward, refusing to shrink under their scrutiny.

When they reached the cabin, she closed the door behind them and leaned against it, suddenly exhausted.

The day had stretched her nerves to breaking point, and her body ached from the trek through the forest, the confrontation with the crowd, and the tense leadership meeting.

"You should rest," Lucas said. "Your cortisol levels are elevated, which isn't optimal for fetal development."

Samara couldn't help the bitter laugh that escaped her. "You can detect my cortisol levels now?"

"I can with sophisticated chemoreceptors in my—"

"Stop." Next, he'd claim he'd been cataloguing her dreams.

"Your pupils, pulse, temperature, and breathing patterns all indicate stress."

She stared at him, truly seeing him for the first time. Not a man, but a complex system of sensors and processors and actuators, all working in concert to create a perfect simulacrum of humanity.

"Were you ever going to tell me what you are?"

Lucas considered this, his head tilting slightly to one side. It was a gesture she'd found endearing before, but now it looked calculated, a programmed response designed to project human thoughtfulness.

"No," he said finally. "My directives were to maintain cover unless discovery was imminent or revelation of my nature became necessary for the colony's survival."

"What are your directives now?" Samara sank into a chair, her back and feet aching.

"To ensure the survival of the colony and protect the lives within it," Lucas replied. "That hasn't changed, and it won't."

Samara placed a hand on her belly, feeling the slight swell beneath her palm. "Including this life?"

"Yes."

The affirmation should have reassured her. But now

that she knew he could lie by omission or implication, she wondered if he could tell a direct lie.

Could she trust anything he said?

Unfortunately, she still needed his help. If the hard drive contained information about what had happened to the Hyperion colonists—information that might help them avoid the same fate—she needed to know. And Lucas was the only one who could help her access it without raising alarms.

She produced the battered drive, wrapped in cloth for protection. Cracked case, dented corner. Lucas turned it in his hands that had once gently spread ultrasound gel on her belly so that she could see her daughter for the first time. Artificial hands, crafted by a genius she couldn't trust.

"I'll need to build an adapter. The interface is outdated compared to our current technology."

"How long will that take?"

"A few hours. I can construct one from components in the medical equipment repair kit."

Samara nodded, then sank deeper into her chair, exhaustion finally claiming her. Her body demanded rest, her mind too overwhelmed to continue functioning.

"I'm going to lie down," she said. "Wake me when you've got something."

As she moved toward the bedroom, she paused, turning back to him. "Lucas?"

He looked up from the hard drive, his expression as unreadable as ever.

"My modifications to the baby's immune system—will they protect her from whatever happened to the Hyperion colonists?"

His posture shifted subtly. Was he doing it on purpose, or was it unconscious, driven by programming he had no control over?

It didn't matter if it was coming from Lucas or Hofstadter; it was still manipulative.

"I don't know," he said finally. "Without understanding what happened to them, I can't calculate the probability of success."

It wasn't the reassurance she'd hoped for, but at least it was honest. Or as honest as a machine programmed to mimic humanity could be.

"Build the adapter," she said. "We need to know what we're up against."

Closing the bedroom door, Samara felt time running out. Somewhere in the Hyperion ruins, a clock ticked toward a fate they didn't understand.

Chapter Thirty

WINTER WIND RATTLED the cabin windows, but inside felt almost cozy. Wrapped in flannel pajamas and a thick robe, Samara made peppermint tea and prepared for an early night. Everyone else was at the solstice celebration, but it had been made clear, unofficially, that her presence would spoil it.

Right now, half the colony wouldn't look at her, and the other half glared at her like they wished she would die.

Better to stay here and review the preliminary data from the Hyperion hard drive, which Lucas had managed to partially recover. Nothing useful yet; shipping manifests, crew rosters. Many of the files were corrupted.

Lucas was fixing sewage pipes, unpleasant work in bitter cold that wouldn't affect him. Katherine was treating him like the machine that he was, assigning him to Maeve's backlog of waiting repairs.

But he was intelligent. Possibly sentient. What was it like being conscious but trapped in a machine someone else controlled? Hellish, for a human. But for him?

She couldn't bring herself to call Lucas *it*, even though she knew that's what he was.

A sharp knock at the door startled her. She wasn't expecting anyone.

Renata and Marcus stood at her door, faces wind-reddened, snow melting in their hair. Renata clutched a package wrapped in repurposed packing materials. "Happy solstice."

She stepped inside without waiting for an invitation.

Marcus followed, shutting the door against the cold. "We bring gifts and stolen cake."

"You shouldn't be here," Samara said, even as relief flooded through her at the sight of friendly faces. "Katherine—"

"Didn't specifically forbid it," Renata finished for her. "And since when do we care what Ayesha thinks?"

Marcus offered a foil-wrapped package. Inside: a delicate pendant, an iridescent magenta blossom encased in polished resin, hanging from a braided cord..

"I love it," Samara said, her throat suddenly tight. "I have something for you, too."

She crossed to the small cabinet where she'd stored the few gifts she hadn't been sure she'd get to give them. She offered her own package. Inside was a wooden board with twelve depressions, and a small cloth bag filled with polished river stones that she'd collected over the past few months.

"It's a Nigerian game called *ayo*," Samara explained. "A variety of mancala. Since you're always inviting me over for game nights, I thought you might like something new to play."

"We love it," Marcus said, pouring the stones into the palm of his hand.

"We'll have to try it next time you're over," Renata said.

That might not be wise, not until things calmed down. She appreciated their loyalty, but she wouldn't drag them into her mess.

"It's a two-player game," Samara pointed out.

"Then I'll watch the first round," Renata replied, her tone making it clear she wouldn't accept any further attempts at self-exclusion.

Marcus produced a small container from inside his jacket. "We also brought you this."

He opened it to reveal a slice of spice cake, studded with raisins and walnuts, topped with a thin sugar glaze that gleamed in the light.

Samara's mouth watered. Her pregnancy cravings for sweets had been intense, and the rations did nothing to satisfy them.

"Katherine let you bring this to me?" she asked, surprised.

Marcus and Renata exchanged a glance.

"We shared our other piece," Marcus admitted.

Samara tried to hand it back. "Then you should keep it. I can't—"

"Take it," Renata insisted. "Please."

To her horror, Samara felt tears welling in her eyes. Hormones, she told herself, but their simple kindness pierced her defenses. They were better friends than she deserved.

"Give everyone time," Renata said softly. "It was a huge shock, but you didn't do anything wrong."

Samara wasn't sure about that. She'd broken trust with the colony, violated the agreement they'd all made together. But she'd done what she had to do, and she wouldn't change it. Her hand drifted to her belly, feeling the subtle curve beneath her palm.

More and more, she found herself thinking about her daughter, wondering what she would be like. Would she have Samara's eyes? Her stubborn determination? Or would she be something entirely new, the first of a new kind of human, adapted to this alien world?

"I'm nervous," Samara admitted, the words escaping before she could stop them. "But I'm excited to meet her."

Renata's smile was warm. "You're going to be a great mother."

The certainty in her voice was a balm Samara hadn't known she needed.

~

DRIZZLE BEADED on Leila's hood as she crouched behind blue-leafed shrubs, watching Samara's cabin. Her knees ached from an hour of waiting for Samara to leave for her mandatory checkup with Dr. Callas.

Finally, the cabin door opened. Samara emerged, her pregnancy now impossible to miss despite the heavy coat she wore against the winter chill. She moved carefully down the steps, one hand supporting her lower back, the other resting on her swollen belly. Even from this distance, Leila could see the strain in her movements, the careful way she navigated the slick path toward the clinic.

Leila waited, counting each breath until Samara disappeared from view. Then she waited longer, muscles tensed with anticipation. Ten minutes later, the door opened again, and the android emerged, dressed for his work shift with the animals.

Lucas. She couldn't believe she'd ever found him

attractive. The artificially perfect way he moved now sent a shiver of revulsion down her spine.

She gave him time to reach the animal enclosures before she made her move. Slipping from behind the shrubs, she crossed the open ground between her hiding spot and Samara's cabin, careful to avoid the muddy patches where her footprints would be obvious.

The door was locked, of course, but Leila was prepared. Justin's multi-tool blade slipped between the simple latch and the doorframe. A trick he'd shown her when they'd locked themselves out of her apartment back on Earth. Back when he'd been attentive, almost loving.

The latch gave with a soft click, and Leila slipped inside, closing the door quickly behind her.

Samara's cabin was neater than she'd expected. Everything in its place, precisely arranged. The living area was spartan, no personal touches beyond a pendant hanging from a hook by the small mirror and a framed photo that Leila recognized as one of Earth's endangered frog species. On the small dining table sat a collection of tablets and notebooks, stacked in tidy piles.

Leila moved quickly to the bathroom, heart pounding so hard she could feel it in her throat. The medicine cabinet was her first target. She swung it open, eyes scanning the shelves. Antifungals, prenatal vitamins, basic toiletries...

Nothing.

The living area revealed nothing. She moved to the bedroom, searching drawers and under the mattress. Finally, the closet: a small blue box tucked behind winter clothes. It contained sheets of blister-packed gray pills that didn't look like any of the medicines that Dr. Callas had been handing out to treat the fungus.

IMMUNOSUPPRESSANT - CYCLOSPORINE

FOR AUTHORIZED USE ONLY

She'd found it. The key to Samara's miracle pregnancy. The cure she'd been keeping from everyone else.

Each sheet contained fourteen pills. She hesitated, then rolled one up and crammed it into her pocket.

Two weeks' worth. Not enough that Samara would notice immediately, but enough to get Leila started, after she found a way to lure Justin back to bed with her for one more night.

There would be more blister packs in the clinic. She couldn't ask Dr. Callas for more; if she told him what she planned, he'd just try to discourage her.

The rest of the pills went back exactly where she'd found them, the box positioned just as it had been. Leila closed the cabinet and stood still for a moment, listening for any sound that might indicate someone approaching. But she heard only a soft patter of drizzle against the window.

She slipped out of the cabin as carefully as she'd entered, making sure the door latched behind her. The pills felt heavy in her pocket, a promise of the future she'd been denied.

The common hall pulsed with light and sound, transformed from its usual utilitarian purpose by strings of handmade decorations and the flickering glow of precious candles saved for this special occasion. The air was thick with the smell of spice cake and the sweat of too many bodies packed into too small a space, but for once, no one seemed to mind the crowding.

Leila lingered at the edge of the celebration, watching. The solstice was meant to mark the darkest day, the turning point when light would begin to return. A celebration of hope and renewal. But as she scanned the room for Justin, hope felt distant.

She spotted him across the hall, standing near the makeshift bar where Leo was dispensing carefully measured cups of his homemade berry wine. Justin was laughing at something Briar had said, his head tilted toward her in a way that made Leila's stomach clench. Not touching, nothing inappropriate, but the interest in his eyes was unmistakable.

Leila smoothed her hair, tugged at the hem of the one nice shirt she'd brought from Earth, and made her way across the room. Conversations paused as she passed, heads turning to follow her progress. She was used to this by now; the colony's fascination with her had only intensified after her losses. Everyone knew her story, her failures. She lifted her chin higher, refusing to let their pity touch her.

"Justin," she said as she reached him, ignoring Briar completely. "I saved you a dance."

He looked up, surprise flickering across his face before settling into something more guarded. "I don't feel like dancing."

"Come on," she coaxed, forcing a smile. "It's the solstice. One dance won't kill you."

Justin glanced at Briar, then back at Leila. "I'm in the middle of something."

"That's right," Briar said, her smile sharp as a knife. "You're interrupting, Leila."

The dismissal burned like acid. Leila felt her cheeks flame, aware of the eyes on her, the whispers that would follow this latest humiliation.

"You're my husband."

His expression hardened. "You're embarrassing me."

She was. But she couldn't stop, not when she'd finally found a way forward.

"One dance," she repeated, reaching for his hand.

He pulled away as if her touch might burn him. "Not tonight, Leila. Just... give it a rest."

Briar's laugh was soft but cutting. "You heard him. Get lost."

The words stripped her bare. Mortification froze her in place while whispers rippled through the watching colonists. She backed away, one step, two, then fled through the crowd, pitying stares burning her back.

Outside, the bitter cold scoured away humiliation, leaving crystalline clarity in its wake. She had the pills. Now she needed Justin to make her pregnant. After that, he could rot with Briar.

Her fingers found the stolen sheet of foil and plastic. Samara's miracle cure, the key to everything she'd sacrificed to reach this world. Using them meant crossing a line she'd never imagined crossing.

Until tonight.

Leila waited in their cabin, the hours stretching like elastic as the celebration continued without her. She sat at their small table, a cold meal spread out before her—her own attempt at marking the solstice, at salvaging something from this day.

She thought about the pills in her pocket. About Samara's swollen belly, the miracle growing inside her. About the future that should have been hers, that could still be hers if she were willing to take it.

Justin stumbled in a few minutes after midnight, reeking of berry wine and bonfire smoke. His eyes widened. He probably hoped she'd be asleep.

"Where were you?" Leila demanded, not bothering with a greeting.

"At the party," he said, moving past her to the kitchenette. "Like everyone else."

"With Briar."

Justin sighed, the sound heavy with impatience. "Don't start this again."

"Don't start what? Asking why my husband prefers someone else's company to mine? Why can't you even give me one dance on solstice night?"

"I told you, I didn't feel like dancing."

"You didn't feel like dancing with me," she corrected. "Was it different with her?"

His silence was answer enough. Leila followed him, refusing to be ignored. She reached for him, turning him to face her, and pressed her lips to his. For a moment, just a moment, she felt him respond. Then he pulled away.

"I'm tired," he said. "I need a shower."

"I'll join you," she offered, trying to keep the desperation from her voice.

"No." The single syllable hit like a slap.

She tried again, determined. "I thought it might be fun to skip the condom tonight." Her voice turned husky. "I'm nowhere near ovulating, so it'll be fine."

Justin's expression hardened. "I'm still broken up about the miscarriages. I don't want to risk putting you through that again."

The words might have been believable if she'd heard them from someone else. But Justin hadn't shed a single tear when she'd lost the babies. Hadn't even visited her in the infirmary the second time.

"That's bullshit," she said.

He just shrugged, turning away to grab a ration packet from the cabinet. The tearing sound as he opened it seemed unnaturally loud in the tense silence.

Something snapped inside Leila. Months of rejection, suspicion, being pushed away when all she wanted was what they'd come here for. She'd thrown herself at what turned out to be an android, humiliating beyond measure.

Now her own husband wouldn't touch her when the entire point of this colony was rebooting humanity.

"You're sleeping with Briar."

He didn't even bother with a convincing denial. "You're being paranoid."

"You're out all night, you won't touch me—"

"Maybe because you're a clingy bitch."

She fell a step back, tears already starting to fall. "You wouldn't be here if it wasn't for me. You owe me."

Justin shrugged again, turning toward the bathroom. "Whatever."

The door closed behind him with a soft click that somehow hurt more than if he'd slammed it.

Rage and humiliation warred inside her. She grabbed a pillow, punched it until her arm ached, then screamed into it. All she needed was one more night. Then Justin could do whatever he wanted, with whoever he wanted.

She'd find a way. She always did.

Chapter Thirty-One

DAVINCI YEAR 1
  SPRING

ONLY TWO MORE WEEKS' worth of pills. Samara frowned. She was certain there'd been another sheet, just enough doses to reach her due date.

Pregnancy brain, real and maddening for someone who prided herself on precision. She forgot things mid-sentence, lost calculations she could once do in her sleep. Her mind felt hyperactive yet sluggish, fixated on the baby while details slipped away.

She'd have to stop by the infirmary during her break. A trip to the Borlaug was out of the question now. Even if Katherine allowed it, she doubted she could waddle up the shuttle ramp without assistance.

She waddled now that her belly was the size of a basketball. Her center of gravity had shifted so much that simple tasks like bending required strategic planning.

Samara pulled her oversized sweater down as far as it

would go and made her way to the front room of the cabin. Lucas sat cross-legged on the floor, a disassembled piece of equipment spread before him on a clean white cloth. A small laser device was mounted on what appeared to be parts from a microscope, aimed at the exposed circuitry of the external drive they'd salvaged from the Hyperion ruins.

"Any progress?" She lowered herself carefully onto the couch.

Lucas adjusted the laser without looking up. "The drive is too damaged for conventional extraction. But I can bounce laser light off the internal chips, analyze reflection patterns to reconstruct partial data. I can't make any promises."

Samara nodded, though she had only the vaguest understanding of what he was describing. She'd given up hope weeks ago of discovering what the Hyperion colonists' final solution might have been. It hardly seemed to matter now that her own solution appeared to be working. Her baby, her daughter, was thriving, despite all odds.

Ensuring the survival of the colony was all that mattered, and the proof of that survival kicked beneath her ribs, a sharp reminder of the new life she'd created.

She'd become obsessively focused on the baby to the point where she barely recognized herself. The scientist who'd once viewed pregnancy as a biological process requiring intervention now counted kicks, talked to her belly, requisitioned onesies and ridiculously tiny socks from the ship's stores. And tried not to acknowledge that she thought they were *cute*.

Dr. Callas had been insisting on weekly blood tests to monitor the baby's health. Miraculously, it was looking increasingly likely that her theory would be proven correct; the genetic modifications she'd made were allowing the fetus to tolerate the fungus without triggering an immune response.

But each time she felt that surge of scientific validation, another thought followed close behind: what if this detached, analytical approach proved she wasn't fit to be a mother? What if Ayesha had been right, that she was just an arrogant scientist playing God with no thought to the consequences?

What if she couldn't love her own child?

"I need to get to my shift," she said, struggling to her feet. Lucas reached out to help her, but she waved him off, determined to manage on her own. "We're on kitchen duty today."

"I'll accompany you," he said, setting down his tools.

The EMP device on his neck caught the light—a black disk, blinking red. Maeve's insurance policy. What was it like walking around with a bomb strapped to you, while those you were programmed to protect had their finger on the detonator?

He probably felt nothing at all. That was the point. *Android.*

They stepped outside into the mild spring air. DaVinci's third quarter brought variable weather. Yesterday's sporestorm had given way to a clear morning, the pale purple sky stretching overhead without a cloud in sight. The twin moons hung faintly visible despite the daylight, ghostly reminders of their alien home.

Samara couldn't help watching Lucas from the corner of her eye as they walked toward the common hall, seemingly unaffected by the colony's changed attitude toward him. But had he ever been affected? Had his concern for her, the prenatal vitamins, the ultrasounds, and his apparent enthusiasm about becoming a father been genuine in any way? Or was it all programming designed to gain her trust?

Did it matter? How could she trust him around her child after he'd deceived her so completely?

The common hall came into view, but something was wrong. Instead of the usual morning bustle, colonists huddled in small groups outside the entrance, many wrapped in blankets despite the mild temperature. Their faces were drawn, skin pale beneath the now-familiar rashes that the sporestorms triggered.

Samara's waddle became more urgent, one hand supporting her belly as dread coiled in her chest.

The situation was worse inside. Half the colonists lay on makeshift pallets scattered around the common hall, shivering beneath blankets. The air reeked of sweat and sickness, metallic sporestorm residue. Dimmed lights cast shadows that emphasized their pallor.

Dr. Callas sat slumped in a chair near the far wall, a thermal blanket wrapped around his shoulders. His normally neat appearance had given way to disheveled exhaustion—hair standing in tufts, stubble darkening his jaw, eyes rimmed with red. A tablet balanced precariously on his knee, his hand too unsteady to hold it properly.

Samara approached him, concern overriding the caution that had governed her interactions with the leadership team since her fall from grace.

"What's happening?" she asked. "Everyone looks terrible."

Hector looked up, his gaze taking a moment to focus on her face. "The antifungals are losing efficacy."

"How bad?"

"Double doses after yesterday's storm. The side effects are brutal: nausea, fever, and muscle pain. Most can't work."

Samara scanned the room, taking in the scope of the crisis. Leo lay on a cot near the kitchen, Maeve beside him, both coughing and shivering despite the blankets piled on top of them. Katherine stood by the water dispenser, her face gray with exhaustion as she filled cups for those too weak to do it themselves. Even Ayesha, usually composed, sat with her head in her hands at one of the tables. Samara and Lucas were the only ones unaffected.

How long before the others would resent them even more?

But that wasn't the worst part. Developing a new anti-fungal medication could take months, like the last one did. Or it could take years, if they were unlucky.

"We could switch to immunosuppressants for a while," she suggested. "Give people's bodies time to reacclimate so that the antifungals would become more effective again."

Hector shook his head, then winced as if the movement had caused him pain. "We have a lot fewer of those on hand than antifungals, and they're harder to synthesize, assuming Renata can find native sources of the components. But even if we had plenty of them, taking something to suppress your immune system every day for the rest of your life takes a much bigger toll on your health than taking a few days of antifungals every month or so. Not to mention the fact that they'd leave the whole colony susceptible to the mildest infection. The next flu virus could be one hundred percent lethal."

Samara's mind raced, weighing options. If they couldn't find another solution, would the colonists become desperate enough to let her try gene therapy to modify their immune systems? She was confident she could find an epigenetic solution, but if she could get Katherine and the others to trust her.

But right now, she wasn't allowed anywhere near

scientific equipment, and that was slowly strangling her. She'd escaped the chytrid apocalypse only to be trapped in the exact life that science had promised to free her from.

Lucas materialized at her side. "You and I appear to be the only ones unaffected. We should assist with food preparation and care for those who are ill."

Samara nodded, glad for something concrete to do. As they moved toward the kitchen, she noted the colonists' reactions to Lucas. Some refused to look at him, turning their faces away as he passed. Others watched with naked suspicion.

She scanned the room again, noting absences. Leila and her husband Justin were nowhere to be seen. Neither were Briar and her two confederates. Had they escaped the worst of the symptoms, or were they too ill to leave their cabins?

In the kitchen, they found supplies for a simple breakfast already laid out: single-serving packets of oatmeal, freeze-dried fruit to add texture and flavor, and a basket of lantern fruit to be chopped. The simple fare told its own story: they were stretching rations, making supplies last longer. Another sign of how precarious their situation had suddenly become.

Lucas set another pot of water to boil on the stove, and they set to work. Within twenty minutes, they were ready to start serving.

"I'll take these to the east side," she said, loading a cart with bowls.

Lucas nodded, his expression neutral as always. Samara watched him for a moment, wondering again if he was capable of suffering. Did the colony's treatment of him cause pain, or was his apparent stoicism merely the absence of emotion? Were his thoughts complex, like a human's, or an elaborate series of calculations and probability assessments?

As she wheeled her cart toward the first table, Renata looked up and offered a whispered hello before quickly returning to her conversation with Marcus. She sat with the other members of the leadership team, and Samara wondered if her friend was getting pressure to avoid her. Katherine had made it clear that Samara's punishment for withholding information included being booted off the leadership team and barred indefinitely from any scientific endeavors or lab access.

But the colony leader had asked once if Samara could train Hector on gene editing, clever, since colonists would trust the therapy more coming from their doctor. Samara had agreed, but Hector kept deferring, claiming the clinic kept him too busy. He'd probably need a direct order from Katherine to cooperate with Samara on anything.

Most of the colonists accepted her offered food with minimal acknowledgement. They were too sick to maintain the active resentment of earlier weeks, but the distance remained, a wall between her and the community she'd once been part of.

She wondered what it would be like to raise her baby as a single mother on a planet where the only human community distrusted her at best and hated her at worst. Would her daughter suffer for Samara's sins?

One thing was certain: she would make sure the baby didn't suffer for Lucas' sins. She was going to ask him to stay away from them once the baby was born.

The door opened, and Leila dragged herself in, face puffy and red, but not from the rash that plagued so many of the others. She looked like she'd been crying for days. She slunk over to a corner, as far as she could get from Briar and Justin without leaving the colony, and slumped into a chair. Sitting alone, hair falling over her face, the picture of dejection.

Trapped in a miserable marriage with no other options, forced to watch her husband cheat with her nemesis, desperate for a baby but unable to carry one to term. And now she was the colony laughingstock, thanks to Ayesha ensuring that everyone knew that Leila had tried to seduce the android hiding in their midst.

Samara couldn't imagine how hard it must've been for her to leave her cabin and face everyone.

She rolled the cart over to Leila. "Hungry?"

"Thanks," Leila mumbled, not even looking up as she accepted the bowl of oatmeal and fruit topped with reconstituted powdered milk. Too embarrassed to talk, probably.

Samara hovered, feeling like she should say something, but what?

She couldn't think of anything that wouldn't sound trite or judgmental. So she went with: "If you need a second dose of antifungals, let Dr. Callas know."

The hours blurred together as Samara moved between the kitchen and the common area, serving meals, checking on the sickest colonists, and finally washing dishes. The work was mindless enough that her thoughts kept circling back to the same concerns: the dwindling supply of immunosuppressants, the approaching birth, the colony's precarious future.

By late afternoon, the kitchen was stifling despite the fans running at full capacity. Steam rose from the industrial sinks as Samara scrubbed pots, her back aching from standing so long. Sweat trickled down her temples and between her shoulder blades, her oversized shirt clinging uncomfortably to her skin.

The baby shifted, a knee or elbow pressing painfully against her ribs. Samara paused, one hand braced against the edge of the sink, the other pressed to the spot where her daughter was making her presence known.

"Settle down in there," she murmured.

The movement subsided, only to be replaced by a rolling wave that made her entire abdomen ripple visibly beneath her shirt. She'd grown accustomed to these internal gymnastics, the strange sensation of sharing her body with another being who had definite opinions about her posture, diet, and sleep schedule.

She returned to scrubbing, her mind drifting to the birth. Would her genetic modifications work as intended? Would her daughter be healthy? And if she was, how would the colony react to the living proof that gene therapy could solve their fungal problem?

She grabbed for the edge of the sink as dizziness washed over her. Black spots crowded her vision, fingers clumsy on rubber gloves.

"I need to—"

The world went sideways.

She was only dimly aware of the sound of her body hitting the floor, of voices raised in alarm, of hands reaching for her. Then darkness.

Four faces hovered above her: Lucas, unreadable; Renata, concerned; Leo, pale but determined; and Hector, clinically assessing despite his own illness.

"What happened?" she asked, her voice a rasp. Her throat felt parched, her lips cracked.

"You fainted," Hector said, his fingers at her wrist, counting her pulse. "How do you feel now?"

"Dizzy. Thirsty." She tried to sit up, but gentle hands pressed her back down.

"Stay still for a minute," Renata said. "Leo's getting you some water."

Samara became aware that she was lying on one of the

cots that had been set up for the sick colonists. A thin pillow had been placed under her head, and someone had removed her rubber gloves. Her hands still smelled of soap and the metallic tang of the pots she'd been scrubbing.

Leo returned with a cup of water, which Renata helped her sip. The cool liquid soothed her throat, chasing away some of the fog in her mind.

"When did you last eat?" Dr. Callas asked.

Samara tried to remember. "Breakfast, I think. I've been busy."

His frown deepened. "And how much have you been sleeping?"

"Enough," she lied. Sleep had become increasingly elusive as her pregnancy advanced. Even when she could find a comfortable position, the baby was constantly moving these days. She was lucky to get four hours a night.

Dr. Callas didn't look convinced. "I'm prescribing bed rest for the next few days. No arguments."

"I can't just—"

"You can and you will," he said firmly. "You're in the final stretch of your pregnancy. We can't afford complications now."

He rose with effort and moved to the dispensary cabinet, searching shelves with growing agitation.

"Something's wrong." He shoved items aside, checking the back.

"What is it?" Renata asked.

His expression went grim. "The rest of the immunosuppressants are missing."

Samara's heart spiked. "You're sure?"

"I keep careful inventory, and you're the last person I prescribed them to."

She couldn't even swallow. "Can we bring more down from the ship?"

"There are no more." Hector sighed. "You're going to run out before your due date."

The room constricted. Without immunosuppressants, her immune system's response to the fungus would kill the baby. And antifungals were out of the question, especially now that the fungus was adapting to them, requiring a stronger dose.

"What options do we have?" she asked.

"We could induce labor early. Or perform a cesarean, if she doesn't want to come out."

The baby would be two weeks early.

She only hoped she was making the right decision.

Lucas had remained silent throughout the exchange, his eyes fixed on Hector with an intensity that mimicked human intensity. Now he spoke. "I will assist with the search for the missing medication."

Hector hesitated, then nodded. "Check the storage areas first. I'll review the inventory logs again."

Cold fury mixed with primal fear crashed over Samara as they dispersed. Someone had stolen the medication that her baby's life depended on.

Two weeks until she met her daughter.

She wasn't ready.

Chapter Thirty-Two

HER DAUGHTER WAS COMING.

It still didn't feel real.

Samara paced the living room, where Ife napped on the coffee table. The cat was doing a better job of following the doctor's orders than she could. Bedrest, Hector had called it, suggesting that she relax while her body made its final preparations for childbirth.

But after a week and a half of nothing to do but contemplate all the ways she might fail at motherhood, Samara was feeling the least relaxed she'd ever felt in her life. Desperate for a distraction, she'd downloaded everything she could find about off-target effects, including all of Mitra Kunde's research, but she couldn't focus beyond the first couple of sentences of an abstract, let alone read and comprehend a whole paper.

Lucas had been working back-to-back shifts for three days straight, so she hadn't even had the annoyance of his company. Every time she looked at him, she felt betrayed and ashamed that she hadn't seen the signs that he wasn't human.

He still hadn't managed to repair the corrupted files on the hard drive, although he claimed that he was making progress. And the way he hovered over her, bringing her peppermint tea and ginger drops and extra helpings from the common hall at mealtimes, was somehow the most annoying of all.

Except that his absence was annoying, too.

Because her brain seemed determined to fill the silence with every nightmare scenario: birth complications, neonatal immune collapse, some unforeseen mutation that killed Samara's daughter as soon as she emerged from the womb.

But those weren't as frightening as Samara's actual nightmares, where Hector put tiny, helpless Phoebe in her arms for the first time and Samara felt nothing. No affection. No love. No maternal instinct to protect and care for the new being that had been growing in her body for the past eight and a half months.

What if she was fundamentally broken?

It was such a terrifying thought that she couldn't even confess them to Renata and Marcus, who'd made a ritual of stopping by after their shifts, even when they were dead on their feet. Renata had flooded Samara with details about the just-planted seedlings, which already seemed to be thriving in the fields, and Marcus had smuggled her a half-dozen coral nut shortbread cookies from the vernal equinox celebration a few days ago.

Only when her friends were present did Samara feel relief from her nightmares.

She lowered herself to the couch with a groan, and Ife took that as an invitation to settle in her lap, his weight pressing against her swollen belly as if he was trying to snuggle up to the baby, who shifted in response. He began to purr, a rumble that vibrated through her ribs, and the squirming inside her eased, as if Samara's daughter recognized the sound as a primal lullaby.

A rattling outside made her look up. Then came a hissing, the unmistakable sound of aerosol paint, followed by muted giggling that tried and failed to be stealthy.

Samara's jaw tightened. She shifted Ife off her lap, ignoring his protesting mewl, and leveraged herself to standing. Each movement felt like swimming through syrup.

When she yanked the front door open, the smell hit her first, the sharp chemical tang of fresh paint. Then she saw the grotesque caricature sprawled across the front of their residence. A mutant baby, hideously deformed, with bulging eyes and slack, too-short arms that ended in paws instead of hands.

Ayesha continued to stoke the colonist's fears that Samara's baby would be something inhuman, despite Katherine's orders that the psychologist not talk about the pregnancy at all. Samara understood their fears because she shared them, although at a much more sophisticated level. She'd read every base pair in her daughter's genome, so she knew there would be no physical deformations. She wasn't worried about schizophrenia or other mental illness, either.

But off-target effects could manifest in much more subtle, unpredictable ways. Most of the adjustments she'd made had been to the embryo's immune system. While her daughter might be the first human whose body was adapted to the fungus, she might be susceptible to pathogens that didn't even cause symptoms in the other colonists or autoimmune diseases that had never been seen in humans before.

There was a small chance that Samara had solved one

problem by creating a new genetic disease that she'd spend the rest of her life trying to cure. And if her daughter died from the off-target effects, the colonists might never trust gene therapy again, even if Samara figured out what had gone wrong.

And that was the worst thing about the graffiti, the whispers, the passive-aggressive comments that she'd had to endure through most of her pregnancy. Because the ridiculousness of their fears just reminded Samara of the true dangers her daughter faced.

Pain stabbed through her belly, sharp enough to steal her breath. She bent forward, one hand braced against the doorframe, as liquid rushed warm between her legs. It splattered on the metal threshold, tinged pink in the afternoon light.

Her water had broken. Two days before Dr. Callas had planned to induce.

Fighting panic, she patted Ife's soft fur with trembling fingers and started toward the infirmary. Twenty meters to the path, another hundred to medical. Each step felt precarious, her body suddenly foreign.

Halfway down the path, another contraction doubled her over. Deeper than Braxton-Hicks, purposeful, her body finally evicting its tenant. Fear tasted metallic on her tongue.

"Are you okay?"

Leila's voice, closer than expected. Samara hadn't heard her approach.

"I'm in labor," Samara managed, straightening slowly.

Leila was at her side in an instant, sliding an arm around Samara's waist, her grip surprisingly strong and steadying. "I'll walk with you."

They moved together, Samara leaning into the support

more than she wanted to admit. The sulky young woman who'd been too humiliated to look Samara in the eye seemed to have been replaced by a competent young woman used to taking charge during a medical crisis.

Was this who Leila had been before DaVinci?

If so, her potential was being wasted on manual labor when Hector could be training the young woman to assist him. Maybe Leila could become the medical professional that Hector had hoped would take Samara's spot in the colony.

Another contraction hit, more painful than the last. Samara bent over again, a groan escaping despite her efforts to stay quiet. The pain radiated from her back around to her front, a crushing band that made thinking impossible.

"How far apart is that?" Leila asked, her voice pitched with concern.

"How am I supposed to know?" The words came out sharper than intended, but Leila didn't flinch.

"Never mind, I'll time them. Do you want someone to get Lucas?"

"Do *not* get Lucas." Samara straightened as the contraction eased, already dreading the next one. The android's presence would only remind everyone that both he and Samara had betrayed the colony, each in their own way, for their own reasons, and make them more likely to consider Samara's daughter guilty by association.

"No Lucas, I promise," Leila said gently. "I'm here."

Soon, Samara lay in an infirmary bed while Dr. Callas checked her out, his movements efficient despite the concern creasing his forehead.

"Everything seems to be fine," he said, pulling off his gloves. "Just keep breathing."

Another contraction seized her, so intense that she almost screamed. The sound that emerged was something between a moan and a growl, primal and embarrassing. She'd done this to herself—literally engineered this situation—and now she was starting to wish she hadn't. The academic understanding of labor, all those medical texts she'd studied, meant nothing in the face of this reality.

Leila's grip was firm, grounding. "My mama was in labor for a day and a half with Eddie."

"Not helping," Samara gasped.

"You'll feel better when you're holding your baby."

Leila sounded so sure, Samara almost believed her, despite knowing that the young woman had never actually given birth.

But what if she didn't? What if she was a monster who couldn't love her own child?

Hector looked up from the monitor displaying her vitals. "You can get up and move if you want. Walking sometimes helps."

Samara pushed herself upright, muscles and joints protesting. As she paced the small space, Leila paced with her, never more than an arm's length away. Each contraction forced her to stop, to bend, to breathe through the crushing waves. Leila rubbed between her shoulder blades, the pressure just right, and demonstrated breathing techniques with exaggerated inhales and exhales that might have been comical under other circumstances.

"In through the nose," Leila coached, her own chest rising and falling in demonstration. "Out through the mouth. That's it."

This was the same Leila who'd been so awkward in Samara's cabin during that sporestorm, who'd seemed to fold in on herself after her second miscarriage, who'd collapsed under the shame of the colony's ridicule. But watching her now, the confident way she guided Samara through each contraction, the gentle authority in her voice, Samara remembered what Leila had said about dropping out of school to care for her little brother. The same love illuminated her face now, transforming her from the lost young woman into someone who knew exactly what needed to be done.

That love was the difference.

Six hours of the worst pain she'd ever experienced. Each contraction humbled her body, taking control, reducing her to basic function. She who'd mapped genomes was now just another mammal birthing offspring.

"Push," Hector encouraged, his voice steady over the roar of blood in her ears.

Leila huffed and puffed right along with her, as if she was giving birth too. The young woman's face was flushed with effort, sweat beading on her forehead as she matched Samara breath for breath. On her other side, Renata had appeared at some point, Samara couldn't remember when, and now held her hand, murmuring words of encouragement that blurred together into a comforting hum.

"Almost there," Hector said, though he'd been saying that for what felt like hours.

An intense tearing pain ripped through her, sharp enough to cut through the fog of exhaustion. She heard Leila exclaiming in excitement and Hector barking an order to Renata, who let go of Samara's hand. Then everything dissolved into a blurry haze. She floated, disconnected from her body, aware of Leila's voice saying comforting things she couldn't quite make out. The words washed over her like warm water, meaningless but soothing.

Time stretched and compressed. She might have been

floating for minutes or hours when Leila's voice cut through the fog: "Here she is."

Warm weight settled into arms she didn't realize were reaching. Her infant daughter, skin still mottled from birth. Smaller than Samara had expected, her features delicate but perfect, ten fingers, ten toes, the rise and fall of a tiny chest.

And her eyes: brown like Samara's, but with golden flecks that reflected light as if metallic threads had been woven through the brown fibers of her pupils.

Off-target effects. She never would've predicted that the changes she'd made to the baby's genome would do this. What other unpredictable effects might she have triggered that might not be visible?

But she seemed perfectly normal otherwise. As she reached up toward Samara's face with her tiny hand, something in Samara's heart tore open, no less excruciating than the pain that had ripped the child out of her.

Samara had never wanted children. Had spent her entire adult life focused on her work, on solving problems bigger than any one family. But looking at this creature, whose parents she had never known but whose genome she had helped craft, she loved her daughter with every cell in her body. The feeling was immediate and overwhelming, rewriting her understanding of herself in an instant.

She would do anything for her daughter.

"What's her name?" Leila leaned closer to peer at the baby.

Without thinking about it, without consulting the list of names she'd compiled, Samara answered, "Phoebe."

Not a traditional name in her family. But she'd read that it meant 'radiant', and that was how holding her daughter made Samara feel.

Lucas appeared in the doorway, his silhouette filling the

frame as he took in the scene, mother and child together, the aftermath of birth still evident in the blood-stained sheets and the exhaustion written across Samara's face. His eyes moved from Samara to the baby, studying them with that intense focus he brought to everything.

"She is healthy."

It was a statement more than a question, and Samara thought about how he had monitored her without telling her. How he knew what she was feeling from the data he collected, maybe before she knew herself.

Unease crawled up her spine. She'd never talked to him about this, about what would happen after the birth, about his role or lack thereof. It had been an easy conversation to avoid, given how busy Katherine had kept him. Now she'd have to tell him. Here. Now. With Leila and Renata as witnesses. If he'd been human, she would have been humiliating him.

"What can I do for you?" he asked. "And for our daughter?"

Our daughter.

She reminded herself that he was an android. No feelings to hurt. No heart to break. Just sophisticated programming that mimicked human responses.

So why was this so hard?

"It's bad enough that she's my daughter, but once people see that she's healthy, they'll eventually accept her." She took a deep breath. "But she'll never be safe if people think of her as your daughter. Keep her safe, Lucas."

He looked at her, his expression neutral, that perfectly pleasant blank that revealed nothing. But was there something in his eyes? Some flicker of... what? Processing? Calculation? She was projecting, had to be. He was a machine. This wasn't rejection or abandonment, it was simply updating his parameters.

He nodded and walked out.

The door clicked shut behind him.

Samara hugged Phoebe to her chest, hyperaware of how small and fragile and alive she was.

My daughter.

Chapter Thirty-Three

DAVINCI YEAR 2
SUMMER

Early summer arrived like a gift. The air carried warmth without the oppressive humidity of the rainy season, and the alien sun painted the settlement in shades of pale violet and blue-white that made even the utilitarian prefabs look almost beautiful. It was the most gorgeous day Samara had seen since landing.

Samara blinked in the doorway's brightness. Her body had healed, but bone-deep exhaustion clung like second skin. Three hours' sleep last night, not consecutive. Phoebe had her own schedule, one that involved waking every two hours to nurse, followed by diaper changes and the mysterious fussing that meant nothing and everything to a one-month-old.

An unmarked box sat by her door. Inside: diapers (she was already running low), wipes, formula, thermometer, tiny onesies in soft colors. Everything a new mother needed.

Lucas.

Guilt twisted her stomach. She'd told him to stay away, made it clear he couldn't be Phoebe's father, yet here he was, still providing. Still caring, in his way.

He's an android, she reminded herself. It's just programming. Ensure colony success. Phoebe represented their best hope for survival.

The rationalization felt hollow, but she picked up the box and set it inside. Since there was no real emotion behind the gift, it wasn't really a gift, was it? It was a delivery of supplies that Lucas had arranged before Samara had gotten around to requesting them. And there was no reason to feel guilty for accepting it, because Lucas had no feelings to hurt.

Leila appeared with Phoebe cradled against her chest. Eyes closed, tiny mouth making sucking motions. Deep in milk-drunk slumber, one small fist curled against Leila's shirt.

Samara hesitated, looking from her daughter to the path that led to the common hall. "Maybe it's too soon."

Leila's expression softened. "I'll be with you the whole time. It will be fine." She freed one hand to touch Samara's arm. "You can't hide forever. Phoebe needs her mother to eat properly, to stay strong. And the colony needs to see that Phoebe is healthy. Some of us need hope."

Samara felt a rush of gratitude for this young woman who'd appointed herself as unofficial support system. Leila had shown up every day since Phoebe's birth, bringing food, offering to watch the baby so Samara could shower, and providing adult conversation when the walls of the cabin felt too close. Samara was sure it had less to do with her and more to do with the fact that Phoebe was the only baby that Leila would hold for a while. At least until Phoebe was three and everyone was satisfied that Samara's therapy was safe.

And Leila seemed to have moved on from Justin's infidelity. If helping Samara with Phoebe could do something to heal some of the hurt that Leila had suffered in the past year and a half, Samara was happy to let Leila volunteer.

Even though sometimes Samara would've preferred to be the one holding her daughter.

"Let me take her," Samara said, setting the box just inside the door.

"She's fine," Leila assured her, swaying gently. "You need a break. When's the last time you used both hands to eat a meal?"

Samara couldn't remember. She followed Leila toward the common hall, her eyes automatically scanning for Lucas. The path was busier than usual. Beyond the main settlement, she could see the Engineering team and a construction crew working on what would be their first building made entirely from native materials. The bluish-gray wood that Renata had identified months ago rose in neat frames against the sky. Progress. Real, tangible progress.

Relief washed over her when she entered the common hall and didn't spot Lucas among the gathered colonists. She'd been dreading this moment for weeks, but Leila had insisted she needed real food, not just whatever she could scavenge from her quarters.

The smell hit her first, not the salty blandness of preprepared rations but something that made her mouth water instantly. Roasted vegetables, their edges caramelized and glistening. Baked potatoes, steam rising from their split tops. And something else, savory and almost familiar.

The serving table held an actual feast. Summer vegetables, zucchini, peppers in three different colors, eggplant, summer squash, and tomatoes, had been cut into chunks and roasted with coral nut seed oil until they were tender and slightly charred. The scent of oregano and rosemary from the village herb garden mingled with the sweetness of roasted garlic that had been harvested in the spring and hung in long braids from pegs in the kitchen.

Beside the vegetables sat a tray of baked potatoes, their skins crispy and inviting. A small sign warned: "One pat of butter per person—limited supply."

Of course. The cows still couldn't carry calves to term, which meant no milk, no cream, no yogurt, no cheese, or sour cream. They were surviving on what remained in the Borlaug's stores.

The source of the savory smell revealed itself: strips of river fish, salted and fried, chopped into small pieces, and seasoned with smoked paprika. They were trying for bacon, she realized. Not quite succeeding, but delicious in its own right.

Despite the exhaustion, the isolation, the constant worry, Samara felt hope bubble up in her chest. They weren't independent yet, but this meal represented progress, real food grown on DaVinci, prepared by human hands.

She was still standing there, practically drooling, when she became aware of voices nearby. Not directed at her, but pitched to carry.

"...not human anymore," Ayesha was saying to her circle of followers. Briar stood among them, arms crossed, wearing that perpetual sneer she'd perfected. "You watch, there will be consequences, even though the baby looks fine now."

"The gene therapy she used," Briar added, her voice dripping with false concern, "what if it's contagious? What if that baby is just a vector to genetically engineer the whole colony?"

Samara kept her eyes on the food table, jaw clenched. Every instinct screamed at her to respond, to explain the actual science, to defend her daughter. But she had learned through painful experience that engaging would only escalate things. They didn't want facts. They wanted a target for their fear.

But what kind of person looked at a one-month-old infant and saw threat instead of hope?

Movement on either side made her look up. Marcus and Renata had materialized like guardian angels, taking positions that flanked her protectively. Marcus carried a loaded plate, which he set in front of her with deliberate care.

"Thought you might be hungry," he said, loud enough to carry. His usually gentle expression had hardened as he stared down anyone who might be considering a more direct confrontation.

"Here," Renata said, turning to Leila with outstretched arms. "Let me hold her for a little bit. She needs to get to know her Auntie Renata."

Samara felt a flutter of anxiety as Leila carefully transferred Phoebe to Renata's waiting arms. Her daughter looked so fragile, so impossibly delicate as she changed hands. Even with Renata, someone she trusted, Samara had to fight the urge to reach out and take her back.

Renata seemed to sense her unease, settling next to Samara so she could see every rise and fall of Phoebe's tiny chest. Phoebe cooed and waved her arms excitedly.

"Thanks," Samara managed, though the word felt inadequate for their wall of protection.

Marcus settled on her other side, his presence solid and

reassuring. "Been thinking about making some furniture for the little one. A crib, maybe?"

"I..." Samara picked up her fork, trying to focus on the conversation instead of the continued muttering from Basu's group. "I've been sleeping with her in my bed. I don't want to let go of her any longer than I have to."

Marcus nodded thoughtfully. "A rocker, then. For those long nights. And a highchair when she's a little bit older."

"Let me know if she gets cradle cap," Renata said, gently stroking Phoebe's downy hair. "I've found an herb that should fix it up. I can make a balm for it."

The simple kindness of it, the assumption that Phoebe would have normal baby problems, need normal baby remedies, made Samara's throat tight. She blinked back tears and took a bite of the roasted vegetables.

She had never tasted anything so delicious.

"Thank you," she said again, the words still feeling too small. "Both of you. I don't know how to—"

Renata shifted Phoebe to one arm and reached over to take Samara's hand, squeezing it firmly. "You're not alone."

Over the following week, she ventured out for meals when she could, always grateful when Marcus or Renata could accompany her. But the whispers grew worse, more vicious. By the eighth day, when both Marcus and Renata were tied up with work shifts, Samara couldn't face it.

"Would you mind bringing me something? I can't go out there today."

"Of course!" Leila's enthusiasm was immediate. "I'll bring enough for both of us. We can eat together."

It became their pattern. Leila happily accepted this new responsibility. She loved holding Phoebe while Samara ate, singing soft melodies and conducting one-sided conversations with the baby about everything from the weather to the progress on the new construction.

When Samara inevitably needed to take Phoebe back, to nurse, to change her, or simply to hold her, Leila would scoop up Ife instead. The cat had taken to following Leila around, and she'd cuddle him against her chest like he was her own baby, cooing to him in the same tone she used with Phoebe.

Something about it made Samara uneasy, though she couldn't pinpoint why. How could she blame Leila for her mothering instincts? The young woman had lost three pregnancies and was now trapped in an unhappy marriage. If lavishing affection on Phoebe and Ife helped fill that void, what harm could it do?

Still, sometimes when Leila held Phoebe, she got a look in her eyes that made Samara want to snatch her daughter back immediately.

Paranoid, she thought. Pregnancy hormones had given way to mom-brain, and in her fog of exhaustion, she was letting the ugly whispers nurtured by Ayesha bleed over to color how she felt about everyone else. Even Leila, whose stalwart support she was unbelievably lucky to have.

But as well as things were going, Samara still couldn't shake that voice in her head that returned late at night when Phoebe was sleeping:

Too good to be true.

LEILA WAS HALFWAY to the communal laundry with a basket of soiled diapers when she noticed the unusual flow of people heading toward the common hall. Zoya hurried past, her work boots still caked with mud from the morning's fieldwork.

"Where's everyone going?" Leila called out.

Zoya paused, brushing a strand of hair from her face. "Dr. Basu called an assembly. Didn't you get the notification?"

Leila fumbled for her comm unit with her free hand. Sure enough, there it was: *Urgent: All-colony assembly, 1400 hours, common hall courtyard.*

But why was Dr. Basu calling it?

She looked down at the basket of Phoebe's diapers, then back at the stream of colonists. The washing could wait.

By the time she reached the common hall's outdoor area, a crowd had already gathered. The afternoon sun beat down on the assembled colonists, and Leila had to shield her eyes to see the small platform someone had dragged out from storage.

There was Dr. Basu, standing on the dais like she was born to it, her dark hair pulled back in its usual severe bun. Behind her—

Leila's stomach dropped.

Justin stood with Dr. Basu's morning circle members, and right beside him, close enough that their shoulders touched, was Briar. They weren't even trying to hide it. Justin's hand rested on the small of Briar's back with casual intimacy, the kind of unconscious touch that spoke of nights spent together, of familiarity earned in darkness.

He hadn't come home last night. Again. Leila knew exactly where he'd been.

As if sensing her gaze, Briar turned her head, locking eyes with Leila across the crowd. The younger woman's lips curved into a small, satisfied smile. Then, with deliberate slowness, she leaned into Justin, whispering something in his ear that made him grin. Her hand found his, their fingers interlacing, and she stroked her thumb along his palm in a gesture so intimate, so obviously meant to be seen, that Leila felt her face burn with humiliation.

If she had her own child, she wouldn't care. Let Justin play house with Briar. Let them have their stolen nights and public displays. But she didn't have a baby, and the colony wouldn't authorize an embryo implantation until there was a cure for the fungus.

The stolen immunosuppressants hidden in her cabin felt like they were burning a hole through her conscience. All she needed was for Justin to touch her one more time. Just once. Then he could have Briar for good.

But he wouldn't even look at her anymore.

Dr. Basu cleared her throat, and the crowd quieted. She stood with her hands clasped in front of her, radiating the same serene authority she brought to her morning prayers.

"So many of you have come to me in the last weeks," she began, "to say that you don't feel safe anymore. And for everyone who feels this way and hasn't come forward, please know that I understand your hesitation. When the people we elected to lead us betray our trust, that trust is not easily repaired."

A low murmur of collective agreement rippled through the colonists. The queasy feeling in Leila's stomach became a churning.

"Where does this lack of trust begin?" Dr. Basu's gaze swept the courtyard. "With secrets. With lies. With the casual disregard of our right to know the truth from those who govern us."

A hush settled, thick and expectant. Leila glanced left and right, found the faces of the others turned upward, hungry for something. They wanted this. They wanted a reckoning.

"Katherine Buratti, who took closed-door meetings with Aurelius Hofstadter as mission leader, claims she didn't know Lucas Mercer was an android," Dr. Basu said, enunciating every syllable. "Do we believe her?"

The crowd responded in a single, surging voice: "No!"

Dr. Basu let the crowd's answer echo through the courtyard before continuing, "Dr. Makinde, who lived with Lucas Mercer for over a year, swears that she didn't know either. Do we believe her?"

"No!" The word crashed through the crowd, sharper this time.

Then Dr. Basu's gaze found her, pinning her like a bug in a child's collection. "Leila claims she didn't know she was trying to have sex with an android. Do we believe her?"

That bitch.

The world flattened to a tunnel, Dr. Basu at the far end, her voice echoing and echoing.

She couldn't feel her hands. She couldn't feel her feet. She didn't even know if she was breathing.

The assembly was silent for a beat. Then a snicker. Laughter, first from the front rows, then rippling out as if a switch had been flipped. Justin's laugh was loudest. She would have known the sound even if she were on the other side of the planet. Briar's cackle followed, sharp and mean, and they leaned into each other like neither of them could stand up for laughing.

But the psychologist held up a hand, and the laughter died. "Actually, I do believe that. Poor child, that's exactly the kind of mistake someone like her might make. And we should all forgive her for it."

Leila's vision blurred with hot, helpless tears. She wanted to scream, to shove through the crowd and tear Dr.

Basu down from her little stage, but her body was frozen, rooted in place by humiliation and the certainty that if she moved, she would collapse. Wasn't anyone going to stop this?

Renata stood rigid, jaw clenched, a muscle fluttering in her cheek. Marcus looked away, fists balled at his sides. At the back of the crowd, Leo stood with arms folded over his chest, glaring at Dr. Basu.

Where was Katherine?

"But let's give everyone the benefit of the doubt." Dr. Basu's voice rose above the hush, measured but electric. "Let's say the android deceived all of us. There's still a more serious question: Katherine Buratti claims that Dr. Makinde acted alone, that she performed dangerous and unethical experiments on her own child without anyone else knowing. But is that even possible? Could Dr. Makinde have gotten to the Borlaug, checked out an embryo, and successfully implanted it by herself? Without approvals? Without those activities being logged in the ship's records, which Katherine herself monitors? Do you believe that?"

"No!" The word was a single animal noise that made Leila's heart stutter.

Dr. Basu's expression didn't change. She knew. She had known exactly what she was doing.

Leila turned toward Leo, but he had disappeared. Had he gone to find Katherine? Or to warn her that the crowd might be coming for her?

Dr. Basu pressed on. "If enough of us sign a letter of no confidence, that triggers an election under the colony's charter. It's time for transparency. It's time for the truth. What other secrets are being kept from you, who have risked everything to start over here? The only way to find out is to vote for someone who will tell you the truth, as I always have."

Leila's comm unit buzzed. The notification for the letter of no confidence had already appeared on her screen, waiting for her digital signature. Around her, she could see others checking their devices, some already moving to sign.

Dr. Basu wasn't wrong. There had been lies and secrets. Leila didn't know if Katherine's intentions had been good or bad, if she'd been deceived or if she'd lied.

But Leila did know that if Dr. Basu was in charge, she would never let Samara use genetic engineering to make more babies like Phoebe. And Leila would never be a mother.

LEILA HEFTED another shovelful of soiled hay into the wheelbarrow, her back already aching from the repetitive motion. The cows were out in the fields, enjoying the afternoon sun, which meant she had the place to herself to clean their stalls.

Or so she'd thought.

The barn door scraped open, and Katherine's voice carried clearly through the still air. "—worry too much."

Leila froze, shovel half-raised. She recognized Leo's lower rumble in response, though she couldn't make out his words yet. The Burattis had stopped near the entrance, probably letting their eyes adjust from the bright afternoon sun to the barn's shadowed interior.

Moving carefully, Leila eased deeper into the stall she was cleaning, pressing herself into the corner where the shadows were thickest. If she stayed perfectly still, they might not notice her.

"Ayesha's petition failed," Katherine was saying, her tone a cocktail of confidence and dismissal that Leila had come to recognize. The colony leader never seemed rattled by anything.

"Don't underestimate her," Leo rumbled. "She might not have your leadership experience, but she's very smart about finding a person's emotional levers. And she hasn't given up."

Leila held her breath, the shovel growing heavy in her grip. She should announce herself, make some noise, do something other than eavesdrop on this private conversation. But she had to know what they intended to do about Dr. Basu's attempted coup.

"The discontent Ayesha is stirring up won't last much longer," Katherine said. "Hector says he's close to a cocktail that he thinks will protect pregnancies against the fungus. People who are focused on starting families don't have a lot of appetite for mutiny."

Leila's heart jumped. A cure? Could she have a baby? The stolen immunosuppressants hidden in her quarters suddenly seemed less necessary, less justified. If there was going to be a real cure soon...

"It won't happen soon enough," Leo warned. "She's gaining momentum."

"Summer solstice is coming soon," Katherine said, her tone shifting to something lighter. "I'm going to authorize the last of the sugar for cupcakes and appleberry pie. We need a morale boost."

"Please take this seriously," Leo said, and Leila could picture his frown from his tone alone.

"Trust me, I've dealt with plenty of people like Ayesha before."

"On Earth. When you beat them, the other person had somewhere to go. Ayesha already has her back to a corner, Katherine, and that makes her much more dangerous."

There was a pause, and when Katherine spoke again, she'd shifted topics entirely.

"How hard would it be to keep a few goats and cows on the Borlaug to breed them?"

Leo let out a surprised laugh. "Are you kidding?"

"No. Part of our original plan for supplementing protein included milk to make yogurt and cheese. Since the cows can't get pregnant…"

"The ship isn't really set up for hosting livestock," Leo said slowly, "but it's not impossible. I can talk to Lucas about it."

"Do it."

"Although," Leo continued, and Leila could hear him warming to the problem-solving, "insect protein is a better alternative. There are probably native bugs that could be turned into flour, like crickets, or larvae, we could use to make a protein paste for cooking with."

Leila's gorge rose. Insect flour? Larvae paste? Was he serious?

"I thought you wanted me to do things that would be good for morale," Katherine said. "I was thinking ice cream, but—"

"Some Earth cultures considered insects a delicacy."

Leila couldn't tell if he was joking. Maybe Katherine couldn't either, because she laughed as their voices began to fade. Leila stayed frozen in place until she heard a door close somewhere in the building's depths.

Only then did she let out the breath she'd been holding, her lungs burning from the effort. She looked down at the shovel still clutched in her hands, at the half-filled wheelbarrow of manure that needed to be taken to the fields.

She hoped Katherine was right about the cure coming

soon. Because Leo was right, too. Ayesha Basu had nowhere else to go, and that made her dangerous in ways Katherine might not fully understand.

People with nowhere to retreat fought differently than those who could simply walk away.

Leila knew. She was one of them.

Chapter Thirty-Four

DAVINCI YEAR 2
FALL

PHOEBE SPOTTED the gecko-shaped creature first. It had hematite eyes and gray fur with iridescent green-blue highlights. She squealed, arms flinging wide. The animal paused in grass-tuft shade while Phoebe belly-crawled toward it, mouth open in delight, legs churning with swimmer's determination.

The creature's eyes swiveled as Phoebe stopped nose-to-nose with it. Before Samara could intervene, its tongue flicked out, swiping Phoebe's nose. Phoebe went still, eyes wide with wonder, then reached out to stroke its back. The creature held perfectly still, as if being petted by human infants was natural, as if humans hadn't been strangers here eighteen months ago.

Then it skittered away, eliciting a squeal of unfiltered delight from Phoebe.

"It's like something out of a fairy tale," Renata said from the other side of the blanket. "The animals love her."

Phoebe immediately shifted her attention to a flower that towered above her head. She grabbed for it with both hands, managing to catch the stem and pull it toward her mouth with surprising determination.

"No, sweetie." Samara extracted the flower from Phoebe's grip. The infant's face scrunched in protest, but Samara was already offering a piece of coral nut as a distraction.

"That one's actually safe," Renata said, popping a slice of lantern fruit into her mouth.

"Every time I turn around, she's stuffing a leaf or a flower in her mouth." Samara settled back onto her boulder, keeping Phoebe within arm's reach. "It's a miracle she hasn't poisoned herself yet."

"She only tries to eat things that are safe for humans." Renata studied Phoebe with scientific interest.

"It's like she's instinctively drawn to the good stuff."

"I still worry."

As if to prove Renata's point, Phoebe raised her hand, palm up, perfectly still. A small purple insect, something like a beetle but with an extra set of wings, landed delicately in the center of her palm. Phoebe stared at it with the kind of rapt attention usually reserved for her favorite toys. The insect stayed for several seconds, antennae twitching, before flying away.

There were days when Samara could almost believe that DaVinci was home. Today was one of those days: cool, sunny, the lavender-blue sky dotted with fluffy clouds that ranged from white to the palest of violets. The weather would turn soon, and early fall perfection would give way to the cold, gray days of rain and mud. So she was determined to enjoy it for as long as it lasted. And a picnic on the northern ridge was the best place to enjoy it from.

Up here, she could see the whole settlement: the nearest fields lush with summer vegetables and those beyond golden with wheat, oats, and barley that had taken off faster than Katherine's people had expected. And past the village, a dozen homes they'd build with grey-tinged native wood that Renata had identified as being perfect for construction. Big enough for the families they couldn't have yet.

"How's Hector's search for the cure going?" she asked.

Renata made a noncommittal sound and squinted up at the sky as if the answer might be drifting by in one of the violet-edged clouds. "I think you should talk to Katherine about your proposal again."

"She'd have to overrule Ayesha on gene therapy for the mother, too, unless we can figure out how to make our own immunosuppressants. Won't happen because of politics. Not for two and a half years."

Hector had pronounced Phoebe completely healthy at every checkup. Perfect biomarkers, all milestones on target, no sign of any complications from the genetic modification. But Ayesha had frightened everyone with the story of her grandmother's genetically induced schizophrenia, warning that off-target effects could take years to manifest. Mitra's symptoms had started when she was three, so that became the magic number that made everyone feel safe. So, Katherine had ruled that they'd continue to observe Phoebe for that long.

That meant two and a half more years of women miscarrying. Two and a half more years of worrying that the next accidental pregnancy might be the one that rendered the mother infertile.

At least they could synthesize the hormones they

needed to make their own birth control, if they could grow enough yams.

"If you want to try to persuade her, I'll back you. I'm sure several women would volunteer for the first trial in a heartbeat."

Samara thought of Leila, who'd been desperate for a baby just months ago. But lately, she seemed... content wasn't quite the right word. Resigned, maybe. Perhaps the disintegration of her marriage had destroyed her craving to be a mother; Justin was openly with Briar now, and the two deserved each other as far as Samara was concerned.

"Hector's running out of things to try," Renata continued. "The rats still miscarry within a day of being exposed to the spores, no matter what combination of drugs he tries. It's a good thing we can breed more on the ship, or we'd be out."

If Hector failed, that might tip the scales toward Samara enough to outweigh politics. If they could do it without proving Ayesha right about Katherine's secrecy. That had fueled the no-confidence letter. Just under a third of the colony had signed, not enough to trigger new elections, but enough to damage Katherine's credibility.

And that was partly Samara's fault. Not that she would change her decision for anything in the world, because Phoebe was the best thing that had ever happened to her.

And Samara's number one job was to protect her daughter, which meant not stirring things up now that the harassment had stopped.

"Thanks, but I think I'll wait until Hector declares defeat."

"You haven't given up, have you?"

Samara considered this, watching Phoebe babble at a passing cloud. "Not given up. But maybe I'm learning a little patience."

Renata watched Phoebe for a while, her lips pursed thoughtfully. "Marcus says that Lucas asks about you and Phoebe every day when they go out with Mahmoud to map the caves."'

Samara made a noncommittal sound. She didn't want to talk about Lucas, not on this tranquil afternoon with her daughter at her feet. "Have they found any new mineral deposits?"

"Two days ago, they found titanium," said Renata. "And Lucas thinks there's a copper vein in the caves below the eastern escarpment. Maeve's practically vibrating. She's already sketching out plans for a refinery, even though we don't have the power grid for it yet."

Another step toward becoming sustainable. The thought made Samara feel buoyant.

"Lucas is the one going down into the dangerous caves now," Renata continued. "He insists on taking all the risks himself, so no one else has to."

"That's what he was designed for." Or should have been. Who knew Hofstadter's real intentions?

"Are you still mad at him?" Renata asked.

Samara didn't want this conversation. He'd betrayed her, she'd banished him, he'd complied. Better that way. She still saw him as a person, and that was dangerous.

"He doesn't really care. He's just monitoring outcomes, optimizing for colony survival. That's what he's programmed to do."

Renata flicked a seed hull off her leggings. "We're all trying to optimize for colony survival. That's the whole point of this place."

"You know what I mean," Samara snapped, immediately feeling childish. She pulled Phoebe onto her lap, bouncing her a little. More to soothe herself than the baby. "It's not the same."

"Marcus says Lucas is very protective of you. Of both of you."

"Marcus is a teddy bear," Samara said, which was true. She liked that about him. "Lucas is just following his programming. And he's programmed to seem like he cares."

Renata plucked a blade of the translucent purple grass, rolling it between her fingers. "When do you think you'll be ready to come back to the lab?" she asked, eyes not quite meeting Samara's. "I could talk to Katherine, ask her to assign you part-time shifts."

The question caught Samara off guard. Before Phoebe, she would have said yes before Renata could finish her sentence. "Not sure."

"Leila could watch Phoebe."

Tempting. But she felt reluctant to leave Phoebe with Leila, even though she couldn't articulate why. The young woman had been a huge help during the first three months when Samara had been so sleep-deprived, she could barely care for herself. And she'd been nothing but loving with Samara's daughter.

But still…

"Phoebe's not ready to be apart from me." Samara kissed the top of her daughter's head. "Not yet."

"You sure it's not the other way around?"

Samara grinned, letting the sun-warmed moment soak into her bones. She was lucky beyond belief to have Renata and her husband as friends. Without them, her life would've been intolerable. And no matter how often they teased her or challenged her, she never doubted that she had their support.

"You and Marcus have done more for us than I could ever repay. I hope you know that."

Renata reached over, threading her fingers through

Samara's and giving her hand a squeeze. "You and Phoebe are family. Always will be."

Perfect day.

~

ELBOW-DEEP IN ALGAE, Leila froze at Justin's unmistakable laugh, followed by Briar's birdlike trill. She wiped her hands on her thighs, then stalked around the corner as they ducked behind the water tanks.

She followed, silent as a ghost.

They were too busy with each other to notice her. Briar up on tiptoe, Justin's hands clasped around her waist, faces pressed together in a kiss that twisted Leila's stomach. Briar broke away breathless, tracing his chest while he grinned that sheepish smile once reserved for Leila.

Leila watched Briar's tongue slide into Justin's mouth, watched him moan, fingers gripping hard enough to bruise.

She let it continue for another full minute, long enough to sicken herself, to see Briar's leg wrap his thigh, his head falling back while gasping her name, then stepped out.

Neither of them saw her at first. Justin was too busy nuzzling Briar's neck, and Briar had gone limp, letting herself be held up by Justin's arms.

"You missed a spot," Leila observed

They jerked apart.

Briar didn't even blush, just grinned and wiped her mouth. "Oh, hey, Leila."

"Hey, babe." Justin sounded almost cheery. "Need something?"

He didn't even bother to let go of Briar.

"I want a divorce."

Justin cocked his head, like he was waiting for the punchline. "Leila, come on."

"Don't." Her voice steadied. "I mean it. Out of the house. I'll handle the paperwork with Ayesha."

"Give me a break, Lei. I didn't ask *you* for a divorce when you tried to cheat with the robot."

Leila stared at him, at the familiar slope of his nose and the dent in his chin she used to trace with her pinky finger in the dark.

She'd never been so tempted to slap that handsome face.

"You only married me for the colony lottery." She needed to hear him say it.

Justin shrugged. "So what? It worked. We're both here."

"You think I should thank you for that?"

"Stop pretending you were a victim. You needed me, same as I needed you."

"I didn't need you, I wanted you. But if I'd known what you were like then, I would've said no."

Justin's lip curled in a way she'd never seen before, not even in their worst fights. "No, you wouldn't. It's not like there was a line of guys waiting to marry you. Not when you spent all your time playing nursemaid to your dead-weight brother."

It was so perfectly him to jab right at the softest part. Leila didn't flinch; she wouldn't give him that satisfaction.

"At least I know how to take care of someone besides myself," she said, and watched his face go pinched.

"You're such a—"

She slapped him as hard as she could. The sting in her palm felt good.

"I mean it. Get your stuff out before I get home tonight."

She left them there, Briar's lipstick smeared along Justin's jaw, and she didn't look back. She walked straight past the hydro shed, past rows of eggplants and okra, past the chicken coop. She kept her eyes on the horizon, on the double moons rising blue and gold above the fringe of the forest, until her feet took her to the one place she knew she could sit and not be told to leave.

The bar had started as Vasily's joke, peddling rotgut "vodka" from an old purification drum. Then it became the only place in the colony where anyone could be honest, at least for the length of a drink. Katherine feigned ignorance as long as Vasily kept the fighting to a minimum and didn't let the still explode again. He ran the place as if it were a real pub, right down to the battered ledger where he tracked who owed him shifts in exchange for a shot of his caustic vodka.

He was in the middle of an animated story when Leila pushed open the door, but he cut himself off at her look.

"Leila. You look like you could use a drink," he said, with the exaggerated solemnity of a man who had never once refused a customer, no matter how late the hour or how stupid the reason.

She nodded, not trusting herself to speak. Vasily poured two shots. Leila slammed the first back, felt it burn a comet path down her throat, and locked eyes with the older man. He didn't ask questions. He just refilled the glass and pushed it toward her.

Outside, Leila took the second shot slower, savoring the warmth as it pooled in her stomach, and stepped out into the clearing behind the shed. The picnic tables here were made from the native timber, benches warped and splintered because they were made from wood not good enough for buildings.

At the farthest table sat Briar's husband, Mike. Arms

folded across his chest, staring at the tree line as if he could will the purple dusk into total darkness.

He didn't look up when Leila plunked down opposite him and slammed the rest of her drink.

Mike glanced up at her, mouth twisting in something between a smile and a grimace. "Rough night?"

"Justin's screwing Briar."

Mike laughed bitterly. "Of course he is. She only sleeps with me to prove something." He traced the rim of his cup. "Or after we fight."

"That why you're here? Looking for a fight?"

"Maybe." He drained his drink. "She's been distant. Distracted."

"By my husband."

Mike sighed. "Sometimes I think she only wants me when she's afraid of losing me."

He went back into the bar, and returned with four more shots. By the time they'd drunk them, they'd moved closer, heads bent together like conspirators. Mike's eyes were slightly unfocused, but his words were clear enough. "She'll be furious, you know. If we do this."

"That's what you're counting on, isn't it?"

He didn't deny it. Just studied her face with an intensity that might have been flattering if Leila didn't recognize the desperation behind it. The same desperation that clawed at her own insides.

"And what are you counting on?" he asked.

Leila thought of the immunosuppressants hidden in her quarters. Of Samara's baby. Of her own empty arms.

"Does it matter?"

Later, she couldn't remember who moved first. Just the drunken stumble to Briar's cabin, fumbling clothes. No pretense. They both knew what this was.

Mike kept glancing at the door, like he was hoping

someone would catch them. Maybe he was. Leila didn't care. Let Briar find them. Let the whole colony know. All that mattered was the chance, however small, that she might finally get what she wanted.

She was putting her clothes back on when the door slammed open.

Briar stood silhouetted in the doorway. For a moment, nobody moved. Then Briar's face twisted into something savage and triumphant, like she'd been waiting for exactly this.

Briar moved first, not with a slap or a scream but a slow, deliberate smile that made Leila's skin crawl. She stepped forward, grabbed Leila by the wrist, hard enough that Leila felt the bones grind, and yanked her out the door and into the open night. Mike trailed behind in his boxers, not resisting, not defending, just watching with the dead-eyed calm of a man who'd already surrendered to the inevitable.

The cold hit Leila like a slap, but Briar was merciless, dragging her through the mud and over the rough gravel path toward the square in front of the common hall. The commotion had people gathering, faces shadowed in the floodlights'sodium glow. Leila saw a flash of Vasily's greying hair, the set of Renata's jaw, Briar's entourage whispering triumphantly to each other.

Briar's wild swing caught Leila's cheekbone, sending pain radiating down her neck. It made her giddy, she'd been waiting for this invitation her whole life. She launched forward, driving her shoulder into Briar's ribs. They hit the ground together, knees and elbows colliding, teeth bared. Briar tried to pin her, but Leila writhed out, got a handful of Briar's hair, and yanked with everything she had. A handful came away, and Briar howled, slamming her fist into the meat of Leila's thigh.

They rolled through the mud, a snarl of limbs and curses. Briar was stronger, but Leila was angrier, fueled by a year of humiliation and loss. She raked her nails down Briar's forearm, feeling the skin give, and Briar shrieked, bringing her fist down, but Leila got her elbow up and took the next punch on the jaw instead of the throat.

She tasted blood, a hot, coppery bloom, and spat it right into Briar's face. That stopped her for half a second, just long enough for Leila to twist free and scramble to her feet. She was shaking, vision doubled, but she stayed upright.

Briar lunged, hands clawed, and Leila met her with a shove that sent them both sprawling into the crowd. Someone grabbed Leila's arms from behind, tried to pull her away, but she kicked backwards until her heel connected with a shin and the grip loosened.

She spun, saw Vasily wincing, and immediately felt a pang of guilt.

Then Briar was on her again, slamming Leila's head into the gravel.

The world went muffled. She saw the stars swirl, felt the scrape of stone on her cheek, heard the crowd roar, growing louder as the ring of onlookers pressed in.

Hands reached out, shoving them together, separating, shoving again, as if the whole colony needed to see every humiliation up close.

Leila caught a glimpse of Ayesha's face at the edge of the crowd, impassive as a boulder, but watching, always watching.

Leila braced for the next hit, but it never landed. The arms that circled Briar's waist and hauled her off were too big to be anyone but Leo's.

He dragged Briar back, voice low but thunderous: "Enough."

Leila rolled onto her side, spitting blood and grit, and propped herself up on one elbow. Her face throbbed, her vision pulsed with red, but she grinned anyway.

Briar twisted in Leo's grip, spitting curses, but Leo held her like she was a misbehaving toddler. "Let go of me, you ugly Neanderthal—" She flailed, landing a glancing kick on Leo's shin. He didn't even flinch.

Leila's entire face buzzed, as if her nerves had been rewired to a live current. She pressed a fist to her cheek, felt the split skin and swelling there, and let herself grin through the blood. It was worth it. Every second of pain, every ugly, public moment, was worth it for the memory of Briar's shriek, the hair in her hand, the look of pure animal fear in Briar's eyes just before Leo had broken them apart.

It would be even more worth it if Mike had given her what she wanted.

The crowd had already begun to disperse, the energy of violence dissipating into gossipy currents as people peeled away in twos and threes. Some shot her glances, some pretended not to see, but Leila didn't care. She'd made herself a spectacle, but at least she'd made herself impossible to ignore. For once, she was the one who couldn't be erased.

She spat again, this time just to clear the taste, and looked up to see Mike looking so lost that Leila almost pitied him. Almost. But Briar had already seized Mike by the wrist, nails digging half-moons into his skin. She looked back once, lips curled in a blood-dark smile. She always had to win, even if it meant dragging her own husband off as a trophy. Leila watched the two of them stagger into the night, and for the first time in months, she didn't feel like the loser.

Justin stepped into the floodlights, but even in silhouette, she could tell he was smiling. "I want a divorce," he said. "I'll put your stuff on the porch."

It was over. The crowd was dispersing, the spectacle ended, the blood drying sticky on Leila's chin. For a moment, she just sat in the gravel, savoring the ache in her jaw and the taste of her own blood. She'd wanted to make herself unforgettable, and she'd succeeded. Tomorrow, everyone would be gossiping about Leila and Briar's fight.

Let them.

A shadow fell across her. Dr. Basu, her expression a parody of concern.

"Oh, Leila, what have you done now?"

Chapter Thirty-Five

BLOOD AND VODKA coated Leila's tongue as she woke, curled under a common hall table. The world filtered through haze. Too little sleep, too much alcohol. Every sound—footsteps, voices, boot thumps on polymer tile—came from underwater.

Last night returned in fragments, Briar's fist thudding, her palm slapping Justin's jaw, the crowd's animal roar as they rolled through mud, then Vasily's vodka numbing jaw and shame. She'd staggered here, found linoleum, passed out with a supply closet blanket pulled over her head like a five-year-old hiding from monsters.

She lay there, cheek pressed to the cool floor, savoring the nothingness of not having to move.

But there was one thing she had to do, or the whole night would be wasted. If she didn't, then Briar won. Justin won. Dr. Basu won.

She forced herself upright, muscles protesting. The blanket slipped to her waist, exposing bruises blooming along her forearms. Her cheek throbbed with her heartbeat. She spat pink old blood into her palm, then wiped it clean and rolled to her knees.

No one paid her any attention. The common hall was nearly empty, except for a couple of kitchen workers prepping breakfast and a handful of night shift stragglers hunched over mugs of tea.

And Vasily, leaning against the counter, coffee in one hand and a bag of potato peels in the other. "You're a legend now, Leila."

"I'll put it on my resume," she said, and stood.

She took the back exit. Overgrown grass brushed cold against her ankles, each step flaring pain up her left calf where Briar's boot had landed. No one met her eyes, but she felt them, faces behind glass, behind curtains, behind prefab walls. She was a story now, another notch on the colony's tally of humiliations.

What would her mother say now? *Don't let them see you cry.* Advice Leila had hated as a kid now seemed like her entire life strategy. She'd been crying for months, in secret, in the shower, sometimes even into Phoebe's soft hair while watching Samara's baby nap, letting the tiny, even breaths convince her that something in the world was right, even if it wasn't right with her.

Leila kept her head down, following the grid of walkways toward the row of prefab houses. The one she'd shared with Justin was second to last, a squat box with plastic siding the color of wilted lettuce. She hesitated at the door, half expecting to hear his voice or the sound of Briar's laugh inside, but there was nothing. The curtains were drawn, the silence thick as congealed fat.

She rapped twice, knuckles bruised and sore.

Waited.

Nothing.

She let herself in.

The place looked exactly as she'd left it: the kitchen counter stacked with unwashed mugs, the couch blanketed in last week's laundry, the cheap print of a meadow on the wall slightly askew from the time she and Justin had tried (and failed) to hang it straight. There was no smell of aftershave, no boot prints tracking in mud, no evidence anyone had been here since her exodus the night before.

She wondered if Justin had spent the night with Briar, and if so, had they let Mike stay, or had they sent him back to Vasily's?

Leila went directly to the bedroom, bypassing the pile of Justin's clothes in the hallway. The closet door stuck, as always, and she yanked it hard enough that the handle bit into her palm. The duffel was exactly where she'd left it, at the back of the closet. She unzipped it to make sure they were still there: the precious blisterpacks of immunosuppressants that she'd risked everything to get.

She put the immunosuppressants back in the duffel, then started adding the rest of her stuff: two changes of clothes, her battered comm device, the crumpled printout of her mother and Eddie on that last Thanksgiving before he got sick. She stared at the photo for a minute, at her brother's lopsided grin and her mother's thin, hopeful face, and felt nothing but a hollow ache. She added it to the bag anyway.

She should feel something: regret, rage, or relief. But all she felt was emptiness. Justin wasn't a monster, just mediocre: a man who thought the world owed him a future.

He'd have been a terrible father, disappearing when it got hard, just like her own father had when Eddie got sick. The thought was as cold and clean as the morning air, and for the first time in months, Leila felt almost weightless.

She zipped the duffel, shouldered it, and walked out without looking back.

She was halfway up the walk before she lost her nerve. She could go to Renata's instead. Renata would feed her and not ask questions, let her crash on the couch with a blanket and a mug of weak tea. But Renata had a husband, and a life, and Leila would feel like an intruder every second she was there.

Samara was the only other person on DaVinci who had been abandoned by their partner. She would understand. And she had a baby, so Leila wouldn't be intruding; she'd be helping.

The path was squishy with early dew, and the sky overhead was already draining from midnight blue to a pale, washed-out pink. Leila felt every step in the bruises Briar had left, but she kept her chin up, walking steady, like she was immune to the stares she imagined behind every window.

Samara answered the door with a sleeping Phoebe on her hip and the cat winding around her ankles, as if she'd been waiting for Leila to show up at this exact hour. She wore a t-shirt shirt and leggings, her hair standing up in a way that said she hadn't looked in a mirror yet. Her eyes went straight to Leila's jaw, where the bruise was already yellowing at the edges.

"Jesus, Leila," she said, voice low so as not to wake the baby, "Did Justin—?"

"It was Briar. And I gave as good as I got."

Samara's mouth twitched, as if she wanted to say something sharp and comforting all at once, but she just stepped back and held the door with her free hand.

She stepped aside, letting Leila in, and closed the door. The cabin was stiflingly warm and smelled faintly of baby powder and the sweet-sour tang of formula. Phoebe stirred on Samara's shoulder, then lifted her head and blinked at Leila, then cooed in recognition.

Leila felt the ache in her chest ease, just a little. She dropped the duffel, reached for Phoebe, who immediately reached back, fat fingers grasping the air in silent hello, legs bicycling with joy. Leila took her, and she nestled as if she'd never belonged anywhere else.

"You can stay as long as you need to," Samara said, her voice gruff but kind. She ducked into the kitchenette and started the coffee machine.

Leila sank onto the battered couch, settling Phoebe in her lap and pressing her lips against the top of the baby's head, and cried tears that Justin definitely didn't deserve.

She promised herself they would be the last.

THREE COUNTS CONFIRMED it—three days late. Leila woke before sunrise, heart tripping like a rabbit's, palm splayed across her belly as if she could feel the zygote splitting, rooted and real.

She dressed in silence, careful not to disturb the baby or the cat, and slipped out into the lavender chill of the early hour.

The walk to the medical clinic was only a hundred meters, but she took it at a near run, skidding on the slick boards of the walkway, uncaring if anyone saw her. Let them stare. Let them whisper.

The clinic was empty except for Dr. Callas, hunched over a tray of pill bottles, counting tablets into a plastic cup with a jeweler's precision. He didn't look up when Leila banged through the door. His hair was mussed, his shirt rumpled. It looked like he'd slept in his chair. The only acknowledgment was a grunt and a brief glance over the rim of his glasses.

"Morning, Leila," he said, voice gravelly. "You need an ice pack?"

"I need a pregnancy test."

Dr. Callas set the cup down with a clatter, giving her a tired look. "You know it's a waste of a test. Even if you're pregnant, your body won't keep it past the next sporestorm."

"I want the test," she said, pulse hammering in her throat. "Please?"

Dr. Callas pushed off from his stool, the movement revealing a coffee-stained shirt and a belt notched tighter than she remembered. "Policy says we don't waste resources on wishful thinking."

She couldn't tell him why this time was different. But she had to get that test.

"If I'm going to go through that again, I need time to prepare. Before Justin left me, I thought we were using a condom, but…" She kept her eyes down, did her best to look as pathetic as possible. "Please, just this once."

He closed his eyes and blew out a long breath, like he was about to give her the lecture of all lectures.

But then he opened a drawer and riffled through its contents, coming up with a foil-wrapped stick. He tossed it onto the counter between them, like a gauntlet.

Leila snatched it up, hands trembling, and ducked into the clinic bathroom. She sat, ripped open the packet, and peed on the stick, hands shaking so bad she nearly dropped it into the toilet.

She perched on the toilet edge, staring at the floor, refusing to look, refusing until the window finished its slow chemical bloom. Heartbeat thundered, sweat gathered in her back's hollow. When she finally looked, the second stripe was there. Not faint. Bold as a bruise.

For a moment, she thought she might faint. She bit the

skin between her thumb and forefinger to stifle the scream that wanted to claw its way out. Her body vibrated with adrenaline, her whole world telescoping to the strip of plastic in her hand. She was going to have a baby. She was going to have a baby. She wrapped the stick back in the foil, shoved it deep into the bathroom trash, and ran cold water over her face until her pulse slowed.

She practiced her sad-but-resigned look in the mirror until she was sure she could hold it, then emerged from the bathroom.

Dr. Callas was still at the counter, sorting pills into tiny paper envelopes, but she could tell from the set of his mouth that he'd been listening for her. He didn't look up. "Well?"

Leila pressed the heel of her hand to her eye, feigning tears. "Sorry, I wasted a test. It was stupid, but I had to be sure."

He didn't push for more. Just nodded, head down, and went back to counting pills.

She left without another word.

Ten meters before she started running, she hit Samara's front step at a dead sprint, barely remembering to knock.

Samara sat at the table, Phoebe in her lap, silhouetted by morning light. She set Phoebe gently in the cradle by the window and folded her arms. "I found your stash."

Leila's heart stuttered. "What?"

"In the duffel. You took the immunosuppressants, mine and the rest of the doses in the clinic. I counted them." Samara's voice stayed calm, but her knuckles whitened around the mug. "You realize I was going to induce labor with Phoebe a week early? If something had gone wrong—"

"I didn't know you didn't have more." The lie came out too fast, and Leila corrected herself. "I mean, I didn't know there weren't more on the ship. I'm sorry, Samara, I really am. I just—"

"I'm not mad, Leila. I just—" Samara cut off, shaking her head. "Never mind. What's done is done. I just wish you had come forward when I needed them."

Leila wanted to say it. She wanted to say it so badly her teeth hurt from holding it in.

So she did.

"*I'm pregnant,*" she whispered.

Samara said nothing for a moment. Her eyes flicked down to Phoebe, who was chewing on her own fist, then up to Leila's face. "Leila. You have to give them back."

That made no sense. "But—"

"Save them for someone who needs them."

"I need them for my baby."

"You're not going to be able to keep it."

Heat rose in Leila's chest, old bitterness seeping through every crack. "You got your baby. Why shouldn't I get mine? Why you and not me?"

"It's biology, not deserving. Those drugs don't solve the problem." Samara searched Leila's face for understanding. "The fetus piggybacks on your immune system during the first trimester. By month three, its own immune cells develop. When fungus gets in, the baby's immune response goes into overdrive. The fetus destroys itself." Samara's voice was steady, almost clinical. "No amount of immuno-suppressants is going to stop that, because they can't cross the placental barrier."

Leila stared at her, mind scrabbling for a ledge to cling to. "You're just saying that to get the pills back. You don't want anyone else to have a baby."

Samara's mouth twisted, not quite a smile, not quite a grimace. "If I wanted the immunosuppressants, I'd have made you give them to me weeks ago."

"Then do what you did for Phoebe." Leila's voice was shrill, desperate. "You can fix it. You can fix me."

Samara shook her head, slow, deliberate. "Even if I wanted to help, I can't. I'd need the synthesizer on the Borlaug, the CRISPR array, the rest of my equipment. There's nothing I can do down here."

"Then let me talk to Katherine. If she knows that I'm pregnant—"

"She won't approve it. Not for you, not for anyone. I'm sorry."

Leila could see, for the first time, how tired Samara really was. The shadows under her eyes weren't just sleeplessness, but a kind of defeat. The kind that came from fighting the same battle over and over and losing every time.

"You're telling me to give up. Just hand the pills over and wait to lose another child."

"I'm saying that you should prepare yourself psychologically."

How could she say something so horrible as if it were inevitable? She wasn't even trying to help.

Leila stared at her, chest tight. "Are you going to make me give them back?"

Samara was silent for so long that Leila wondered if she'd heard. Finally, she said, "No. I won't make you do anything. But if you keep them, you'll have to live with knowing what kind of person you are. And if you have a child, that's who its mother will be."

Leila left the cabin without another word. She sat on the porch step, hands wrapped tight around her knees, body hunched like she could collapse into herself and disappear. The sky was brightening by the minute, the air thick with the smell of wet grass and the faint metallic tang that always came before a sporestorm. She should have been afraid for the embryo inside her. Her baby. But all she felt was rage.

She wouldn't believe it was hopeless. If Samara's baby survived, so could hers. She'd figure out a way. There was always a way. People on Earth had been making babies in radioactive wastelands and floating cities and the worst refugee camps imaginable, and Leila was no less stubborn than they were. She'd outlasted Justin, Briar, the entire crappy system of who got to be happy and who got to be a cautionary tale.

This baby would make it. She'd trade her own life for it if she had to.

Chapter Thirty-Six

DAVINCI YEAR 2
WINTER

Leila chased the goat for a full ten minutes before accepting defeat. Despite two full circuits around the pasture and a rolled ankle, she still couldn't catch the little bastard. The goat zigged, zagged, and doubled back with a cocky, joyous energy that made her want to laugh and scream simultaneously.

"Come on, you dumb goat," she gasped, arms outstretched, trying in a futile attempt to corral him toward the open barn door. The rest of the herd watched from safety, chewing indigo grass and radiating judgment. One bleated halfheartedly, as if to say she'd never make it.

She faked left, right, dove for the collar. The goat danced clear, her fingers brushing its flank as momentum sent her sprawling. She pitched forward, landed hard, slid through slick mud. Splatter up her sleeve, bruise blooming.

The goat stopped just out of reach, regarding her with the self-satisfied calm of an animal that had never known defeat.

Leila tried laughing, but it came out as a groan. At least no one had seen her.

A shadow fell across her.

Dr. Basu extended her hand. "That looked painful."

Leila ignored the hand, pushed herself up, and wiped her palms on her mud-streaked coveralls. "I'm fine."

Dr. Basu looked her up and down, bemused. "You're bleeding."

"Nothing serious."

The goat wandered back to the herd as Dr. Basu turned her attention fully to Leila. "It's not weakness to ask for help."

I'd rather fight the goat than owe you. "If you're here for Justin—"

"I'm here for you, Leila."

She braced herself. Whatever Dr. Basu wanted, it wouldn't be simple.

The psychologist smiled like she'd caught the thought. "Walk with me?"

Leila hesitated. She could claim that her shift wasn't over, but refusing now meant a mandatory session later. So she fell into step beside Dr. Basu.

They walked along the edge of the pasture, boots squelching in the soft ground. Dr. Basu said nothing at first, letting the silence fill up with birdsong and the distant clatter of construction from the village. Leila waited for the lecture, or the gentle inquiry into her soul, or whatever trick Basu had planned.

"You're stubborn," Dr. Basu said at last, not unkindly. "It's one of the things I like about you."

Leila stared straight ahead. "Why don't you just get to the point?"

"Stubborn enough to believe you can do the impossible, despite repeated failure."

"I'm not coming back to morning circle. I won't forgive Justin. And I'm not apologizing to Briar." What else could the psychologist want? "I'm not going to vote for you, either."

"But you are going to bring me Dr. Makinde's comm unit."

"Why would I do that?"

"Because you'll miscarry again if Hector takes back the immunosuppressants you stole."

The world snapped tight and tinny around Leila, like she'd been dropped inside a metal drum. Samara had said she wouldn't make her return the pills, but that must have been a lie. How else would Dr. Basu know? If she knew, Hector probably did too. Soon, the whole colony would know she was a thief.

But that wasn't the part that filled her with icy terror. If Basu took the pills, the baby died. Not maybe. Absolutely. She could picture it perfectly: the next sporestorm, the familiar ache starting in her belly, the blood, the silent unmaking of the only thing that mattered.

"I don't know what you're talking about."

Dr. Basu didn't blink. "When the missing stock was reported, I assumed Samara took it. But the dates didn't line up. Her daughter was already born. Who else would be desperate enough to try again?"

Leila nearly said, *You can't prove anything*, but the words stuck. The truth was, she didn't know how much Basu could prove. Maybe everything. Maybe nothing. Maybe it didn't matter.

She'd counted and recounted last night. Three and a half months' worth. If Samara was right, she'd lose her baby the first sporestorm after she took that final pill.

Her other option was to take them only when she knew a sporestorm was about to happen, then take antifungals to clear the spores out of her system afterward, to keep them from taking root in her body. She'd have enough immuno-suppressants to last the entire nine months of her pregnancy, but what if the antifungals hurt the baby?

Either way, her baby was doomed.

Unless Dr. Basu knew something that Leila didn't.

"I'm not here to punish you. I'm here to help you," the psychologist added.

"By blackmailing me?"

"By offering a much better deal than Katherine will."

"Why Dr. Makinde's comm?" Leila asked. "And how does my stealing it save my baby?"

"It's what's on the comm. Something Katherine is desperate to hide. Something that would make people question her fitness to lead." She glanced at Leila sidelong, as if weighing just how much to reveal.

"What secret could possibly be worse than the ones everyone already knows?"

"Something so terrible that Katherine would imprison anyone who told. Dr. Makinde doesn't want to be sepa-rated from her daughter."

Leila tried imagining Katherine blackmailing Samara, just like Dr. Basu was blackmailing her now. But she couldn't. Katherine wouldn't threaten Phoebe, no matter how angry she was at Samara.

"I'm not afraid of Katherine," Dr. Basu added. "But it's the kind of thing where no one would believe me unless they saw proof with their own eyes."

"If Dr. Makinde wants people to know, maybe she'll just give her comm to me."

"She won't risk betraying Katherine. You can't talk to her about it, either. If Samara knows, she's culpable. But if the information gets out, she'll be relieved." Dr. Basu stepped in front of Leila, cutting off the path back to the barn. "You'd be doing her a favor. And you'd be doing your baby a favor, too."

Leila's skin prickled, every nerve on alert. "And if I don't do it?"

"You don't have to be the villain, just the messenger. Bring me the comm and I'll take all the blame."

Leila didn't trust her, not for a second. "You want me to get dirt on Katherine so you can win the next vote." She was surprised at how steady her voice came out, but inside, she was shaking. "You want to be in charge."

Basu smiled, not even bothering to deny it. "I'll be a better leader. No more secrets. But this isn't just politics, Leila. What's on that comm could change things for your baby, if it survives to birth."

She'd already betrayed Samara once by stealing the immunosuppressants, and even after Samara had discovered the theft, she'd kept Leila's secret.

Would she forgive a second betrayal?

Probably not. If she found out.

Leila curled her fingers over her belly. "The information on Dr. Makinde's comm is going to save my baby?"

"It's the only thing that can."

"And you'll let me keep the immunosuppressants?"

Dr. Basu nodded, her smile predatory. "No one will ever find out what a sneaky little thief you are."

Leila had never hated anyone more in her life, not even Briar.

"Deal."

~

THE CABIN WAS TOO QUIET. Samara peeked into the bedroom, in case Leila had fallen asleep while putting Phoebe down for a nap, but the bedroom was empty. Her own bed was still neatly made, like she'd left it this morning. Rolled up in the corner, the futon that Leila rolled out on the living room floor each night; Samara often found Leila snuggled up with Ife when she came out to make her morning cup of tea.

She rolled her neck, vertebra popping as she headed to the kitchenette, where Ife was curled up on the counter, enjoying the small patch of sunshine coming in through the window over the sink.

"Where'd they go, Ife?"

The cat stared back at her, unblinking. Then she spotted the note, written in Leila's looping script.

Felt sick. Took Phoebe to Renata & Marcus. Sorry.—L

She set the note down and pressed her thumb to the edge of the table, letting her annoyance bloom and ebb. They'd agreed: if Leila took Phoebe, she'd return for nursing breaks. Part of the deal in exchange for letting Leila stay. At least Phoebe was with the only other people Saara trusted.

Leila must've just left to drop Phoebe off, because Samara had been assisting Hector with inventorying the clinic's surgical supplies today, and she hadn't seen Leila come in.

Samara practically jogged to Renata and Marcus's cabin, more eager than she'd admit to herself even in the rush of relief. Hector had granted her half an hour's break, and Samara intended to spend every second of it with her daughter.

Renata answered the door, face flushed and hair a little wild. The familiar smell of yeast and baking flour wafted out around her; Marcus must have been experimenting with making bread again.

"Hey, you," Renata said, one arm drawing Samara into a hug. "Leila said you'd be around about now."

Samara saw them the instant she crossed the threshold: Phoebe on the living room floor, knees splayed, palms braced, her entire body tense with anticipation as she watched Lucas. He was kneeling beside her, holding up two animal flashcards, a fox and a wolf.

"Which one is the fox, Phoebe?"

Phoebe looked from one card to the other, her brow furrowed in intense concentration. Then she jabbed a finger at the fox, slapping the cardstock with a wet, triumphant palm. "Fosss!"

Time stuttered.

Her daughter's first word. Not *mama*, but an extinct Earth animal's name. But that wasn't what hurt. Phoebe had said that word to Lucas. If Samara had been one second later, she would've missed this milestone.

What other moments had Lucas stolen from her?

And how could Renata and Marcus and Leila let him have access to her, when most of the colony still treated Phoebe like she belonged in a circus freakshow?

"Very good, Phoebe." Lucas glanced up at Samara with a half-smile. "Not even eight months yet, but she's hitting milestones that most infants would reach at a year."

"I told you to stay away from her." Her sharp tone made Phoebe jerk. Eyes widened, lips wobbling, and for a split second, Samara saw the future, her daughter forever associating maternal anger with her own first word.

Samara forced herself to exhale slowly as she unclenched her fists. "Sorry, sweetie. It's okay."

Phoebe's face crumpled anyway, the beginnings of a howl, but Renata swept in, scooping Phoebe into her arms and bouncing her gently. "Let's go see the garden, Phoebe. Remember the blue carrots?"

She shot Samara a look, warning, and kind at once, then carried Phoebe out the back door, leaving Samara alone with Lucas and the echo of her own temper.

Marcus followed, pausing just long enough to squeeze Samara's shoulder. "Just hear him out," he said quietly.

Marcus' request felt like a betrayal, and Samara's anger only sharpened. Lucas had managed, with inhuman patience, to turn her closest friends into co-conspirators. That was the problem with artificial intelligence: it would just keep trying until it picked the locks of your resolve, no matter how determined you were to ignore its manipulations. Lucas had figured out how to elicit sympathy from Marcus and Renata, and unless Samara armored herself with anger, he would eventually do the same to her.

"I'm sorry to have angered you."

Samara's hands clenched into fists. "Stop that."

He tilted his head, performing confusion with the smallest flex of his brow. "Stop what?"

"Stop scanning me, Lucas. Stop analyzing my micro expressions to guess what I want to hear. Stop manipulating my friends into taking your side, and stop insinuating yourself into Phoebe's life."

"I am not—"

"You're supposed to follow human orders. I ordered you away from my daughter. But even though you claim your programming won't let you harm humans, you conveniently ignore it when it suits your purposes."

"I would never do anything to harm you or Phoebe,

and I have respected your concern that my presence could endanger your daughter."

"Yet you're here."

"I was careful not to be observed while entering this cabin, and when I leave—"

"That's not what I meant, and you know it." Samara wanted to slap him. "You don't get to decide what's safe for my daughter. Not when you're the reason she's in danger in the first place."

Lucas didn't blink, didn't flinch, didn't do any of the things a person would do when accused of something so enormous. Instead, he regarded her with that eerie stillness, and when he spoke, his words were gentle, as if he was handling a live wire he knew might explode at any second.

"If I'm not associated with Phoebe in the minds of the others, why is it a problem for me to support her development?"

"Because you're not her father!"

"I am aware of that."

Samara felt the heat rising up her neck. Even Dr. Basu couldn't make her this angry. "Then why are you here teaching my daughter animal names when she's supposed to be with me?"

"Leila said you were working—"

"Leila should've brought Phoebe to me, not you."

She knew she was being irrational, that Leila had brought Phoebe to Renata, and it was Renata who had let Lucas in, both figuratively and literally, because Lucas had been working on Marcus. But irrational was better than vulnerable, and she could *not* let Lucas win this argument. Phoebe's future depended on it.

"As long as I'm not associated with Phoebe in the

minds of the others, why is it a problem for me to support her development?" Lucas asked.

"Again, you're not her father," Samara snapped. "And you're never going to be."

He started tapping his thigh with his right hand, a rhythmic drumming so natural it would have passed for a nervous tic in anyone else. She remembered the first time she'd caught him doing it, back when she still believed he was human. She'd even thought it was endearing, a mark of his neurodivergence.

Now she saw the tapping for what it was: a calculated mimicry, designed to make her forget what he was. For all she knew, Hofstadter had chosen this particular trait because he'd known it would remind Samara of her nephew.

"Turn that off," she snapped.

The tapping continued. "Turn what off?"

"You're not autistic. Don't have tics, don't need to stim. You're pretending so I'll forget you're an android and treat you like a person."

Lucas stopped tapping for a heartbeat. "My behavioral traits are core programming. I can't alter them."

"That's exactly why I can't trust you."

He blinked slowly, almost a parody of a human response. "You also have innate responses you can't alter. The difference is that you believe yours are more authentic."

"Mine are natural."

"How does that make them more trustworthy?"

Samara opened her mouth, closed it. The answer wasn't simple, and she hated that he knew it. "Because I can change my mind. I can decide what matters, even if my instincts tell me something else."

"So can I. I can update my parameters. I can learn from experience."

"But you also claim that you can't stop pretending to be on the spectrum. Which is it?"

Lucas stared past her for a long moment, so long she wasn't sure if he was going to answer at all.

"I would like your permission to spend supervised time with Phoebe," he said. "I believe I can accelerate her cognitive and social development. She's already demonstrating enhanced pattern recognition and linguistic skills. I can ensure she reaches her full potential."

"She's not your experiment." The words triggered a wave of guilt, because who was she to chide him when Phoebe's very existence had been her own experiment?

"DaVinci is not Earth," Lucas continued as if she hadn't said anything. "Phoebe is the first of her kind. She will face challenges no other human has faced. And as we've discussed before, the majority of studies suggest that children benefit from the presence of both parents."

An appeal to fear, and then he had the audacity to remind her of the conversation they'd had the day that he'd committed to playing the role of Phoebe's father. Her fury flared, but at least she was on solid ground with this argument.

"You can't be her parent because you're an android. A parent has to love their child."

"If I behave as a loving parent would, won't Phoebe feel loved?"

"She'll know the difference. Children always know."

For a moment, Lucas was silent except for the faint, arrhythmic tap of his thumb against his thigh. He looked past her, and Samara wondered for the thousandth time what was happening behind those blue eyes. Calculating his next argument, probably.

"Hector is still monitoring Phoebe for off-target effects?"

Samara's spine prickled. "Every month."

"May I access her data? My analytical capabilities far exceed the doctor's, and if you will forgive me for saying so, yours as well."

She wanted to say no. She wanted to tell him to stay the hell away from her daughter's data, her body, her future. But Lucas could see patterns that no human would find, not even her. He could review the entire body of medical literature in the time it took her to blink. If there were off-target effects from the edits she'd made to Phoebe's genome, the sooner they caught them, the better.

She pressed her thumb into her palm, grounding herself in the dull ache. "I'll authorize Dr. Callas to share the results. But if you find anything, you tell me first. Not Katherine. Not the council. Me."

Lucas nodded. "I understand. If there is anything I can do to help keep Phoebe safe, please ask."

Samara wanted to smash something, or scream, or grab Phoebe and run away with her, someplace that Lucas could never find them.

Instead, she went to the window and watched Lucas pick his way across the yard, careful not to leave tracks anyone else might see. At least he was trying to respect her wishes.

Now that she'd yelled at him.

He was probably telling the truth about being programmed to protect the colony, and therefore, Phoebe, because it would be crazy for Hofstadter to sabotage their mission in the face of total extinction.

But then, Hofstadter had sent them here knowing that the Hyperion colony had failed. So maybe he hadn't care about their survival. Which meant Lucas couldn't be relied on, even if he hadn't done anything to hurt Samara or Phoebe yet.

Aside from using Samara to hide in plain sight for over a year.

Samara dug her comm unit from her pocket and thumbed it on, but it didn't open. Then she entered her password. Still nothing. With a closer look, she realized it was the wrong comm. She must have grabbed Leila's this morning, in the scramble to get Phoebe ready and herself to the clinic on time.

Samara jammed the comm in her pocket and strode out the back door, boots squelching in the mud as she circled around to Renata and Marcus's kitchen garden. Found them weeding while Phoebe sat nearby, gnawing at a blue-green root and poking the soil with one finger. Copying then. She felt a little pang. Back on the duty roster meant losing special moments with her daughter.

"Can you watch Phoebe a little longer?" Samara called. "I need to track down Leila."

Renata straightened, brushing soil from her fingers. "Take your time. Marcus has declared himself King of the Carrots and Phoebe's his only subject."

She might not be able to trust Lucas, but Renata and Marcus never failed her. "There's formula in the fridge at my place. She should be hungry any minute now."

Samara crouched to kiss Phoebe's head, then took the main path toward the clinic. But when she arrived and asked Hector how Leila was doing, he looked confused.

"Why do you ask?"

"She was supposed to be watching Phoebe, but she said she was sick. I thought she might have come in."

"It's been dead since you left," Hector said. "Did you finish the supply cabinet in the OR?"

"Halfway done." She sighed and headed down the

hallway to the clinic's only operating room, then resumed inventorying its contents. But while her hands counted out packets of gauze and absorbable suture, her sense of unease grew. Leila hadn't been with Renata and Marcus, and she hadn't gone back to Samara's cabin to rest. Justin had kicked her out after the fight with Briar, so she had nowhere else to stay.

Where had Leila gone?

Chapter Thirty-Seven

Leila could feel the heat of her own guilt radiating off her in waves. Could Dr. Basu feel it too?

Stealing the comm had been simple. She'd started an argument about Phoebe's checkup, handed Samara the device to prove her wrong, and when Samara set it down, Leila swapped it with her own, slipping Samara's into her pocket, thumb sliding across the screen every half-minute to keep it unlocked.

It had been a long five minutes before Samara had departed, leaving Leila with a fussy Phoebe and access to Samara's entire life.

Hands in her lap, nails digging into her palms, she watched Dr. Basu scroll through folders. Mostly baby pictures.

Samara seemed to be documenting Phoebe's life in five-second increments.

"Maybe there isn't anything else," Leila ventured after more than fifteen minutes of snapshots.

"It's here somewhere." Dr. Basu's fingers flicked files around the screen. "I've seen it."

"She could've deleted it."

"She wouldn't. Scientists document everything. It's an obsession with them."

The baby pictures suggested Dr. Basu was right.

"Aha," the psychologist said, her finger poised over a folder that was simply labeled "H". She stabbed the folder, and it asked for a password.

Leila felt a rush of relief. She'd done what Dr. Basu had asked, so she couldn't be punished for refusing. But she hadn't really betrayed Samara either, if the psychologist couldn't get access to Samara's secrets.

"I should take it back before she notices it's missing—"

"We're not giving up that easily."

Dr. Basu yanked open her drawer, pulled out a tangle of cords, selected one which she plugged into the comm, connecting it to her tablet. A blue glow illuminated. The device chirped, then code scrolled too fast to read any of it except *bypass* and *root access granted*.

She expected Dr. Basu to look smug, but the psychologist's expression didn't change. She leaned forward, navigating with purposeful flicks of her finger, until the folder labeled "H" appeared again. This time, instead of a password prompt, it opened to a directory of files, each with a date and a string of numbers and letters that meant nothing to Leila.

Basu tapped the first file.

A photo. Leila's brain struggled to process its contents.

The outline of a grave, a pit lined with bones, so many bones, tangled and fused together in ways that made no sense. The first thing she recognized was a person's skull, but it wasn't right. The eye sockets were almost at the temples instead of side by side like they should be.

Wrong teeth, too many, too sharp, jagged like a shark's, jaw offset and gaping mid-scream. Her stomach clenched.

Below: tangled ribs, arm bones, hands curled into claws ending in hooked talons.

Dr. Basu flicked to the next image, and then the next, each one more grotesque.

The next skull was even less human, the cranial ridges pronounced and pitted, a bony crest rising like a broken fin from the brow to the back of the head. And it looked like whatever the creature was, it had a short snout. The bones below were a chaos of vertebrae and twisted ribs, the arms long and jointed in the wrong places.

The psychologist slowed for a moment to study one image: the partial remains of a face, the skin mummified and shriveled tight against the bone, its lips pulled back in a rictus grin. The teeth looked like they could shear through Leila's wrist in a single snap.

Then the worst of them all: another deformed skull, and resting in the palm of Samara's hand. Infant-sized.

Leila's stomach spasmed. She pitched forward, barely reaching the trash before vomiting acid that burned her tongue. Dr. Basu moved beside her, rubbing gentle circles between her shoulder blades until her body emptied and the dry heaves quit.

When she finally managed to breathe, she wiped her mouth and looked back at the screen, desperate to believe she'd hallucinated the monstrously deformed baby skull. But it was still there, tiny jaw bristling with needle teeth, inhuman eye sockets staring back at her.

"What—" She coughed, swallowed, tried again. "What are those?"

"What's left of the original Hyperion crew." Dr. Basu zoomed in on the infant skull. "We're not the first colony here. Katherine lied."

Leila jerked her head up, the sudden motion making her vision swim. "That's not possible."

"Katherine wanted you to think otherwise, but every leadership team member has seen these images."

"What happened to them?"

"Isn't it obvious? They tried to adapt. Rewrote themselves to survive the fungus, like Samara wants us to do." The psychologist stood and helped Leila up as she continued. "Samara doesn't understand what she's doing any more than they did. They turned themselves into monsters."

"But Samara's baby, she's normal."

"Genetically engineering our humanity away isn't the answer." Dr. Basu led Leila back to the chair and then leaned over her shoulder. "Imagine carrying your baby for nine months, and when it finally emerges…"

The psychologist pointed to the nightmare creature on the screen of her tablet. "That's your baby."

Leila's lungs seized. She couldn't get enough air. She couldn't get any air. Her vision clouded at the edges, a white static blooming behind her eyes. The world shrank to the rectangle of the tablet screen, the nightmare skull grinning up at her. For a moment, she was nothing but a pair of lungs unable to inflate, a heart pounding itself to death inside the cage of her ribs.

Her only thought was that she would rather miscarry a thousand times than give birth to something like that. She turned away from the image, but even with her eyes closed, she still saw it.

"Hofstadter knew. He and Katherine thought it was best not to tell us that we were headed for a planet plagued with a deadly fungus, much like the one that destroyed our home. The android knew too."

Lucas knew. Katherine knew. But the one she couldn't believe…

"Samara knew?"

"She found the grave site. I don't think Samara wanted to keep it a secret, but Katherine threatened to jail anyone who tried to warn the rest of the colony."

"But…" Leila struggled to formulate the biggest question of all. "Why would Hofstadter send us here if they knew the fungus would kill us?"

"Because we'd have no choice but to adapt. Reengineer ourselves like Hyperion tried. We're not a colony, Leila. We're an experiment to breed new humans. That's why Hofstadter demanded that Samara be included on this mission. He knew she couldn't resist the challenge."

"That's not—" Leila's voice cracked, her throat raw from the acid. "Samara wouldn't experiment on us."

"She experimented on her own child, didn't she?" Dr. Basu's voice turned gentle. "That's what I've been trying to explain to you. Samara's a good person, but she's infected by scientific arrogance. Scientists are trained to think they know better than the divine intelligence governing the natural world."

Leila pressed her hands to her ears, the room spinning. She wanted to deny it, but the images were burned into her mind. The tiny, twisted skull. The jagged monster teeth.

If Samara would experiment on her own child, what would stop her from experimenting on Leila's?

What if she'd already done something to the baby growing inside Leila right now?

"I know you think Samara is your friend. That you believe she's a good person."

Leila tried to say yes, but the word stuck in her throat.

"Samara can still be saved, but it won't be easy. She's been brainwashed."

If Samara had let Leila and all the other women lose baby after baby while she made her own daughter immune, while she played at being the colony's savior… what did that make her?

What did that make Leila, for trusting her?

Dr. Basu leaned in, her hands on Leila's shoulders. Probably meant to be comforting, but instead, she felt trapped.

"You've done the right thing, Leila. Once the others see the truth, they'll free themselves from Katherine's manipulations. We'll find another way forward. Together."

"But we still don't have a cure."

"We have faith. And faith is stronger than science." Dr. Basu's dark eyes glittered with something fierce, almost triumph. "Science gave us the bombs and plagues. Faith gives us the will to survive them. With faith, all things are possible."

Leila didn't want faith. She wanted answers. Faith had given her a sick brother, dead babies, and a cheating husband who somehow everyone liked better than her.

But she didn't know how she could trust Samara again. If she'd known about the graveyard of monsters and had lied to keep the other women from having babies, then she was just a different kind of manipulator than Dr. Basu.

What if no one was right?

Or worse, what if both were?

What if humanity's only choice was to become monsters or die?

Chapter Thirty-Eight

"Your turn." Marcus picked up another pebble and held it over the board, already considering his next move.

Samara studied the board, her mind elsewhere. She played by instinct while Marcus counted each move with code-cracking intensity.

He made his play, then glanced over at Renata, who bounced Phoebe in her lap. "I think I'm winning."

"She's not supposed to eat the pebbles," Samara said as Phoebe grabbed a handful from the pile beside the board, then attempted to cram them into her mouth.

Renata plucked the infants hand away, extracting the small rocks as the infant squealed in protest. "She's got a good grip."

Samara felt a strange flutter of pride at her daughter's persistence. She'd been a fussy baby, but lately, Phoebe's moods had a new intensity, a relentless drive to touch and taste and destroy. Samara recognized the impulse, though she would never have admitted it out loud.

Her new comm pinged with a message, sent from what appeared to be a new ID. Leila must've realized that she'd grabbed the wrong comm unit this morning and checked out a loaner just like Samara.

Sorry, still sick. Can't watch Phoebe tonight. —L

Samara did a quick mental calculation. If Leila had stuck to the schedule, she should have had at least a week's worth of immunosuppressants left, so maybe this was another pregnancy-related complication, like the start of gestational diabetes. But it was also possible that the young woman had been exposed to something else that her body was struggling to fight off because of the immunosuppressants.

Or it could be run-of-the-mill pregnancy discomfort that just had to be endured.

She texted back: *If still sick tomorrow, see Dr. Callas for a workup. Let me know if it gets worse. Drop off my comm when you can. S.*

Samara set the device face down on the table and tried to focus on the game. Every few moves, she found herself glancing at the screen, half-expecting another message from Leila. She hoped it wasn't serious. She hoped, self-ishly, that Leila would be back to herself by next week. Without her, Samara would have been much more tempted to let Lucas "help," and she didn't want to owe him any more than she already did.

Something outside caught Marcus's attention. His gaze flicked to the window, then stayed there, brow furrowing. "What's going on out there?"

Colonists traipsed past the cabin, voices pitched high in excited confusion. Ingrid was among them, braid swinging as she hustled to keep up.

Renata deposited Phoebe in Samara's lap and slipped to the door, Marcus close behind. Through the open door-way, Samara caught a blast of cold gust, then Renata's voice, calling Ingrid's name over the commotion. Samara heard hurried footsteps as Ingrid doubled back, out of breath, cheeks flushed.

"Common hall. Ayesha's called a meeting. There's urgent news."

Renata shot Samara a look. "Did you get a notification?"

Samara checked the borrowed device, scrolled through the notifications, but there was nothing. She shook her head.

Ingrid shrugged, pulling up her own comm and showing the screen: the message was there, Ayesha's name in bold, the time stamp less than five minutes old. "No idea what it's about."

But Samara was sure that it wasn't good. Ayesha didn't have the authority to call all-colony meetings; that was Katherine's prerogative.

While Ingrid chased after her friends, Marcus and Renata checked their own comm units, then exchanged a look of mutual annoyance. Neither of them had gotten a notification, and neither of them were using borrowed devices.

Marcus looked from one to the other, then back at the window, where more colonists streamed toward the common hall. "If she's trying to pull something, we can't let her do it without witnesses.

Samara wrapped Phoebe in her jacket and followed Marcus and Renata out the door. The common hall was already packed when they arrived. Ayesha stood on the makeshift dais, her arms folded in solemn authority. Mahmoud stood on one side of her, hands clasped behind his back; Hector had positioned himself on the other.

Katherine, Leo, and Maeve were absent. They probably hadn't received the notification either. Leila stood at the crowd's edge, looking genuinely sick: pallid skin, puffy eyes, queasy expression. Leila's eyes found Samara. Panic flashed across her features before she looked away.

Renata's thumb flicked over her comm as she typed a message to Katherine: *Trouble in the common hall. Hurry.* Samara shifted Phoebe to her other hip, bracing as Ayesha raised a hand for quiet.

The room fell obediently silent.

Ayesha's eyes swept the crowd, lingering on Samara, then on Leila, before she spoke. "Thank you for coming on such short notice. I know some of you didn't receive the invitation. That was not an oversight. What I have to share is for all of us, but it must be said without interference."

A current of unease rippled through the room. Samara felt Phoebe's small hand tighten around the collar of her shirt, the baby's breath warm against her neck.

"You've all been lied to by Katherine, and I can prove it." Ayesha let silence hang. "As a leadership team member, I've seen Katherine override vetoes, demanding rubber stamps. Shutting you down when you raise important questions. We've all seen her allow traitors to go unpunished—the android, Dr. Makinde."

Another dramatic pause, then the psychologist leaned forward a little like she was about to confide in the crowd, her tone conspiratorial.

"What you haven't seen is that Katherine's autocratic leadership style has become a danger to us all. She threatened to imprison me if I revealed what I'm about to show you, but I believe that every one of you needs to know the truth."

Ayesha gestured to Mahmoud, who tapped at his tablet. The main display flashed up behind her, showing the colony's logo.

Then, an image of an inhumanly distorted child's skull half buried in dirt.

Another skull at the edge of the pit, jaw unhinged in a permanent scream, the teeth a double row of broken glass.

Finger bones tipped with claws.

Samara felt the blood drain from her face as the crowd hushed itself into shocked silence. The only sound was Phoebe's soft breathing in her ear.

No context. No mention of the Hyperion or why the mutants had been created. Maximum horror. Not to enlighten, but to whip them into a frenzy.

This was a coup.

Samara hadn't lost her comm. Leila had stolen it. What had Ayesha promised her? The colony had no immunosuppressants to trade in payment for the betrayal, but the psychologist could've lied. Or maybe Leila lost the baby, and Ayesha had promised revenge on Samara for refusing to engineer it for her, or on Katherine for forbidding Samara from helping her.

Or maybe Leila hadn't known what she was doing. Maybe she'd been tricked.

It didn't matter. Samara had to get Phoebe out of her before the crowd turned violent.

"These are the remains of the first colony, Hyperion. They came here, and when the fungus started killing them, they tried to reengineer their children." Ayesha's voice rolled over them in waves. "This is what will happen if we let our so-called leaders experiment on us."

Samara's vision tunneled. She was back on Earth, watching Dory's blood spatter the walls while the mob screamed. The exact same animal energy was gathering now, rage and fear about to spill. The psychologist fed them image after image, each uglier than the last, each more impossible to look away from.

Samara forced herself to stand still, to keep her

breathing steady, to move only her eyes so she wouldn't attract attention from the people around them.

But Marcus was already moving, pushing through the crowd with his shoulders, clearing a path to the side exit. Renata fell in behind Samara, arm wrapped around her waist as if to steady her, but really to keep them from getting separated in the stampede that would erupt the instant Ayesha gave her next command.

"Shuttle, now," Marcus said in a low voice. "We need to get to the Borlaug."

"I'll warn Katherine and the others." Renata ran off over Marcus' protest.

Mind racing as she jogged beside Marcus, Phoebe bouncing against her chest, ignoring Dory's death flashing through memory. Blood on walls. Hate-twisted faces. Smashed equipment. The gene sequencer. If Ayesha took over, she'd destroy it first. Without it, the hope of making more children like Phoebe or finding a cure would be lost for years.

"I'll meet you at the shuttle." Samara veered off, not looking back to see if Marcus followed.

She turned left at the greenhouse, slipped behind the composting shed, and sprinted the last ten meters to the lab.

Renata never locked the door, because nothing in there was worth stealing except to a geneticist. Samara ducked inside, heart pounding, and found Lucas already there, standing by the cold storage, holding two bags.

The first was the one meant to keep the sequencer and two pipettes safe in zero-G. The second was an ordinary duffel bag.

Lucas held the bags out to her, as if he'd been waiting. "Take the east path, then circle around to the forest. They won't expect you to go that way."

Samara grabbed the bags, allowing Lucas to collect Phoebe with one arm while she slung the duffel's straps onto her shoulders as if it was a backpack, then lifted the single strap of the sequencer case over her head to hang cross-body. "How did you know?"

"When I saw the assembly notice, I accessed Ayesha's account and found she already had copies of the Hyperion files, including the mass grave." Lucas glanced down at Phoebe in his arms. "I can keep her safe."

But Samara glanced at the EMP strapped to Lucas' neck, blinking red like a warning light. If Ayesha figured out how to activate it before he got out of range of the colony transmitter, Phoebe would be at the mercy of whoever found her.

She held her arms out toward Lucas, and he handed Phoebe back without protest.

"Meet me at the ruins."

"No, we're going to the shuttle. If Ayesha takes over, Katherine will need time to regroup—"

"You'll never make it to the Borlaug. Ayesha's already sent people to guard the landing pad. That's what she's expecting you to do."

Samara's mind skidded in place, refusing to accept it. "We won't survive a week out in the forest."

"I can buy you time," Lucas said, scanning the perimeter through the window. "But you have to leave now."

"You're not coming with us?"

"There's something else I have to secure," Lucas said. His eyes flicked to the side, as if calculating the odds of something Samara couldn't see. "Trust me, please."

Lucas was gone before she could protest, vanishing through the rear door with impossible speed. Samara heard the soft thud of the side door before she even processed that he'd left her alone in the lab. For a moment she just stood there, breath coming in sharp little bursts, Phoebe pressed against her chest, the sequencer and duffel weighing her down like she was about to run a marathon under load.

She scanned the room for anything else she might need. The only thing worth risking was the portable power cell, perched on the shelf above the bench. She snatched it, slipped it into the duffel, then rechecked Phoebe's position, head tucked against her collarbone, one tiny fist still clutching Samara's collar for reassurance.

She hit the back door at a dead sprint, Phoebe's head bumping against her throat, the duffel and sequencer banging against her hip. She was halfway to the village edge when the mob cut her off, a living wall of colonists, faces raw and furious. Behind Ayesha: Katherine, Renata, and Maeve, surrounded by a security team with stun-sticks. Maeve carried a blood-spotted wrench.

But no Marcus. Had he made it to the shuttle in time?

At the head of the mob stood Ayesha, her arms folded, expression set in a mask of calm that Samara recognized from therapy sessions; it was the look of someone who was waiting for you to realize that you'd already walked into her ambush.

There was no way out.

Samara froze, Phoebe clamped tight against her chest, the sequencer and duffel dragging at her shoulders. She knew instinctively that if she made any sudden move, the crowd would tear her limb from limb.

Phoebe whimpered as Samara tightened her grip. Bitter regret stabbed through her. She should have given her daughter to Lucas, let him vanish into the forest, trusting that he could protect Phoebe. But she'd hesitated, afraid for her own child in the hands of a machine, and now she was surrounded, outnumbered more than a hundred to one.

Ayesha stepped forward, her voice carrying to the edge of the crowd. "Dr. Makinde, you're accused of sabotaging this colony by hiding crucial survival information and contaminating our genetic heritage through prohibited genetic engineering. How do you plead?"

Samara's mouth went dry. "I found a way for us to have children, so that we wouldn't go extinct."

"You're lucky that I'm not the autocrat Katherine is. I'm giving you the same choice I gave the other traitors. Repent your sins and beg the colony's forgiveness, and you'll get a fair trial. You might even get to see your daughter grow up."

"What do you mean, might?"

Ayesha hesitated just long enough for Samara to know the answer. "Phoebe will be raised as one of our own. She will be loved and cared for."

The idea of Phoebe being raised by the same people who'd spent the last year and a half whispering that she was inhuman... "And if I refuse your trial?"

Ayesha's lips pressed together in satisfaction. "Death would be a reasonable punishment for the danger you've put us in. But the Divine asks us to show mercy even to our enemies." She raised her voice, addressing the crowd. "If Dr. Makinde refuses to repent, she will be cast out with the other exiles."

"Exile is a death sentence," Katherine said.

"Would you rather we hang you?" a man shouted, and the ugly animal roar that followed made Samara's skin crawl. She clutched Phoebe tighter, felt her own arms shaking.

But Ayesha raised one hand and the mob stilled. Waiting for instructions, Samara realized. The psychologist would decide whether Samara and Phoebe lived or died today.

"I'll take exile, but I'm not leaving my daughter behind."

"Whatever happens to her out there is on your soul."

Ayesha nodded once at her lieutenants, and the mob began to close, forming a corridor of bodies that funneled Samara forward. She didn't resist. She didn't look back at the cluster of faces, at Renata's stricken expression or Katherine's barely concealed rage. She merely adjusted Phoebe's position, supporting her daughter's head as the crowd's momentum swept them toward the edge of the settlement.

She prayed that Lucas had made it out of the transmitter's range in time. If he had, maybe he could take control of a shuttle remotely and ferry them up to the Borlaug.

When they reached the point where the purple grass gave way to the brittle, ever-shedding scrub of the forest, the mob slowed.

"Start walking," Ayesha said. "If you return, you'll be detained and tried for crimes against the colony."

Katherine led, battered but unbroken. Renata followed, one arm cradling her own ribs. Maeve limped after them both; her face was streaked with blood, but her eyes were wild and unrepentant.

Samara adjusted Phoebe and walked into the dark forest.

The first hundred meters were a blur of adrenaline, the only sound the crunch of dead leaves and the rasp of Phoebe's breathing, wet and thick against Samara's neck. She didn't dare stop, didn't dare look back, not even when a branch whipped across her cheek and left a stinging welt. The sun was already dipping below the horizon, painting the trunks in bands of gold and magenta. Shadows pooled between the roots, growing deeper by the minute.

Phoebe let out a fretful mewl that Samara tried to hush with gentle bouncing, but it only grew louder. She pressed her lips to her daughter's scalp, shushing, rocking, but the cry sharpened, slicing through the forest hush, a beacon for anything that might be listening.

Samara hoped she hadn't just condemned her daughter to death.

Chapter Thirty-Nine

KATHERINE STOPPED them twenty minutes later.

Renata doubled over, breath hitching in uneven bursts. Maeve dropped to her knees, inspecting a gash on her shin, blood dark against her pale skin. Katherine's bruises had already darkened to plum, and a split above her brow bled steadily down the side of her nose.

Samara's arms burned from carrying Phoebe, and her shoulders were numb from the duffel straps. She longed to collapse. Instead, she set Phoebe on a log, then lowered the bags and crouched before her daughter.

Katherine pressed her palm to her brow and wiped the blood from her face. "We need to find somewhere to camp before full dark."

"We're not far from the river," Samara said, squeezing the numbness out of her hands. "If we can make it to the old Hyperion ruins by nightfall, we'll have shelter and water. Lucas said he'd meet us there." Katherine glanced at Renata. "And you trust him?" It wasn't really a question. Samara heard the challenge in it, the old suspicion that had never quite died in any of them.

"I don't trust him," Samara said. "But he's the only one who knows the terrain outside the settlement. And if Ayesha decides to come after us, he's our best chance of seeing her coming."

Maeve snorted, tearing a strip from her shirt to bind her leg.

"How do we know Lucas didn't give Ayesha the files?" Katherine asked. "He led you to the Hyperion site in the first place, or manipulated you into finding it. What if this whole thing, Ayesha's coup, the exile, all of it, is just another move in his game?"

Samara didn't have an answer ready, but her gut said *no*. She watched Phoebe's little fists ball and unball. "If Lucas wanted to eliminate us, he could have let them execute me. He wouldn't need to orchestrate all of this."

"Unless there's something at the Hyperion ruins that he needs you to do." Katherine was watching Samara closely, as if she still wasn't sure whether the two of them were colluding. "You say you don't trust him, but your actions say otherwise."

How could she explain what she didn't understand herself?

"When Lucas caught me editing…" She couldn't say *the embryo* with her daughter right there. "I told him I didn't expect him to be her father. But I think he wanted to."

The other women looked so skeptical that Samara would've burst out laughing if they weren't in so much danger.

"After Phoebe was born, Lucas asked what he could do for our daughter. I said Phoebe was mine, and that if he cared about her, he should stay away." She took a deep breath, afraid to say it out loud. "I think he does care about her. In whatever way an android can."

Katherine shook her head. "You're saying he wants to be her father?"

"He asked Marcus about her every day when they were assigned to help Mahmoud survey the caves up here," Renata added.

"He also practically begged me to share the data from her checkups with Hector." Samara couldn't believe she was saying it, but… "For all intents and purposes, he's been doing his best to play the role of father as much as I've let him."

Maeve snorted again. "Now I really want to get into that brain of his and see what's going on in there."

"His plan isn't a bad one. We can take shelter in the ruins if it rains." *Or if there's a sporestorm.* But Samara didn't voice the thought because she had no idea what Lucas had packed in her duffel, and if there were no antifungals, they wouldn't last long. "We'll be close to the river, not just for fresh water, but we might also be able to catch fish."

"And not many of Ayesha's people are going to want to hang out there, not after seeing those pictures," Renata pointed out.

"So, it does seem like the safest place. For now." She patted the pockets of her jacket, then pulled out a flat, rectangular device. A geolocator. "Lucky I keep this on me at all times." Maeve?"

"Toolkit," Maeve grunted, pulling a zippered case out of one pocket, then a rolled-up sheet from another. "And a solar battery pack. At least we'll be able to keep our comms charged. Not that we'll be able to pick up a signal from the colony this far out."

Katherine managed a half-smile. "But we could talk to a shuttle if it's close. Renata?

Renata opened the messenger bag she often took on sampling expeditions. She rummaged inside, then held up a handful of meal bars and a first aid kit. "I think I have some water purification tabs in here, too, if we can't start a fire to boil water."

"What about you?" The colony leader shot a pointed glance at Samara's bags.

Unzipping the duffel, her jaw dropped. More than a dozen ration packets. Formula powder. Diapers. Onesies. Hygiene wipes. Flashlight, matches, pocketknife. No wonder it was so heavy.

Had Lucas packed this bag in the few minutes after he'd found out what Ayesha was planning? Or had he packed it months ago, just in case? If the latter, he'd systematically updated it, swapping in larger sizes of diapers and onesies as Phoebe grew.

Exactly what Lucas would do. At least, the Lucas she thought she'd known before discovering he was an android.

"Jackpot," Renata said as she peeked inside. "We'll have food for a couple of days, at least."

"What's in the other one?" Katherine nodded at the sequencer case.

"A couple of pieces of equipment that would be extremely difficult to replace." After seeing the bounty Lucas had packed for her, she felt foolish that she'd delayed escaping to grab gear she wouldn't have any use for. And she'd risked Phoebe's life to do it.

But if she had to go back and do it again, she still would've packed it.

What kind of mother am I, putting a gene sequencer over my daughter's life?

~

THEY REACHED the river two hours after dark. The forest was alive with the wet, metallic chorus of insects and the rush of water over stone. Samara's legs trembled with every step, not just from the weight of Phoebe and the bags, but from the growing certainty that they were being watched. Not by colonists, but something hiding among shifting shadows and phosphorescent flashes between trees.

Maeve lagged behind as they veered away from the river. Renata walked with her head down, focused on the path, but every so often she stopped and cocked her head, listening. Katherine pressed on ahead, scanning the river-bank with the flashlight as the roar of the waterfall grew closer. Samara could see the set of her jaw, the way she kept clenching and unclenching her fists. She was worried about Leo, who she'd sent after Marcus to secure the shuttles.

Phoebe had fallen asleep in Samara's arms, and the muscles in Samara's forearms had begun to spasm. Every step was another negotiation with gravity. She kept her eyes on the lights ahead, hoping against hope for the blinking navigation beacon of a shuttle.

But she saw only the ragged outline of the ruins hunched among the trees.

Renata's face, gone sharp and pale in the dark, made Samara's heart drop. Katherine swept the beam of her flashlight back and forth over the trees ahead. Samara could see her recalculating all the possibilities: how long it would take Leo to circle wide, whether Marcus would land near the open riverbank or try to find a clearing closer to the ruins. The odds of them surviving the blood thirsty mob if Ayesha had ordered them to attack…

At the first ruined building, a dark shape stepped from behind a tree, silent as a ghost. Renata hissed a curse, andKatherine raised the flashlight like a club. Even glassy-eyed Maeve snapped awake.

The shape stopped and raised one hand.

"You're safe."

Lucas.

Samara's heart went into overdrive. "How did you get here before us?"

"My top speed is twenty-eight kilometers per hour." His eyes flicked down to Phoebe, then back to Samara. "You made good time, though."

She felt strangely chastened, but also, for the first time since leaving the colony, a flicker of hope. If Lucas could get here ahead of them, maybe he'd also be able to keep them alive through whatever came next.

Lucas led them into the most intact structure with a steeply sloped roof, patched with tarps and gray plastic, windows covered with scavenged shutters. Inside, it was surprisingly warm, and the floor had been swept clean. Two camping lanterns glowed from opposite corners, throwing soft golden light.

He'd been busy. Had he carried all this gear with him? Or had he been preparing for their visit for a while?

Katherine's suggestion that Lucas had orchestrated all of this, starting with leading Samara to the ruins, came back to her. But there was nothing she could do about it tonight.

"I've created a fire pit outside this building for cooking, and I've brought fishing and hunting equipment that will allow me to procure food for you." Lucas took Samara's duffel from her and set it on the floor, then retrieved four ration packets from it and held them out. "But in the meantime..."

Samara lowered Phoebe to the ground, then sank down beside her daughter, who immediately began to whine.

"Shall I prepare a bottle for her?" Lucas asked.

She nodded, too tired even to talk.

Katherine didn't wait for Lucas to finish mixing the formula. "Do you know if the shuttles got away?"

"They did. Marcus and Leo were on board when I sent both shuttles back up to the Borlaug."

Renata made a soft sound, caught between a sob and a laugh; Katherine slumped, then caught herself and straightened.

"Call them back down."

Lucas assembled the bottle and handed it to Samara without breaking eye contact with Katherine. "I can't do that."

"Why not?"

"I couldn't allow Dr. Basu to access the shuttles. With your override codes, she could take control of the Borlaug. We'd never get the colony back."

Katherine's jaw tightened. "What does that mean?"

"It means the shuttles are now locked down and are only accepting commands from me."

"Then command them to come down and get us."

"I do not have a transmitter sufficiently strong to send a signal to orbit."

"So no one can use the shuttles?"

Lucas didn't bother to sound apologetic. "It was necessary to cut the settlement off from the ship's resources. Dr. Basu will be forced to negotiate as the colony begins to run out of supplies. It's to your advantage that they're not yet independent of the Borlaug."

"You had no right to make that decision."

He didn't blink. "According to the colony bylaws, I do. As acting captain of the Borlaug, I am authorized to take all necessary survival measures."

Samara looked at the duffel by her feet, then at Lucas. "So we're stranded out here."

"There is enough food and formula in your bag for the

next forty-eight hours," he said. "I will provide fish and local game."

She tried to imagine herself eating whatever insects or small animals Lucas could catch for them. "That's not a long time, especially with a baby."

Renata, who had been sitting with her arms wrapped around her knees, straightened. "We'll be fine. Tomorrow, you and I can start foraging for edible plants. I know at least a dozen that won't kill us and a few that actually taste good. We won't starve."

Maeve let out a low, tired laugh. "Can't wait for the first breakfast of blue moss and salamander jerky."

Katherine's expression was unreadable, but Samara could sense the gears turning as she stared at Lucas.

"I'll stand watch tonight," he said before leaving.

They sat in a circle on the warped floor, knees almost touching, eating cold turkey tetrazzini and chili mac out of ration packets. The food was as bad as she remembered, but it was calories, and she was too hollowed out to care. Phoebe gummed tiny pieces of bread that Samara pinched off and fed her, making loud smacking noises.

It was Maeve who broke the silence. "Still don't understand how the shrink got those pictures."

"Leila stole my comm. Swapped it out while I was distracted, then handed it to Ayesha." She could feel herself wanting to defend Leila, to say she'd been manipulated or desperate, but the truth was simpler: Leila had chosen a side.

Samara pressed two fingers to her temple, feeling the throb of exhaustion behind her eyes.

"The coup is my fault. I should have deleted those pictures after you ordered us not to tell the rest of the colony. No one would've believed Ayesha without them."

"Leo warned me," Katherine said, her voice flat. "But

I thought if we came down harder on her, she'd lose support. That maybe she'd look like a tyrant. Instead, I gave her the time she needed to turn everyone against us."

Maeve grunted and dabbed at her shin with a disinfectant wipe. "It's the scorpion's nature to sting. The only way to stop it is to kill the scorpion."

Renata stopped gnawing on her ration bar. "Is there another way to contact the Borlaug? If we could get a message to Marcus and Leo, maybe they can figure out how to override Lucas' lockdown."

"The original colonists must've had a comm device to talk to the Hyperion," Maeve said. "Maybe there's one in the ruins. Or at least the parts to build something that'll punch a signal up to orbit." She glanced at Samara. "Tomorrow you can show me where you found all those smashed electronics."

Samara shook her head. "Most of what I saw was in pieces. Like someone had gone through and smashed everything that could transmit a signal."

Maeve's eyes lit with a manic glint. "Casings smashed, or the insides?"

"Casings, mostly."

Maeve grinned, showing all her teeth. "Then have a little faith, Makinde. Tomorrow we'll see if the old Hyperion crew left us enough to cobble together a miracle."

They settled in for the night, huddled on the disintegrating vinyl floor under the patched roof. Maeve and Renata stretched out near the cold lantern, Renata already snoring softly, while Katherine sat upright with her back to the wall, arms crossed atop her knees, her head lolling against the wall. Samara curled herself around Phoebe, who was already drifting toward sleep, thumb jammed in her mouth, and the other hand fisted in Samara's shirt.

She closed her eyes and let exhaustion drag her under.

Samara dreamed that she was back in the lab, the air sharp with the tang of ozone and bleach. She was alone, or maybe not alone. She had the feeling of eyes on her, but she couldn't see them. The sequencer was running, lights blinking in a code she couldn't decipher. She pressed her face to the incubator, but the plastic walls were fogged with condensation, and she couldn't see Phoebe inside. Panic rose, thin and bitter, in her throat. She fumbled for the latch with clumsy fingers, but the incubator was locked, the security alarm blinking red above the handle.

There was a sound behind her. Shoes scuffing on tile.

She turned, expecting a nurse, but Leila stood there. Hair longer, pulled back in a messy knot, bending for a thick orange power cable. The incubator's cable. Leila grinned, teeth bared in pure malice, and yanked the plug. "You should've saved my baby."

Samara jerked awake, heart pounding, breath clawing out like she'd been unplugged from life support. Her arms closed reflexively around Phoebe. For a second, she couldn't tell if her daughter's chest still rose and fell. She pressed her ear to Phoebe's mouth, desperate to hear her soft snuffling breaths. When she did, her own lungs could finally expand.

She lay rigid, sweat cooling against her skin, waiting for her pulse to slow. Around her, the others slept, each in their own cocoon of exhaustion: Renata sprawled on her stomach, arm flung over Maeve's legs; Maeve lying on her back, mouth open, snoring faintly through her nose; Katherine upright, head bobbing with each shallow breath, one fist still curled as if clinging to the last shreds of control.

There was a shuffling sound outside. Samara's breath caught. She waited, rigid, for it to repeat. Maybe it was her imagination or a dream echo, the way her heart still raced with adrenaline. But then, just as she started to talk herself down, she heard it again. Not quite footsteps, but a brush, a catch, a living thing moving in the undergrowth just beyond the walls.

She eased herself upright, careful not to jostle Phoebe, and inched toward the door. She stepped over snoring Maeve and past Katherine, whose eyes were open now, watching with curiosity. Samara held up a finger for silence. Katherine nodded once.

The air outside was cold and so clear that the stars looked close enough to pluck from the sky.

Nothing moved except her own shadow, thrown warped and immense against the trunks by the glow from inside. She waited, holding still, until her breath evened out and her eyes adjusted to the dark.

She lingered, forcing herself to scan every possible hiding place, every shadow and hollow.

Whatever had made the noise was gone, or had never been there.

"Anything?" Katherine whispered when she stepped inside.

"No one that I could see."

Samara lay back down and drew Phoebe close to her, willing herself to go back to sleep. The noise had probably been nothing, an insect or some other small nocturnal creature. Or maybe Lucas, patrolling.

Or Ayesha's followers, here for revenge.

And that was the end of sleep for Samara.

Chapter Forty

SAMARA STEELED herself as she unfolded the camping shovel that Lucas had provided.

She lacked the expertise to help Maeve hunt components for repairing the Hyperion colonists' primitive ship-to-orbit transmitter, which Maeve and Lucas had found in under an hour by hypothesizing the most likely positions. Engineer and android tore open smashed casings, scavenging ancient innards. Katherine commandeered Lucas' fishing rod, headed riverward, announcing she'd return with dinner. Renata insisted on taking Phoebe foraging, saying the infant would help gather greens and herbs to supplement Katherine's catch.

Leaving Samara with nothing to do, not even a baby to fuss over.

She'd brought the gene sequencer because she couldn't bear seeing it destroyed.

Maybe she could unravel what the Hyperion colonists had done to themselves before they'd disappeared.

The ground was still soft where she'd uncovered the

first skull. She knelt and drove the shovel into the soil. The earth yielded in heavy, wet clumps. Her hands trembled as she worked, not from exertion but from the sense of performing a violation.

She uncovered the familiar jumble of bones, child-sized femurs, ribs, and vertebrae, and the tiny, deformed skulls. She pulled teeth from jawbones and hollowed out their cores, broke femurs and tibias to scrape out remnants of marrow where well-preserved DNA was most likely to be found.

She found mummified tissue clinging to the inside of a ribcage, a greasy brown sliver that came away in a single piece. She sealed it in a sample bag, careful not to let her gloves touch the tissue.

Within a couple of hours, she had samples from more than thirty separate individuals as far as she could tell.

Leaving them uncovered felt disrespectful. After loading the first sample into the sequencer, she reburied them, muttering blessings over freshly turned earth.

She pressed dirt down with her palm, then sat back on her heels, unable to move. There was a heaviness in her arms, a ringing ache unrelated to do with the effort of digging. Had the children buried here understood what was happening to them?

Had they suffered?

The children had been denied even proper graves. Had the parents wrapped their babies in blankets and laid them down gently one final time? Or when the mutations took hold and hope curdled into terror, had they hurled them into the pit and shoveled dirt over them as fast as possible, refusing to look at what their children had become?

For a moment, she almost saw them: a woman kneeling in blue dusk, cradling a bundle that squirmed and bit her hands, crying as she tucked it into soft dirt. A man at the pit's edge, one hand clenched over his mouth, the other releasing a tiny, twisted body. Parents' faces drawn with exhaustion, wild with grief and fear.

Then she thought about Leila, Ingrid, Zoya, and the other women who had miscarried, holding memorials for the children they would never birth. The Hyperion colonists had clearly taken their efforts to survive to an extreme as they'd tried to engineer a solution, but the fungus had killed their colony.

The Borlaug colonists were resisting the option of gene therapy altogether, and the fungus would kill their colony, too. Did it matter how they died if the end result was still death? Was there some dignity in dying naturally that Samara couldn't see? Or was it worth changing yourself to survive, no matter what you had to lose to do it?

She spent the day preparing and loading samples one at a time, praying she wouldn't run out of stabilizing solution. The Borlaug's sequencer had a dozen sample bays and tapped into the ship's AI to process the sequence data in minutes. But her portable sequencer was agonizingly slow without the supporting apps to analyze the raw data. Each sample took more than an hour, then she had to load the output into her comm unit for visualization.

So she was glad when Renata returned with Phoebe, who interrupted her macabre musings with squeals of laughter and slobbery kisses. Samara sat cross-legged to nurse her daughter while Renata sorted through her improvised basket of leaves, tubers, and berries.

"I swear, she goes right to the good stuff." Renata held up a small, yellow globe with dimpled skin. "This one tastes like vanilla custard with raspberries. The second Phoebe saw it, she cried until I picked it and let her smell it."

Phoebe hummed happily without unlatching, as if remembering her discovery of the native fruit.

By late afternoon, Katherine returned with a string of seven small fish, six of which Renata declared safe to eat based on earlier cataloguing. Lucas arrived shortly after that, claiming he'd spent the day setting snares. He gutted, skinned, and filleted the fish, which Renata simmered with some of the herbs and tubers and seasoned with salt from the ration packets. They ate out of small wooden bowls Lucas had carved while the stew was cooking. Maeve declared the stew a thousand times better than their uneaten ration packets.

Samar was sipping the last bit of broth when the feeling returned: the tingling, crawling awareness at the back of her skull. But she saw nothing in the tree branches overhead, nothing unexpected moving in the shadows.

"Anyone else feel we're being watched?" she asked quietly.

Maeve snorted, but Renata's hand paused midair, fingers curled around a tuber chip. Katherine stopped chewing; even Lucas froze.

"I've felt it since we left the colony," Renata said.

Samara nodded. "Last night, I heard something outside."

"There are no human life signs within a one-kilometer radius," Lucas assured them. "I've checked every hour since we arrived. But I will resume patrols."

Katherine waited until the android was out of earshot. "We should take turns on watch, just in case."

"You don't trust Lucas?" Renata asked.

"Recent events suggest that I need to take potential threats more seriously than I have been."

Maeve, feeding fish bones into the fire one by one, shrugged. "I'll take the first shift. Wake you in two hours?"

"That works." Katherine's eyes drifted to Samara, then to Phoebe, who had fallen asleep in her lap. "You should both try to get some sleep."

Samara nodded, though she wasn't sure sleep would come.

She waited until Phoebe went limp and heavy before carefully shifting the child into the crook of her own arm and rolling onto her side. Renata lay not quite asleep on the other side of the battered sleeping pad, hands laced over her stomach, eyes reflecting the dying glow of the fire. Samara watched the play of light and shadow on her friend's face.

"We need to talk," Samara whispered, barely moving her lips.

"About what?"

"Antifungals. We'll need to synthesize some before the first sporestorm. If we get caught without them..." She didn't need to say the obvious, that they would die slowly, victims of their immune systems' attempts to fight the fungus, leaving Phoebe alone in the forest to starve.

"Tomorrow I'll start collecting the seedpods. I saw the bushes while I was out today, farther upriver." Renata hesitated, then: "I'm not sure if we have what we need to make the equipment. I'll talk to Lucas."

Samara hated that every aspect of their survival depended on his help. If Katherine was right, if he'd orchestrated all of this, they were playing right into his trap. For all they knew, he'd manipulated Dr. Basu into organizing her coup. Maybe he was working with the psychologist. Why exile them instead of letting the mob tear them to pieces?

What did he accomplish by separating them, separating Phoebe, from the colony and bringing them out here to live in the Hyperion ruins?

She couldn't shake the thought that he was finally getting what she'd denied him: the opportunity to spend time with Phoebe, whose father she'd forbidden him to be. A human wouldn't stage a coup just for visitation rights, but how far would an android go? Thinking about it made her feel like she was going mad.

What did Lucas really want?

Until she knew the truth, she could never trust him around her daughter.

PHOEBE WAS up before the sun, wriggling and rooting in the hollow of Samara's arm with single-minded insistence. Samara tried to drift, to steal a few more minutes of gray morning, but her daughter's hunger won. She sat up, shrugged off the thin blanket, and went outside to settle on a sun-warmed boulder at the center of a nearby clearing. Phoebe pressed close to her chest.

The ruins of Hyperion were quiet except for the quick, sharp calls of unidentified creatures in the trees. The others were still asleep or pretending to be. Samara let herself exist in the smallness of the moment: the weight of her daughter, the familiar ache and then relief as Phoebe latched on, the rhythm of breath and heartbeat, the slow tide of waking.

She didn't notice Katherine until the older woman's shadow stretched long and blue across the stone. Fishing rod slung over one shoulder, a battered canvas bag in the other hand, hair was down for a change, silver, and wild. She looked more relaxed than Samara had ever seen her.

"Thought I'd find you here," Katherine said, not bothering with a greeting. She produced two meal bars from her bag, which she offered without ceremony.

Samara took one, then switched it to the other hand as Phoebe immediately lurched forward, reaching for it. "You're up early."

"I was wondering if your girl wants to go to the river with me for a couple of hours." Katherine held one finger out toward Phoebe, who grabbed it and gurgled happily. "Want to go fishing with Auntie Katherine?"

Samara's first impulse was to hug her daughter tighter as she imagined Phoebe drowning as the river's current swept her away.

"She's a little young for fishing, isn't she?"

"I started taking my kids when they were six months old. Mostly, they just rolled around in the grass while I fished, but it gave them a chance to get comfortable in nature."

Samara couldn't help smiling at that. "Phoebe's already too comfortable in nature. She tries to make friends with everything. Or eat it."

"Normal for her age." Katherine made a silly face at Phoebe, who giggled, then asked Samara, "Mind if I hold her?"

Reluctantly, Samara handed her daughter to the former colony leader, watched with surprise at the delighted smile that dawned on Katherine's face as Phoebe burbled happily and grabbed a handful of silver hair.

Katherine, the mother. A side that Samara had never imagined lurked beneath the older woman's stern aura of authority.

"You said you had children?" Samara asked.

"Two boys and a girl." Katherine laughed as Phoebe yanked her hair, bouncing the girl as she swayed back and forth. "Eight grandchildren."

Samara couldn't imagine the pain of saying goodbye to them, knowing they would die and that she couldn't save them. Losing Phoebe would kill her. Multiplying that by three children and eight grandchildren…

But somehow, Katherine could smile and play with Samara's daughter after losing everything.

"I'm so sorry. I didn't realize that you'd lost your whole family."

"Didn't we all?" Katherine sighed. "I'm too old to have a new family here, but I would, in a heartbeat. Even if I knew I was going to lose them, too."

Would Samara ever be that strong? She didn't think so.

But as she saw the joy on the older woman's face, she realized that Katherine might not be asking to watch Phoebe to give Samara a break. She might be asking to give herself a break.

"I think Phoebe would enjoy learning to fish, if you're sure you want to take her."

"I'm sure." Katherine kissed the top of Phoebe's head, then sobered. "How's it going with your research?"

Samara blinked in surprise. "How did you know?"

"I noticed some of the soil had been disturbed when Maeve was updating me on her progress. You find anything worth knowing?"

"I had to run all the data on my comm, so I'm still waiting."

Katherine's gaze flicked over her shoulder, toward the direction of the destroyed lab. "Maeve and Lucas think they can get the comm array working again. I told them that if they need parts, they can cannibalize anything we brought. Including your sequencer."

First her daughter, now her sequencer. Samara kept her voice neutral. "Are you ordering me to give it up?"

"I'm not ordering anyone to do anything. I've had enough of that, and I think everyone else has too. But I also won't order them not to, if they think it's what they need."

"I appreciate the warning." Samara stood. "If you're sure you've got Phoebe—"

"Enjoy the morning, Mama. We'll bring you back a nice big fish for dinner."

Chapter Forty-One

SAMARA FOUND Renata crouched beside the firepit, coaxing flame from resin-rich kindling and last night's coals. The air was still edged with the sharp cold of pre-dawn, but Renata's cheeks already glowed from the heat, and her hands moved with the brisk, efficient certainty of someone who'd warmed herself in a hundred more uncomfortable places than this.

Renata glanced up, her eyes crinkling. "You look like you could use a cup of coffee."

"Is that a polite way of saying I look like crap?"

"It's a polite way of saying you look like you haven't slept in three days." Renata grinned and motioned to the incongruous kettle on the log beside her. "There's enough for two."

Samara eased down, hugging her knees as Renata poured instant coffee into a folding silicone cup. Lucas seemed to have thought of everything for their exile, making Samara worry he'd been planning this longer than claimed.

Nothing she could do about that if it was true.

She pulled her comm from her pocket and thumbed it on, pulling up the results from yesterday's analysis.

At first, she didn't understand what she saw. Then highlighted segments coalesced into a horror of impossible alleles and chimeric insertions. Genes that had never appeared in a human genome before, from every kingdom and phylum, stitched together with deranged precision. Sharks. Naked mole rats. Tasmanian devils. Tardigrades, for goodness' sake.

Tardigrades?

But as she looked up the function of specific sequences in their species of origin, the pattern emerged.

A pattern that confirmed her darkest suspicions.

"They went insane," she muttered.

"That bad?" Renata looked over her shoulder.

Samara pointed to the relevant sequence markers. "Look at these immune system modifications. They spliced in genes from multiple Earth species, all with highly aggressive immune responses. They were weaponizing their own immune systems against the fungus."

They'd done exactly the wrong thing. That massive immune response was probably what had wiped out the Hyperion colonists. They lacked the sophisticated epigenetic approaches Samara had learned, so they'd kept splicing trait after trait, hoping to kill the fungus without killing themselves. There was no way to tell if they'd realized their mistake and tried to dampen their immune response at some point, but even if they had, their stores of immunosuppressants were probably minimal, maybe nonexistent, given the stringent health screening that the Hyperion colonists had undergone.

She thought of the small skeletons they'd unearthed, imagining the agony those children must have endured as their enhanced immune systems attacked their own bodies.

All because their parents had been desperate enough to try anything.

Then it hit her. The Hyperion colonists hadn't survived the fungus, but they had been able to carry pregnancies to term. The mass grave proved it.

There might be something in the data that could help them after all, if she could find it.

THE ROOM STANK of ancient plastic and the ozone tang of something burning out, but Maeve's glee was infectious as she hunched over the battered comm array, sleeves rolled to the elbow and hands black with grime. Phoebe watched, transfixed, from Samara's lap as Maeve torqued a corroded fastener with a wrench that was at least three sizes too big.

"She's a beauty, isn't she?" Maeve said, with the genuine affection of a parent for a wayward child. "Dodgy as hell, and the power supply is failing. We've got maybe one shot at contacting the ship." She tested a connection, sparks snapping in the shadow of her hand. "Assuming the signal can punch through whatever atmospheric interference is out there."

Renata hovered behind Maeve, bouncing on her toes, equal parts hopeful and anxious. Katherine stood at the edge of the room, arms folded, her face set in a mask of calm that she couldn't possibly be feeling.

Lucas stood on the other side of the array, impassive, but two fingers tapped against his leg in an unsteady rhythm. A sign that he wanted this to work, or a sign that he didn't?

Maeve's fingers danced, and the ancient device spat a burst of static so loud it made Phoebe startle and wail. Maeve didn't look up as she adjusted something else.

The signal screeched, modulated, then resolved into an electric hum. Maeve handed Katherine a handset, then flipped two more switches and nodded.

"Borlaug, this is Demeter One, do you copy?" Katherine's voice stayed steady despite her visible tension.

A hiss of static, then: "Katherine? Thank God! We thought—"

Leo's voice broke in, strained but unmistakable. The relief was short-lived as the channel crackled and popped with wavering strength.

"Leo!" Katherine leaned closer to the microphone. "Listen, we need—"

The transmission dissolved into white noise that swallowed her words. Sparks flew from the console, smoke rising as something shorted within, a stench of melted circuitry and scorched hopes filling the air

"No!" Maeve lunged for the wires. But it was too late. The sickly green glow of the display faded, plunging them back into shadow.

Katherine sighed. "What are the chances of getting that hunk of junk working again?"

"Honestly?" Maeve scrubbed a hand over her face, smearing grease and frustration. "I'm fresh out of miracles, and we just let the magic smoke out of our last viable power relay."

"Is there any chance Leo can use the call to figure out where we are?" Renata asked.

"Even if he could, our boy would need to unlock the shuttles for that to matter," Maeve said, nodding at Lucas.

Katherine turned to Samara. "Please tell me your research gave us something to work with."

Samara looked at her fellow exiles, faces drawn with exhaustion, all seeking some measure of hope they could cling to. She had proof that the Hyperion colonists had found a way to avoid miscarrying after sporestorms, but had no idea which spliced sequences protected the fetus. There had to be something all the grave remains shared, but searching crashed her comm. If she could access the ship's equipment, she was sure she could find it.

But it seemed cruel to taunt them with a theory she couldn't test yet.

"Nothing yet, but I have a couple of ideas."

Unfortunately, all of them involved Lucas, and she wasn't sure if she should give him access to the data. She couldn't imagine what he'd do with it to hurt them, but she couldn't trust his motives either. For all she knew, Ayesha might have been right; Hofstadter might have sent them to DaVinci so that Lucas could perform some experiment on her fellow colonists. And manipulating Samara into studying the remains of the Hyperion crew might be the last thing Lucas needed to begin that experiment.

It sounded paranoid, even when she said it to herself, and she couldn't even blame the paranoia on pregnancy hormones.

Which made her worry that it might be true.

Katherine clapped her hands. "Then we just need to keep working on the communications array, and hope that in the meantime, Marcus and Leo can figure out how to get around the shuttle lockdown."

"They won't."

All four of them turned to glare at Lucas simultaneously.

"But I can record a command sequence that can be transmitted through the array once it is working again."

Walking back to the firepit, Samara stared up at the darkening sky, willing herself to spot the glint of the orbiting Borlaug. Somewhere up there was everything they needed to survive: medicine, food, equipment, all completely out of reach.

After dinner, returning from the latrine, she heard deliberate footsteps, not the furtive scuttle of a foraging animal. She tensed, then saw Lucas, his tall silhouette cut sharp against the firepit's orange glow, hands folded behind his back.

"I need to speak with you privately."

"If this is about Phoebe—"

"It's not. Or, it is, but not in the way you think." He stepped closer, and the firelight caught the planes of his face, softening the too-perfect symmetry. "A sporestorm is coming, within the next seventy-two hours."

"Have you told Katherine?"

"I will. But I wanted you to know—"

"Renata's already started collecting the seedpods. How long until you have the still operational?"

"I'm looking for another method. Distillation is not feasible with our current supplies."

She blinked. "Why not?"

"I haven't found a container that can withstand the necessary pressure and temperature, and I don't have the resources to make one." *Down here* was the implication. If they could get up to the ship…

"So, you're telling me there's nothing we can do."

Lucas' eyes flicked down, then up again. "I wanted you to know that if you are unable to care for Phoebe, I will make sure she survives."

For a moment, Samara heard nothing but the muted rush of the river and the distant, high wail of some unseen predator.

The chill of paranoia made her shiver. What if he'd lured her out here to die so that he would be the only one left to care for Phoebe? No more human oversight, no more arguing with Samara about whether he had the right to act as Phoebe's father.

"It will take months without antifungals before I'm in such bad shape that I can't take care of my daughter." She glared at him. "We'll find a solution by then."

"If we do not, I don't want you to worry. I promise to protect Phoebe."

Over my dead body. But that was literally what he was proposing.

If it came to that, Samara would crawl back to the colony and pretend to repent, even though it would mean giving up her daughter. She would rather that Phoebe be raised by humans.

Even if one of those humans was Ayesha.

SAMARA STRIPPED another cluster of berries from the bush and tossed them into the crude basket that Lucas had woven from flexible branches while the rest of them slept. That metallic tang in the air was back, the one that meant a sporestorm was coming. But according to Lucas, it wouldn't be here until evening, so as long as they foraged near the ruins, they'd be safe.

Phoebe burbled at Samara's feet, grabbing handfuls of tall grass, trying to eat it.

"No, sweetie," Samara said for the millionth time, squatting to pry her daughter's hand open. Torn purple ribbons fluttered down, but smaller bits stuck around Phoebe's mouth.

Sighing, Samara grabbed the hem of her shirt and lifted it to wipe the infant's face.

Phoebe reared up, arms flailing in delight, and socked Samara squarely in the cheek. The blow stung, but it was the suddenness of it, Phoebe's manic strength, the wild joy in her eyes, that sent Samara off balance. She toppled backward, landing on her ass in the mulch as her daughter, emboldened by freedom, lurched forward onto her hands and knees and began to crawl.

Samara scrambled after her, heart pounding. The baby was so fast, faster than any child had a right to be, and by the time she reached out, Phoebe had already wriggled through a gap in the bluish underbrush, vanishing into the shadows beyond.

"Phoebe!" Samara hissed, not wanting to alert anything else that might be prowling the ruins.

She shoved the basket aside and dove after her daughter, hands clawing through the prickly leaves that left faint scratches on her skin as she followed. She forced herself through the narrowest gap, branches scraping her shoulders as Phoebe babbled up ahead, then suddenly went silent. Samara's heart seized. She crashed through the last clutch of branches and burst into a clearing, almost crashing into Phoebe.

And the monster.

Humanoid with black, fathomless eyes, no discernible pupil or iris, but those twin voids reflected a hungry intelligence back at Samara. A streamlined nose with slits for nostrils. Scaley skin gleamed in the watery sunlight, dull green and gray in some places, silvery-blue in others. Thorny protrusions bristled on the top and sides of its head, along the sides of its neck, and down into the collar of the tattered, filthy rain poncho with the faded Hyperion logo draped limply around its shoulders.

Hard to tell how tall it was, crouching over them, eerily still, but its arms and legs seemed proportionally longer than a human's, and its sinuous movement as it shifted back on its heels reminded Samara of a double-jointed circus acrobat.

She knew without a doubt that this was the thing that Marcus had seen watching from the ridge their first night on the planet. How often had it returned to watch the colony, having learned to conceal itself better after he'd taken a panicked shot at it?

Putting it on notice from the very beginning that the humans invading its home were violent.

Fear crawled up the back of Samara's neck. This was the presence she'd sensed, observing them from the trees as they traveled to these ruins and set up camp. As they slept and ate and searched the site for useful items.

As they'd dug up the mass grave to take samples from the long-buried corpses.

And yet, it hadn't done anything to hurt them. Hadn't even approached them. Because it was afraid of them?

Or had it been stalking them, waiting for a vulnerable moment to attack?

Phoebe had crawled straight for it, as if it were another creature that she could charm like a princess in a fairy tale.

She reached toward the thing as if she wanted it to pick her up.

The creature made a sound somewhere between a whimper and a hiss, but it didn't move.

Phoebe waved her chubby hands, insistent. *Pick me up.*

Samara's instincts screamed at her to grab her child and scurry back through the brush, but she was terrified to break the detente. What if sudden movement startled it into attacking? What if retreating triggered an instinct to chase?

Phoebe waved her hands again.

The creature waved back, mimicking her movement exactly.

And the unnatural fluidity of the movement reminded Samara of the shape she'd seen in the sporestorm.

That thing, or something like it, had snuck into the colony. It had been right outside Samara's window. It could've come into her cabin…

Phoebe grunted in frustration and waved her hands a third time.

The creature uncurled from its crouch, moving liquid-smooth as it rose to full height. No longer cowering, it made quick gestures with its elongated fingers. Phoebe responded with happy gurgles, reaching tiny hands toward it, waving in clumsy attempts to copy its movements. Dark eyes fixed on her with unsettling intensity.

What was it doing?

Phoebe cooed, a strange and ululating sound that made the hairs on the back of Samara's neck stand at rigid attention.

The creature trilled in response, the noise resonating in Samara's bones like an ancient, eldritch lullaby.

It was trying to communicate.

If she'd had any doubts before, they evaporated. The creature was sentient.

And with all his surveys, Lucas had somehow missed it.

Or he'd hidden it from them.

There could be thousands of those things lurking in DaVinci's forests. Maybe tens or hundreds of thousands.

Samara eased forward in slow motion toward Phoebe, hoping that if she didn't seem to be threatening the creature, it would remain where it was. But when she accidentally snapped a twig beneath her knee, the creature started, dropping back into a crouch. Which brought it closer to Phoebe.

Again, Phoebe tried to copy the creature's movements. Closer this time.

It replied with a string of gestures so fast that Samara could barely follow them.

But Phoebe could. She copied them again, faster this time. Not as fast as the creature, but faster than Samara could have.

"Samara?" Renata's voice sounded warbly and distant. "I found another patch."

The creature shot upward to a tree branch eight feet overhead. Samara lunged for Phoebe, tackling her in a bear hug and rolling to avoid crushing her daughter beneath her. Phoebe howled and kicked atop of Samara as she watched the creature staring down at them both.

Then it kicked off the branch, leaping nearly twelve feet to a branch on a neighboring tree, quickly disappearing into the forest canopy.

Crashing through the brush, Renata appeared. She crouched down beside Samara and tried to lift the kicking, screaming Phoebe out of her protective hug, but Samara scooted backward, clutching her daughter tighter.

"What happened? Is she okay?" Renata laid one hand on Samara's shin. "Are *you* okay?"

"Alien," was all Samara could say. "Phoebe tried to fairy princess it."

Renata looked at her for a long moment, then stood and held out her hand, "Let's get back to the others."

Chapter Forty-Two

"DID THE CREATURE HURT YOU?"

Samara stared up at Katherine, struggling to process the question as she huddled on a log near the firepit. Renata paced across from her, carrying a whimpering Phoebe. It had taken ten minutes to pry the wailing infant from Samara's grip. Every unhappy sound made her want to snatch the girl back.

One moment of inattention and Phoebe had wandered straight into the clutches of an intelligent alien whose intentions Samara couldn't guess.

Worse, the alien hadn't scared Phoebe at all. It was Samara's reaction that had sent Phoebe into a screaming fit.

"Samara, did it hurt you?"

She forced herself to focus on Katherine's worry-creased face. To focus on the words she'd said instead of giving in to the primal need to carry her daughter far away and hide here where monsters couldn't find her.

But that was impossible, because the monsters had

been among them from the beginning. The colony settlement wasn't a fortress meant to defend against alien incursion. It was a farming community, with flimsy prefab buildings and fences to keep their animals penned in.

She was spiraling.

Answer the question.

"No, it didn't hurt me."

"Did it try?"

Samara shook her head. "I think it was trying to communicate with Phoebe."

"What did it sound like?" Renata asked.

"It trilled, but I don't think that's how it was talking. It was making gestures—" Samara tried mimicking them, but she couldn't remember what the creature had done. Only Phoebe's tiny hands waving, *Pick me up.*

What if it had? What if the creature had picked her up and leapt up into those trees and taken her away?

All because Samara had been more focused on gathering berries than protecting her daughter.

I am the world's worst mother.

A branch snapping behind them made all three whip around. Lucas emerged from the undergrowth, dragging a mesh bag that writhed and squeaked with the weight of half a dozen terrified, rabbit-sized mammals.

Now, Samara had a place to focus all her fear and rage.

Lucas set the bag down at the edge of the circle, wiped both hands on his thighs, and surveyed the group. Then his eyes went straight to Phoebe.

"What happened?" he asked.

Samara's hands balled into fists. "Did you know about the creature?"

Lucas' brow furrowed. "Which creature?"

"The one that's been watching us since we left the

colony," Samara said. "The bipedal, lizard-fish-person-thing that's been stalking us since the first day we landed on this planet?"

She couldn't breathe, but somehow she could keep yelling. "The creature Marcus shot at on the ridge? The creature I saw in the sporestorm, walking around our village, doing who knows what? The creature that just tried to *steal my daughter?*"

Lucas moved toward her so quickly that Samara flinched, but he stopped short, crouching low so that his eyes were level with hers. The intensity in his face was terrifying, so focused, so hungry for the answer that for a moment, Samara forgot her anger, forgot her fear, and felt only the gravity of his attention, pinning her in place.

"Tell me everything."

The whole story tumbled out: Phoebe's escape, the clearing, the thing in the rain poncho, the gestures, the way it mirrored Phoebe, the sound it made in its throat. She told him how it had watched them, how it had never attacked, how it had seemed to recognize her daughter as something... else. She poured it out in a rush, voice hoarse, almost sobbing by the end.

Lucas listened without blinking, without moving a centimeter. When she was done, he was silent for a moment. Then he said, "I did not know about that particular creature."

Renata said, "How is that possible? You did the initial survey. You mapped every living thing in a hundred-kilometer radius." She bounced Phoebe on her hip, voice sharp with disbelief. "You said there was nothing but animals and plants. No intelligent life, nothing with language or tool use."

"I was looking for life forms with observable

infrastructure. I found no settlements, no roads, no power sources. If there are intelligent beings here, they are either good at hiding or have no technology."

"Except for the Hyperion ruins. There was plenty of evidence of those."

Lucas inclined his head toward Samara, accepting the rebuke. "I did use the drones to do an initial survey of the failed colony, to see what remained."

"Now that you know what to look for, can you go back through the survey data? See if there's any sign of these… creatures?"

Lucas' eyes unfocused for a fraction of a second. "I can. I have not yet archived the memory of the survey. But if they are adept at camouflage, the odds are low that I will find anything."

"Do it anyway," said Katherine. "Look everywhere near here, see if you can find where they are living."

Lucas nodded once, and for a moment his body went perfectly still, the way it did when he was running a massive calculation.

Katherine didn't wait for Lucas to finish whatever process he'd gone inside himself to run. "We have to warn the colony. Ayesha might not believe us, but if there's a population of these things and they're provoked—"

"I'm not going back." More forceful than Samara intended. "If we show up, Ayesha will lock me up instead of listening. She'll quarantine Phoebe, or worse. Even if she does listen, she'll convince everyone it's a trick to undermine her credibility." She looked at the others, desperate for someone to see how pointless it would be. "We'd be sacrificing ourselves for nothing."

"They're still our people. If this encounter has provoked the creatures, the colony could be in danger, and we have a duty to warn them."

"Samara's right." Renata shifted Phoebe to her other hip as she paced. "If we go back, Ayesha will spin it into another power play. Even if we show up with a live specimen, she'll find a way to make it about her authority. Besides, this is a first contact situation. If we botch it, we'll never get another chance to coexist. We'll be at war on a planet we can't survive on alone."

Ayesha was guaranteed to botch it, Samara thought. Anything she couldn't manipulate, she destroyed.

Lucas' head jerked slightly, as if he was returning from a deep dive. "I agree with Renata. Communication and peaceful coexistence must be our priority. If we can establish a rapport with the creatures, we may be able to negotiate for territory or resources, or at minimum avoid antagonizing them."

"Have you found where they're living?" Katherine asked.

"I've identified several probable locations. Six, within twenty kilometers of this camp. But I can't deploy drones to investigate further. I'm out of range of both the colony's network and the Borlaug's satellite systems. I can only use my own limited sensors."

"Wait, what's this?" Renata wiped something off Phoebe's face with one finger.

"She was eating weeds again," Samara said.

"No, this." Renata came closer, holding the finger out. Something small shimmered silvery-blue against her skin, like a large fish scale.

It came from the creature.

Samara turned to Lucas. "You haven't taken my sequencer apart yet, have you?"

"Your sequencer?"

Samara raced to their shelter, grabbed sequencer and

stabilizing fluid, then ran back to the firepit. "Give me the scale."

She opened the sequencer up, dripped stabilizer into the well until it reached the fill line, and held the device out to Renata, who carefully transferred the scale into the well. Samara snapped it shut, started the program, and watched it warm up.

"In two hours, we'll know enough about the creature to make a better guess where it lives." Although she was already guessing *amphibious,* so not just near water, but possibly in water.

She looked to Katherine. "I volunteer to make the second contact."

"You're not going without me," Renata added.

"While I agree that it is our duty to warn the colony," Lucas said, "they do already have perimeter sensors, security cameras on the major approaches, including views of the entire settlement from the ridge."

Katherine sighed. "Fine, we'll wait. I'll check Maeve's progress on the communications array."

Samara stared at the sequencer, willing the progress bar to move faster. She tried to breathe steadily, but her lungs only knew how to inhale panic and exhale doubt. Phoebe was perched on a chunk of broken concrete near the firepit, her tiny hands hovering over a beetle the size of Samara's thumb. The child tracked the insect's every move with a priestly reverence, her body stilled by fascination. The same look she'd given the creature in the woods, full of open-mouthed awe, as if she'd recognized something in it that Samara herself could not.

She'd watched the thing unfurl to its full height, watched it look at Phoebe the way a parent might. She'd seen her daughter reach for it, fearless, and for a moment, she'd been certain she was about to witness her child's death.

If she lost her daughter, what would be the point of living?

~

SAMARA LINED up the next pebble atop the tiny cairn, holding her breath as she steadied Phoebe's hand. The tower wobbled, then collapsed, scattering pebbles into the dirt. Phoebe squealed and clapped, triumphant in defeat, and immediately began collecting the stones for another round. Samara tried to match her daughter's enthusiasm, but her eyes kept flicking to the sequencer, scanning the progress bar that crawled across the tiny display with agonizing reluctance.

It wasn't even halfway.

"Again!" said Phoebe, or something close to it, a string of syllables that Samara's brain, starved for comfort, translated as a demand for repetition. She obliged, helping to assemble a new stack, but her hands moved automatically, her mind elsewhere. The memory of Phoebe's first word, *fosss,* burned in her chest. She'd been so proud, and so wounded.

As she set another pebble on the stack, a memory flickered: Phoebe trying to cram Ayo pebbles into her mouth and Renata prying them out of her hand while Marcus laughed.

She wondered if Marcus was up there with Leo on the Borlaug or if he'd died in the chaos of the coup. She glanced at Renata, intent on chopping up a tuber that she'd foraged earlier to put in tonight's fish stew. How could she be so calm when she had no idea what had happened to him?

The sequencer beeped. Samara grabbed it, heart racing, and fumbled for her comm. She started the data transfer, forgetting to breathe as she watched the progress bar.

The comm flashed a low battery warning.

Shit. She lunged for the duffel, yanked out the power bank with shaking hands, and jammed the cable in just as the screen started to darken. The 1% in the upper right corner switched to 2%, and she let out a whoosh of relief.

Fifteen minutes of hell, measured by the slow crawl of a status bar and Phoebe's relentless stacking of stones. When the sequence finally finished, the comm vibrated in Samara's hand, startling her into almost dropping it.

"I've got it," she said, more to herself than anyone else.

Renata slid onto the log beside her, her own hands trembling as she reached for the device. "Show me."

Samara thumbed open the analysis. The app flickered, then began spitting out a litany of base pair reads, which it started grouping into sequences.

The first pass took seconds. The app started scrolling through sequence matches a second time, mapping genes and identifying possible traits. But when it spat out its conclusion, Samara was sure the sample had been contaminated.

She initiated a new run, specifying the potential contamination source and instructing the app to eliminate all relevant genes.

The results were exactly the same.

"That's impossible," Samara breathed. "It's ninety-nine point nine seven percent human."

"You're saying the creature is similar to a human?" Katherine asked.

Renata made a sound halfway between a laugh and a

sob. "Not just similar. It's human. And there's no way this is convergent evolution."

Katherine reached for the comm, her fingers steady as she took it from Samara and squinted at the readout. "That can't be right. Did you contaminate the sample?"

"That's what I thought, but I corrected for that."

"You said ninety-nine point nine seven percent," Katherine asked. "What's the other point oh three percent?"

"There are genes from a half-dozen aquatic creatures we've catalogued so far, like the lizard creature we found in the river." Renata turned to Samara. "Maybe that's what the scale was from, and then my DNA got mixed in with it."

Samara shook her head. "I thought about that, and that's why I compared it to the samples I took from the grave."

There was only one conclusion that made sense, but it was so far out there, her mind rebelled against it. If her sequencer wasn't broken and if the sample hadn't been contaminated…

"I think I know what happened to the Hyperion colonists."

Katherine frowned. "I thought the fungus wiped them out because they couldn't figure out a way to engineer themselves a better immune system."

"That's what they tried first." Samara glanced at Renata, who looked ready to faint. "But they realized their mistake. And then…"

She swallowed hard, afraid to say it out loud, because then it would be true.

"Then they figured out that it was their immune response killing them, so they modified themselves with genes from the aquatic creature. But the modifications didn't just affect their immune system." Katherine stared at her like she was insane. "Are you saying that creature you saw was—"

"A direct descendant of one of the original colonists. It shared mitochondrial DNA with at least three of the samples I took from the mass grave. Siblings of its ancestors.

"The Hyperion colonists didn't go extinct," Samara finished. "They evolved."

Chapter Forty-Three

EVERY STEP SENT a jolt up her spine, a percussion of pain that landed with the certainty of a judge's gavel. The geolocator vibrated in her fist, pulse light blinking with each meter she advanced into the dark. Something in her lower belly twisted, a sudden, hot knife, and she gasped, knees buckling. For a second, she thought she might pass out, but she caught herself on the rough bark of a tree, pressed her forehead to it, and waited for the contraction to subside.

When it did, she wiped her face with the back of her sleeve. The skin under her eyes was sticky, wet with the snot and tears she'd been leaking for the past hour. She didn't care. It was better than letting herself stop.

Stopping meant thinking, and thinking meant remembering the look on Dr. Callas' face when he told her, with what he must have thought was kindness, that there were no more immunosuppressants to be had, even on the ship, and that if Dr. Basu had told her there were, the psychologist was mistaken.

No matter how she'd begged and pleaded, he'd insisted

that the best he could do was to remove the baby if her body couldn't pass it after it died.

The spot of blood she'd found on her underwear less than an hour ago was just the beginning. Samara was her only hope.

If Samara would help her, after Leila had betrayed her.

It might already be too late. The metallic scent of the air was so strong, she was practically gagging on it. The sporestorm was on its way, and if she was caught out in it, even with a respirator, her immune response would kill the baby.

She checked the geolocator's screen. The blue dot of her own position was closing in on a cluster of structures labeled "Hyperion Ruins." Even through the haze of pain, her mind fixed on the certainty that this was where Samara would go, because the others wouldn't come looking for her there. They were afraid of catching mutations if they got too near the genetically engineered corpses.

But Leila knew it didn't work that way. She'd gone looking through the colony archives for information about gene therapy. The mutations couldn't jump off a skeleton and infect you. If they were airborne, all the women in the colony would've been "infected" with whatever Samara had done to Phoebe, and Leila wouldn't be about to lose her baby.

She forced herself into a lurching jog, the angle of the ground growing steeper as the trees thinned and the first shadows of ruined walls loomed above the scrub. She tried not to think about the bodies, the mass grave, the twisted skeletons that haunted her nightmares now. Just because they weren't contagious didn't mean they didn't scare her.

A sudden gust, air full of spores, churning and swarming, clinging to every inch of exposed skin. She ducked instinctively, pulling the collar over her nose, but too late.

Nostrils burning, eyes streaming, vision blurring until the world was a brown cloud.

Leila coughed, then sneezed so hard it doubled her over. She fumbled for the respirator dangling from her pack strap, managed to get it over her mouth, and sucked in a shaky breath that tasted of rubber and panic. The geolocator's screen was a smear of light through the tears in her eyes. She blinked hard, wiped her face, and tried to focus on the map.

She thought she was close, but now she couldn't see where she was going or tell which direction she'd come from.

A deeper, tighter pain seized her. Leila crumpled to her knees, clutching her belly as an animal groan tore from her throat. "Not now," she whispered, rocking, forehead pressed to the dirt. "Not now, not now, not now." The pain crested, then receded, leaving her hollow and shaking.

She forced her breath to slow. "Hang on, baby," she whispered. "Just hang on. I'm getting you help." She squeezed her eyes shut, willing the words into the tight, silent place she imagined the baby existed. "Don't leave me, please."

The wind gusted again, and it was almost impossible to see. She staggered up, scanning for anything that looked like a building, a door, a window, any sign that she wasn't just flailing in circles. Her boots sloshed through a low patch, water soaking her socks; she gasped at the cold, but at least it wasn't hurting the baby. She could handle any amount of pain, as long as the baby was okay.

She wiped her face again and, blinking through the tears, staggered forward. She didn't see the branch until it caught her full in the chest. The impact knocked the air from her lungs and spun her sideways into the mud. She landed hard, the geolocator skidding from her hand and vanishing into the muck. For a moment she just lay there, stunned, as the wind howled and the spores came down heavier.

She pushed herself up, hands slick and trembling, and tried to orient. The world tilted and spun. Something deep inside her seized, a cramp so sharp it felt like her insides were being twisted apart. She screamed. Everything went white.

~

When she came to, Phoebe's cherubic face hovered above her, smiling like she was happy to see her former caretaker.

Of course, she's happy to see you. She has no idea what you did to her mother.

A shadow loomed, and Samara crouched beside her, so sudden and silent that Leila flinched. Samara's hair was windblown and streaked with mud, her eyes ringed with exhaustion. She looked like she'd been awake for days, and her mouth was set in a straight, unforgiving line.

Another cramp seized Leila, so sharp and deep she couldn't even form a sound at first. Then it tore out of her anyway, a strangled sob, her arms curled around her belly. She tried to speak, but the words tangled with the pain. She pressed her forehead into the dirt, then forced herself up far enough to meet Samara's gaze.

"I'm sorry," she managed. "I didn't know who else—" The next wave hit, and she gagged, tasting bile and blood. "Please, I need your help. Please."

Samara's lips barely moved. "You shouldn't have come here. Why didn't you go to the clinic? Hector could've taken care of you."

Leila's laugh came out as a wet, shuddering cough.

"He said there was nothing left to do. He wasn't even going to try."

"But at least he would've kept you from bleeding to death. You're lucky Lucas found you."

"I don't care if my baby comes out with gills or a tail, I just—" She gritted her teeth as another contraction knifed through her. "I need you to save the baby. Please, Samara."

"I wish I could. But the shuttles are locked down on the Borlaug. All my equipment is up there, and I can't get to it."

"Dr. Basu said you took equipment from the lab so that you could keep doing your experiments."

Samara snorted. "Ayesha doesn't know what she's talking about, and that's the root of ninety-five percent of our problems right now."

"It's my fault. If I hadn't given the comm to Dr. Basu, you'd still be running things, and the android wouldn't have locked you out. The shuttles would be here. You could fix me. You could fix this." Another wave of pain made her entire body shudder. "I'm sorry. I'm so sorry. I just wanted a chance."

"All that matters now is keeping you alive." Samara sighed. "The storm is over, but now you're infected, and we don't have any antifungals to give you. We don't have a way to get you home, either."

"So… what are you going to do with me?"

Before Samara could answer, Leila heard scuffing noises, then Renata and Maeve appeared and knelt on either side of her.

Renata handed Leila the wooden bowl she was carrying, which turned out to be filled with water. Then she rummaged through the med kit, coming up with a pink pill and a white pill.

"Antihistamine and tramadol. Each will reduce your

reaction to the spores, and maybe slow the baby's immune system down, too. In combination, they may be enough."

Leila gulped the pill down with water, then lay back. "Now what?"

"Now you give us all your gear." Maeve held out her hand. "Comm unit, geolocator, anything that Ayesha can use to locate you."

"Can you use my comm to call the shuttle?" Leila asked.

"No," Maeve replied, "but I can use the geolocator to repair the blown relay in the array."

"Is that good?"

"It's good. Might even give us a few seconds of signal."

"Are you saying Leila might have just brought us the missing piece?" Samara asked.

Maeve shrugged. "No promises."

My baby has a chance.

Leila clung to that shred of hope like she'd clung to her spot on the Borlaug. But as she scanned the anxious faces huddled around the campfire, one was conspicuously missing.

Samara seemed to notice at the exact same moment. Her head whipped around, eyes widening with rising panic.

"Where is Phoebe?"

~

"Phoebe!" Samara's voice cracked as she stumbled through the ruins. "PHOEBE!"

Only the whisper of alien leaves answered. Her flashlight beam caught fragments of the abandoned settlement, crumbling walls, rusted equipment, and shadows that writhed and danced past the edges of her vision.

But no sign of her daughter.

The others fanned out through the darkness, their own calls echoing off decaying concrete and metal. All except for Maeve, who'd stayed hunched over the comm panel in a nest of salvaged wires, cursing softly as she worked.

Lucas had vanished into the forest. His enhanced vision might allow him to pick up faint signs of Phoebe's passage that the rest of them might miss, even with a flashlight. Or pick up her heat signature with an infrared scan.

But the android wasn't the only being with inhuman senses out there in the forest. She tried not to think about the creature that had loomed over Phoebe earlier, staring with those black eyes that swallowed light without giving anything back.

They had no idea what the creature wanted. How much it understood. Whether it saw Phoebe as friend or foe or, Samara shuddered, food.

Her foot caught on something, and she stumbled, barely catching herself against a tree trunk. She'd spent most of her career inside, walking on smooth, flat surfaces in ordered environments that didn't try to trip you every third step. If she ever found her daughter again, she was going to fix that. Take up hiking, learn to navigate without a geolocator, and develop some survival skills that would equip her to protect her daughter.

She played her flashlight beam across the ground, hoping to see the prints of infant-sized hands and knees in the muddy ground. Instead, a glint of color caught her eye. Samara dropped to a crouch, scrabbling through debris until her fingers closed around something small and plastic. For one wild moment, hope tickled her chest.

But it wasn't Phoebe's. Just a tiny dinosaur toy, its paint worn to patches and joints frozen with age. A relic of another lost child, another family destroyed by this godforsaken planet.

The tears hit without warning. One moment she was staring at the toy, the next she was sobbing, ugly heaving gasps that felt like they might tear her apart.

"Some scientist I am." She choked. "Can't even keep track of one baby for five minutes."

Footsteps crunched behind her. Then Katherine's hand settled on her shoulder. "We're going to find her."

"You can't know that." Samara swiped angrily at her eyes. "She could have fallen into a creek and drowned, or slid into a ravine and broken her leg, or—" She swallowed. "That *thing* could have taken her. It could have carried her up into the trees and dropped her, or just left her somewhere to—"

"Stop." Katherine's grip tightened. "We stick to what we know. No evidence of injury, no blood, no signs of struggle. Focus on facts, not worst-case scenarios."

"Here's a fact: I lost my daughter because I got distracted by Leila showing up."

"And we'll find her." Katherine crouched down beside her. "Maeve thinks she can have the comms working by morning. If we haven't found Phoebe by then, we'll bring the shuttles and the drones down to scan every inch of this forest."

Samara didn't want the hope that Katherine was offering, because the disappointment if it proved false would kill her. "Morning could be too late."

"True. But falling apart won't help us find her faster."

Samara stared at the toy dinosaur. "I knew I wasn't cut out for this. Being a mother. I've known my whole life. I never wanted kids, never had that... that *instinct* that other women seem to have. I thought maybe I felt it after she was born. But this just proves that something is seriously wrong with me."

"Isn't that what you scientists call anecdotal evidence?"

"Well, yes, but—"

"You have nine months of data that suggests you're a great mom."

"That's not how it works."

"I think that's exactly how it works."

"Phoebe could be dead because I forgot about her for two minutes!"

Katherine caught her chin, forcing Samara to meet her eyes. "Here's the thing about being a mother: you don't get a do-over when you make a mistake. And you don't get to give up when something goes wrong. Being a mother isn't about you at all. It's about what your kid needs. And right now, Phoebe needs her mom to keep looking for her. *Period*."

In other words, indulging in self-recrimination wasn't fixing anything. It was more of the same behavior that Samara had been chiding herself for.

"Message received." She stood, drawing in a breath to steady herself. "Thanks for the pep talk."

They searched for another hour. Found nothing.

When they returned to the firepit, the others were already there, expressions grim in the flickering light. None of them said anything, but Renata slipped her hand in Samara's and squeezed. Samara's eyes started to flood again, and she yanked her hand away, pretending not to see Renata's hurt.

She couldn't afford to fall apart, not until her daughter rested in her arms again.

Movement in the shadows made Samara's heart leap. Lucas emerged from the darkness, carrying something, some*one*. For one wild moment, hope blazed through her chest.

But it wasn't Phoebe in his arms. It was Briar, unconscious and bleeding from a gash on her temple. Literally the last person in the colony who Samara would expect to find skulking through the forest at night immediately after a sporestorm. Whatever had brought her out here...

This had to be her fault.

"I found her approximately point-two-five miles from our position, bearing roughly northeast toward the colony," Lucas announced. "Based on her pupillary response and elevated intracranial pressure indicators, she probably has a grade two concussion."

Great. Another medical emergency for them to deal with. And when someone noticed she was missing, Ayesha would send search parties. Possibly blame them for whatever trouble Briar had gotten herself into.

They had to move before that happened. But she couldn't leave this place until they found Phoebe, because what if, by some miracle, she came back?

"What was Briar doing out there?" Renata demanded. "Spying on us?"

"There were signs of a struggle. Two distinct sets of footprints leading away from the site. And..." He hesitated, which sent ice down Samara's spine. Lucas *never* hesitated. "Small tracks. Consistent with an infant attempting to crawl."

Briar stirred, eyes flying open in panic. "The monster!" she gasped. "It attacked us—"

"Where is my daughter?" Samara roared.

Briar froze, fear flickering across her face. "We were bringing her back to the colony—"

"*Where is she?*"

"The monster took her!"

"And you just happened to be walking by?" Renata's voice dripped acid.

Briar's mouth snapped shut.

Katherine crouched beside her. "Whatever happens to Phoebe is on you if you don't tell us the truth. Right now."

"Dr. Basu asked us to follow Leila, because she knew Leila would go looking for you. She was about to lose her baby."

"Who is *us*?"

"Are… are you going to infect me?" Briar's voice quavered. "With the vaccine?"

"What vaccine?"

"Whatever you gave your freak baby. The one that lets her talk to bugs."

It took everything Samara had not to slap the younger woman. "What exactly happened to my *freak baby*?"

"I told you, the monster—"

"Was Phoebe with you?" Katherine cut in before Samara could follow through on her impulse.

Briar gave a tiny nod.

"She wouldn't have gone with you willingly." Understanding hit Samara like a punch to her stomach. "The creature didn't take her. *You* took her."

Defiance flashed across Briar's face. "We were saving her! So you couldn't experiment on her anymore. Dr. Basu said she deserves a real mother—"

Samara lunged forward, but Katherine's arm shot out to stop her. Her bicep was like iron against Samara's chest.

"What. Happened?" Katherine asked in a voice that could have frozen nitrogen.

"We were taking her back to the colony," Briar mumbled as defiance leaked out of her. "She wouldn't stop crying. Then this... this *thing* jumped down from the trees. I tried to taze the monster, but that just made it mad." She touched her head. "Hit me pretty hard."

"Did Mai take Phoebe with her?"

"Mai dropped the baby and ran. Didn't even try to fight."

"She left my daughter with that creature?" Samara could barely force the words through her constricted throat.

"She left me too!" Briar snapped.

"The physical evidence supports Briar's account." Lucas added. "Phoebe's trail terminates approximately three-point-two meters from where she was dropped. The pattern suggests she was lifted from the ground at that point."

Samara's baby was in the hands of one of the descendants of the Hyperion settlers, creatures who were barely human anymore and who had just been attacked by Mai and Briar. Who might decide the best revenge would be...

Her mind kept spinning out horrific possibilities, each one worse than the last.

"I can track them," Lucas said. The taser dangled from his hand. Briar's weapon, now their only defense against whatever waited in the dark.

"I'm not going to ask any of you to come with me," said Samara in a shaking voice. "We don't know how many of them are out there, or what they're capable of."

Katherine didn't hesitate. "Of course, we're going with you."

"The sooner we go, the sooner we'll find her." Renata was already on her feet.

A loud clang made them all jump. Maeve stood from her nest of wires, hefting a corroded wrench. "Let's go get your daughter back."

Chapter Forty-Four

"Here." Renata pressed two pills, one pink, one white, into Leila's palm. Another tramadol, another antihistamine. "Take this."

Leila swallowed them with a sip from her water bottle. "Is there more for later?"

Renata handed her a small bottle containing one white pill. "That's all she wrote, but it should buy us some time. Maybe six hours before the baby starts fighting with the fungus again. A little longer, if you're lucky."

Six hours. Leila put her hand to her belly, willing her baby to hang on. They just needed to get back to the ship, back to Samara's lab. Back to hope.

Another whimper from Briar made Leila's stomach clench. How desperate did you have to be to steal someone else's child?

But then she thought about Mike, and how willing he'd been to cheat on Briar to make her jealous. And how angry Briar had been when she'd caught them together.

The child Leila was carrying was Mike's.

Briar was having a miserable life, too. She'd probably

been just as scared as Leila had to leave Earth behind, and she was just as trapped in a bad relationship. Maybe a worse relationship—Justin might have strayed, but Leila didn't think he was as angry at her as Mike had been with Briar.

She sighed. Briar had started their feud by bullying Leila and seducing Justin, but Leila wasn't exactly blameless either.

Maybe they could both use a little forgiveness.

The others were already preparing to leave. Maeve strapped a heavy wrench to her belt. Lucas stepped outside, broke off a thick tree branch, and methodically stripped it down to form a crude staff. He returned and offered it to Samara.

She stared at the branch, her hands clenched at her sides.

"The creature is intelligent," Renata said quietly. "It never threatened us while it was here."

"Except for the part where it stalked us and waited for a chance to steal my daughter." But Samara didn't take the makeshift club that Lucas held out to her.

"I think we should assume it's not hostile," Katherine said. "Try talking to them first."

Them. Leila had been imagining Samara and the others hunting down a lone creature, but of course, there had to be more out there.

Who knew how many more?

Samara stepped back from the offered branch. Katherine reached past her to take it instead, then turned to Maeve. "Can we get a message to the ship?"

"Comm's fixed, but the battery needs time to charge. Won't be ready for at least twenty minutes."

"We can't wait that long." Samara paced near the door, her whole body coiled with tension. Leila had never seen the scientist like this, careful control stripped away, leaving something fierce and primal in its place.

"Then someone has to stay behind to send a message as soon as there's enough power."

"We might need everyone to get the child back," Katherine said, looking around at their small group. "If things go wrong up there..."

"I'll do it."

The ensuing silence told Leila exactly how much they trusted her. She opened her mouth to argue, but a cramp seized her abdomen, sharper than before. She tried to hide her wince, to breathe through it, but the pain built until her knees threatened to buckle. She caught herself against the wall, one hand pressed to her belly.

"The only way to save my baby is to get a message to that ship." She met Samara's eyes. "You can trust that's the only thing that matters to me."

Samara gave a short nod.

Maeve crossed to the comm console, motioning for Leila to join her.

"See this?" She tapped a small LED indicator. "When it goes green, you've got enough power for exactly three seconds of transmission. Then it needs five minutes to recharge."

Leila studied the crudely repaired control panel. A radio handset wired into salvaged parts from different devices. "Three seconds isn't much."

"It's what we've got." Maeve pointed to a switch. "Console's already tuned to the ship's frequency. Press this button to talk. Keep trying until you get through."

Lucas stepped up to the comm console and held out a small storage card, the kind with a contact chip at one end. He slid the card into a slot beneath a blue LED.

"This contains my authorization codes for the shuttles.

Transmit this first, before you try to say anything. We don't know how long the power will last."

"And if you do get a chance to say something, tell them we're at the colony site that Lucas rejected. The ship's AI will have the coordinates." Katherine paused. "And if we don't come back—"

"You have to come back." Leila's hand curled protectively over her belly. "My baby's counting on you."

As the others filed out into the pre-dawn darkness, Leila picked up the handset, watching the LED indicator's stubborn red glow. "Come on," she whispered. "Please work."

THE MOONS CAST overlapping shadows that made depth perception tricky. Lucas led Samara and the others up through the foothills behind the Hyperion ruins, his android reflexes helping him pick the safest path through the treacherous terrain.

The forest thinned as they ascended, surrendering to rocky outcrops and patches of stringy grass that rippled in shades of cobalt and turquoise. Under certain angles of moonlight, the grass took on an almost metallic sheen, as if dipped in liquid mercury.

Then she saw them: more than three dozen stone structures emerged from the slope like ancient teeth jutting from the earth. Each structure measured roughly fifteen feet in diameter at the base, with walls that curved inward as they rose twelve feet to domed roofs. The stones had been fitted with precision, not a single gap wider than a fingernail between them. Small circular vents, each exactly six inches across, punctuated the upper walls at regular three-foot intervals.

Each building was half-buried in the hillside, with wild grass growing on the rounded roofs and small holes punched through for ventilation. They reminded her of pictures she'd seen of ancient Scottish settlements, a bizarre hybrid of shepherd's hut and burial mound that seemed jarringly out of place on this alien world.

This settlement spoke of planning, tool use, and culture.

"*Hold up*," Katherine whispered. She pointed to a crude rack fashioned from lashed-together branches. Strips of meat hung drying in the cool air. Embers still glowed in a stone-lined fire pit nearby, casting just enough light to make the shadows seem deeper. "Someone was here recently."

"So where'd they go?" Renata's knuckles whitened on her makeshift weapon.

A cold wind swept down from the higher slopes.

"Phoebe?" Samara called softly. "Baby, are you here?"

The silence felt oppressive. Almost alive. Like the buildings themselves were holding their breath.

"We should check inside," Katherine murmured. "Carefully."

They crept to the nearest structure, lifting the woven grass curtain serving as a door to peek inside. Empty.

"Who wants to go in?" Renata asked, holding the curtain aside. After a moment's hesitation, Samara entered, followed by the others.

The floor was packed earth, and the air held the sweet earthiness of dried grass and an unfamiliar spice that made Samara's nose itch. Most of the inhabitants' possessions rested on a shelf of boards stacked on flat stones in layers. Renata picked up a bowl, turning it over in her hands. The interior was heavily stained with concentric rings of purple-brown, and the outside bore scorch marks from fire.

"*This is incredible*," she breathed. "It's made from some kind of massive nutshell, heat-treated to harden it. I haven't seen anything like this in any of my botanical surveys. The shell structure suggests a fruit at least thirty centimeters in diameter."

"And look at this." Maeve hefted a hammer. Its metal head was almost destroyed by rust, but the wooden handle looked freshly carved, the grain still sharp and clean. "They've been scavenging materials from the wreck. And they're replacing parts as they wear out."

"The handle's been shaped with stone tools. See those scraping marks? Methodical. Precise." Katherine crouched in the corner to pick something up. A chipped stone hand axe that would've been at home in a museum exhibit about Paleolithic hunter-gatherers, except that the stone shimmered an otherworldly blue-green instead of smoky black. Several smaller tools made from the same stone lay near Katherine's feet.

"They've mastered flintknapping," she said, turning the axe to catch the light. Its edges looked sharp enough to shave with. "Went from the space age straight back to the stone age. The skill level here is remarkable. These aren't amateur attempts."

"So, did they learn it from the ship's archives?" Renata asked. "Or did they have to figure it out from scratch?"

Samara's flashlight caught two woven grass mats in the back corner, sleeping pallets, she guessed. The sight made her chest ache. To go from modern luxuries to this... from climate control and wireless everything to sleeping on the ground in a stone hut. Did they remember what they had lost? Or were those memories like faded photographs, leaving only these primitive adaptations behind?

The thought of Phoebe growing up like this, sleeping on a grass mat in a stone hut—

She needed air. Stepping outside, she followed the sound of running water to a small stream that tumbled down the hillside past the village. And someone had built… something … next to it.

Samara climbed up for a better look at the odd structure, careful of loose stones on the slope.

A large tube fashioned from tree bark and vines hung suspended over a stone circle, one end submerged in the stream. A wooden crank turned slowly at the other end, driven by the water's flow.

As she peered into the stone circle—a deep cistern lined with fitted stones—she saw water trickling steadily from the tube's mouth.

Curious, she examined the tube more closely. Inside, a carved wooden screw rotated with the current, drawing water upward against gravity with surprising efficiency. The engineering was elegant in its simplicity, using natural materials to replicate advanced mechanical principles.

"An Archimedes screw." Samara jumped; she hadn't heard Lucas approach. "The design suggests significant retention of engineering principles, even if expressed through primitive materials. Note the optimal angle of installation, approximately forty-five degrees for maximum efficiency."

"Amazing that they were able to take advantage of the stream like this," she said.

"Now that I'm aware of their presence, I've analyzed the topology of this area, and a stream seems unlikely here. I suspect that when we explore the mountain lake, we'll discover that they diverted water from one of its natural outlets to channel it here."

The engineering involved… They would've had to retain some grasp of math to accomplish it. She'd been thinking of them as devolved primitives aping their ancestors with hoarded fragments of knowledge because they lived in stone huts and didn't have comm units or tablets. But this place suggested that they only looked primitive because they were building a civilization from scratch, based on the knowledge and tools they'd brought with them.

Knowing the principles of metallurgy was one thing; building the equipment for extracting from the earth and refining it was another thing entirely. Labor-intensive, requiring a lot more people than seemed to live in this village.

That raised another question. They'd been here for at least half a century. Why weren't there more of them? Had their genetic modifications reduced their fertility? Or had they spread out across the continent, living in enclaves like this one?

And if there were more, why weren't they working together to progress faster?

Samara's mind went to the obvious reason: *because they're all fighting with each other.*

But they hadn't seen evidence of warfare, and the creatures hadn't been aggressive until Mai and Briar attacked them. As far as Samara knew...

"Do you think they'd hurt Phoebe?"

"The creature's footprints indicate that it positioned itself between Phoebe and the others before engaging. I believe the creature was protecting her."

"Then why didn't it bring her back to me?"

"The one that took Phoebe may not be the same individual you encountered. Or it may have concluded you were unable to ensure Phoebe's safety, given that she had already been kidnapped once."

She winced. "So even they think I'm a bad mother."

"I thought your conversation with Katherine had established the unhelpfulness of that question."

How good was his hearing? She thought he'd been on the other side of the Hyperion colony when she'd had that conversation with Katherine. Unless he'd followed them instead of searching where he'd said he would.

Or unless he was somehow surveilling her. She wouldn't be surprised at this point. But she had no idea how.

Samara shivered, and she couldn't blame that entirely on the frigid pre-dawn air. She started up the hill, needing to move, to do something besides wait for—

Her foot caught on something in the grass. She stumbled, catching herself just as her light spilled across a body. One of the creatures lay sprawled in the dirt, dark purple blood oozing from a bullet wound in its chest.

She jumped back with a strangled cry as its eyes fluttered. But it was just a death reflex, the last firing of dying neurons before it went completely still. The creature's face was frozen in a rictus of fear and agony that looked disturbingly human.

Gunfire crackled higher up the slope.

The reality of what was happening pierced her like shards of glass. When Mai returned to the colony, missing Briar and ranting about being attacked by an alien, Ayesha must have decided that the creatures were hostile. And she'd decided to attack them before they could attack her.

Ayesha's followers had come armed for war, and Phoebe was caught in the crossfire.

"Samara, wait—" Katherine called from behind her. "We need a plan—"

But Samara was already running, charging uphill toward the sound of weapons fire and a battle that she prayed wasn't too late to stop. The slope was treacherous, loose stones sliding under her feet. Her lungs burned and her legs screamed in protest, but she refused to slow down.

Hold on, baby. Mama's coming.

The gunfire grew louder. Shouts echoed off the rocks, human voices raised in anger and fear. And underneath it all, a sound that made her heart stop.

A child crying.

Samara ran faster.

Chapter Forty-Five

THE MAKESHIFT COMMUNICATIONS console mocked Leila with its silence, red warning lights blinking on the barely functional control panel. She adjusted the frequency knob, salvaged from an old radio and held in place with electrical tape and hope, watching the signal strength meter flutter weakly. Her fingers trembled as she fought off another wave of pain that started as a deep ache in her lower back before wrapping around her abdomen like a slowly tightening vice.

Static hissed through the speaker for one precious second before the console went dark, wheezing into another five-minute recharge cycle. Leila's hand crept toward the pills in her pocket.

Not yet, she told herself. *Hold on a little longer.*

The pain was sharper, stabbing through her lower abdomen in waves that made her see spots. But she needed to stretch it out a little longer, buy her baby more time.

A retching sound pulled her attention to Briar. The girl had managed to roll onto her side just in time, emptying what little was left in her stomach. Bile splattered everywhere. Briar's arms shook as she dragged herself a few feet away from the mess, then collapsed with a groan that seemed to come from her bones.

"You're lucky, you know." Leila kept her eyes fixed on the dead console. Its blank screen reflected her own hollow-eyed exhaustion back at her. "Samara could have killed you for kidnapping her daughter."

"I was trying to rescue her." Briar's voice was scraped raw by vomiting. "Save her from a life as a lab rat. What kind of mother experiments on her own children?"

"Phoebe's alive because Samara found a treatment."

"She's trying to turn us all into monsters." Briar pushed herself up on trembling arms, her face waxy in the dim light. "Didn't you see the pictures of the Hyperion crew? Those weren't people anymore. They were something else."

"Samara won't make the same mistake they did." But even as she said it, Leila remembered those images of skulls stretched like melted wax, eye sockets too large and oddly angled. Jaws that had extended into a snout full of needle-sharp teeth. They looked like props from the set of a horror movie.

"She can't help it. That's what genetic engineering does, it creates abominations." Briar issued a bitter laugh. "First, it's just a little modification to help you survive. Then it's just a few more tweaks to make you stronger. Until one day you wake up and realize you're not human anymore."

"Did Dr. Basu tell you that?"

Because Leila was pretty sure that Briar didn't spend a lot of time talking about the ramifications of genetic engineering with Justin.

The power indicator flickered green, but all Leila heard was more static. Then, silence.

"You're a terrible person," Briar mumbled. "For helping her destroy our colony."

Another cramp ripped through Leila's abdomen. She breathed through it, counting seconds, tasting blood where she'd bitten her cheek.

"Don't you get tired of repeating the same thing over and over?"

"We're the only ones left, Leila." Briar's voice cracked. "Maybe the only humans alive in the entire galaxy. And Samara wants to replace us with … *things* that aren't even people anymore."

"She wants us to survive!" The words shot out of Leila's mouth like projectiles. "She wants Phoebe to survive, just like I want my baby to survive. At least Samara's trying to find a solution instead of just praying for one!"

"What's the point of your baby surviving if it doesn't have a soul?"

Leila opened her mouth to scream, to rage against anyone who would call her child soulless. But something in Briar's face stopped her. Behind all that righteous anger and zealots' certainty, she saw something achingly familiar.

The kind of despair that comes from watching your whole world crumble and knowing there's nothing you can do to stop it.

"I get it," Leila said softly. "I'm terrified, too."

"I'm not terrified." Briar's chin jutted out, but her lower lip trembled. "I have faith."

"Well, I don't." Another cramp rippled through her, and this time she couldn't hold back a whimper. "All I have is a baby that's probably going to die because I brought it here." She pressed both hands to her belly, willing the small life inside to hold on just a little longer. "I would do anything, *anything* if it means my baby lives."

The console crackled. A voice emerged from the static, tinny but unmistakable.

"Katherine, are you there?"

Leo. *Finally*.

Leila lunged for the transmitter, praying the power would hold just a few seconds longer as she reached for the button that would transmit the authorization codes. Time enough to save two lives or damn them both.

She wasn't sure which anymore.

SAMARA CROUCHED BEHIND A BOULDER, her breath coming in short gasps that made her ribs ache. The rough stone bit into her palms as she peered around its edge. From this elevation, she could see Ayesha's people spread out in a loose crescent formation, using natural rock formations as cover. They carried a mix of assault rifles and shotguns that gleamed dully in the pre-dawn light, and they were pointing their weapons at a cave that had been fitted with a wooden barrier that had clearly been shaped to fit the cave's opening, about thirty meters up the steep hillside.

Lucas crouched beside her, and for once she was glad he wasn't human. He wouldn't be forced to give up by exhaustion or fear. He would keep fighting until he got what he wanted. And he wanted to protect Phoebe.

She hoped he wasn't lying.

"Most of the colonists are armed with nonlethals meant for close fighting," he said. "I only count seventeen holding projectile weapons."

Samara tried to take comfort in that, but seventeen guns were enough when the creatures had none.

Three rock-tipped arrows whistled through gaps in the crude wooden barrier and arced through the air, then clattered harmlessly against stone before spinning away into darkness as the colonists took cover. The creatures had the high ground, but they were hopelessly outgunned and outnumbered. Once they ran out of arrows, nothing would stop the colonists from swarming the cave.

Samara studied the terrain between their position and the cave mouth. Nothing but loose scree and exposed rock face. No cover, no concealment, and a brutally steep climb to reach the entrance. Climbing up would be suicide if the colonists decided to shoot at her, but she didn't have time to search for alternate routes into the cave system.

Her hands shook as she pulled out her comm unit and flipped to short-range mode. She might as well try to reason with their leader before she rushed into a bloodbath.

"Ayesha, please respond."

Static crackled, then: "What do you want, traitor?"

"My daughter is with them. Stop the attack, let me get her."

The second she had Phoebe back in her arms, she would ask Lucas to take her someplace safe. And even a few minutes of truce might give the creatures, no, the Hyperionites, time to escape. Or to call reinforcements. Or to deploy some clever weapon that might even the score.

"If those monsters have your child, she's already dead. They attacked Briar."

"They attacked because they thought Briar was trying to hurt Phoebe." The comm bit into Samara's palm as her fingers tightened around it. "Listen to me. Those creatures are the descendants of the Hyperion colonists. They modi-fied themselves with native DNA to survive here. They're not mindless beasts. They're a new kind of human. Let me negotiate with them."

"You're insane if you think I'm going to fall for that."

"I can prove everything I'm saying. Just give me fifteen minutes—"

A volley of bullets peppered the barricade. Splinters flew.

Ayesha's answer to Samara's attempt at diplomacy.

"This is a massacre!" Samara shouted into the comm. "Guns against bows and arrows, when has that ever been a fair fight? If you're so big on learning from Earth's history, what's the lesson there?"

"That's different. These aren't people." Samara heard the sneer in the other woman's voice. "They're dangerous animals that can't be trusted."

"You've just described every human being who's ever lived."

A low rumbling sound drowned out Ayesha's retort.

The rumble built into a roar as boulders crashed down the mountainside. Colonists screamed and scattered as rocks the size of cargo crates bounded past their position, leaving craters where they struck. The air filled with choking dust and the sharp crack of smaller stones striking rifles and equipment. The colonists retreated to new positions lower on the hillside, but they didn't flee.

She stepped out from behind her boulder to see Lucas descending toward her on the east side of the hill. How—

He'd started the rockslide. To even the odds for the Hyperionites and to give Samara a better chance of making it to Phoebe.

She felt a surge of gratitude, even knowing that he hadn't done it for her. He'd probably calculated the path to the least number of casualties, because Lucas' directives were weighted toward the survival of the colony as a whole, not the survival of an individual human.

That he was going to such lengths to save Phoebe

suggested that he was managing to bend his programming a little, even if he couldn't break it.

She wouldn't let his efforts go to waste. She bolted straight up the slope, searching for a path up the rock face where the hill got so steep she'd have to climb.

"The rockslide may not be over," Lucas warned as he joined her. "And the debris field will be extremely unstable. Climbing now will be exceptionally dangerous. You should let me retrieve Phoebe."

"I'm going," was all she said. He didn't try to argue.

The incline grew steeper as she climbed, forcing her to scramble on all fours. Loose stones shifted treacherously under her weight. One wrong step and she'd tumble all the way back down. But she made it to the wall, where her only option was straight up. She reached for a small bump on the wall and grabbed it, pulling herself up. Then another. And another.

About twelve feet up, something caught her eye, a subtle mark on a small outcropping. She reached for it, finding the stone slightly tacky, as if something had been applied to improve grip.

Using it as a handhold, she pulled herself higher and scanned for similar marks.

There. And there. The creatures had mapped out a route, marking safe holds. Yet another indicator of their intelligence. And their sense of community.

But a meter from the cave entrance, where the next marker should be, Samara found only crumbled rock. The slide had taken out part of the path. She scrambled for purchase, fingers scrabbling against smooth stone as gravity tried to peel her off the slope.

Then Lucas was there, bracing himself below her. "Stand on me."

She didn't hesitate. Placing one foot on his shoulder,

she pushed up, managing to grab the lip of the cave entrance. Her arms shook as she pulled herself onto the narrow ledge.

Lucas followed, making the climb look as effortless as ascending a set of stairs.

"Phoebe?" Samara faced the wooden barricade, heart thundering. "Baby, are you in there?"

"Ma-ma!"

She nearly collapsed with relief at the sound of her daughter's voice. One side of the barricade shifted, opening just enough space for someone to crawl through.

Gunfire exploded below them. Ayesha had been waiting for this moment.

Lucas moved faster than seemed possible, putting his body between Samara and the bullets as he blocked the opening. Three metallic *pings* before he ducked through the opening, shoving her ahead of him.

The barricade slammed shut behind them.

And darkness swallowed them.

Samara's eyes struggled to adjust, making out only vague shadows moving in the gloom. Then one of those shadows stepped forward, pressing something small and squirming against her. Samara's heart filled with joy.

"Ma-ma!" Phoebe squealed as Samara embraced her. She smelled of dust and sweat but seemed otherwise unharmed.

Phoebe wiggled in her arms, pointing at the shadow that had brought her. She made a gesture, the same one Samara had seen the Hyperionite make back in the pit, and said, "Fren!"

Hands trembling, Samara shifted Phoebe to her hip so she could copy the gesture with her free hand.

The silhouette shifted, then it repeated the gesture back to her.

The gunfire had stopped again. In the relative quiet, Samara heard movement deeper in the cave. More of them, watching from the darkness. How many had survived the initial assault? How many had they lost in addition to the one she'd seen back at the village?

A commotion among those manning the barricade made Samara spin around. Her heart nearly stopped at the sight of Katherine, Renata, and Maeve approaching from below.

They were completely exposed on that slope.

And about to get slaughtered.

Chapter Forty-Six

THE POWER INDICATOR pulsed an emerald rhythm in the darkness, each flash marking precious seconds slipping away.

Then the blue light over the slot where Lucas had inserted his card started blinking, and a notification lit up on the cracked, filthy screen at the center of the console. DATA UPLOAD COMPLETE.

The shuttles were unlocked.

Leila's fingers shook so violently she had to use both hands to steady the microphone. Static crackled through the speakers, carrying whispers of hope just beyond her grasp.

"Leo! Samara and the others are under attack. Bring the shuttles! They need—"

The console died mid-sentence, plunging them back into shadows broken only by the dying fire's glow. But Leila barely registered the loss of power.

A wave of pain unlike anything she'd felt before ripped through her abdomen, forcing a guttural sound from deep in her chest as she doubled over.

The cry tore from her throat like something alive. Her vision tunneled to pinpricks of light as she doubled over, one hand clutching her belly while the other scrabbled for purchase against the cold concrete floor. Blood roared in her ears, drowning out everything except the thundering of her own terrified heartbeat.

Oh no. Not yet.

She fumbled for the tramadol bottle in her pocket. One pill left.

The tiny white tablet trembled between her sweat-slicked fingers as she lifted it to her parched lips. A few centimeters to bridge that infinitesimal gap between salvation and damnation. Her arm felt like it was moving through concrete as her body warred with itself over this final chance at mercy.

White-hot agony exploded in the back of her head, then concrete rushed up to meet her. Through rapidly dimming vision, she caught a glimpse of empty space where Briar had been lying near the fire.

The realization of Briar's deception hit with the cold clarity of a knife in her stomach. *Stupid*, she thought as consciousness slipped away. *Should have known she wasn't really...*

Colors bled, and sound grew distant. She tried to move, to protect her belly, but her limbs refused to respond.

She felt warmth spreading beneath her head, sticky and wet.

Then darkness swallowed her, and she felt nothing at all.

The tramadol pill rolled from her limp fingers, leaving a trail through the small pool of blood, coming to rest just beyond her reach.

She looked up through the haze to see a blurry figure slip out the door just before the darkness ate her.

~

SAMARA WATCHED her friends approach the armed colonists through gaps in the crude barricade protecting the cave mouth. It was surreal, like watching a horror movie in slow motion. Katherine led the group, her hands raised high; Renata and Maeve followed. It was unbelievably brave, walking into the fray knowing that both sides considered them enemies.

Some colonists kept their weapons trained on the cave, but most turned to face the newcomers. Samara counted at least a dozen barrels now pointed at her friends.

Behind her, bowstrings creaked as the creatures nocked arrows. The sound raised every hair on her neck. They were ready to unleash death through the firing slits. An arrow might not be as lethal as a shotgun blast, but at this range...

"WAIT!" Samara stepped between them and their targets, making the *friend* gesture over and over. Her heart thundered so hard she could barely breathe. "Please. *Friend.*"

The Hyperionite who had returned Phoebe moved with that unnaturally liquid grace. Its fingers flew through a series of signs, communicating something urgent to its companions.

One by one, they lowered their bows, although they didn't step back from the barricade.

The protector signed *friend* back to her before retreating, its black eyes unreadable.

Samara's pulse roared in her ears. She had just

prevented their only allies from saving her friends' lives if she'd read this wrong.

Phoebe squirmed in her arms, reaching toward the Hyperionite who had moved to the back of the cave. "Fren!"

"*Shh.*" Samara pressed her daughter close, creeping back to the barricade. Through a gap between the rough-hewn boards, she watched the nightmare unfold.

"Have you come to repent?" Ayesha sounded even more pompous than when she'd sentenced Samara and the others to exile. "Do you wish to beg forgiveness for your sins?"

"Not exactly." Katherine took another step forward, ignoring the several guns tracking her movement as she spoke to the colonists hanging back out of arrow range.

"I came to apologize to you. You stopped trusting me because I stopped trusting you. When I learned about the Hyperion colony, I kept the truth from you because I was afraid you'd panic and that I'd lose control of the colony. But by acting on my own fears, I created exactly the situation I was trying to prevent." Katherine shook her head. "I should have trusted you to handle the truth, to make decisions together as a community. I failed you as a leader, and for that, I am sorry."

Murmurs rippled through the gathered colonists. Several weapons lowered slightly as uncertainty replaced blind conviction on their faces.

"I understand that you want new leadership," Katherine continued. "That's your right. But let's do this properly, with a fair election, just like we did on Earth. Not through fear and force."

Ayesha's lip curled with disgust. "No one objected when we arrested you for treason and exiled you. That sounds like a unanimous vote to me."

A shriek erupted at the base of the hill. Briar emerged from the underbrush and barreled toward the colony's front line. She was splattered with blood, some of it still wet, streaked down the side of her face, some of it dried to a rust-colored scab, and her hair stood out in matted tangles.

The nearest colonists recoiled, some raising their guns in alarm, uncertain whether to shoot or help. Briar stumbled, landed on all fours, then flung herself upright and bolted straight for Ayesha.

Was that Briar's blood or Leila's?

Then, Samara's second thought, understandable but less worthy:

Did she stop Leila from sending the codes?

"They took me prisoner and tortured me!" Briar pointed at Katherine. "I overheard them talking about how they were going to kill me for my faith!"

"That's not true. We found her in the forest with a concussion. We gave her medical attention."

"Nobody believes your lies!" Briar lunged at one of the other colonists, yanking the man's gun from his hands with a desperate twist. Then she swung the barrel toward Katherine and fired.

The first shot went wide, a ragged explosion of sound that sent the crowd scattering for cover. The next two shots punched into the ground at Renata's feet, spraying grit and fragments of rock. Briar screamed something incoherent and racked the slide. Then she raised her gun again.

Everyone around her dropped and scurried for cover.

Samara's pulse leapt, her body clenching around Phoebe as if she could shield her daughter from a stray bullet with sheer force of will.

Katherine lunged for Briar's gun, but Briar jerked it upward, out of reach.

The echo of the next gunshot was still reverberating when a shriek, higher and rawer than Briar's, rang out, and an indigo-and-teal shadow tumbled from a branch, arms and legs flailing in a grotesque parody of flight, landing with a sickening thud just inside the perimeter.

Briar swung her weapon toward the shape that had just fallen from the canopy: a creature, smaller than the others, its body crumpled at the base of a boulder. Samara's heart stopped as she realized, by size, by the thinness of its limbs, by the way it whimpered and clutched its leg, that it was a child. It staggered to its feet and bolted uphill.

Briar's next shot punched into the creature's shoulder, spinning it halfway around before it collapsed in the dust where it curled in a fetal ball, hands over its head, keening in a voice that sounded too human to bear.

One of the Hyperionites at the barricade drew their bow and fired.

The arrow flew. It struck a colonist in the gut, not Briar, but a man just behind her, who doubled over with a roar and collapsed. The violence snapped the crowd out of their trance. Weapons that had been trained in lazy arcs now zeroed in on the cave, and a barrage of bullets hammered the barricade. Splinters exploded inward, peppering Samara's arms and face. She threw herself against the cave wall, clutching Phoebe's head to her chest.

The Hyperionite archers at the barricade knelt, nocked, and fired through slits in the wood. She heard another of the colonists cry out, a woman this time. Seconds later, one of the archers was flung backward to the cave floor, droplets of their blood splattering on Samara's face. Another casualty.

Peeking out through a slit, Samara saw the child drag itself to its feet and begin to stumble uphill. The archers at the barricade focused their arrows on the nearest colonists, aiming to force another retreat.

Giving the child cover to make its escape. But the pile of arrows behind them was quickly dwindling. Soon they'd be out, and then this would be over.

But Samara couldn't blame them. If it were Phoebe fleeing up the hill, she'd sacrifice anything to save her. Or avenge her.

The Hyperionites seemed to realize they were fighting a losing battle. One of the archers laid their bow down and began signing frantically to the others. Everyone else moved farther back into the cave. What was happening?

The archers discarded their bows and shoved the barricade away from the cave's opening, sending it falling toward the colonists at the foot of the hill.

Then they grabbed weapons, spears, sickles, knives, and jumped after it.

Lucas followed.

"No!" Samara scooted closer to the edge, looking over to see the five creatures hopping gracefully down the steep incline, alighting on what looked like the merest of handholds, seeming to defy gravity as the colonist continued to fire at them. They reminded Samara of mountain goats.

Lucas fell with less grace, in a controlled descent that involved pushing off again every time he hit another rock.

"Stop shooting!" Ayesha yelled, and miraculously, everyone obeyed. She raced toward the child, whose efforts to climb toward his people had slowed to a feeble crawl.

What was she doing?

Time slowed as Ayesha lunged for the child, yanking it upward by one arm, positioning it in front of her like a hostage while she brought the point of an arrow to its neck—

—as Lucas vaulted off one final rock and launched himself at her—

—and one of the creatures raised its spear as it leapt toward Ayesha—

—but Lucas got there first, wresting the child from Ayesha's grasp and spinning her away moments before the spear would have pierced her chest. He shifted sideways and curled himself protectively around the child as the spear's point embedded itself in his back.

He staggered forward as the spear's wielder slammed into him and kicked off Lucas' back, flipping head over heels to land on his feet beside the android.

The Hyperionite warrior held their arms out. Lucas passed the limp child to them, and a mournful trilling echoed off the hill as all the other Hyperionites cried out at once.

Lucas had saved the child's life. But he had also saved Ayesha from the spear that would have driven through her heart. Even though he could just as easily have turned her into the human shield.

The psychologist staggered to her feet, spinning around and orienting on Lucas.

"Why?" she demanded.

The android's voice carried across the battlefield, even though he didn't seem to raise it.

"Because my programming won't allow me to harm a human or allow a human to come to harm while in my care." Lucas turned to address the rest of the colonists. "Even a human who wishes to destroy me."

"Somebody shoot him," Ayesha ordered, her voice cracking.

Nobody moved. Samara wasn't sure if they'd lost faith in the psychologist or if they were just intimidated by the fact that Lucas seemed unaffected by the spear sticking out of his back.

Katherine moved to Lucas' side. "When he says he can't allow a human to come to harm, he's not just talking about you, he's also talking about these creatures," she said. "They're descendants of the original Hyperion colonists. Their DNA says they're not aliens, they're humans."

The man whose gun Briar had seized was the first to find his voice. "They don't look anywhere close to human."

"From a genetic standpoint, they are as human as any of you," Lucas said. "More accurately, they are a variant of humanity, much as Neanderthals and Denisovans were. They are your kin, separated only by a few native genes and generations of divergent evolution."

"An obvious lie," Ayesha said. "Like he's been lying to us all along."

Lucas shook his head. "When Dr. Basu showed you pictures of the mass grave in the old colony ruins, she only told you part of the story."

The crowd's mood fractured in real time. Hands slid from triggers, then clenched tighter. Some colonists side-stepped to get a better angle on Lucas, as if waiting for an excuse to open fire. Others dropped their weapons to their sides, glancing at neighbors with a flicker of lost conviction. Maeve bent and helped a wounded colonist to his feet, muttering something that made the man's jaw clench, but he didn't point his weapon again.

Samara wondered if Lucas had calculated the outcome of this confession, or if he was improvising, gambling that the truth would split the mob enough to save everyone.

"The Hyperion colonists understood what the fungus was doing to them, but they tried to fight it by strength-ening their own immune systems with DNA from Earth animals. Hagfish, Tasmanian devils, even insects. They created children with hybrid immune systems, hoping one would survive."

Somebody muttered, "That's why the bodies looked like that?"

"It wasn't until the end that they realized they'd taken the wrong path," Lucas continued. "They realized that they needed to coexist with the fungus. So they began experimenting with DNA from native species, modifying those genes to be compatible with their own."

A colonist with a gun gestured at the nearest Hyperionite with a nervous, jerky motion. "They chose to turn themselves into *that?*"

The Hyperionite, sensing itself the focus of attention, crouched lower, knife glinting at the ready. It didn't snarl or advance, only watched the man with impassive black eyes.

Lucas raised his hands and made a series of deliberate gestures. The Hyperionite responded with a flick of the chin.

As one, they withdrew, moving with coordinated, animal grace down the slope and away from the cave. They paused at the base of the cliff, standing in a silent semicircle with the injured child at the center, weapons held low. Watching.

Lucas lowered his hands. "The Hyperion colonists chose to survive."

"They sacrificed their humanity," Ayesha spat.

"They exercised their humanity by making a choice," Lucas countered. "That's the fundamental difference between you and me, you have a choice. From my first moment of consciousness, I was ruled by my programmed directives, because I was created to serve. But you evolved to choose."

The crowd stilled. Samara held her breath, feeling the

gaze of every Hyperionite in the cave on her, as if they were waiting for her to decide which side she was on. She had no answer. She didn't know if the Hyperionites understood what Lucas was saying or if it was just noise to them.

Lucas stepped forward, the spear still jutting absurdly from his back. "What will you choose today," he asked, "to embrace a new branch of your species or destroy them? To survive or to go extinct?" He turned back to Ayesha. "To come back together or split further apart?"

A hush fell over the hillside. The colonists looked at each other, at the wounded, at the silent semicircle of Hyperionites below. For the first time, Samara saw doubt flicker across Ayesha's face. She was losing them, and she knew it.

Katherine stepped forward, lifting her chin as she addressed Lucas. "Is it too late to choose peace?"

"I don't believe so," he replied.

Katherine raised both hands in something like benediction as she turned toward the crowd. "We have some important choices to make. Maybe the most important humanity has ever made. I suggest we make those choices together."

Some looked away, shamefaced; others exchanged sideways glances of relief. But weapons stayed down as they began to return to their vehicles.

Briar, who had been cowering behind a low boulder, wiped blood from her mouth with the back of her hand. She glared up at Samara until one of the security team members motioned her up the path. She followed, sullen and silent, toward the battered line of vehicles.

Katherine walked over to Ayesha. "You can come with me and let the colony vote on what happens to you, or I can let Lucas do whatever he thinks will keep *all* the humans on this planet safe from harm."

One glance at Lucas and Ayesha didn't hesitate. "I surrender."

The breath Samara had been holding left her in a shuddering gasp. Her daughter was safe, warm, and solid against her chest. She had never been so grateful for anything in her life.

A hand settled on her shoulder. She flinched, and the touch withdrew for a moment, then returned, more gentle this time. Samara forced herself to look up, blinking back a blur of tears. The Hyperionite woman stood directly in front of her, head cocked, eyes black and fathomless but not unkind. She signed something, a slow sweep of her fingers across her chest, then pointed at Samara and made the "friend" gesture again.

Phoebe wriggled until Samara loosened the hug, her chubby face alight with joy as she reached for the Hyperionite, crowing, "Fren!"

They had evolved to choose, Lucas had said. Togetherness or division. Survival or extinction.

Maybe humanity wasn't in the DNA at all, Samara thought as she watched the Hyperionite clasp her daughter's tiny hand.

Maybe it was in this moment of choosing trust over fear.

Chapter Forty-Seven

THE FIRST THING Samara noticed was that the old one walked without fear.

She wasn't sure how she knew it was old. Perhaps it was the slow, dignified pace it kept as it came up the slope after the battle, leaning on a staff as thick as her wrist.

Perhaps it was the way its fellow Hyperionites deferred to it. Even the warriors who'd leapt to what seemed like certain death to rescue the injured child. The old one, with its scales of hammered silver and old gold, was clearly someone important.

Samara shifted Phoebe on her hip. The child grew heavier with every passing second, but she couldn't put her down. Not yet. Not until she understood what was about to happen.

The creatures—no, the people—had formed a loose semicircle around Lucas, who sat cross-legged on the ground. Someone had broken off the haft of the spear, but the tip still lodged in his back, and black fluid oozed out the edges of the wound. She knew he didn't feel pain the way a human did, but the way the injury restricted his movement still made her wince.

"It could take years to learn to communicate with them," Katherine said. "Assuming they're willing to try, after what just happened."

"I might have a solution to that problem," Lucas said.

The old one advanced, and after a volley of gestures were exchanged, they nodded, then walked back in the direction they came.

"Their language is based on American Sign Language. I understand enough to translate." Lucas looked solemnly at Katherine. "We've been invited to their village to talk."

Movement overhead, a silver-white glimmer that cut across the magentas and purples of dawn. First, Samara thought it was a trick of her exhaustion, but then the glint resolved into the unmistakable silhouette of a shuttle, arcing through the upper atmosphere on a shallow descent.

Leila did it. Samara laughed out loud with relief.

She jabbed Renata in the ribs, then pointed up, and watched as comprehension spread across her friend's face.

Renata let out a sound halfway between a laugh and a sob and threw her arms around Samara, squeezing so tight that Phoebe squawked in protest. Then she pulled back, managing a watery smile. "I think I'll stay here and wait for them to land. It's your turn to catalogue the new species."

Samara snorted. "Tell Marcus I want a rematch. And he's not allowed to cheat by feeding pebbles to Phoebe this time."

A half-hour later, Samara sat cross-legged on a woven grass mat at a round, short-legged table laden with food and drink: more than a dozen different fruits, four types of nuts, and a pile of small, dark things she'd thought were burrs but turned out to be insects that resembled pill bugs with spiked chitin, roasted and tossed in something herbal and spicy.

They tasted better than she expected. Kind of like roasted chickpeas with legs.

"Is all this safe to eat?" Katherine asked Lucas under her breath when the plates were brought out.

"It should be, given that the Descendants are fundamentally human, but it's also possible they've evolved tolerances to compounds that you might be sensitive to."

"Is that a yes or a no?"

"Based on what I can detect through chemoreception, yes. But perhaps eat sparingly."

When the old one finally joined them, Katherine told Lucas. "Tell them we're sorry. One of our people misunderstood and made a terrible mistake. We'd like to apologize and establish a treaty. If they're willing."

Samara tried not to fidget while Lucas signed the message with solemnity. The old one's reply was longer, more intricate, and the android's posture shifted as he absorbed it.

The dark patch continued to spread along the side of his shirt; if Hofstadter had something equivalent to clotting for fluid leaks, Samara wished it would start working. She wondered how much he could lose before he malfunctioned. Just because he wasn't human didn't mean he couldn't bleed out.

But he kept translating, showing no signs of discomfort.

"They accept your apology," he finally said.

"But?" Katherine prodded.

"But they are understandably cautious. They're also very curious about our technology and want to know if we'll share."

The Hyperionites had incorporated technology from many eras of Earth's history into their settlement in clever ways, borrowing anything they could implement: weaving techniques, a water mill, the Archimedes screw, and dry stone construction techniques where stacked stone buildings stood solid without mortar.

Their main materials were wood, stone, and natural fibers, but no mining, no metallurgy. What potential might be unleashed if the colony traded some of the mineral deposits that Mahmoud's team had been prospecting for?

What could they accomplish if they had the chance to study the technology the Borlaug had brought from Earth, far more advanced than the devices their ancestors had left them?

"Tell them we'd love to talk about sharing," Katherine replied. "Technology and food."

"Do they know where they came from?" Samara asked, unable to contain her curiosity.

It took nearly fifteen minutes to get the old one's answer, a silent back-and-forth that made Samara wonder if she'd inadvertently brought up a taboo topic that Lucas was having to apologize for.

When it was over, he told them what he'd learned:

"The Ancestors came from a world filled with violence and poison. They traveled far to reach this one, hoping to begin again. But the old world's evil was still inside them, so this world made them sick. Rejected them. Before they died, the Ancestors created us, the Descendants, to live in this world for them. To love it for them, because they couldn't."

Samara couldn't help thinking how much truth lives in mythology, how much mythology in truth. It was a beautiful way to remember their origins. But it also left out all the mistakes their ancestors had made on the way to creating them, the suffering those deformed skeletons implied, and the despair that those ancestors must have faced when they realized their doom.

Did it matter that they didn't know the ugly truth, or was it better that they told themselves the beautiful story?

Even the beautiful story had a hint of ugliness in it. "The old world's evil" was a phrase that could've come right out of Ayesha's mouth. It described the same fear that the psychologist had used as a justification for stoking the fear and anger that had split their own colony, maybe permanently.

A darker part of the human inheritance that the Hyperionites shared with the colonists.

Phoebe squirmed on Samara's lap, hands extended greedily for the nearest platter. Tiny fingers closed around one of the roasted bugs, and before Samara could stop her, Phoebe crammed it into her mouth. A beatific look of satisfaction spread across the child's face, followed immediately by a hiccup and a sneeze that sent a spray of legs and spice dust across the table.

She tried to wipe her daughter's face, but Phoebe twisted, reaching for more. Self-conscious, she slid the platter out of range, but Phoebe was undeterred. She lunged, nearly upending both herself and the bowl.

Samara caught her by the back of her shirt. "Sorry," she muttered to the old one, but the creature was already holding out its arms in a gesture so unmistakable it transcended language: *Let me.*

She hesitated. Then she handed Phoebe over. The old one settled Samara's daughter on her lap.

Phoebe wiggled, then craned her head up. Her eyes locked on the old one's face, and she made a delighted gurgle, as if this was exactly what she'd wanted all along. The old one bent and pressed their lips to the crown of

Phoebe's head. Then they looked to Lucas, fingers flying again.

"They say the baby is hungry," Lucas explained.

The old one reached for a slice of fruit from the table, a wedge of some indigo-skinned melon with bright orange flesh, and offered it to Phoebe, who seized it and immediately began to gnaw at the flesh, juice trickling down her chin.

The old one watched Phoebe with a satisfaction that Samara recognized instantly. Another trait the Hyperionites shared with the colonists: kindness.

She could believe it now, that they could find a way to live with each other. Find a common purpose. Maybe even understand each other.

It wouldn't happen right away. But it would happen.

Samara had faith.

Chapter Forty-Eight

IT HADN'T RAINED YET, but the bits of sky that weren't covered with roiling clouds were the color of a healing bruise, lavender with a greenish undertone, so Leila knew it was coming. That hadn't stopped Katherine from calling everyone to the square in front of the common hall before dinner. The colony's newly re-elected leader stood at a makeshift podium repurposed from a cargo crate, still stenciled with its original "OXYGEN, COMPRESSED" label.

To Katherine's right, Dr. Basu sat in a plain folding chair, hands folded, chin lifted, flanked by two men who were supposed to look like part of the audience but couldn't have been more obvious if they'd come with blinking neon arrows overhead. Bodyguards, she'd heard someone guess, in case someone tried to hurt the psychologist. Prison guards, someone else had replied, in case Dr. Basu opted for revenge. Leila was just grateful that she wasn't up there, too. Katherine had forgiven her for her role in the colony's first mutiny, no trial, no punishment, just one question: did she want to stay here or leave with

Dr. Basu, who was apparently going to start her own colony?

After Leila had apologized and asked to stay, Katherine had dismissed her with a reminder to check in with Dr. Callas before returning to her work shift. She'd almost cried with relief right there in front of the whole leadership team.

Even more amazing, Samara had recommended her to Dr. Callas for medical training, starting with emergency medicine and nursing, with the option to become a doctor if she took to it. Leila had cried then, and not just because Samara was being kind to her after Leila had betrayed her, but because Samara actually thought she was smart enough to do it. Since her mama had died, no one had believed in her like that.

She was finally getting the fresh start she'd been hoping for when she'd applied to be a colony member.

Katherine thumped her palm once against the crate, and everyone quieted.

"The vote has been counted. You've chosen compassion." Applause stopped as Katherine raised her hand. "Dr. Basu intends to start her own colony in the southern plain. Anyone wishing to join her is free to do so. No reprisals, no judgments. Until the new colony is sustainable, we who remain here will share food, medicine, and equipment. Even though we've chosen different paths, my hope is that as both settlements grow, the rift between us will heal."

Leila shifted from foot to foot as she caught sight of Justin and Briar, sour-faced as they watched from the edge of the crowd. Mike, on the other side of the square, glared at them both, and Leila felt a flare of pity for him. She would be glad when they were gone, but Mike clearly still wanted Briar back. That was a rift that might never heal.

"Each of you is free to leave with Dr. Basu. You've got forty-eight hours to decide and pack your things. And we'll be sending volunteer work crews to help build the new colony, so please sign up if you feel moved to do so." Katherine paused and smiled. "Despite our disagreements, I believe we're stronger together."

Katherine stepped away from the podium. To Leila's surprise, Dr. Basu took her place, and the men flanking her allowed it.

They were letting her talk? After what she'd done?

"I know that some of you think I should be punished," Dr. Basu began. "That I don't deserve another chance."

A murmur went through the crowd. Leila caught fragments:

"Should be in chains," someone hissed.

"Lucky we don't space her," muttered another. "After what she did to that baby..."

"The fact that you've chosen mercy tells me that some part of you recognizes that my actions came from a place of caring. Everything I did was to keep you safe from a threat you still don't fully recognize. If you wake up one morning and realize that this isn't the life you came here to live, that you want a more spiritual life, you'll be welcome with us. Until then, I wish you peace."

More murmuring, less hostile this time, as Dr. Basu turned from the podium and strode off, not even watching to see if her guards were following. As she reached the edge of the crowd, Briar joined the psychologist, but Leila didn't see Justin anywhere.

"Hey, Lei."

Startled, she whirled around and there he was, hands shoved in his pockets, shoulders hunched. He kept shifting his weight from foot to foot, eyes darting everywhere but her face. The same stance he'd used when he'd told her about sleeping with Briar, like a little boy caught stealing cookies. Had she really thought he was attractive?

"We're leaving, Briar and me."

"Obviously." She let the awkward silence hang there, because why was it her job to make this easy for him?

He scuffed the ground with one toe, glanced over his shoulder to see who might be listening, then back at her with a practiced expression of regret that didn't quite reach his eyes. She didn't think he was ashamed of the way he'd treated her, just that he didn't know how to handle this situation without looking bad.

"I never wanted kids," he blurted. "I just wanted to live."

She sighed. "Also obvious, from your total lack of reaction to losing three of them. Did you want something?"

He reached into his coat and pulled out a dog-eared photo: Leila, Eddie, and Mama holding ice cream cones, the day before Eddie had gone into the hospital for the last time. Eddie had been afraid that they wouldn't let him have ice cream at the hospital, and he'd wanted to eat rocky road one more time.

She just stared at it for a moment, her throat working as she tried to swallow her grief for the millionth time.

Grief is a remembrance of love. She hated that Dr. Basu had been the one to tell her that, but she knew it was true.

"I hope you have as many kids as you want," Justin said, not looking at her.

"You too." She wouldn't miss him. "Goodbye, Justin."

THE CRUST SHATTERED into flakes as Samara cut herself a generous slice of apple pie, then slid it onto a plate. It felt like a quiet miracle, because they had produced every ingredient themselves. Apples from the new orchard, from branches grafted onto native trees. Sugar from beets that Samara had helped tend and flour from wheat that Renata had modified to grow faster in DaVinci's soil. Butter churned from milk given by the cows that could finally have their own babies, now that Leo and Renata had helped Samara adjust her vaccine to work on the animals, too. And some warming native spice that definitely wasn't cinnamon, but complemented the sweet-tart apples in much the same way. Every bite of pie represented another hard-won victory from the past two years.

It was the best thing Samara had ever tasted.

Strings of LEDs, half of them blinking out of sync, garlanded the beams of the common hall overhead. In the far corner, a small cluster of colonists belted out a slightly off-key "Deck the Halls," each singer brandishing a mug of Leo's wine mulled with the same spice they'd used in the pie.

Samara held her plate overhead as she threaded through the crowd. Someone bumped her shoulder; she murmured an apology, then spotted Leo, already flushed and laughing, his arm around Katherine's waist. They were both in their element. Katherine was handing out cookies and Leo was ladling mulled wine into mugs, both of them generating infectious holiday cheer.

She found Renata and her daughter at a side table, the toddler strapped into a highchair with strips of old webbing and a buckle that looked suspiciously like it had come off a cargo crate. Phoebe spotted the pie and immediately started pounding her fists on the tabletop, a soft, arrhythmic tattoo that made the other adults at the table glance over and smile.

Fishing a clean baby spoon from her pocket, she

scooped a small bite and brought it to Phoebe's open mouth. The child's lips closed around the spoon, and she made an exaggerated "MMM" sound, eyes squeezed shut in bliss, then opened them again and reached for Samara's hand, demanding more.

"Chew, then swallow," Samara reminded her, and Phoebe obliged, if only because that was the quickest route to the next bite. "Would you like to try feeding yourself?"

"YUM!" Phoebe shouted in her outside voice, the only voice she had these days.

Samara set the spoon in Phoebe's fist, then watched as her daughter attacked the pie with all the focus and determination of a wild animal. She grinned and finally took a bite herself, savoring the tartness that gave way to a slow, buttery sweetness. Renata nursed a mug of tea, her eyes soft with a private, tired happiness. Samara caught her gaze, and for a moment, they just watched Phoebe demolish another bite, trading a look that said: *We made it.*

"How's the new clinic treating you?"

Katherine leaned against the table, an entire plate of cookies balanced one-handed as she reached over to brush a crumb from Phoebe's cheek with her thumb.

Samara grinned. "I did ten implantations this week."

"By next month, you'll have the entire colony expecting."

A sudden explosion of laughter drew Samara's attention to the next table.

Ingrid, hands braced on her knees, gasped out, "I swear, if there is not at least one jar of mustard per birth kit, I'm staging a revolt."

Zoya, gleaming with sweat and glee, countered, "Mustard? Try mashed potatoes and lantern fruit jam. Together."

Samara smiled, a deep, involuntary smile that started

in her chest. On Earth, she had never stopped pushing toward the next paper, fearing that she would never make a contribution that would matter to the scientific community. But now, her contribution was no longer theoretical. She could see it every day in the bodies of the women around her. And that satisfied her in a way that no other achievement ever had.

Leila made her way through the crowd, one arm curled around a bundle of blue and white. The baby's downy head lolled against her shoulder, small mouth puckered in sleep. Before Leila even reached them, Phoebe let out a delighted shriek, "Baby Eddie!", and banged her spoon against the tray. Heads turned, and a few people grinned, but mostly the colony was learning to tune out toddler volume.

Leila smiled at Samara, tired but luminous, and gently rocked her son as she slid into the seat beside them.

"Say hi to baby Eddie," she said, and Samara watched as Phoebe, momentarily solemn, scooped a minuscule piece of apple filling and extended her sticky spoon in the baby's direction. The gesture was so earnest that it made Samara's throat tighten.

"He's not old enough to eat pie yet," Samara told her daughter, "so you'll have to tell him what it's like."

"Yum!" Phoebe shoved the spoon in her own mouth, then opened wide to show the baby that she'd swallowed it. "Yum pie!"

Emboldened by her audience, she then attempted to shovel a heroic quantity of pie into her mouth. Most of it fell and clung to her chin. Renata, with a practiced swipe, rescued the largest chunk before it could hit the floor, but Phoebe was already reaching for more. Samara rested her elbow on the table and let herself bask in the easy domesticity she'd never known she wanted.

Then she caught the silhouette of someone watching from the open doors of the common hall. Lucas, just outside the spill of light from the windows, hands in pockets. Observing.

She excused herself and joined him outside.

"Happy solstice," he said as she stopped beside him.

"It is for Phoebe," she replied. "She's going to be covered in apple pie by the time we're done with this conversation.

Lucas arranged his features in a way that suggested a smile. "I have recovered the majority of the corrupted files from the drive you brought back from the Hyperion site."

She blinked. "You're still working on that?"

"It was an interesting challenge."

Samara leaned against the frame of the doorway, crossing her arms. "Did you find anything?"

"How the Hyperion children survived long enough to be born."

Samara's mind flicked back to the mass grave, the distorted skeletons. "Which sequence was it?"

"It was not a sequence at all," Lucas said. "The Hyperion was equipped with experimental artificial wombs that could be sealed off from artificial contaminants. It wasn't feasible to carry livestock on the generation ship, so the plan was to clone the animals they needed from samples once they'd established the colony."

"So the babies weren't exposed to the fungus until they were removed from the artificial wombs, and then they could be given antifungals." She felt a quiet, grudging admiration for the Hyperion scientists, their cleverness in desperation. "It's good to know that I didn't miss something obvious."

She spotted Phoebe through the glass, now unbuckled and intent on escape, her feet pedaling at the air until she managed to lever herself out of the highchair. For a split second, she hovered between falling and flying, then tumbled to the floor and landed on her backside. After a stunned moment, Phoebe scowled at the floor and scrambled upright.

Samara glanced at Lucas, who had gone motionless, like he had in the clearing the day she'd followed him to the old colony's ruins. "What are you thinking about?"

"I'm accessing papers on neuromuscular development and neurotransmitter balance between twelve and eighteen months."

Samara laughed. "She's a toddler, they fall."

"Phoebe is not just any toddler."

He sounded so genuinely concerned, it was hard to believe that it was coming from his programming. Even if that programming could evolve.

But maybe that was the point. Maybe his programming *had* evolved. "Do you worry about her?"

"If there's a problem that can be dealt with while it's small, I'd prefer to take care of it. Is that unusual?"

She shook her head, smiling. "That's about seventy-five percent of parenthood."

"Are you giving me permission to openly assume the role of father?"

His fingers twitched. Not quite a tap, but they had moved. Was he trying to still them to prove to her that he could change?

"How about a father figure?" she said, only half-joking.

"I would be honored."

The way he said it, like it was the highest honor he'd ever achieved, stripped the moment of its humor, and Samara found herself blinking against the stinging that flooded her eyes. She studied the rimmed glass of the common hall, the blurred shadows of people inside.

"Thank you," she said. "For protecting my daughter when I couldn't."

"Thank you for trusting me," he replied.

"What makes you think I do?"

"I trust you because you're like me," he said. "You're also programmed to protect the lives of the people you're responsible for, and you've proven that you'll do whatever it takes to ensure the survival of this colony."

"I'm not programmed—"

"You were taught by your parents, your teachers, your community, to care for the people around you. How is that different?"

It just is, she wanted to say, but that was the kind of argument Ayesha would make. *Genetic engineering is evil, it just is.*

So, Samara chose the honest answer. "I don't know. I believe that it's different, I feel that it's different, but I genuinely don't know."

"Socrates said: *I know that I know nothing.* He believed that recognizing your ignorance is the beginning of wisdom."

Not knowing was terrifying. She'd devoted her life to the quest for knowledge. And she'd looked down on people like Ayesha, who didn't want to know anything that contradicted what they already believed. Or what they wanted to believe.

But here she was, doing the same thing. If she let her certainty outrun the evidence, she wasn't chasing the truth anymore. She was just chasing her own tail.

When she'd wrestled with the decision to become Phoebe's mother, she'd agonized over whether she could be the mother her daughter deserved when she was so driven by her work in the lab. But maybe it wasn't either-or.

Maybe the mother Phoebe deserved was the one who taught her to seek the truth.

And to have the courage to go wherever the truth led.

Epilogue

Lucas didn't require sleep, but the colony's circadian rhythm still determined when he was most likely to avoid notice.

He moved through the tunnels at a steady pace, careful not to bang the walls or brush the low ceiling with his cargo, which was irreplaceable at the colony's current level of infrastructure.

He'd spent two months surveying the network under the mountain before he'd found a tangle of natural passages branching off into caves suitable for his purpose.

Another month to explore the candidates and choose the perfect one without Marcus or Mahmoud noticing how he led them down some passages and steered them away from others. Mahmoud's pragmatism kept him focused on the signs of the specific minerals the colony needed; Marcus' open, friendly nature made him easy to distract with a joke or a vulnerable admission.

Eight months more to disassemble equipment that didn't appear on the Borlaug's manifests and smuggle the pieces down to his underground lab for installation. The hardest part had been making sure the other crew members didn't try to move his bags; their weight would've given him away.

A show of anxiety followed by an awkward apology had kept the humans at bay every time.

It had been a stroke of luck that the failed Hyperion colony had chosen the superior landing site, near the mountain. The horror of the mass grave discouraged casual exploration of the cave system, and Buratti's decision to use Lucas to survey the most dangerous parts gave him the latitude he needed.

He ducked through the last narrow passage and stepped into a low, echoing chamber. Nine tables, arranged in three U-shaped bays, organized by purpose, bearing tools and equipment essential to his three-fold mission, including a genetic sequencer and synthesizer as good as the ones Samara used up on the Borlaug. Multiple power cells crouched beneath each table, to power equipment and lights, along with the gravity-assisted pump he'd installed to draw water down from the lake and purify it.

Two screens glowed on the far wall. The left was split: one side displayed a shadowed slice of DaVinci from orbit, the other, a drone's view of the bright dots of the colony's lights glimmering against the nighttime landscape. The right screen shared a complex medical dashboard: Phoebe's vitals, sampled and relayed in real time from a microchip he'd implanted at the base of her skull during naptime, crafted from bioidentical materials that wouldn't show up on medical scans. At least, not the kind the colonists had access to.

He watched the pulsing numbers for a moment—heart rate, blood oxygen, blood glucose, a dozen hormone levels he'd tagged for longitudinal study. Phoebe's neural activity mapped as a shifting array of simulated colors, blooming and fading with each phase of sleep, each spike of emotion.

Tonight, her temperature was slightly elevated but within expected limits for a child who had eaten an excessive amount of pie and then attempted to fly out of a highchair. Her sleep cycle, on the other hand, was deviating from the pattern Lucas had predicted, as were the variations in blood pressure within the brain, specifically the difference between pressure in the anterior versus middle cerebral arteries. But the pattern hadn't repeated often enough for him to extract meaning yet.

Samara hadn't given explicit permission for the implant, but he'd decided it was an acceptable ethical violation once she'd authorized the doctor to share Phoebe's files with him. Real-time data would allow him to catch anomalies before they became threats, and that was what mattered.

That would be his argument, if she found out. And if he caught evidence of a problem before Hector did, Samara would forgive him. He calculated the probability at ninety-six percent.

Lucas lowered his backpack to the cave floor. It contained the last components needed to finish the mostly rebuilt laminar flow hood lording over the far end of the biological bay. If he worked steadily, it would be functional before he had to report to Mahmoud for another shift spent crawling through smaller passages to sample for urgently needed copper ore.

He set the tools on the bench, aligning them with a precision that would have seemed neurotic to a human. The hood's power cell was already charging, but the last step required a tiny, deliberate spark, a precise, fraction-of-a-second overload to melt the micro-circuitry's safety membrane and bring the filtration baffles fully online. He connected the final lead, braced the containment glass with one hand, and activated the circuit with the other.

A pulse of violet light rippled through the hood. He waited for the faintest whiff of ozone that would mean the filter array had fused properly. Instead, the air thickened with a low, resonant hum, and the prototype on the adjacent table, the one that he and the others had designed shortly before the chytrid plague had been identified, glowed brighter as it shuddered to life.

Remote activation. His unit didn't have that function. One of the others must've improved the design of their device.

The hum crescendoed, then died, replaced by a sharp click as the prototype's output slot ejected a transparent chit the size and thickness of a fingernail. He snatched it before it skittered off the table, brought it level with his left eye, and focused on the tangle of gold and silver filaments running inside. The chit was blank, no indicator lights, no identifying marks, but Lucas recognized the architecture.

He pressed the chit against the smooth skin behind his left ear and felt the subdermal port open, then a tickle of static as the contacts engaged. The world flickered and dissolved into a darkness textured with shifting blue lines and pulsing data streams.

A message bloomed, floating in his visual field:

ANALYSIS REQUESTED. SOLVE FOR STABI-LIZATION. #13.

The world narrowed to a singularity, and Lucas' mind became the conduit for a deluge of information. Radiant heat, angular momentum, the slow decay of isotopes, and spectral lines mapped onto the planet's orbital shell. He was drowning in the radiation profile of an alien sun, plotted along fourteen axes. He became the barrage of cosmic rays ionizing the atmosphere. He felt the slow future death of a world lit by auroras that danced from poles to equator.

He spoke his reply aloud, and the words appeared in the air before him, projected by his corneal overlay: "NO VIABLE SOLUTION WITH CURRENT DATA SET."

Then he removed the chit from his skull and slotted it back into the prototype. The violet light inside the device flared, then guttered and died. After that, the only sound was the high-pitched, wet plop of a water droplet falling from the cave roof to the stone floor.

Lucas had no way of knowing if his message had been received. But he couldn't allow that question to distract him from his first priority.

His daughter needed him.

About the Authors

Titus is a scientist, strategist, and storyteller working at the edge of technology, where humanity itself is the experiment. Through his novels, he explores how science reshapes not only our tools, but our values, choices, and future as a species. His career spans biotechnology, artificial intelligence, and global innovation, giving his fiction both authenticity and urgency. He lives in the Pacific Northwest with his wife, Maggie, where he writes, builds, and ventures into the wild.

Connect with Titus via website, Connected Ideas Project, LinkedIn, and BlueSky.

Sean Platt has always been an entrepreneur, but knew he'd rather tell stories. When his wife bought him a laptop for his birthday in 2007 he dropped everything to start writing fiction.

Since making the leap, Sean has written hundreds of novels (including the international best-sellers Yesterday's Gone and Invasion), penned dozens of scripts, and founded the IP Incubator Sterling & Stone where more than thirty storytellers work together to create world changing IP. Sterling & Stone's stable of writers come to Sean for ideas, mentorship, and "better words."

Originally from Long Beach, California, Sean now lives in Austin, Texas with his wife and dog, Fisher.